ATLANTIS LEGACY

David Gibbins

Cover design: Alan Gibbins

Copyright © 2024 David Gibbins

The right of David Gibbins to be identified as the author of this work has been asserted in accordance with the UK Copyright, Designs and Patents Act 1988.

All rights reserved. No part of this publication may be reproduced, stored in a retrieval system, or transmitted in any form or by any means, electronic, mechanical, photocopying, recording, or otherwise, without the prior permission of the publisher and author.

All characters in this publication - other than the obvious historical characters - are fictitious, and any resemblance to real persons, living or dead, is entirely coincidental.

ISBN 979 8 8796 0527 3

Cover design: Alan Gibbins

Throne Tree Productions
www.davidgibbins.com

Illumina praeteritum melius futurum
'Illuminate the past for a better future'

The motto of The International Maritime University

'Immortality, to live as a god, was a fool's dream, but if there were something in what they had found that might ease illness and misery, some ancient lost wisdom that might allow those who were suffering to enjoy another day, then what they were doing would have been worthwhile.'

Jack Howard

PART 1

CHAPTER 1

The Giza Plateau, Egypt, present-day

'Jack. You won't believe what I've just found. It's gold. *Solid* gold.'

Jack Howard breathed hard on his regulator and stared at the diver silhouetted on the surface some ten metres above. Of all the extraordinary places he and Costas had dived in over the years, from the sacred wells of the Mayans to the sewers of ancient Rome, this one surely took the cake. *They were diving beneath the pyramids of Giza*. He pressed the intercom on the side of his helmet, trying to contain his excitement. 'Roger that. I've reached the bottom of the shaft.'

Costas' voice crackled in his ears. 'I'm coming down now.'

Jack stared up through the veil of bubbles from his regulator exhaust, trying not to look directly into the beam of sunlight that shone through a ventilation shaft in the pyramid above. He had only just recovered from his own tumble into the shaft from the burial chamber, and he quickly felt around to make sure his equipment was all in place. He and Costas had come here not in the hope of finding gold, but for proof that an image carved into a three-thousand-year-old temple in the desert in Sudan really was a plan of this place. Six months earlier they had entered the underground complex at Giza the other way, through a long-lost tunnel from the Nile. They had seen extraordinary things, artefacts to parallel the treasures of Tutankhamun's tomb. They had seen the sarcophagus of a pharaoh with a golden mask that seemed straight out of a Hollywood film. And they had seen papyrus scrolls in jars, hundreds of them, a library where the greatest wisdom of the ancients had been preserved from changes in religion and dynastic rivalries, taken there by a heretical pharaoh who knew that the days of his new religion of the one god were numbered and that all he could do was to preserve the knowledge he had collected for a future world where reason and science might prevail.

Jack watched the silt in the water settle, revealing the polished granite walls around him. Finding the hidden shaft beneath the burial chamber in the pyramid had been amazing enough, but when they had seen the shimmer of water in the darkness below, water at the same level as the Nile some three kilometres to the east, they knew they had hit pay-dirt. If they were right, if their gamble had paid off, somewhere beyond those walls might lie another entrance to the underground complex, a route to the pharaoh's mortuary chamber and treasures greater than anything they had found before.

He saw the familiar spread-eagled silhouette of his friend descending at his usual alarming rate. In the narrow confines of the shaft Jack had nowhere to go, and he braced himself for impact. Seconds later Costas hit him, forcing him back in a tangle of limbs and regulator hoses. Costas' mask was only inches from his face, tilted and half-full of water, but his eyes glinted as he pressed his intercom. 'Now that's what I call an uncontrolled descent.'

'So what's new,' Jack said, extricating himself and checking his gear again. 'The first time we dived together, you were in free-fall. Twenty-five years on, nothing's changed.'

'Normally I'd blast some air into my buoyancy compensator and pull up just before hitting bottom. This time I was carrying some unexpected extra weight.'

Jack remembered Costas' excitement and pushed himself away until he was floating in the beam of sunlight. 'What have you got?'

'Put out your hands and close your eyes.'

Jack felt something heavy being placed in his hands. He opened his eyes and stared in astonishment. For a few moments he was mesmerised by the gleam of gold, and then he forced himself to be the sober archaeologist, bringing the object up to eye level and inspecting it closely. It was about twice the length of his hand and shaped like a cross with a loop at one end. 'It's an *ankh*,' he said. 'The ancient Egyptian symbol of life.'

'That's why I was so excited,' Costas said. 'Maurice showed me one just like this in the Cairo Museum a few days ago from the tomb of Tutankhamun.'

'And there I was thinking you were only interested in submersibles and remote-operated vehicles.'

'I *get* Egyptology,' Costas said. 'I can see why it fires Maurice up. It's not about theories, but about artefacts. It's about gold.'

'Well, there's gold in this artefact, and a lot of it,' Jack said, feeling the weight of the ankh. 'At least a kilo, I reckon. The Tutankhamun ankh is only a wooden box with a veneer of gold, though there are hieroglyphs on it and I don't see any here.'

'Turn it over.'

Jack did so and angled the surface of the gold into the light for a better view. He stared again: Costas was right. At first glance the symbols looked similar to those on the Tutankhamun ankh, hieroglyphic cartouches surmounted by solar disks and flanked by the *uraeus*, the rearing cobra that was the pharaohs' symbol of divine authority. It showed beyond doubt that they were looking at a royal inscription. But it was something else that made Jack so excited. On the loop of the ankh was the arc of the sun, the rays extending outwards and each one terminating in the shape of a hand. The cartouches contained the name not of Tutankhamun but of the man known to have been his father, the heretical pharaoh who had cast aside the old religion in favour of the new, the pharaoh whose vision had been shared by a slave named Moses who had taken it with him to his ancestral homeland on the eastern shore of the Great Middle Sea beyond the mouth of the Nile.

'Incredible,' Jack said, barely believing it. *'The sun-disk of the Aten.'*

'It's the same image we saw carved into the submerged temple in Sudan. This is the guy we're after.'

'The pharaoh Akhenaten,' Jack said, turning the object over in his hands, his mind racing. 'Where exactly did you find this?

'It was below the ledge at the top of the shaft. When you jumped into the pool, you dislodged a loose block of stone. The ankh was beneath it, in a depression carved into the rock. Almost like a key under a mat.'

'The Tutankhamun ankh was a box for a mirror,' Jack said, thinking aloud. 'The ankh symbol itself can also mean mirror, so the symbol is a metaphor, meaning that the afterlife mirrors life, is a reflection of it.'

Costas had been staring beyond Jack, and now he turned back to face to him, his eyes gleaming. 'Not a metaphor, Jack. Sometimes it helps to be an engineer, to think practically. Look behind you.'

Jack followed Costas' gaze. *Of course.* He could just make out a slab of rock in the silt at the base of the shaft, its surface at an angle. The beam of sunlight that lit up the water came from a ventilation shaft high above them in the pyramid and was reflected into the burial chamber by angled blocks of highly polished basalt. The slab below must be another of those, its reflective surface covered by silt. He felt a rush of adrenaline. It was all beginning to fit together. Maurice had discovered and unblocked the shaft beneath the burial chamber only two days before; in the few hours preceding their dive he had located the ventilation shaft, part of an ingenious system that not only aerated the chamber but also directed sunlight into the depths of the pyramid. A simulation by their computer genius Jacob Lanowski had stoked his excitement. It showed that when the sun was in the right position, at the right time of year, the basalt mirrors would have directed a beam intense enough to light up an underground complex far larger than just the burial chamber and the shaft below it. Jack was now certain of it. *There had to be something beyond.*

They had brainstormed the discovery with Maurice in the burial chamber the night before, waiting on tenterhooks as Maurice's Egyptian wife Aysha drove from the Institute of Archaeology in Alexandria with their diving equipment concealed in the back of her truck, hoping that Maurice's pass from the Antiquities Director would give her access to the plateau. They were in Egypt on a wing and a prayer, and the clock was ticking. Three weeks earlier the new regime in Cairo had closed the pyramids to tourists, swayed by militants who had infiltrated the Antiquities Department and begun to shut down archaeological sites to westerners. They were driven not by religious ideology but by a brutalised worldview that came from their origin in the gang wars of the Sudan. They had hated western intervention in the piracy and drug running that had sustained them, and now they were exacting a price. Archaeology was switching off in Egypt like the lights of a failing power grid, and Jack knew it could only be a matter of time before their projects were ended by the authoritarian control that was engulfing the country.

It was only the presence of medieval Arabic graffiti in the burial chamber that had kept the militants from dynamiting the entrance. Maurice had highlighted the importance of the inscriptions in his bid to have his permit to survey the pyramid extended for a few days longer, to allow him to complete his work and record any new discoveries. Aysha was an expert in the archaeology of early Islamic Egypt and was able to add her voice to the argument. The Antiquities Director owed them a favour, and they still had a small amount of leverage with the new regime. But smuggling Jack and Costas on to the plateau had been a huge risk for Maurice.

They had already been booted out of Sudan by the warlord who controlled the country, and Jack had made himself *persona non grata* in Egypt by publicly criticising the regime for closing museums in the south of the country and allowing their contents to be ransacked. He knew that if they were discovered at Giza not only would they be summarily expelled from Egypt but also Maurice's thirty-year career as an Egyptologist, his lifelong passion, might come to an ignominious end. The writing was on the wall for archaeology in Egypt, but Jack desperately hoped that what they found here today would allow Maurice to finish his work knowing that he had done his utmost to reveal Egypt's greatest remaining treasures. What Jack and Costas did next would be their one chance to prove that his hypothesis was right.

Jack remembered the energy of their discussion in the flickering candlelight of the burial chamber the night before, fuelled by apprehension about what lay ahead for Egypt. Ideas that might normally have taken months to gestate had come tumbling out in the space of a few hours. It was Maurice who had first suggested that the pyramid, built in the third millennium BC for the pharaoh Menkaure, could have been reused a thousand years later by Akhenaten as a centre for his new cult of the Aten, the sun god. Maurice had been astonished by the image of the wall carving that Jack had sent him six months earlier from the temple in Sudan, showing a plan of the three pyramids at Giza with a line running from the Pyramid of Menkaure to the river Nile; they had guessed that the depiction of the Aten overlaying it somehow formed part of the plan. They had managed to enter the underground complex from the Nile just as the militants seized power in Cairo, and their fleeting sight of the riches within had been tempered by the desperate need to keep the discovery secret and escape before the gunmen were on to them. Maurice had been allowed to remain in Egypt only because of Aysha, whose brother was an influential historian of Islam in Cairo and their uncle an engineer responsible for the Aswan Dam, but they all knew that time might be running out and the decision to expel him could be made on a whim.

And then a few weeks earlier Maurice had found hieroglyphs on the stone block that had been used to seal up the ventilation shaft into the burial chamber, showing that it had been put in place at the time of Akhenaten. Someone, the priests of the Aten perhaps, had carefully concealed all evidence of this place, knowing that those who were resurrecting the old religion after Akhenaten's death would attempt to destroy everything associated with his reign. The fact that no record existed in subsequent Egyptian records for a cult complex beneath the pyramid suggested that the priests had been successful, and that what lay below might remain intact and undisturbed by looters. If so - and if this truly was Akhenaten's fabled repository of knowledge - then they could be on the cusp of one of the greatest archaeological discoveries of all time.

The clue to the pool beneath the burial chamber had come when Maurice had unblocked the ventilation shaft and seen the beam of light fall on one block in the floor of the chamber. He had persuaded Jack and Costas to return to Egypt, bringing them secretly by the Nile on a boat and then to his dig headquarters on the Giza plateau where they had spent the previous night. He had paid off his Egyptian workers two days before, knowing that they could include spies for the militants, and it had been left to the three of them to prise out the block using a pulley and ratchet that Maurice had brought into the chamber. When Jack had first seen what lay below, when he had seen the light reflect off the surface of the pool, he had known that his instinct had been right. And now that he was in the water his excitement mounted further as the silt settled and he saw that the basalt slab below him was angled towards the side of the shaft facing the eastern edge of the Giza plateau, in the direction of the Nile.

He sank to the bottom of the shaft and wafted the silt from the block, revealing the polished surface. The beam of light from above reflected off it, at first opaquely through the suspended silt and then with the intensity of a powerful torch. Whereas the other three sides of the shaft were rock-cut, quarried from the bedrock, the side lit up by the beam was made from finely joined blocks of granite. He looked back at the opposite side of the shaft as he waited for the silt to settle, his eyes following an incised line that he had spotted leading from the surface of the pool down the side of the shaft and over the basalt mirror towards the masonry wall. The line ended on the floor of the shaft in the shape of a hand, with the forefinger pointing in the same direction as the beam of light. The hand was identical in shape to those radiating from the image of the Aten. He reached out, put the palm of his own hand on the cold polished surface of the rock and felt a sudden frisson from the past. 'Well I'll be damned,' he said. 'It's not often that the hand of a god points you in the direction of treasure.'

Costas sank down beside him, looking at the light playing on the surface of the rock and then peering at the basalt mirror. 'The angle's not quite right,' he said. 'Given what we know about Egyptian engineers, you'd expect the light to shine off the mirror directly at the centre of that wall, but it's off to the left. It's exactly where it would go if you'd failed to take account of the refractive index of water. There's no way the Egyptians would have made that mistake.'

'What are you saying?'

'I'm saying that this shaft was dry when the mirror was put in place. It must have been dry for a good part of the year, when the Nile was low. That fits the paleoenvironmental model that our geologists proposed for later second millennium BC, at the time of Akhenaten. The shaft is only flooded now because of the permanent high water caused by the completion of the Aswan Dam in the 1970s.'

'Meaning that whatever lies beyond here under the plateau was also dry at the time of Akhenaten for at least part of the year, with any chamber at a level higher than we are now possibly being dry all year round.'

'And also meaning that the shaft of light we're seeing here, diffused by the water, would have been far more intense, enough to illuminate a large underground complex using a system of reflective mirrors such as this one. A true City of Light.'

Jack's mind raced again. *City of Light.* Costas had taken those words from the hieroglyphic inscription they had found in the temple in Sudan, beneath the depiction of the pyramids. Then, the idea had seemed ethereal, perhaps referring to a mystical city of the afterlife, but after their discoveries six months ago it meant a real place, as real as the immense blocks of granite in the wall in front that were preventing them from exploring what might lie beyond. He turned back towards the mirror and sank down in front of it, holding the ankh in one hand and sliding his other hand over the surface. He could see his own helmeted head reflected in the basalt, an otherworldly form like some Egyptian demigod alongside the shimmering reflection of the ankh.

He remembered what Costas had said about the niche where he had found it. *Like a key under a mat.* He switched on his headlamp and panned it over the surface of the basalt, looking for more clues. He glanced at his pressure gauge. The small five-litre cylinders they were using had been easy to conceal in the truck and bring into the pyramid, but only allowed half an hour underwater. He had breathed heavily trying to disentangle himself from Costas, and only had about ten minutes of air left. He felt a rising sense of frustration. He pushed back from the rock, wondering if they should try to smuggle the ankh out, risking its discovery if they were held up by the militants, or leave it concealed here for some future archaeologist lucky enough to work at a time when Egypt and her treasures were once again open to exploration and discovery.

'Bingo,' Costas said.

'What is it?'

'I mean, *bingo*.'

Costas was on the floor of the shaft wafting silt from the lower edge of the basalt slab. He jabbed his finger into the silt. 'Check this out.'

Jack sank down through the sheen of exhaust bubbles and came to rest beside him. Where Costas had been wafting he could see a low bevel at the point where the slab joined the floor, perhaps twenty centimetres high. In the centre was a depression, its form unmistakeable. 'That's it,' he said. 'It's exactly the shape of the ankh.'

Costas reached into the canvas tool belt he wore around his waist, the last tattered remains of the beloved boilersuit that had melted around him during a dive into a submerged volcano a few years before. He extracted a water-jet device the size of a small automotive oiler and aimed it at the bevel. 'The aperture's full of silt,' he said.' Give me a few seconds and I'll clear it. Then we can put the key in the lock and watch the door to the treasure chamber open before our eyes, just like in the movies.'

He twisted the valve on the miniature high-pressure cylinder and pulled the trigger to activate the water jet, testing it a few times before aiming it into the aperture and blasting away the silt. *Just like in the movies.* For a moment Jack wished they were on a film set, that the dangers they faced in the world outside were just fiction. His excitement was tempered by a moment of uncertainty, something he had rarely felt even in their worst predicaments. He had to be confident in their ability to battle against the odds, to rely on their own grit and determination. He refused to bow down before the forces of crime and exploitation that had dogged their steps since they had left Sudan, and now threatened to eclipse not only this quest but all archaeological exploration in the heart of the ancient world.

Costas pushed away from the bevel and Jack could now see the recess more clearly. He sank down and handed over the ankh. 'This had better work. We've got less than five minutes of air left.'

Costas placed the ankh in the recess and pressed on it. Suddenly it disappeared inside, and Jack felt a tremor in the water. He looked up and saw that the block in the centre of the wall had dropped about half a metre, leaving an opening about two metres wide, exactly the right size for the beam of light to shine through. They quickly swam up to it and peered through. 'You were right about the light refraction in the water,' he said. 'You can see the beam playing off the left side of the tunnel about ten metres in, when it should have been shining directly through.'

Costas pushed his head into the gap and activated his headlamp. He immediately pushed backwards, his exhaust bubbles swirling around his head. 'An image from my worst nightmare. A crocodile attacking me underwater.'

Jack took his place and cautiously peered inside. Directly in front of him was a polished granite life-sized image of a crocodile, staring at him with fierce eyes and its jaws menacingly agape. But it was more than just a crocodile. It wore the black and gold striped headdress of a pharaoh, had the cobra Uraeus on its forehead and held a crossed crook and flail over its front. It was Sobek, the crocodile god of the Nile, feared by all who went on the river and worshipped at a temple near Thebes. Below it was the hieroglyphic name of Akhenaten in a cartouche, with another symbol of the Aten radiating outwards. Jack pushed back, coming to rest again beside Costas. 'Sobek was one of the old gods that Akhenaten banned. Odd to find it here.'

'Maybe it was carved by the workmen who made this place,' Costas said. 'This was a ventilation and light shaft, right? Probably none of the priests of the Aten would have come along here and seen this. The workmen would have had to make their way here along the Nile, and maybe they were hedging their bets. Crocodiles would have been the biggest danger on the river.'

They already knew that the water they were in was an

inflow from the Nile to the east. They knew that the ancient Egyptians had built canals to the funerary temples beside the pyramids and had even dug a harbour. But before now nobody had guessed that there might be a secret extension beneath the plateau. And now Jack knew who was responsible: Akhenaten, the pharaoh of the Old Testament, whose vision of the one god may have led him to create a legacy greater than all the other treasures of Egypt combined. The scientist in Jack knew that he should reserve judgment, that he should wait until he could see it with his own eyes. But the adventurer in him, the explorer, recognised the familiar feeling that was coursing through his veins, the result of instinct borne of years of discovery. He *knew* that something lay beyond.

'You're not going to make me try to get into that shaft, are you, Jack?' Costas said. 'You know how I feel about crocodiles.'

'It's too narrow. You'd get stuck.' He peered inside again. He had seen something lying beside the crocodile, and he switched his beam to high intensity for a better look. The light shone through the object, a deep blue colour with a hint of green. He could see a marking on it, perhaps a hieroglyph, but he could not make out the shape. 'There's something on the floor, a polished stone or jewel. It's just beyond my reach.'

'No problem.' Costas reached into a pouch on his belt, producing a small device about the size of a mobile phone. 'Little Joey Five can record it. My latest nano drone.'

'I should have known.'

Costas released the drone and it whirred off into the tunnel. Less than thirty seconds later it returned, and he extracted a microchip from its base. 'A full spec survey of the crocodile and that jewel. We should be able to see it when we're back on *Seaquest*.'

'If we ever get back,' Jack said. 'Maurice predicted that we had half an hour before the gunmen roll up, so our time is pretty well finished. They'll have been tipped off by someone on the way. We're not getting out of this pyramid without being strip-searched and having everything confiscated. Little Joey Five, for a start.'

'Not again,' Costas said. 'All four of his predecessors have been sacrificed in the name of science.'

Jack felt his breathing begin to tighten. 'And I'm running on empty. We need to surface now.'

Costas thought for a moment, then pulled up his mask and regulator, put the chip in his mouth and swallowed it. He put the mask on again, purged air into it to clear the water and then activated Little Joey again, stroking it and sending it back into the tunnel. He quickly swam down to the aperture where the ankh had disappeared and put his hand inside to retrieve it. 'Once this is removed that opening is going to shut. I'm hoping there will be enough time for me to toss the ankh inside. That will keep it out of the bad guys' hands and make sure nobody else sees this place.'

He reached as far as he could inside. A dull clatter of noise filled the shaft, and Jack looked up. He heard the banging of SOS in Morse code that was the prearranged signal from Maurice and Aysha if the militants were closing in. Flashlight beams played across the surface of the water, showing that they were already inside the pyramid. He sucked hard on his regulator, knowing that he had only a few breaths left. Costas moved back from the aperture holding the ankh, and the tunnel entrance began to close. With only seconds to spare Costas swam up and thrust the ankh inside the gap, pulling out his arm just in time. As the stone shut he signalled to Jack that he was out of air and ascending. Jack remained for a moment longer, his tank empty and having taken his last breath, but transfixed by something extraordinary that he had just seen. The shaft of light had reflected off the gold of the ankh as Costas had thrust it in, and in a flash had illuminated the jewel in a way that he had not seen before. In that moment he saw the symbol on the jewel with absolute clarity. It took him back to another revelation by Maurice and Aysha in the desert of Egypt, to a dive with Costas into a lost citadel that had shown the world the truth of one of the greatest legends of all time.

He stared at the stone wall in front of him. He had never given up on any quest, and he was not about to do so now. Whatever darkness might be about to descend on this country, one thing was for certain. *He would be back.*

CHAPTER 2

Egypt, 1334 BC

The funerary barge slid quietly down the waters of the Nile, letting the current take it through the night from the royal city of Memphis towards the pyramids on the plateau to the north-west. The two men on board had been fearful of being followed, straining their eyes in the darkness for the telltale shimmer of paddles on the river behind them, knowing that they had committed a crime against the goddess Isis by breaking into her temple and taking the body that now rested on the thwarts between them. With the sail furled and the mast lowered nothing of the boat would be visible from the surrounding desert, but even so the farmers along the banks working the irrigation channels in the cool air of the night could report their presence. Only now could they begin to feel safe, knowing that they were close to the tunnel that led to the pyramids and that once inside nothing would bar the way to their destination. It was the rightful resting place for the pharaoh, a secret tomb dug out of the rock by the toil of countless slaves over the years, far from the temple at Memphis where the priests had performed their horrifying final ritual.

The boatman leaned on the tiller and turned the prow towards the bank. A huge crocodile swam by, its tail sweeping languidly from side to side, leaving a widening ripple on the surface of the water. It had accompanied them since they had passed the temple to the crocodile god Sobek just beyond Memphis. It had seemed like their protector, and yet they knew that if they fell into the river it would devour them in an instant. He reached down and flung out the carcass of a small goat, part of the supply of carrion that all boats held for this purpose, and watched as the crocodile snapped at it and the carcass disappeared in a tumult of water. From here the crocodile would leave them and swim north to the place where the worn-out slaves from the quarries were bound up and launched into the water, a feasting place for all of the sacred creatures of the river.

The boatman's companion in the prow scanned the riverbank for the stone blocks that marked the entrance to the tunnel, but still he saw nothing. On his wrist he bore the brand of a slave, the hieroglyph of a bowed-over man, and hanging from his neck was the symbol of the pharaoh, a golden disk of the Aten with its arms outstretched like the rays of the sun. Yet when he reached beneath his tunic it was not the Aten that he grasped but another pendant beneath, the six-pointed star of the god of his people, Yahweh. It was he who had convinced the pharaoh that the two gods were one and the same, that the followers of Aten and of Yahweh would be stronger together than apart. It was this heresy above all that had stoked the rage of the Hemnetertepi, the high priests of Isis, who had stolen into the royal bedchamber while the pharaoh was ill and taken him to their temple on the edge of Memphis, who had inflicted on him the dreaded ritual of akhet-re, mummification alive.

The slave turned back to look at the shrouded form lying in the middle of the barge. He could no longer see the mist of exhalation rising above the head, and he quickly scrambled over, his heart racing. *The pharaoh could not die now.* He leaned over the hole in the linen above the mouth, pressed his ear close and felt the faint warmth of breath. He was still alive, but only just. They needed to get him to the underground chamber near the pyramids as soon as possible. The linen that was wrapped tightly around the body was oozing red and yellow, red from blood and yellow from nacre, the embalming fluid used by the priests. They had known exactly how much of his body to take and yet still leave him alive: his eyes, his tongue, one each of his lungs and his kidneys, and the front of his brain through a hole in his nose. They had fed him with poison from a spider that had left him paralysed and yet still able to feel pain, wrapping his face in linen as it contorted in agony and preserving his expression of torment forever. They had re-enacted Osiris' death, and then Isis' success in restoring him back to life, but they had given the goddess extra pleasure through the akhet-re, using the still-living spirit of a mummified pharaoh sucked half of life to give virility and power to her consort and brother, making Osiris a fit husband for the queen of the gods.

When the slave and his companions had broken into the temple and found him after the ritual was over it would have been an act of mercy to plunge a knife into his heart and end his life there. But they had sworn to the pharaoh during his long weeks of illness before the priests of Isis had taken him that they would bring him here to die, to the place that he had prepared for his ascent to join the Aten, the Sun-God. To have killed him in the temple would have been to condemn his soul to imprisonment for all time in the afterlife under the yoke of the gods he had come to revile and spurn.

But the slave had another reason for wanting to keep the pharaoh alive, to bring him to a place where he might hope to hear his whispered last words. From a priest at Saïs on the Nile delta the pharaoh had heard rumours of an ancient citadel lost beneath the sea, of a people who had escaped long ago and sailed south to Egypt and brought with them the secret of immortality. He had come to despair of ever converting Egypt to the Aten, of breaking the hold of the priests of the old order, and instead had become fixated on the story told by the priest and on the hope of a new land where his followers could begin afresh. He had known that his time was short, that the illness that had afflicted him all his life, that had caused his enemies to mock his elongated face and misshapen limbs, would soon claim him. He would be unable to lead his followers on the exodus himself, and instead he had come to pin his hope on the Hebrew slave and his people. For the slave the place was their ancestral land of Canaan to the north, and they had been willing to continue to toil under their Egyptian masters until the pharaoh had found enough hope of personal salvation to release them from their servitude and allow them to leave on their quest.

For months before he had become bedridden the pharaoh had secreted himself away in his library, the repository of ancient wisdom that he called the Pr-Ankh, the City of Light, knowing that his final illness was upon him, feverishly searching among the papyrus scrolls and inscribed tablets that had been brought to him from all of the temples in the land, looking for everything he could find about the people from the sea. He had cast his net further afield, sending gifts of gold and ivory to the kings of other lands in return for their knowledge, promising alliances and trade. From the island of Keftiu to the north, the place of the bull-worshippers, had come ancient stones with strange symbols on them, one of them identical to a symbol that the priest of Saïs said had been brought from the drowned citadel. From the land of the two great rivers to the east, from the ancient archives of Babylon, had come clay tablets with accounts of the hero Gilgamesh and his escape from the flood, but also of an earlier deluge, a great exodus at the dawn of time. It had been tantalising but had still not given the pharaoh what he so desperately yearned to find.

And then from the Temple of Isis at Memphis had come something extraordinary, something that had caused the pharaoh to send word for the Hebrew slave to travel at once from the new city of Akhetaten, the Horizon of the Aten, where his people had been labouring on the buildings. By expelling the priests from the Temple of Isis the pharaoh had gained access to the Holy of Holies, to a secret that had been kept since the priests had first worn the falcon head of Horus and worshipped the goddess as the supreme deity of Egypt. An ancient tablet in the temple showed the arrival of the men from the north, tall and bearded, their leader Shamash named after the sun god of their drowned citadel. The pharaoh had been mesmerised, seeing in Shamash an early manifestation of his beloved Aten. With the Hebrew slave he had sought out the place where the refugees had landed after their voyage over the Great Middle Sea, and they had dug from the sand a pillar that had been constructed in thanks for their survival. The pharaoh had affixed a plaque to the pillar and ascribed his own symbols beside that of Shamash, making the site a shrine to the Aten. The revelation had given him a greater sense of purpose as one who would merge with the Aten itself, to shine down with beneficence on a new world that he now knew was rooted in the oldest and purest civilisation of all.

The pharaoh had found out more from a priest of the temple of Isis who had been tortured and talked. Shamash and his companions had brought with them knowledge of masonry and metal-working and agriculture and had rebuilt in Egypt much of the civilisation that they had lost in the floodwaters to the north. And they had brought with them something else, something that promised to fulfil the greatest dream of humankind and yet also threatened the existence of the gods themselves. It was a metal called orichalcum, mined in the fiery depths of a volcano beside the lost citadel. Consuming a powder made from the metal had made Shamash and his companions live longer than anyone ever known, many generations beyond the normal span of men, allowing them to see the great monuments that they had started come to completion, living so long that they came to be worshipped by the people of the Nile as gods themselves.

No others could consume the orichalcum safely; those who attempted it died a horrifying death. To the priests of Isis, the orichalcum became sacred and feared, something that threatened the power of the goddess and their own role as priests. It promised eternal life, a substance that could expel disease and revive youth, the hope of all humankind. To the followers of Isis, the punishment for those who sought immortality was to embark on the journey to the afterlife still half-alive, suffering the worst torment for having aspired to a state that was only the preserve of the gods. Fearing its power, the high priests ordered the orichalcum to be concealed in the Holy of Holies of the temple at Memphis, under the statue of the goddess whose ascendancy would thus be assured. But then knowing that Akhenaten had ordered the temples to be opened they had secretly sent it to a new place of concealment, putting it in a stone box and sending it in one of the ships that traded for tin with the peoples beyond the western edge of the Great Middle Sea, to an island whose location would be their sworn secret for all time. The priest who had been tortured told them that the shape of the island had been drawn by one who had returned from the voyage, but that too had been sent to a secret location that the priest had not divulged before he had died.

To Akhenaten, the promise of orichalcum seemed the fulfilment of a dream, a promise to free him from the shackles of his illness and to make him a living god, one who did not need to wait until the afterlife to take his position alongside the Aten. But the dust of the archives had been his undoing, settling in his lungs and making his illness worse, sending him back to Memphis to his bedchamber weak and near death. In the months while he had been obsessed with his quest and taken his eyes off the kingdom the banished priests had secretly returned, infiltrating Memphis and gathering once again in the underground chambers of the temples, bent on revenge. Already they had begun to desecrate the symbols of the Aten, burning and ripping down the temple façades and defacing the statues of the pharaoh. Akhenaten's own wife Nefertiti, high priestess of Isis, had turned against him when she knew that he had desecrated her temple and when she discovered what he had found out. The pharaoh had summoned the slave to be with him, wanting to tell him something, but by the time the slave had arrived in Memphis the priests had taken the pharaoh from his bedchamber and performed the terrible ritual. All that he could do was to join the pharaoh's son Tutankhaten and his most loyal followers in rescuing his half-mummified body, and then to pray to Yahweh for a miracle, clutching the Hebrew symbol of the star under his tunic through the long night of their boat journey down the Nile.

He stared through the gloom at the riverbank. He saw the stone blocks of the tunnel entrance and gestured for the boatman to look. He had been to this place near the pyramids before, to the rock-cut complex that served as the pharaoh's repository of knowledge and his future tomb, when he had helped the pharaoh to decipher texts in the ancient Hebrew script and had first told him about Yahweh. He remembered watching the workmen cut the rock face to enlarge the mortuary chamber at the entrance, and the little alabaster jars of potion that the foremen had kept nearby to revive them when the air became stifling. If he could use the potion to wake the pharaoh now, even just for a moment, there might be a chance that he would tell him what he had wanted to pass on. He prayed that the embalmers had left enough of his brain intact, that the pharaoh would be able to talk before the slave led his people to a place of safety, to a land where they would be able to worship the one god and defend themselves against those who saw them only as slaves.

The boat nosed into the bank of the river, bumping a low wharf. The ghostly forms of the pyramids were just visible in the desert to the west, huge and otherworldly, difficult to imagine as the works of men. The slave jumped ashore, took the rope from the prow and caught the boat as the current swung it around, pulling the rope hand over hand until it came alongside. The boatman jumped out, crouched in front of a rock and reached into a hole in the bank. He had done this many times before, bringing the pharaoh from Memphis when he had wanted to spend time in his repository of knowledge. He pulled a lever and a circular slab rolled aside to reveal the tunnel and another dock. Together they drew the boat inside and tied it to stone bollards on the edge. The boatman reached into the hole from the inside and the slab rolled shut again, leaving them in darkness. From a rack beside the entrance he pulled out a wooden pole wrapped with rags soaked in naphtha, the oil that oozed from the desert. He struck a flint and lit it, sending spluttering flames into the chamber; it would burn long enough to light the way to their destination. In the torchlight the slave could see another smaller craft moored at the entrance to the tunnel, and together they heaved the linen-wrapped form out of the river boat and placed it on the thwarts of the smaller vessel ready to take down the tunnel.

The slave checked again anxiously for signs of breathing, and then turned to the boatman. 'I am the one who gave Akhenaten succour when he became ill as a young man, using the medicine of my people. I must be allowed to try again when we reach the tomb chamber.'

'I have my instructions from Tutankhaten, the new pharaoh,' the boatman replied. 'And now you must help me to pull the boat through the tunnel. The distance is great, and we do not have much time.'

They sat down at either end of the boat and began to pull hand over hand on a hemp rope that had been hung along the length of the tunnel for that purpose. All that the slave could hear was their breathing and the spluttering of the torch, the sounds magnified down the tunnel as if they were part of a procession of boats. They turned a corner and the tunnel constricted further as it went through an outcrop of hard stone that the workmen had struggled to penetrate. The water was only knee-deep and they went overboard to guide the boat through, one pushing and the other pulling, crouching low. The torch flickered and the slave felt faint, but then the flame leapt up again and he revived as they passed under a ventilation shaft. After what seemed an age they reached another rock-cut dock on the right side of the tunnel. The boatman took the torch and got out, standing before another circular slab like the one at the tunnel entrance and putting his hand into an aperture on one side. The door was slow-moving because of the weight of the stone and the time it took for the pulleys to grind into motion. The slave joined him, his legs aching and his body dripping with sweat from the exertion in the tunnel, and they waited while the slab rolled open and the chamber inside was revealed.

The slave remembered his previous visit here, when he had stood beside the pharaoh and watched the barges being unloaded. This was not a place filled with gold and jewels like the tombs in the Valley of the Kings, where as a boy he had watched the procession of carts laden with riches being taken to the tomb of the pharaoh's grandfather Thutmose. Here, the alabaster jars that lined the rooms were filled not with precious substances and offerings to the gods but instead with treasures of another sort, scrolls and clay tablets and stones carved with inscriptions. And instead of going with him to the afterlife they would remain here until the people of Egypt were ready to bask in the rays of the Aten, to receive the wisdom of the ancients. The pharaoh would return from his seat beside the Aten just as the prophecy of the slave's own people foretold that the son of Yahweh would one day alight on earth and guide their way.

The boatman put the torch in a slot by the door and they lifted the body out of the boat. They were entering the mortuary chamber, the place where the pharaoh's body was meant to be prepared before being moved into the tomb itself, beyond a wall blocked off with massive slabs of granite that could only be removed by teams of masons. It was a way of keeping the treasures within as secure as possible, and was only to be opened during the mummification ritual that the pharaoh and his priests had envisaged; with the wall blocked off, all that the slave and the boatman could do now was to lay the pharaoh on the mortuary slab, but it was still a sacred place where the Aten would ensure that the pharaoh would ascend to take his seat beside the god in the afterlife.

In the wavering light they could see jars around the edges of the chamber and in the centre a polished white slab, with carved lines representing the rays of the Aten radiating out on the floor all around it. They placed the body on the slab, and then stood back. The boatman drew his knife, a curved dagger with a blade of obsidian. Now that Akhenaten was in his rightful place he could finally be put out of his torment. But before that the slave desperately needed a few moments with him. He stepped forward, his heart pounding, but the boatman barred his way, and then rolled up his left sleeve to reveal his forearm. There were two puncture marks beside the veins of his wrist, and the skin around them was purple and swollen. 'I told you that we did not have much time,' the man said, his voice rasping. 'The poison from the asp of the Erythraean Sea is slow acting, killing only after several hours have passed, but is always fatal. It was to allow me time to get here and complete my task, but no more. The others who helped to rescue the pharaoh took much quicker poison, and Tutankhaten pledged to do the same. Our pact with the pharaoh was that after his death none would remain alive who knew of this place, so that his site of resurrection would not be violated.'

The slave swallowed hard, feeling his mouth go dry. 'But I must lead my people to safety. That was *my* pact with the pharaoh. He was to release me from servitude.'

'I know who you are. The Israelite they call the child of the Nile. But I know nothing of a pact. Submit to me now and I will make it painless. I have done this many times before. It was my task to ensure that the slaves who had finished their work here did not leave the tunnel alive. Tonight was not the first time the crocodile had followed my boat down the Nile, expecting to be fed.'

He gripped the knife and advanced on the slave, who stood transfixed, not knowing what to do. The boatman's eyes were bloodshot, and his face was dripping with sweat. The poison was taking effect faster than he had anticipated. He lurched forward and slashed wildly, spinning and falling to the floor, and then got up on his knees and launched himself forward again. The slave caught him by the wrists and used all his strength to prevent the knife from being driven into him. The boatman shuddered violently and fell on his front, the knife beneath him. The slave sprang out of the way and watched as the end of the blade appeared out of the man's back. He gurgled, the blood from his mouth streaked black with the poison, and then lay still, his eyes wide open.

The slave stood in stunned silence, his hands shaking. Then he heard a low grinding noise. The boatman's last act before drawing the knife had been to activate the door again, causing the slab to roll slowly shut. The slave quickly went over and put his hand in the aperture, reaching down for the handle that operated the mechanism, but felt nothing. He remembered being shown the mechanism when he had been here before. Once activated for the final time the handle was designed to be pulled off and dropped into a deep well below, to ensure that the tomb would never be entered again. The boatman had made sure that if one of them were left alive, if he failed with the knife or the poison did not work, they would both be locked inside for all time.

He had only a few minutes to act. He grasped the torch and stumbled towards the mummy of the pharaoh on the platform, and then veered off to a shelf on the wall where he remembered seeing the foreman put the potion for the workmen. He searched frantically among the alabaster jars on the shelf, sweeping them aside and knocking them over until he found the right one. He turned back towards the pharaoh and jammed the torch in a holder beside the platform. In the flickering shadows the pharaoh seemed elongated and supernatural. He leaned over the face, trying not to recoil as he saw the congealed brain tissue in the nose and smelled the blood and the nacre. He knocked the top off the jar and poured the contents into the hole in the linen above the pharaoh's mouth. He knew that it was far more than a normal dose, having seen the effect that a small spoonful had on the workmen, but this was his only chance to awaken the pharaoh and if it then killed him it would be a mercy.

The pharaoh coughed and issued a terrible noise, a long-drawn-out moan. The slave leaned over him, saying the pharaoh's name over and over again and then his own, and pressed his ear against the linen. The mouth was just a bloody hole with the stump of a tongue inside, and the words that came out were barely audible. He listened hard, trying to be sure of what he had heard, and then glanced back at the entranceway, seeing that the stone was rolling shut with little more than an arm span to go. He quickly turned to the mummy's right arm and began pulling away the binding, unwrapping it until the shape of the hand was revealed. Beneath the bindings were bandages that had been on his limbs for weeks now infused with medicaments to treat his illness, and the Hemnetertepi had left them there when they had wrapped him in linen to mummify him. The slave had been present when the doctors had treated him and he had seen the jewel clasped in his hand under the bandages, an object that had remained in the temple of Isis from the time of Shamash. When the pharaoh had broken into the temple the orichalcum had already been despatched in its stone box by the priests to the harbour for its voyage to the west, but the priests had kept the key to the box to stop anyone on the voyage from getting inside; the key was the jewel that the pharaoh was clasping in his hand now, revealed to him under torture by the last remaining priest. If Akhenaten could not have the orichalcum, if he could not have immortality on earth, then he could at least have the jewel to ease his entry to the afterlife as promised by his vision of the Aten. Now the slave, he whom Akhenaten had named Moses, wanted it for himself, to take away and light up the path for his people on their way to the promised land.

He looked at it now, luminescent in the flickering light of the torch, and quickly prised it out of the pharaoh's fingers.

It was an extraordinary colour, blue like lapis lazuli but with a shimmer of green that he had never seen before. Incised on one side and picked out in gold was a symbol that looked like a hieroglyph but that he knew was much older, made up of two parallel lines with smaller lines extending from them at right angles. The priest had told Akhenaten that it was a jewel brought by Shamash that bore the symbol of their ancient citadel, the name that the slave had heard the pharaoh whisper just now, a name that he could scarcely believe to be true.

The door made a grinding noise again and the stone rolled forward until the gap was barely wide enough for him to get through. To his horror he saw that the pharaoh was writhing and jerking like an animal in its death throes, struggling against the binding as the potion took full effect. What had been an agony of paralysis was now an even worse torment, with the potion giving him a superhuman burst of energy. The slave glanced at the knife in the body of the boatman. There was no time to use that now. He took the torch and thrust it against the pharaoh, watching the flames leap and swirl over the linen as the volatile elements in the embalming fluid ignited. He turned and ran towards the entrance, the torch in one hand and the jewel in the other. At the last moment he stumbled and fell, dropping the jewel. He reached frantically for it, but it rolled away towards the ventilation shaft below the pyramid, the place where sunlight was reflected through in daytime. As he pulled himself through the gap he glanced back and saw the body of the pharaoh roll off the platform and curl up on the floor in the flames. The crack closed and he was alone in the tunnel beside the boat, the torch now burnt down to its final flickers of light.

He shut his eyes and leaned back on the tunnel wall, trying to control his breathing. By hastening the pharaoh's end he had carried out his last whispered request, an act of mercy. Moments from now the pharaoh would rise out of his tomb to take his rightful place beside the fiery orb of the Aten. But in so doing, in violating the akhet-re and allowing the pharaoh to ascend to the afterlife, the slave knew he had also brought down a curse on himself and his people. The priests who had been enraged by the pharaoh's heresy and thirsted for revenge would come to know that the slave had survived from the tomb and would do all in their power to hunt him down. The pharaoh's son Tutankhaten was weak and would lack the resolve to poison himself, and would soon enough tell all he knew to the Hemnetertepi. Their wrath would be felt by any who dared to take up the quest of Akhenaten for immortality. All that the slave could do now was to get as far away as possible, to take his people beyond Egypt to safety and fortify them against the vengeance that would come.

And the pharaoh had kept his pledge to him as well. The promise of the Aten, of the one god, was the promise of a return to the world before gods that people had created in their own image, before priests and priest-kings. In his dying breaths, in his final moments of torment, the pharaoh had thought only of the quest that had consumed him, of the dream that they had shared and the secret that he would pass on. The slave may have lost the jewel but the pharaoh had told him of the map to the remote island and the name of the drowned civilisation from which Shamash had come. He repeated it to himself now, hearing it echo up and down the tunnel like an exhalation from a past almost too distant to contemplate: *Atlantis*.

CHAPTER 3

Cornwall, England, present-day

Jack Howard stood up from his desk, stretched and walked to the window overlooking the wooded shore of the Fal Estuary, watching the sunlight glinting off the water and seeing the western reaches of the English Channel and the open Atlantic beyond. He was in the drawing room of the old manor house in Cornwall where his ancestors had shared the same view, planning forays to distant oceans and defending these shores against the threat of invasion. From here John Howard had sailed out against the Spanish Armada in 1588, commanding one of the privateers owned by his cousin Charles Howard, Lord High Admiral under Queen Elizabeth I. Howards had later been present at many of the famous naval engagements of British history, from the Battle of the Medway against the Dutch in 1667 to the Battles of the Nile and Trafalgar under Nelson and the sinking of the *Bismarck* during the Second World War. They had fought pirates in the Caribbean, plundered treasure ships in the name of the Crown and explored to the very limits of the earth. For Jack this legacy was never far from his thoughts, especially when there was a new adventure in the offing. It was as if he were drawn into an ongoing voyage of discovery that had begun all those centuries ago in the age of sail, one in which the destination, the prize, was always just beyond the horizon, beckoning him on just as the promise of riches and acclaim had done for his ancestors. His instinct today told him that he was again on the trail of something momentous, something that had been dominating his thoughts ever since he and Costas had seen the jewel beneath the pyramid the year before and the symbol that was carved on it.

Until twenty years ago the house had been a place of dilapidated grandeur with the drawing room serving as his father's painting studio, but with the foundation of the International Maritime University it had become the heart of a thriving campus that stretched from the dock on the estuary up the slope over much of the former estate surrounding the manor house and farm buildings. The collection of books dating back to John Howard's time in the sixteenth century that had once filled the drawing room was now housed in a state-of-the-art library on the other side of the courtyard, part of a complex that including an engineering department and conservation labs extending down to the shore.

On the field adjacent to the campus he could see the scaffolding and cranes where the new museum was taking shape, with construction due to finish that summer. Once the museum was complete Jack's vision of IMU would be close to being realised, with the endowment from his old friend Efram Jacobovich covering all operating costs and allowing him to plan projects without having to seek external funding. It was the people as much as the money that made it work, some of them with him from the time when IMU was little more than a dream; for him a big measure of success was the momentum that now existed in IMU beyond his own expeditions, with projects underway around the world for which he played only an advisory role. It meant that he could concentrate on the projects that most fired up his imagination, on the unsolved mysteries that had driven him to push the boundaries of exploration and make some of the greatest discoveries in archaeology of the past decades, projects that had only been possible because of his core team of scientists and explorers who had taken the IMU flag to the most remote regions of the world's seas and inland waterways.

He glanced at his watch and ran through his plans for

the day. The class of high school interns was due here at any moment for their meet-and-greet in advance of their summer programme in the campus. He had brought out some artefacts to show them and had thought of what he would say. Elsie, the programme co-ordinator, had suggested that Atlantis would be a good place to start, as they had all read his book on the discovery and would be full of questions. After that he was planning to go down to the equipment store to check over his dive gear, something that he always did personally despite the technical team ensuring that everything was fully serviced and ready to go. The dive he had planned for tomorrow would be his first since the winter storms had shut down their projects along this coast, and he wanted to make certain that everything ran smoothly and the dive would be the best possible start for the season to come.

It had been almost a year now since he and Costas had been summarily ejected from Egypt following their escapade under the pyramid. For a few unpleasant days after their arrest it had seemed as if they might be condemned to one of Egypt's harsher prisons for the foreseeable future, but then an old diving friend who worked in the Foreign Office in London had pulled a few strings and a deal had been struck with the new regime. The price was that IMU should fund an ecological survey of the shoreline salt flats of the northern Sinai, something that Jack had agreed to as it meant a toehold back in Egypt and the possibility of renewed archaeological work. The regime itself had little interest in the ecology of the region, but like most autocratic governments had realised that being completely inward-looking was not good for their economy and that an environmental project might bring in renewed foreign investment.

The outcome of the deal had been good in the circumstances, but Jack had returned chastened by the experience. He had spent several days in solitary confinement in a cell in the Egyptian Ministry of the Interior, not knowing what had happened to Costas, thinking about his daughter

Rebecca and for the first time in his career wondering whether the price of pushing the boundaries had been too high. If the press had learned about his arrest then the reputation of IMU might have been in jeopardy, compromising the work of colleagues trying to get permits in other places ruled by totalitarian regimes. He had kept a low profile for six months, disappearing to his cottage in northern Canada to write while Costas worked on a new property he had acquired in the Caribbean. Eventually after it had become clear that there would be no significant fall-out he had put his qualms behind him and refocussed on what they had glimpsed that night under the Giza Plateau. It had come to preoccupy him, to be uppermost in his mind first thing in the morning and last thing at night. There was a burning question about how the jewel with that symbol came to be under the pyramid that he was determined to resolve.

The door opened and Elsie poked her head around. 'Are we OK to come in?'

'Yes. Please do.' Jack tapped the keyboard to activate the display screen on the wall at the back of the room and picked up his laser-pointer. The students entered, and Elsie ushered them to the chairs that had been set up in front of a table facing the screen. They sat down and looked expectantly at him, some with notebooks out and phones ready to record. 'You will all recognise Dr Howard,' she said. 'He's generously agreed to give us half an hour as part of your introductory tour. Dr Howard?'

'Call me Jack,' he said, smiling at them. 'I'm delighted to see you here, and congratulations on winning your internships. I'll look forward to meeting each one of you properly at the beginning of your course in the summer. Meanwhile, who can tell me about the image on the screen?'

A hand shot up from the back. 'It's the Atlantis symbol,' the girl said. 'It was already known from the symbols on the Phaestos Disc, a pottery disc from Crete that was thought to be Bronze Age but we now know was much older than that. The breakthrough came when Maurice Hiebermeyer and Aysha found the same symbol on a papyrus fragment reused as a mummy wrapping in the Faiyum Oasis in Egypt. The papyrus turned out to be the lost account of Atlantis by the Greek scholar Solon, who had been told the story by an Egyptian priest and then gave a partial version of it to his disciple the philosopher Plato. The *Timaeus* and *Critias* by Plato are the only sources we had before this for the story of Atlantis. Anyway, translating the papyrus and the Phaestos disc led you and Costas to a site on the southern edge of the Black Sea that had been inundated when a land bridge over the Bosporus Strait breached in the sixth millennium BC and the Mediterranean flooded in, raising the level of the Black Sea by over 100 metres. What you had found was a Neolithic citadel that turned out to be Atlantis. You had a big fight with a warlord called Aslan who wanted his share of the loot. He was your friend Katya's father. What he actually wanted was the nukes on a Russian submarine that had sunk at the site. Oh, and it was also the location of an active volcano. The rest is history.'

Jack cracked a smile. 'Well, you've been doing your homework. Anyone else?'

A boy in the front row tentatively put up his hand. 'Five years later you and Costas went in search of the priests who had escaped Atlantis and gone west. What you found confirmed your theory about Atlantis being the cradle of civilisation, that agriculture and Indo-European language and metalworking technology spread out from the area of what's now Turkey all around the world.'

'Not only that, but also science and medicine,' Jack said. 'What's been amazing since our discovery is the other archaeological finds showing that Atlantis was not just a one-off but part of a wider early Neolithic civilisation.' He reached over and tapped a key, bringing up an image of circular stone structures under excavation, and aimed his laser-pointer at it. 'This is the so-called temple complex at Göbekli Tepe, in southern Anatolia overlooking the cradle of civilisation in Syria and Mesopotamia. It's the earliest stone structure of this type found anywhere in the world. It dates three thousand years *before* the inundation of the Black Sea and the end of Atlantis. That's five thousand years before Stonehenge. If anyone had suggested when I was your age that something like this would be found, dating ten thousand years ago when most people were still living as hunter-gatherers, they would have been laughed at. Nobody then would ever have taken the idea of Atlantis seriously. But look where we are now. And that's all a result of hard science, not fantasy and speculation.'

Another hand shot up. 'My Dad says old divers never retire. What are your plans?'

Jack smiled. 'Well, I'm not old yet, and I have no plans to retire. It may be that my greatest discoveries lie ahead of me. There are still treasures on my bucket list that I haven't even begun to research yet.'

'Will you ever return to Atlantis?'

Jack tapped a key and brought up an underwater picture showing a mottled rocky outcrop devoid of vegetation. 'We've been monitoring it, but further excavation is not likely for a while. That's what it looked like from a remote-operated vehicle three months ago, buried under tons of lava from the volcanic eruption that took place shortly after we found it. What fascinates me is where the survivors went and what they took with them. We've already found evidence for one group making their way over the Atlantic to the Caribbean. We know that some of the priests relocated to the island of Crete in the Aegean and that their descendants were behind the Minoan civilisation of the Bronze Age. If you go to the Minoan palace of Knossos you'll see images of bulls in the wall-paintings just like the ones we found in Atlantis.'

Several hands went up at once and Jack pointed at one of them. 'It must be tricky having a settled domestic life when you're a famous international explorer,' the girl said. 'Are you going to marry Katya or Maria?'

Elsie cleared her throat and looked down, suppressing a smile. Jack was used to questions like this, the price to be paid for all the books and films that had charted his projects over the years. 'Well, Katya runs the Institute of Palaeography in Moscow and Maria is a professor of ancient linguistics in Spain. It might be a bit tricky for them too.'

'Next question?' Elsie said, smiling at Jack.

A hand shot up from the same row. 'Is Rebecca really going to follow in your footsteps? Is she still with Jeremy?'

'Well, you'll have to ask her that,' Jack said. 'She's currently in East Africa working for the Jacobovich Foundation. As you know, Efram has been our main benefactor, an old diving friend of mine when I was a student who decided to fund IMU when Costas and I came up with the idea nearly twenty years ago. But he's put most of his software billions into famine relief and poverty programmes, and that's what Rebecca is doing this summer. What she does in the future is her call. She's already made some amazing discoveries with me and directed her own shipwreck excavations.'

A girl in the front row spoke up. 'There are always bad guys in your adventures. It never seems to be an easy ride. Why is that do you think?'

Jack smiled. 'It's human nature. Costas calls it gold fever. For every archaeologist there's a treasure hunter only interested in personal profit.'

'Aren't you treasure hunters too, really?'

'Any person calling themselves an archaeologist who's not excited by the idea of treasure should be doing something else. But treasure doesn't have to be gold and jewels. A single potsherd can be just as exciting if it opens up a revelation about the past.' He paused, putting down his laser pointer. 'The black-market trade in antiquities has got worse as deep-water technology has allowed easier access to wrecks in abyssal depth, beyond national jurisdictions. The United Nations convention on maritime archaeology is only as good as the ability to police it, and that's very difficult in international waters. Antiquities and stolen works of art continue to be used in the criminal underworld to oil deals, as gifts between drug kings and warlords. And there are other kinds of bad guys too. Organisations such as the Nazi Ahnenerbe, the Department of Cultural Heritage under Hitler, have modern-day followers who still want to find artefacts to support their racist ideologies. And there are organisations going far back in history that act as guardians of ancient secrets they are sworn never to divulge. As those of you who have read my books and seen the films will know, we've had to battle many of these. And there will be more to come.'

'What's your latest project, Jack?' Elsie asked.

Jack went over to his desk and picked up a tray of artefacts, bringing it back and placing it on the table. 'It's a ship called the *Santo Cristo di Castello*, but we call it the Mullion Pin Wreck. That's because it was wrecked near the town of Mullion just a few miles from here, and among its cargo were thousands of brass clothing pins found all over the site. The ship dates from 1667, during the reign of King Charles II, and was wrecked on her way from Amsterdam to Spain and Italy. Her captain had delayed sailing to load up with more cargo and didn't reach the waters off Cornwall until early October that year, when the ship was caught in a south-westerly gale and blown into the cliffs. He and some of the crew survived, but many of the passengers died and most of the cargo was lost, either dispersed by the sea or sinking to the bottom where we've been finding it since rediscovering the wreck a few years ago.'

He returned to his desk, tapped a key and the image of Atlantis was replaced by a stormy view of the wreck site in the inlet of Pol Glas, with Mullion Island in the background and the open Atlantic beyond. He turned to the tray and picked up the artefacts one by one, handing them to Elsie to pass around. 'This little box contains a few of those clothing pins I was just talking about, all made by hand in Amsterdam and quite valuable at the time. Women and men wore elaborate outfits and these pins that held them together. The next artefact is a small circular ingot of copper, part of a consignment of raw metal in the cargo. And this beautiful brass candlestick dates from the fifteenth century, more than two centuries earlier than the wreck. If you look at its base you can see that it's damaged, so it was part of a barrel of scrap metal being taken to a foundry in Spain for recycling. We've found lots of items like that, candlesticks, pieces of chandeliers, candelabras, most of them probably originally church fittings. And here's a beautiful little brass swan that seems to have been an ornament on one of those chandeliers.'

The girl who had spoken first put up her hand again. 'You've excavated along the west coast of the Lizard peninsula before. I've read your two most recent books, on the Phoenician wreck in Church Cove and the wreck of the *Schiedam* in Jangye-ryn on the other side of the headland. Also the wreck with the silver pieces of eight at Kynance Cove. How does the Mullion Pin Wreck stack up against those?'

Jack smiled. 'You *have* done your homework. Every wreck has a fascinating story to tell if you can put it in a wider historical context. You could write a history of the world in shipwrecks, if you could focus on wrecks that provide portholes into technology, exploration, trade and society at significant periods, as well as on the great events that shaped world history at the time.'

'You mean *you* could write a book,' the girl said. 'Is that your next writing project?'

'Well, it would be an interesting one, wouldn't it?' Jack said. 'With everything we've done over the past few years we've got more than enough wrecks to choose from. But in answer to your question, the Mullion Pin Wreck provides a remarkable glimpse into the world of the mid-seventeenth century. I'm fascinated by that period because it was half-way between the medieval and the modern. Europe was in religious turmoil because the wars sparked by the Reformation were still panning out, with Protestants fighting Catholics. Some of those brass ornaments you're passing around now had been pulled out of Catholic churches in Holland by Protestant reformers who objected to the wealth of the Church, and so they ended up in a barrel of scrap being taken to be melted down and reused. But as well as war and turmoil it was also a time of great scientific revelation and exploration. The ships of the English and Dutch East India Companies were going further than mariners had ever gone before and exposing Europeans to the cultures of the east. The *Santo Cristo di Castello* was carrying spices from as far away as the islands of Indonesia, and only a few days ago our lab was able to prove that the copper in that ingot you are passing around came from Japan. Can you believe that? Other cargo on the ship included ebony wood from the Spanish and Portuguese colonies in the Americas. And Amsterdam where the ship had been built was in the midst of the Dutch Golden Age, perhaps the greatest period of artistic endeavour the world has ever known. As well as the other cargo, we know that the ship was carrying two paintings by none other than Rembrandt himself, destined for a wealthy buyer in Italy.'

Elsie collected the artefacts and put them back on the table. Jack waited while they finished making their notes, glanced at the clock and nodded at her. Another student put up a hand. 'When will we meet Costas?'

'After you visit the library Elsie is going to take you on a tour of the conservation lab and the site of the new museum, and then Costas is going to meet you outside the engineering department,' Jack said. 'That's when the fun really begins. And there will be lunch in the canteen along the way.'

'Thank you, Jack,' Elsie said.

'My pleasure. I look forward to seeing you all again soon.'

They trooped out of the room and Jack turned back to what he had been doing before they arrived. He sat down behind his desk, tapped a key and stared at the computer screen in front of him. It showed an image sent to him that morning by Jeremy, who was in The National Archives at Kew researching the *Santo Cristo di Castello*. This document in the *Calendar of State Papers* for King Charles II of August 1666 was his best discovery so far, and Jack read it through again:

To the King's Most Excellent Majestie. The humble Petition of Giovanni Lorenzo Viviano Genoese, Captain of the Ship St Christo de Castello. Most Humbly Sheweth that your petitioner did cause to be built at Amsterdam the said Ship St Christo de Castello upon the Account of himself, and other Genoeses resident in the State of Genoa, and paid for her with their owne moneys, as by the Certificate annexed appeares. That having fitted the said Ship with 46 Gunnes and 120 Seamen your Petitioner is by Order from the said Genoeses to Lade severall Comodityes at Amsterdam aforesaid, & thence to proceed on a Tradeing Voyage for Lisbon, Cadiz, and other Ports on the Coast of Spaine, and from thence to Saile for Legorne & Genoa. The truth of the Premisses further appearing by a Letter to your Sacred Majestie from the State of Genoa, He humbly Prayes that youre Majestie would be graciously Pleased, to graunt Your Royal Pass-Port for the said Ship and her Ladeing, to Pas from Amsterdam aforesaid, to the several Places above mentioned, without any Molestation.

He clicked open a file from Maria, who was researching the ship in the Sauli family archive in Genoa. The Saulis were a wealthy Genoese mercantile family, and one of them, Francesco Sauli, a future Doge of Genoa, had been Viviano's main patron. Maria had found a letter confirming Viviano's appointment to the ship and showing that he was to travel to Amsterdam in 1665 to oversee her construction and the lading of her cargo. Amsterdam was not only a hub of international trade but also the best place to have ships constructed, with the expertise of the shipwrights of the Dutch East India Company to hand. No expense was to be spared in her construction, which was to be to the same standards as an East Indiaman. She was to be 32 metres in length and armed with

36 iron and 6 bronze guns as well as 18 swivel guns on the rails of her top deck.

The armament reflected the threat facing merchantmen sailing in and out of the Mediterranean at this period, running the gauntlet of the Barbary corsairs of North Africa every time they went through the Strait of Gibraltar. 1665 also marked the beginning of the Second Anglo-Dutch war, the conflict fought mainly at sea that would rumble on until just before the ship sailed in the autumn of 1667. Strictly speaking she was neutral, a vessel owned by a consortium of Genoese merchants and commanded by a Genoese captain, but such niceties were unlikely to be observed by the English privateers who stood to profit from prizes and regarded any ship coming out of Amsterdam as fair prey. Had she been captured and deemed a prize her cargo would have been forfeit and auctioned off at the earliest opportunity, and by the time the English High Court of Admiralty came to judge the case there would be little recompense for the merchants whose property had been taken. Being heavily armed meant that the captains of the smaller privateers would think twice before taking her on, something that had also led the Dutch East India Company to construct their vessels to look as nearly as possible like warships.

The connection with the East India Company was not just in the ship's appearance. Jack tapped a key and brought up a list of the consignments known to have been laden on the ship. There were no surviving bills of lading, as those would have been on board and gone down with her, but the Amsterdam Notarial Archive contained a claim of recompense by a merchant with goods on the ship and there were also records of material salvaged in Cornwall shortly after her wrecking. By far the most valuable consignments were the spices that had been brought by the Indiamen from the islands of the Far East, their value greatly increased by the risk of the passage around the Cape of Good Hope and up the eastern Atlantic. On arrival in Amsterdam the spices were bought by merchants and shipped out again in vessels such as the *Santo Cristo di Castello*, destined for France and Spain and Italy as well as Constantinople and the other Ottoman ports of the east Mediterranean. Jack was staggered by the prices they commanded once they reached their destinations, with pepper, cinnamon and cloves being practically worth their weight in gold. The cargo of cloth and spices alone was estimated by the Vice-Admiral of Cornwall to be worth over £50,000 – almost four million pounds in today's money - making her one of the richest vessels ever to be wrecked on the shores of Cornwall.

He glanced at another entry sent by Jeremy from the *Calendar of State Papers*, this one a summary of a letter from the Admiralty agent in Falmouth dated 9 October 1667: 'The *Santo Cristo di Castello*, a new ship built at Amsterdam, and laden with cloth and spices to the value of 50,000 pounds, has been cast away near the Lizard, and 25 men and women drowned; the captain and crew got ashore in their boat.' Later accounts put the number of people lost higher, with the fate of the captain uncertain. Before setting sail Captain Viviano had been held up in Amsterdam, waiting for the ship to finish her sea trials, icebound during the harsh winter of the 'Little Ice Age' in 1666-7 when the Zuider Zee froze up and then waiting for the final consignments to arrive, delays that placed her squarely in the face of the autumn storms as she sailed through the English Channel towards the Bay of Biscay. The sea trials had been more extensive than usual owing to a problem with the hull caulking that needed to be addressed, and the holdup while icebound was unavoidable. But Jack pondered the possible reason for that final delay to await more cargo. Viviano was a highly experienced captain, entrusted by the merchants with cargo worth a king's ransom and himself a part-owner of the ship. Whatever it was that he was awaiting must have been of great importance for him to take such a risk with the weather, a risk that did not pay off as he clawed his way down the channel against the westerlies and then trusted to good fortune as he set off in a lull from Falmouth towards Spain, only to be blown back against the cliffs of the Lizard Peninsula a few days later.

He and Jeremy had decided to split the research into two parts, with Jeremy seeking further evidence for the lading of the ship in Amsterdam and Jack searching in the Cornwall archives for anything he could find on the salvage and the whereabouts of cargo that was saved. Even for a ship as rich and noteworthy as the *Santo Cristo di Castello*, there were yawning holes in the documentary evidence that made the archaeology a vital a source of information. He looked again at the image he had left on the main screen of the spray-lashed cliffs adjacent to the wreck and felt a wave of excitement as he thought about tomorrow. He knew from the reports of IMU divers at the site yesterday that there would be some groundswell, but nothing to deter him. It was a spring tide at this point in the month, with a tidal range of more than 5 metres and low water in the early afternoon. By getting there a good hour before low water he would be able to reap the maximum benefit, with the site being less than ten metres deep and therefore giving him more time on the seabed. He stretched again, already feeling the cathartic effect that diving would have on him, a feeling of well-being that seemed to sweep through him. He had plenty to occupy himself for the rest of the day, but he knew that he would soon begin counting down the hours before setting off tomorrow morning for the site. *He could hardly wait.*

CHAPTER 4

Off south-west England, 5 October 1667

Captain Giovanni Lorenzo Viviano braced himself as the ship pitched forward even more violently, straining at the anchors and causing the ink pot to slide across the table in front of him. He quickly blotted the letter he had been writing, folded it and scrawled the name of his patron Francesco Maria Sauli on the front. There was little chance that the letter would ever reach Genoa now, but he had fulfilled his obligation to report on their progress. He sat back, listening to the timbers creak and groan, to the boom that resonated through the hull each time a giant Atlantic roller struck the stern. She had been the envy of the other captains anchored off Texel Island near Amsterdam as they had waited out the winter, nearly 800 tons burden with 48 guns, enough to fight off the Barbary pirates of the Mediterranean and even the English privateers in the Channel. But she had been a new ship, built at Amsterdam and never at sea before, and her timbers had not yet had time to settle. Viviano knew what a well-found and tight ship sounded like in a gale, and this was not one. Every time she pitched forward and her timbers shivered he expected the worst. It did not help that they were clinging on for their lives in the face of the worst Atlantic storm he had ever experienced, entirely dependent on the anchor cables to hold them from being swept to near-certain death against the forbidding rocky shore in front of them now.

  The harsh winter that had kept the ships icebound at Amsterdam was not the only reason for their delay. It had taken almost a year to accumulate the cargo, more than 150 consignments from 60 merchants, all of it bound for Spain and Genoa. Viviano had never before had to deal with such a wide range of goods: metal ingots, exotic hardwoods from Brazil, Guinea and Japan, bale after bale of cinnamon, pepper and cloves, all of it brought originally to Amsterdam by the ships of the United East India Company, large quantities of expensive cloth from Bruges and Leiden, hundreds of skins of Russian leather, and all manner of manufactured items, ranging from gun barrels and candlesticks and pins to globes and books and pens and pencils, and even, for one Genoese merchant with a very particular client, an elaborate multi-door mousetrap.

Such a range of merchandise had brought with it inevitable problems and delays. 50,000 pounds of Swedish iron, needing to be laden before everything else as a paying ballast, had to be sent back because a flaw in the flux required all of the ingots to be resmelted. Thirty 300-pound lead ingots taken legitimately as prize by a Dutch privateer from an English ship, sold at auction but suspected by an over-zealous customs inspector to be contraband, had to be laboriously offloaded to show him the stamps. A Flemish painter with far too high an opinion of himself in Viviano's view had endlessly procrastinated and demanded ever-more exorbitant expenses, until finally delivering his creations only when they could delay their departure no longer. And then there was the bookseller Pieter Blaeu, a good friend of his, tearing his hair out waiting for the Jesuit scholar Athanasias Kircher to finish writing his latest magnum opus, for it to be delivered overland from Rome to the printer Johanssen in Amsterdam and then to reach the wharfside literally hot off the press – and to be leather-bound in a feverish haste by Pieter himself in this very cabin, fulfilling just in time an order from yet another Spanish dilettante. And the list went on. By the time they had finally weighed anchor and sailed from Texel his mind was so cluttered with facts and figures, with values in ducats and pieces of eight, with volumes and weights and numbers of barrels and casks and bales, that he had been in an unaccustomed daze for the first few days of the voyage, until that lifted and was replaced by euphoria their departure and the small fortune that would be coming his way with the payment of freightage by the merchants who would be receiving the goods in the ports of Spain and Italy as the voyage progressed.

That optimism had changed ten days ago. The wind that had been in their favour for a swift passage down the Channel had suddenly veered to the south, making it difficult for them to make headway. After days of beating fruitlessly against it they had sought refuge in the port of Falmouth in Cornwall, in the lee of the Lizard peninsula. It was already late September and Viviano had become jittery about getting on before the autumn storms. At the first shift of the wind to the east he had set out once again, giving wide berth to the dangerous rocks at the end of the peninsula and striking out for the Bay of Biscay. But after only a day the southerlies returned, veering south-south-west and building up to gale strength, forcing them to run before the wind and seek shelter again. They were too far west to return safely around the peninsula to Falmouth, so they had found refuge off the dangerous west coast in a small anchorage called Mullion. They had been here for two days now, anchored in the lee of a little island, praying that the wind would not continue to veer westward and catch them again in full force. Viviano had only to listen to the ship and feel the changing movements to know that those prayers were not being answered.

He reached over and picked up the little statue of the Crucified Christ that had often been in his hands over the past few days. He had rescued it from a barrel of scrap brass that had been among the last consignments to be laden from the quay at Amsterdam before they had warped over the sand bar at Pampen and sailed past their old moorings off Texel to the open sea. Some industrious merchant's assistant had sheared off the statue's arms and legs, cutting it down into smaller pieces as he had done with all of the other scrap metal in an attempt to fit as much as possible into the barrels. The Calvinist Dutch had little regard for the devotional art of the Roman Church, and during the decades of war with the Spanish in the Low Countries they had done their best to eviscerate the old churches of the trappings of the papacy. Even with the war over and restrictions on Roman worship in Amsterdam lifted, rescuing the statue had seemed to Viviano like an act of defiance and its mutilated state an even greater image of Christ's suffering. He kissed it and whispered his own personal devotion. He was not accountable to God for the goods in the cargo, whatever some of the merchants might think. In signing the bills of lading he put his hope in God's Grace for the safe passage of the ship and acknowledged that it might be divine Will that they succumb to the dangers of the sea. But it was his responsibility as captain to do all that he could to safeguard those on board, and if his own personal piety helped to save those souls in this world or the next, his own included, then he would have fulfilled his contract with the people and with God.

'*Capitano.*' A man stood at the doorway, drenched in spray and holding a sounding lead. He was one of the English sailors they had recruited in Amsterdam from a ship that had been taken as a prize by the Dutch, the same ship that had been carrying the lead ingots that ballasted the hull beneath then now, lead that had once been destined to make shot for the English navy but was now part of the richest cargo to sail from Holland to Italy in his lifetime. Viviano braced himself against the surge and looked at the man impatiently. 'Well? What is it?'

The man ducked into the cabin and showed him the sounding lead. Viviano could see where the depression in the base that held a dab of pitch to pick up a sample of the seabed was filled with coarse-grained sand. 'I know these waters, *capitano*,' the man said, his Italian heavily accented in the English way. 'It is deep sand from here all the way to the shore. Even with two anchors the ship will not hold against the south-westerly for long. And even if the wind abates, the swell will linger and may even get worse. With each wave the ship will lurch closer to the shore, dragging her anchors on the way.'

Viviano stared at the man. 'Well? What do you suggest?'

The man put the lead on the deck and braced himself in the doorway. 'Where we are pointing, less than half a mile away now, is a stretch of high cliff with sandy coves on either side. You might think that we could cast away our anchors and steer into either cove with the hope of grounding, but you would be wrong. To the left close to shore is a rocky reef that will gouge the hull out. To the right the current sweeps round the bay towards the north, meaning that even with the helm hard a-port we would never make the beach and we would be driven into the cliffs.'

'So we may as well continue to trust in our anchors, and in Providence.'

The man shook his head. 'The anchors will not hold. The sand is coarse, as you could see, and therefore loose. And nobody wrecked against those cliffs survives. *Nobody*.'

'Are you saying we should abandon ship in the boats?'

The man stared at him intently, and then nodded. 'I have concealed my identity, as otherwise I would have been imprisoned by the Dutch. I was master of the *Peter and Rebecca*, the ship from which the ingots were taken. I know the agony of a captain about to lose his ship, and why you may be reluctant now to think about taking to the boats. But I swear you have no choice.'

Viviano pursed his lips and shut his eyes for a moment. He knew the man was right. He had been thinking this for several hours now. He opened his eyes and took a deep breath. 'The boats would make for the cove ahead, to the right of the cliffs?'

The man shook his head. 'That cove has a long shallow reach and the swell rolls up it to a great height. The boats would be overwhelmed and there would be no chance of putting out to sea again to return to the ship for more people.

We must instead make for another cove further to the right, in the lee of the island. With the wind veering from sou'sou'-west to sou'-west the island will soon no longer protect the ship, but it would protect the boats once they had pulled out of the wind into its lee. As we stand, the boats would have less than a cable length of exposed sea to navigate before then. We have a strong crew, and it could be done. But every moment that we delay the opportunity will diminish. Another half-cable of drag on the anchors and we will be too far to the north-east, too close to those cliffs. The oarsmen in the boats would have to pull directly against the wind and would never make it.'

'Then we have no time to lose. I will go below to warn the passengers. You muster the men from your crew and we will break out the boats. Together we will choose the strongest oarsmen.'

'There is another danger,' the man said. 'The local Lord of the Manor and the King's men will be kind and solicitous, but it may be hours before they arrive and the people hereabouts may be of another moral standing entirely. They live by wrecking, and word of a rich Genoese cast ashore may set them in a frenzy. You may not be able to keep the powder in your pistols dry in the boats, but you would be well-advised to have daggers and swords at the ready.'

'I will set my quartermaster to it. And thank you, *capitano*.'

'There is only one *capitano* on this ship. I will continue to follow your orders.'

'I will see you on the main deck.'

The man nodded and quickly left. Viviano waited for the ship to roll level, and then hurried across the cabin to his strongbox. The fact that the ship was not just pitching with the swell but rolling and yawing was an alarming development and would put more strain on the anchor cables. He opened the chest, dug through the clothes and finery and pulled out two heavy purses of gold ducats, shoving them into pockets on either side of his doublet. He would leave the ship's supply of silver pieces-of-eight, but the gold was his own personal treasure and might be vital in the days ahead to make his way to his agent in London and then back home to Genoa, and to pay off any surviving crew. He lifted up a sumptuous cloak of fine Liege cloth and then hesitated, casting his mind back to a dark night twenty years before in the Bay of Biscay, to another ship and another wrecking. It had been his first-ever voyage as a boy, and he had learned that heavy clothes that seemed so important for warmth only became waterlogged and hastened death in the sea. If there were people living hereabouts as the English captain said, then gold in one hand and a dagger in the other might dissuade them from plundering the survivors and help to pay for warmth and lodging for himself and the others who made it ashore.

He thought of what the captain had said, and then reached into the chest again and pulled out a beautiful German brass-barrelled flintlock pistol that he always kept loaded. It was one of a pair, but he could only sensibly fit one beneath his doublet. The lock was of a new design meant to keep the priming powder dry when the steel closed on the pan, but even so he wrapped a silk stocking tightly around it and over the steel for added protection. The gunsmith had done his best to make the lock waterproof but had probably not envisaged his creation being taken into the teeth of a north Atlantic gale.

He tucked the pistol inside his doublet and quickly sifted through the papers at the top of the chest. He glanced at the plague passport, issued at Amsterdam to show that the ship was free of pestilence, and for a moment he felt the hollowness of loss. Plague had ravaged London a year ago and Genoa before that, taking his wife and young son and many thousands of others. It seemed that Divine Providence was once again wreaking vengeance on humankind as it had done in the days of ancient Egypt, that the sins of avarice and greed of which he was a part had turned the eye of God away. The joy of being at sea and away from the throngs of people on the wharf had made him forget his loss for a few days, but the storm had brought it back again. He took a deep breath, tossed the document aside and pulled out the one he had been searching for, the passport from the English king Charles II that had guaranteed his ship safe passage through the Channel unmolested by English warships. It might prove vital to prove his identity and to lay claim to any cargo that was salvaged or washed ashore, to show that it was Genoese and not Dutch. He rolled up the vellum sheet as tightly as he could, wrapped another around it and pushed it in beside the pistol, and then buttoned up the doublet and wrapped another stocking around his neck in the hope of keeping water from dripping inside his clothing.

He remembered the night five months ago in this very cabin when his friend Antonio Basso had presented him with the pistols. Antonio has been one of those who had envied Viviano his ship and its guns, and he had joked that he hardly needed the pistols when his ship was armed like a galleon. He could never have guessed that the pistols might have their first use not against pirates but against wreckers on the Cornish shore. Just before they had left Amsterdam, word had come that Antonio's ship, the *Sacrificio d'Abramo*, had been taken as a prize by the English, her cargo sold off and Antonio himself dangerously ill in London with the plague, now presumed dead. He had taken the risk of leaving without a passport while the war between England and Holland was still at its height and had thought to evade the English by risking the weather around Scotland and Ireland, only to fall foul of an English squadron off Galway. Without a passport and coming from Amsterdam he would have had no hope of convincing the English that he was Genoese rather than Dutch, and they had therefore thought him fair prize during time of war. Little could either of them have imagined as they drank wine late into the night the fate that would befall them both before the year was out, and the immense wealth of cargo on which their own fortunes and those of so many merchants had depended.

The ship lurched again, more violently this time, and

Viviano felt the timbers strain and creak against the cables. If the cables parted before the boats could be got out - a possibility that he and the English captain had known but not voiced - then all on board would be doomed. He looked round the cabin one last time, walked out under the main deck and slid down the rails of the stairwell into the hold. The passengers were all there, cowering miserably on top of the bales and barrels, where he had told them to go while the ship rode out the storm. There were twenty-five altogether: the families of two merchants returning from Amsterdam to Genoa, the youngest a child of five years, and a dozen English men and women picked up in Falmouth bound for the English colony of Tangier in north Africa. One of them was a secretary to the English Admiralty official Samuel Pepys, whose acquaintance Viviano had made two years previously when Antonio had also been in London and they had spent an uproarious evening with Pepys in the taverns of Fleet Street. The secretary was a garrulous man like his master, and it struck Viviano now that his friendship with Pepys might prove useful if it came to a claim to the High Court of Admiralty for what might survive of the cargo. At the moment the man was doubled over retching with seasickness on one of the merchant Tensini's bales of silk. Tensini himself seemed to care little that the contents of the Englishman's stomach might be tainting his precious wares irreparably, a small concern given the circumstances they were now in.

Viviano braced himself against the base of the mainmast and raised his voice so that they could all hear. 'You must go on deck immediately,' he said, gesturing emphatically upwards for the benefit of the English passengers who might not understand Italian. 'We are preparing to cast off our boats to take everyone ashore.'

Tensini, a well-fed man wearing too many clothes, rose from among his collected personal belongings with bags and purses hanging from him, evidently having anticipated a precipitate departure. 'When will we be returning to the ship, *capitano?*' he demanded.

'That is in the hands of Providence. For now you may only take what you can carry with ease on your person. Coins, jewellery, nothing else.' The English secretary crawled off the bale and lurched towards Viviano, who caught him and directed him to the stairway, trying not to gag on the smell of vomit. 'Anything to end this,' the man said hoarsely in English. At that moment a deafening report like a cannon resounded through the hold, and one of the women shrieked. A crack several fingers wide had appeared along the port side just below the waterline, and seawater sprayed the bales and the people. An even greater fear of Viviano's than the anchor parting was that the strain would break the ship. She may have been impressive in size and armament, built with a speed that pleased the merchants who financed her, but the Italian captains had complained that the recent ships of Amsterdam were not as well-built as those of Genoa; commissioning them from the cheaper Dutch yards was a false economy. Already she had sprung a leak in the Zuiderzee that had forced them to turn back to Amsterdam for repairs and delayed her departure further, obliging Viviano to sail into the Atlantic just as the autumn storms were brewing up. Now with the hull splitting apart in front of him the quality of her build was all too apparent. Whether she sank here at anchor or was blown into shore, God in his infinite wisdom had decreed that the maiden voyage of the *Santo Cristo di Castello* would also be her last.

There was another ominous cracking sound, this time from the base of the mainmast. Viviano helped the last of the people up the ladder and then stood for a moment alone with the doomed cargo, staring at the marks branded on the barrels and stencilled on the bales, thinking of all the merchants who would be affected by this loss. He glanced at the strongroom beside the mainmast, thought for a moment and then made his way determinedly towards it, stepping over bales already waterlogged and ruined by seawater. The strongroom was built above the hold into the floor of the gundeck and was meant for valuable items requiring careful handling for which extra freightage cost had been added.

He took a key from his belt, unlocked the door and stepped inside, steadying himself against the lurching of the ship. The room was packed from floor to ceiling with cases and boxes, testament to the faith of the merchants who believed that the *Santo Cristo di Castello* was a good bet for their most valuable merchandise because her size and armament made her less vulnerable to capture. It had been good business for Viviano, too, and he felt slightly ill as he thought of the freightage fees at the destination that would now no longer come his way. But this was no time to dwell on losses; he had come here to see one thing only. He pushed apart two barrels containing a pair of globes from the workshop of Blaeu, one representing the heavens and the other the earth. Stacked above them were two wooden cases containing the paintings that had taken so long to procure, the name of the artist emblazoned on the packaging – Rembrandt van Rijn. Beyond that was a crate containing a complete set of Pieter Blaeu's *Atlas Maior*, the most expensive books ever produced. And beyond that lay his objective, a barrel containing the collection of Father Kircher's books whose delay had caused Pieter such consternation, that had been the last items of cargo to be sealed up before the ship had set sail.

He stooped over the barrel in the gloom, reached for a hammer and chisel among the tools left in the room and used them to prise open the lid. The *Mundus Subterraneus* was at the top, still smelling strongly of printer's ink, but that was not what he was after. Beneath it spaced with wooden slats to prevent the ink from being pressed by the heavier work above was another document, a single sheet of vellum bound in leather. It had not gone to the printer Janssonius but direct from Kircher to Blaeu, who had added some annotations in his own hand drawn from the extensive geographical knowledge that he had accrued from sea captains coming into Amsterdam who had contributed to his *Atlas Maior* and navigational globes. There had only been one copy of the document, and that was in Viviano's hands now.

He stared at the vellum and remembered when Sauli had first spoken to him about Father Kircher, just before Viviano had set out from Genoa for Amsterdam to oversee the construction of the *Santo Cristo di Castello*. Sauli had wanted him personally to take charge of acquiring the paintings and books he had ordered, chasing up the commission for the paintings and making sure that his name was at the top of the list for the *Mundus Subterraneus* when it came off the press. But there had been something else, something secret. Sauli was a great admirer of Kircher and had funded his excavation of the ruins of the Temple of Isis in Rome, where Kircher had been seeking anything that might help in his quest to translate hieroglyphics. Among the statues and inscriptions brought in the Roman period from Egypt was a Roman copy in bronze of an ancient Egyptian map. To Kircher's astonishment it showed Atlantis, the lost citadel that he had studied extensively from the accounts of the ancient Greek philosopher Plato describing its inundation in a flood. It was shown on the tablet as an island in the Atlantic Ocean that might equate with the Azores or one of the archipelagos off the west coast of Africa.

In great excitement he told Sauli of his discovery and they agreed to mount an expedition to find the island. They brought Blaeu into their confidence, as he was to package and annotate the map, as well as the Genoese merchants Cornelissen and Porrata in Lisbon, as they had dealings with the Portuguese and Spanish settlers on the islands. Viviano was to be the lynchpin in the plan, as he was to take Kircher's drawing of the map from Genoa to Amsterdam and then convey the printed version to Cornelissen and Porrata when the *Santo Cristo di Castello* reached Lisbon. He had sworn to Sauli that he would protect this consignment above all others. There had been others after the map, a mysterious priesthood whom Kircher believed still worshipped the Egyptian goddess Isis and whose land in Rome he had apparently violated when he had begun digging. And now to honour that promise Viviano was making the decision that no captain should ever have to make, to put the rescue of a material object above his duty to remain with his ship and his passengers to the end, something that he knew would live with him for the remainder of his days if the worst should happen.

He took out the volume and traced his hand over Pieter Blaeu's precise writing in red lettering on the cover. He quickly opened it up, seeing again the map that had made him stare wide-eyed in wonder. What it showed might be nothing, a flight of fantasy by Kircher, a man known for straddling the line between hard science and imagination. But Sauli had been convinced and so had Pieter, a man whose opinion Viviano greatly respected. He closed the volume and looked at the lettering on the cover. The larger volume, the *Mundus Subterraneus*, was subtitled *Atlante*, an old Italian word for Atlas. The title on this smaller volume was *Insula Orichalcum,* the Island of Orichalcum, a word that Kircher said came from the ancient Greek texts and referred to a miraculous material of the Atlanteans, an elixir of life. Beneath it was a word nearly the same as the one on the first volume, a word that Viviano himself had seen in Plato's account of the lost civilisation, a word that all explorers who sailed the uncharted oceans knew: *Atlantis.* If he could find that place, if he could bring back the fabled substance that was meant to cure all plagues, then his name would be greater even than the Genoese and Portuguese who had first rounded the capes and circumnavigated the oceans; he would bring a world beset with pestilence a treasure far greater than all of the merchandise carried by all of the ships that had ever set sail in his lifetime.

The ship rolled again, the timbers gave another ear-splitting crack and the hull seemed to shimmer and shift. He opened a page of the *Mundus*, took out a pencil made of English graphite that he kept in his pouch and quickly wrote a note. He picked up several thin sheets of leather beside the barrel all inked with his personal monogram and wrapped them around the book, trying to make it as watertight as possible. It seemed a futile gesture in the circumstances, but he was thinking of his friend Pieter and the efforts he had made to get it printed and on board the ship. At least he would be able to tell him if he survived that he had done everything possible to keep it preserved, if by some miracle the barrel might be salvaged. He hammered the lid back on, tore a length of baling material off the package with the paintings, wrapped that around the map and slid it inside his doublet beside the pistol. The next lurch sent a tremor through his body as well and was followed by a terrible grinding noise from one end of the ship to the other. It was time to go.

He sloshed over the bales to the stairwell and climbed through the hatch to the main deck. He stepped out into the full force of the gale, the rain lashing the deck around him and foam flecking his face. He could just make out the island off the stern, the headland off the starboard bow and the line of the cliffs dead ahead, all shrouded in spray. The English captain came up to him, one hand shielding his eyes from the foam. 'You will see that the wind has edged round fully to the west and is now against us,' he shouted in Italian. 'We no longer have the advantage of the island. It is as we feared.'

Viviano leaned close to him, bracing himself against the starboard railing. 'There's a split in the hull below the waterline,' he shouted in reply. 'She's taking on water fast. And the base of the mainmast is cracked.'

The other man gestured overboard. 'The boats will take ninety people off. That's the number of the crew. There is no room for the passengers.'

'Then a boat must return for them. I will see to it.'

The man pursed his lips, looking at the women and children clustered against the railing. 'God willing, *capitano*. God willing.'

Two of the ship's three boats had already been swung out from the mainyard and had set off for shore, each under the command of a ship's officer. The third was still swinging precariously with the boatswain and oarsmen already aboard. The boatswain bellowed a command and the yardmen released the tackle, the boat hitting the sea only inches from the side of the hull. The sudden release of pressure on the tackle caused the mainmast to crack and come crashing down, hanging up against the foremast with the spars and rigging dangling over the side. The mass of cordage swung back and forth as the ship pitched, narrowly missing the boat each time. Viviano leaned over the side, shouting and gesturing at the hanging wreckage so that the boatswain would see. A man at each end of the boat held a rope attached to the ship's railing, and they pulled on them to draw the boat closer and allow the remaining crewmen to clamber down the rope ladder that had been rolled over the side. The English captain was the last to go, and as he sat in the boat he made space on the thwart beside him for Viviano. 'Capitano,' the boatswain yelled, his voice barely carrying above the wind. 'Come aboard *pronto*.'

Viviano could not in any conscience leave the passengers to their fate, but by going in the boat he would serve that purpose best. Staying aboard with them would only seal their fate as well as his; the only likelihood of a boat returning would be under his command. They were a good crew, but he knew they would not choose on their own volition to set out once again into the maw of the sea after having made landfall. He would need a dozen strong men on the oars, and if needs be he had the gold to induce them. He felt certain that the English captain would join him, along with some of the English crew who had befriended the English passengers over the past few days. He turned to the merchant Tensini, who had slumped beside the railing, and leaned close to make himself heard. 'I will go with them,' he shouted. 'And then I will return for you all, God willing. Be strong and pray.'

Tensini was beyond replying and looked up at him with vacant eyes, his hair matted and his face streaming with water. Viviano hesitated for a moment, and then reached into his doublet for the little devotional figure of Christ and thrust it into Tensini's hands. He turned to the rail, grasped the rope and vaulted over, kicking off as the boat rose on the crest of a wave and dropping into the hands that were reaching up for him. He sat on the middle thwart wedged between the men on either side as the boat pitched and rolled. 'Release the lines,' the boatswain yelled, grasping the tiller while the oarsmen fended the boat off to prevent it from being dashed to pieces against the ship's hull. One oar cracked, and the oarsman shrieked as a splinter went through his arm. And then they were away, the oarsmen pulling with all their might and the boatswain leaning hard on the tiller to keep the bow into the wind and the boat from swinging broadside-on to the waves. Slowly they made headway, with the island in front of them and the headland to the left. Another cable's length and they would be in the lee of the island and out of the worst of the gale, able to swing round the headland and into the safety of the cove.

Viviano looked back at the ship, still only a stone's throw away. The English captain was doing the same, and then turned to Viviano, shaking his head. They both knew that the chances of returning to the ship and coming alongside to take off the people were diminishing by the second. The wind had strengthened even more, and the swell was now so high that it was breaking in whitecaps. As the ship pitched forward the mainmast slid off, taking the spars and canvas but with the rigging still holding it on. Viviano watched in horror at what he knew must happen next. The mass of flotsam would be pushed by the waves in front of the bow and act like a sea-anchor in reverse, keeping the ship at right-angles to the waves but placing intolerable strain on the anchor cables off the stern. He watched the fallen rigging became taut and then heard two cracks like gunshots as the anchor cables parted, sending the cables whipping around in the wind. The stern rose high, enough to see the rudder down to the keel, pushed up by the swell. The ship seemed to balance on the crest, as if between life and death, and then it plunged forward, quickly receding as the wind drove it towards the black line of cliffs just visible through the spray in the distance.

For a moment Viviano had seen a line of stricken faces staring at them from the rail, an image that he knew would be seared in his memory for as long as he lived. But there was nothing he could do to save those people now, and he tried to put it from his mind. He felt the document under his doublet and remembered his promise to Sauli. The wind shrieked and howled above their heads, drenching them with spray with each crest of the swell. They were not out of danger yet, and he needed to look to his crew. He and the English captain each took the end of an oar, doubling up with the sailors. Divine Providence had shown its hand already today, a hand that had turned resolutely against them, and now it was up to them to use all of their earthly strength to pull for their lives.

CHAPTER 5

Off the Lizard Peninsula, Cornwall, present-day

Jack eased himself into his kayak and leaned back against the seat, wedging his legs into a gap in the equipment in front of him and picking up the paddle. He glanced back at the pebbly shoreline of the cove to make sure that he had left nothing behind, and then took his first stroke to pull the bow round towards the exit of the little harbour. As he paddled out past the stone wall of the pier he felt the swell take him, and saw it slap against the outer face of the masonry. Ahead of him beyond Mullion Island the horizon was lined with dark clouds, the leading edge of a storm that was slowly heading in his direction over Land's End, but for now it was a beautiful day and the sea was crystal-clear, the reflected sunlight radiating up from the sand and rock a few metres below him.

He swung past a fishing boat heading back into the harbour, waving at the fisherman and giving a thumbs-up, and headed to the right past the jagged serpentine rocks rising fifteen metres or more that marked the outer limit of the promontory. Around the rocks to the right lay the cove of Polurrian with its sandy beach about a kilometre away, and about half a kilometre beyond that to the north lay the wreck site. He paused for a moment to take in the scene, Mullion Island now behind him and the coast of the Lizard peninsula trending away to the north beyond Polurrian and Gunwalloe coves, and then he began to paddle determinedly across the open water of the bay, making directly towards the cleft in the cliffs that marked the inlet of Pol Glas and the site of the wreck.

He had decided to make his own way this morning by kayak rather than joining the project rigid inflatable boat at the larger harbour of Porthleven because he had wanted to retrace the route that the *Santo Cristo di Castello* had taken on that fateful October night in 1667. He knew that Captain Viviano had tried to hold the ship in the lee of Mullion Island, not far from his position now, casting anchors in the hope of riding out the storm that had blown them to this place from the open sea to the west. The lee of the island might have seemed safe, but the wind veering even a few points could have caught the ship and pushed her back out into the exposed waters of the bay, causing her anchors to drag on the sandy seabed and the ship to be pushed inexorably into the full force of the storm.

The records showed that Viviano had gone ashore in the ship's boat with most of his crew, making landfall in Mullion Cove where Jack had set off a few minutes before. He tried to put himself in Viviano's mind, imagining his thoughts as the storm waters rose. He would not have abandoned his ship as long as there was hope of recovery, not with merchants and their families still on board as well as cargo on which his future depended. But if the crew were insistent on leaving he may have had no choice other than to accompany them so that he could ensure that a boat under his command returned to rescue those still on board if there seemed no hope of the ship holding ground. It would have been a gamble, and it was one that Viviano lost. Jack tried to imagine him watching helplessly from the boat as the cables broke and the ship plunged away towards Pol Glas, dooming the passengers. For a captain to lose his ship that way would have been tantamount to death, leaving him plagued by guilt and knowing that his career was now forfeit, the rest of his life to be lived in the shadow of a calamity for which he would have felt personally responsible.

Jack paddled out further into the bay, the wide sweep of Polurrian beach to his right and the cliffs sharply outlined ahead where they rose above Pol Glas. He remembered the rush of excitement two years earlier when he had first seen the wreck. In his long career exploring wrecks around the world he had rarely gone in search of a richer cargo. All he had to go on was a tantalising document in the Admiralty papers for 1667 and the account of a local diver who had snorkelled out to Pol Glas in the late 1960s and seen cannon. In the years since then the site had been buried in sand and shingle, but it had never been far from his mind while he was focussed on other projects.

The spur to search for it had been a lull in their work in the Mediterranean and a violent winter storm that had shifted the sand on many of the wrecks along this coast. He and Rebecca had snorkelled out together from Polurrian that spring, following the same route taken by the diver who had discovered the wreck almost half a century before. The water had been cold but clear, with the annual growth of kelp that obscured much of the seabed not yet having taken hold; they could easily make out the sandy gullies and rocky reefs below them. Just before the entrance to Pol Glas they had passed over a gully containing iron concretions and copper piping from the *Boyne*, an inward-bound East Indiaman wrecked here in 1873. Wreck had piled on wreck along this coast since the beginning of the age of sail, creating a litter of artefacts half-revealed on the seabed; to some it was a chaotic jumble but to Jack it was like stratigraphy on a land site, a chronology of world history. In Pol Glas itself there were the remains of at least two other wrecks that had taken place since the *Santo Cristo di Castello*, but almost every vestige of them had disappeared in the violence of their wrecking and the sweeping of the inlet by the sea that occurred with every storm that beset this coast.

As he and Rebecca turned into the inlet they had swum under the shadow of the cliffs, a darkening of the seabed that made it seem deep and forbidding. He had felt the familiar excitement as he approached a new site as well as the respect that he always felt at a place where so many people had lost their lives. Only a few weeks before he had stood at the top of the cliff looking down on a seething cauldron of white water and spray, watching the swell suck in and out and imagining what it would have been like for the people in their final moments being blown into the cliffs. As a diver he had a strong empathy with the mariners of the past, as he was subject to the same vagaries of wind and tide and took the same risks every time he went into the sea – those same forces that dashed people to their deaths could be felt in the sea even in the best of conditions, and he had felt them that morning as they swam under the cliffs and into the inlet that had been a place of no return for so many on that day in 1667.

Their chances of seeing anything exposed at the site had been small. Years earlier after word of the snorkeller's discovery had leaked out treasure-hunters had used explosives to try to get at the cargo, inadvertently bringing down tons of rock from the cliff face and blocking up the entrance to the gully. But it was that act of vandalism that had driven Jack to relocate the site, as the fallen rock had prevented the shingle from dispersing and left much of the wreck buried, protecting it from further looting. The severe storms of the past winter might have driven the shingle further into the inlet, revealing areas of concretion and loose artefacts that had not been seen before.

Rebecca had dived down first and surfaced brimming with excitement, pointing to an area where boulders and other shapes could be seen among the shingle. Jack followed her straight to a cannon, its muzzle orange with rust and poking out of the sand. Certain artefacts had an electrifying effect on him: in the Mediterranean it was pottery amphoras, the ubiquitous transport containers of antiquity, and in the sea off Cornwall it was cannon. To find a cannon meant that they were almost certainly looking at a shipwreck, and the surrounding seabed took on a new meaning. His vision was sharpened, and shapes that might have been dismissed a few moments earlier were suddenly worth closer inspection.

He had put his hand on the cannon, as if to reassure himself of its reality, and then surfaced giving Rebecca the OK sign, the adrenaline coursing through him. A few metres further on he saw another cannon, and then another beyond that. They had dived down again and again, photographing each gun in turn and measuring them using their dive knives as crude rulers. And then an astonishing vista opened up before them: the seabed seemed to be glittering with gold. The shingle had been swept clear and the concretion beneath it was embedded with artefacts of brass and copper, including thousands of brass clothing pins. It was incredibly exciting – this part of the site had never been seen before. He knew then that the wreck would be his sole focus while the good weather lasted, that he would dive on it over and over and not let go until he had got as much as he could out of it and begun to tell its full story.

He remembered the following days of diving as he steered the kayak towards Pol Glas. He had immediately assembled a crack team of divers, with Rebecca able to give the remaining few days of her university vacation to the site and using local divers affiliated to IMU who were familiar with the waters of the west Lizard. Because of the shallow reefs and unpredictable weather he had decided against committing an IMU research vessel to the site – bringing a deep-draught vessel close to this shore would risk exactly the same fate that befell the *Santo Cristo di Castello* - and instead had used inflatable boats from Porthleven and Mullion or shore-dived it from Polurrian, making the arduous trek with their gear up and down the coast path from their vehicles. They had known that time might not be on their side – another storm and the shingle might shift back again – and they had put maximum effort into the recovery of artefacts, systematically excavating the exposed area of the wreck that they had seen on that first dive.

Rebecca had made the first finds, a beautiful candlestick and part of an elaborate chandelier. As more and more similar artefacts appeared Jack realised that they were looking at church decorations, from a time when the Catholic churches of Holland had been stripped of their ornaments by the Protestants and many of the items were cut up and sold as scrap. It was his first real glimpse into the historical backdrop of the wreck, and he was hooked – there were few periods of recent history more fascinating for him than seventeenth century Europe, a time of religious strife and war but also of exploration and discovery and extraordinary achievements in culture and science. The site was providing exactly what he yearned for in a wreck, artefacts that were not just intrinsically interesting but also portholes into the past that opened up bigger pictures to explore.

Later that autumn when the weather had closed in and diving had ceased he had travelled with Rebecca and Jeremy to the Metropolitan Museum of Art in New York, where they had examined paintings of the Dutch Golden Age in which similar objects were depicted - often the best way of dating a particular style of candlestick or church ornament if the date of the painting was known. Standing in front of a celebrated triptych from the workshop of Robert Campin of Tournai, dated to 1427-32, they had seen exactly the same shape of 'lavabo' or holy-water vessel that they had found on the wreck only a few weeks before. It was thrilling to realise that they had discovered artefacts more than two centuries older than the wreck itself, among the oldest artefacts ever to be found underwater off the south coast of England.

He refocused on the present as he paddled up to the buoy with the IMU flag that had been moored at the entrance to the inlet, and then looked in the direction of the CCTV camera that had been positioned on a building above Polurrian with a view of Pol Glas. The IMU campus was close enough that a security team could be here within an hour if illicit diving were recorded at the site; the days of treasure hunters using explosives were thankfully long gone. He had decided to go to the site this morning ahead of the RIB that would arrive shortly with the final team who would close the excavation and retrieve any tools in advance of the heavy seas that were expected that evening. He had wanted to see the site again as he had on that first day with Rebecca, and to finish excavating the sector where they had made their first discoveries two years before.

The rocks at the entrance were just awash, appearing and disappearing with each surge. He had been right to arrive early before the sea picked up. With the bottom only eight metres deep at low tide a significant swell on the surface meant a groundswell on the seabed, making it difficult to hold position while excavating as the water swept in and out. The furthest point of the inlet, where he planned to anchor the kayak, was a backwater protected from the swell by rocks on either side of a narrow entranceway, a bottleneck that he needed to navigate carefully in order to prevent the boat from scraping the sides. At the back he could see the jumble of boulders where a section of the cliff had fallen three years before, and above that a stretch of fencing showing where the coast path had been diverted. Each time a westerly storm battered this coast there was the threat of another fall; the possibility of a massive collapse lent further urgency to their work at the site.

He paddled over the main part of the site and then steered the kayak towards the gap at the back, bringing it broadside-on and then pulling round hard to the right to get through. He passed the rock with inches to spare, and then came to a halt in the middle of the backwater. He waited for a few minutes, letting the residual swell push him gently to and fro, making sure that the worst of it was blocked and that it was safe to anchor as he had planned. He tossed his paddle on its retaining line in the water and then knelt up to cast out the small grapnel anchors from either end of the boat. It was nearly low tide and his dive would be at slack water, so he did not need to worry about the lines tightening up and the anchors dragging as the sea level rose.

He knelt again in the centre of the boat, put his arms in his wetsuit and reached back to zip it up, wriggling his shoulders until he was comfortable. He preferred diving in a wetsuit to a more bulky drysuit at shallow sites in the summer, when the temperature was tolerable for several hours underwater. After making sure his knife was secure on his calf and strapping his dive computer to his wrist he heaved up his cylinder rig from where it had been lying between his legs while he was paddling. He checked that the valves were fully open, blasted some air into the buoyancy compensator so that it would float and then rolled it over the side of the kayak into the water, clipping it with a carabiner to a metal ring on the side. The single 12-litre cylinder with a 3-litre pony bottle as a safety backup would give him the time he needed, with the area that he planned to excavate being less than half a metre square and mainly loose shingle that could easily be cleared.

He put on his weight belt and fins and dangled his feet over the opposite side of the kayak to the rig, making it less likely when he dropped into the water that he would flip the boat over. For a few moments he looked down, feeling the boat swinging lightly against the anchor ropes, enjoying the cool of the water on his legs after the exertion of paddling in the heat of the sun. Earlier in the bay he had not been able to see into the water because of the glare of reflected sunlight off the surface, but now that the sun had risen higher he could see more clearly. Small jellyfish and filaments of tentacles and weed bobbed around him, and he could make out the rock and kelp below. The refraction and the shimmering light seemed to enhance the interface between the air and the sea, between the world from which he was about to depart and one that was more his natural element, where he had found the greatest excitement as an archaeologist in the search for sites such as the one that lay spread out below him now.

He put on his hood and mask and gloves and slipped into the water, dropping down under the boat and coming up beside his rig. He unhooked it from the boat and eased himself into it, tightening the straps and clipping the regulator second stages in place on his front. He began snorkelling towards the main part of the site, passing through the gap between the rocks and then riding the swell over a boulder that came within a metre of the surface. Beyond that the bottom levelled out into smaller boulders and shingle, with the sunlight reflecting in radiant lines off patches of sand and the seabed to the left obscured by the shadow of the cliff. He saw the first cannon, rusty orange against the light-coloured rocks, and then two more, scoured down by centuries of shingle movement so that they were barely recognisable. And then he saw the edge of the excavated area where the cliff on one side and the rocks on the other formed a wide gully, with the reef on the outside of the inlet that he had passed on the way in marking the seaward limit of the site. Almost all of the artefacts had been caught within this gully, many of them loose in the shingle but others seized up in a great matte of concretion that had formed when a consignment of iron bars had corroded. One end of that matte below the seaward reef was exposed, and it was there that he planned to excavate today. From the finds that had been made already he had a hunch that this part of the site might include artefacts from the captain's cabin, and he wanted to dig down to bedrock to be sure that they had found everything.

He reached a point directly over the excavation and floated still for a few moments, slowing his breathing in preparation for diving. He raised his head above the water and saw the IMU boat approaching from out at sea. It would be at least half an hour before the divers on the boat were ready to descend, enough time for him to do what he wanted before they would need to get into the area to cover the excavation with sandbags to protect it from the coming storm. He took out his snorkel and put in his regulator, raised the inflator hose of his buoyancy compensator to empty it and sank below the surface, blowing on his nose to equalise the pressure as he dropped to the seabed. He injected a blast of air into his jacket to achieve neutral buoyancy as he swam towards the excavation and then emptied it completely once he was in position, wedging his legs in a cleft in the rock and coming to rest just above the edge of the concretion where the shingle still covered an unexcavated area of artefacts.

He scanned the concretion, listening to the suck of his intake and the bubbles of his exhaust, feeling the slight movement of groundswell pushing him forward and back. The surface of the concretion had been smoothed by the shingle and was shiny with brass pins and other objects embedded within it, just as he and Rebecca had seen on that first dive. Today he was intent on what lay beneath the concretion, in the half-metre or so of sediment that had been trapped underneath when the concretion had formed. The artefacts there were generally in better condition because they had not been tumbled to and fro in the shingle; he should be able to reach underneath and pull them out. He turned to where tools had been stashed beside the excavation and took a weighted bucket, filling it with shingle as he scooped it out from the seabed while carefully looking for artefacts that might be loose within it.

As the shingle gave way to sand he began to find fragments of crudely cast copper ingot, some the size of his hand but mostly in small pieces. He took a weighted finds box and put the artefacts inside, and then returned for more. Once he had reached bedrock he began to find heavier items caught in fissures and cracks, including lead musket shot and several one-inch balls for the ship's swivel guns. He wafted carefully in one crack, knowing that the smallest finds were often the most interesting, and was rewarded with a lead seal used to identify bales of cloth. He peered closely and saw that it bore the crossed-keys stamp of the city of Leiden, one of the main cloth-exporting centres of the Netherlands and the source of several of the consignments being carried on the ship. It was an exciting find, a small porthole into the manufacturing and trade that had fuelled this venture and underpinned the maritime world of the seventeenth century.

He put the seal in the mesh bag that he carried in his buoyancy compensator pocket for more delicate items and turned back to the excavation, seeing the bases of two embedded candlesticks sticking out. While he waited for the silt to settle he looked around at the site. For a few moments it was as if he were in the nave of a great church, the candlesticks and chandeliers suspended in ghostly form in front of him as they would have been affixed to pillars and arches, the rocky sides of the gully transformed into apses and alcoves hung with the cloth and other finery that had been carried on board. Reconstructing a ship and its cargo from a wreck site was always an act of imagination, but a point could be reached where they appeared in front of him as if reconstituted, spirited out of the seabed like a hologram. The image of the church transformed into the hold of the ship, with bales of cloth and spices and in the centre the captain's strongroom, its door locked but containing the most precious items of all – paintings and globes and books, bound up in leather and sealed in barrels that may have kept them watertight during the passage but were no protection against the destructive power of the sea once the ship was wrecked.

He looked down again and reached beneath the concretion almost as far as his shoulder, feeling for any artefacts loose in the sediment. His hand closed around a cylindrical object and he carefully pulled it out. It was a one-pound brass merchant's weight for a steelyard, part of a set that had been on the ship. That was exciting enough, but when he angled it he could see that the top had been stamped by the Dutch regulating authority with three dates – 1663, 1664 and 1665. The last date, 1665, was the very latest that he would have expected to find on a ship that had been built and equipped in 1665-6 and had been due to depart on its maiden voyage that year, only to be delayed. There had been no need for further evidence that the wreck was the *Santo Cristo di Castello*, but it was exciting to find an actual date like this on an artefact that clinched the ship's identity.

He placed the weight on the finds tray and reached into the hole again. This time he pulled out a small brass chisel of the type that had been used to knock wax seals off letters, an essential desktop tool in the seventeenth century. It was another rare find, few such items having survived from that period. Could this have been a tool that Viviano himself used, to break open correspondence from his patron in Genoa and from the merchants and agents whose cargo he was transporting? It seemed entirely plausible – Viviano had been living on board the ship during the long cold winter in Amsterdam before she set sail, and his cabin would have served as his office. Jack had felt something else in the hole and pulled out the gilt-brass end of a pair of nautical dividers, a valuable piece of equipment that Viviano might have used to measure distances on the charts that he acquired from the Amsterdam booksellers. Jack was now certain that he was excavating a part of the site that contained objects from the captain's cabin. Holding those two artefacts, the chisel and the dividers, he felt as close to Viviano as he ever had been, as close as when he had touched Viviano's signature on the petition to King Charles II for safe passage through English waters.

He put the artefacts in the finds bag and checked his pressure gauge and computer. The arrow on his gauge was nearly in the red, showing that he was down to his final fifteen minutes or so. He pushed off from the seabed, injected air into his buoyancy compensator and unclipped his camera so that he could photograph his progress. Among the shingle that he had shifted from the hole he could see what appeared to be another piece of copper ingot, green with verdigris and irregular in shape. For a moment he debated whether or not to collect it. They had several thousand pieces of copper ingot already; the metallurgy lab at IMU was inundated with samples for their programme of isotope analysis to determine the origins of the metal, and they did not need more.

But his instinct as an archaeologist took over and he

reached down to pull it out, lifting it towards the finds tray with the other artefacts that would be collected by the divers later that day. As he did so he sank to the seabed, staring in astonishment. It was not a fragment of ingot but a brass figure of Christ on the Cross - a Corpus Christi - with the ends of the arms and legs missing but the musculature of the torso and the downturned face preserved in detail. It was not just a cheap devotional figure but a work of great beauty by a master. During his visit with Rebecca and Jeremy to the Metropolitan Museum of Art he had seen a similar figure attributed to the Genoese sculptor Guglielmo della Porta, and inspired by the famous sculpture of Christ the Redeemer by Michelangelo in the Church of Santa Maria sopra Minerva in Rome. It dated a full century before the wreck, to the time of the Counter-Reformation in the sixteenth century, and showed Christ at peace rather than in agony, following the instructions of the Catholic Church that images of Christ should be more compelling to those who might be tempted by Protestantism, and to encourage private devotion that could focus on such figures.

Nestled in his hand the figure seemed vulnerable and human. He took several moment-of-discovery photographs, showing the spot where he had found it with a cannon in the background. Could this, too, have been a possession of Captain Viviano's, perhaps deliberately left on the ship when he had accompanied the crew to shore, evidence that even a hard-edged mariner who would have known that God rarely bestowed favours at sea had realised that the passengers remaining on board would have needed all the help they could get? Jack saw that his air was now well into the red and he put the figure in his finds bag, tying the top and clipping his camera back on his webbing. As he finned off from the seabed he saw the first of the dive team round the corner from the seaward side of the reef, the bubbles from their exhaust advancing towards him like a curtain in the water. He gave an OK sign to the first diver, pointed at his finds bag and then made a thumbs-up to show that he was surfacing, and the diver made an OK sign in return. Jack turned back for one last look at the wreck below him. The *Santo Cristo di Castello* had given up another secret, one of the most beautiful finds he had ever made, but he knew there was more to her story, much more, and as the silhouette of his kayak came into view he knew he would not stop until he had coaxed everything he could from the ship and her cargo.

CHAPTER 6

Early the next morning Jack sat in his study in the IMU campus with his papers spread out in front of him and keeping half an eye on the weather. The storm that had been threatening the day before had built up momentum during the night, with rain lashing against the windows and drumming on the roof. He was still basking in the afterglow of his dive on the wreck and had enjoyed his usual cup of coffee first thing in the morning. He felt on top form creatively, and was looking forward to what Jeremy had to tell him when he arrived.

He went over to the table in the centre of the room and scanned the tithe maps of western Cornwall in the seventeenth century that he had brought from the library. They showed the division of the land into manors and hundreds, and the familiar surnames that cropped up throughout Cornish history: Godolphin, Trelawny, Tremayne, Vyvyan, St Aubyn. The Vice-Admiral of South Cornwall at the time of the *Santo Cristo di Castello* was Francis Godolphin, but he was often absent in London and deputised the salvage of wrecks to men who were locally based. It was in the records of those men that they were most likely to find reference to the wreck, men such as the lord of the local manor of Winnianton and Godolphin's deputy for the Lizard peninsula, who would have arrived with soldiers on the scene of a wreck within hours to drive off wreckers before they had made away with property that was claimed by the crown. Even those records were often partial and sometimes deliberately misleading, with some landowners being wreckers themselves and removing valuables without declaring them. One name that appeared often in the records was William Paynter, whose manor was some distance away in Penwith near Land's End but was one of Godolphin's most reliable lieutenants, appearing with his guards at wreck sites around Cornwall as soon as he could ride to them. Jack made a mental note to order all of the documents of the seventeenth century in the Paynter Archive in the Cornwall Records Office. He had a hunch that the paper trail could yield important evidence for the salvage of the ship and the whereabouts of any artefacts that were removed at the time.

The door opened and Jeremy came in, his laptop bag slung over his shoulder and carrying a large book swathed in bubble-wrap that he put carefully on the table. Jack poured him a coffee and gestured at the book. 'I see you've been raiding the library as well.'

'On threat of excommunication. The librarian said that this is one of the most valuable books in your ancestor's collection. A splash of coffee on it would be fatal for me.'

Jack put the coffee on a side-table. 'What's the title? When I was growing up I used to pore over those books.'

Jeremy took out his laptop and placed it on the table beside the book. 'All will be revealed.' He pointed to the projector at the end of the table. 'All right if I set up PowerPoint?'

Jack went over and pulled down the screen while Jeremy busied himself with his laptop. 'Heard anything from Rebecca?' Jack said. 'She was going to send pictures of Cape Coast Castle in Ghana for our exhibit on the Royal Navy and suppression of the slave trade in the Falmouth Maritime Museum. It's due to open next month.'

'She got held up at the airport at Accra. She's flying from there to Cyprus, and then in the IMU Lynx to *Sea Venture* off the Nile Delta. She wants to join Maurice Hiebermeyer's team in the Sinai but felt that flying directly into Alexandria might be a bit risky.'

'That was my advice,' Jack said. 'With her surname if they make the connection to me she'd be vulnerable. Even though it's now a year since we were expelled and IMU has the new agreement with Egypt for the Sinai project, there are still some in the regime who will take a dim view of Jack Howard and his Greek American buddy.'

The door swung open and Costas appeared, looking unshaven and dishevelled as usual. 'Who's talking about a buddy?' he said.

'Well, it's better than sidekick,' Jack said, smiling at his friend. 'That's what the Egyptian newspapers called you.'

'I remember,' Costas grumbled. 'I'll never forgive them for that.'

'Coffee?' Jack asked.

Costas reached down to the floor outside the door and picked up an extra-large paper cup. 'Got my Americano from the canteen. Always made to perfection.'

'Of course.'

He sat down heavily behind the projector with his coffee, and then looked at Jeremy. 'How long is this going to take? I've got an appointment with a friend.'

'Let me guess. Mechanical, not human?'

'Little Joey Six. Can't keep him waiting too long or he gets fidgety.'

Jeremy tapped a key and an image of an old woodcut appeared on the screen, showing a man in religious attire surrounded by vignettes with strange symbols and in the background a flowing volcano. He took a sip of his coffee and leaned forward with his elbows on the table, staring at the image and turning to Jack and Costas. 'What do you know about Father Athanasius Kircher?'

Jack sat down and looked at the image. 'Seventeenth century Jesuit scholar and polymath, from Germany but lived most of his life in Rome. Prolific author of books on almost every subject imaginable. Exuberant curiosity. I last came across him when we were researching Atlantis, as his book

Mundus Subterraneus has a map of Atlantis as an island in the Atlantic Ocean based on his reading of Plato's account as well as other Egyptian sources that he claimed to have seen. We dismissed him as a source after Maurice and Aysha found the papyrus in the mummy necropolis that led us to the citadel in the Black Sea.'

'He's in Umberto Eco's novel *The Name of the Rose*,' Costas said, taking another slurp. 'I've just finished reading it.'

'He was interested in a grand unifying theory of everything, at a time when the evaluation of knowledge was more an art than a science,' Jack continued. 'He gathered together all of the intellectual flotsam and jetsam he could find in Rome, as well as ancient inscriptions and manuscripts and observations of natural phenomena, and tried to corral them into overarching theories of how the world worked. Until recently he was largely discredited, but he's now seen as important for stimulating people's imagination and opening the way for Newton and the other scientists of the Enlightenment. His books were among the biggest bestsellers of the seventeenth century, essential in any cultured person's library and approved by the Jesuits who sent them to their missions around the world.'

'And a maker of machines,' Costas said. 'Devices for modelling the workings of time and gravity and the universe. We tried to replicate one when I was an undergraduate at MIT. He was a kind of seventeenth century Leonardo da Vinci.'

'What's the connection with the *Santo Cristo di Castello*?' Jack said.

'You sent me to find out everything I could in The National Archives about the wreck and her cargo,' Jeremy replied. 'There is nothing indexed on the wreck, but I knew that the papers of the High Court of Admiralty contain many random documents relating to shipwrecks in which the Admiralty took an interest, anything with cargo of value that might be salvaged for the Crown or returned to the owners if they made a claim. I struck it lucky in the second box of papers I ordered.' He tapped a key and another image came on the screen, showing a letter in a seventeenth century style of handwriting. 'This was written in Cornwall in March 1668 to the Admiralty, summarising the state of salvaged material some six months after the wrecking. The writer is one William Paynter, a local squire.'

'Aha,' Jack said, getting up and peering closely at the screen. 'I've just been looking at his landholdings in western Cornwall. He was an Admiralty agent responsible for wrecks.' He read out the letter:

'William Paynter of Sitney in the County of Cornwall gent maketh oath, that in the month of October 1667 and most particularly on or about the fifth day of the said month a certain ship named the St Christo de Castello was splitt in pieces and cast away near Mullion to the westward of the Lizard and many of her Company were lost, but one Lorenzo Viviano who was her Commander and Maister of the said shippe and some others who did belong to her came ashoare, and indeavoured to save what they could to carry away with them or to dispose of the same but they stayed there not long, the said Commander going from there within two or three days and most of the Company about a week after and the rest of them stayed about a month at most. And after they had disposed of some Cynamon Cloth and Corall which was saved whilst they stayed there, they forsook and left all the rest. And since their departure a quantity of Iron and of Leade was recovered out of the Sea, and some Cynamon, some parts of the Ship and masts and other ffurniture.'

He paused, staring at the words. 'The final sentences after that are a bit unclear and will take some deciphering, but basically he's talking about the whereabouts of the goods and their condition. The material he just listed as having been recovered from the sea was in the hands of Francis Godolphin. He was Paynter's boss, the Vice-Admiral of South Cornwall. Here we go: *Some also in the hands of some other who have not yet delivered it to said Vice Admiral.* He's referring to the wreckers, who would have made off with what they could before Godolphin's men arrived. And it seems that even the goods in Godolphin's hands were in a sorry state, *the cynamon and cloves and Russian hides deteriorated by their long lying undisposed of.*'

'I couldn't find any evidence in the archives that the owners in Genoa and Amsterdam made a claim of salvage,' Jeremy said. 'That's odd given the value of the cargo. Before the cinnamon and cloves deteriorated, they'd have been worth a king's ransom. They would have been brought by Dutch East Indiamen to Amsterdam all the way from the Moluccas Islands in Indonesia.'

Costas finished his drink and put the cup down. 'It's especially odd given the fact that Viviano seems to have survived the wrecking. You would have thought that a captain with his future reputation and livelihood at stake would have done all he could to seek recompense for the merchants who had entrusted their goods to him.'

'I couldn't find any subsequent record of him,' Jeremy said. 'It's as if he disappears from history. But that was a time when the plague was still rampant, only a year after the Great Plague of London, and a man weakened by the experience of shipwreck might have been especially vulnerable. When people died of plague their bodies were usually disposed of unceremoniously without record of their identity, regardless of their status and wealth. That's my best guess.'

'So what's the Kircher connection?' Jack said.

'After finding the Paynter letter I hit a dead end. I searched all of the Admiralty papers for that year but there was nothing more. After reading the letter I began to think that the *Santo Cristo di Castello* had become something of an embarrassment, that the Vice-Admiral's men had failed to get to the wreckers in time to confiscate the more valuable items and the spices and hides that they did recover had all spoiled.

By 1668 there were other wrecks to deal with and the *Santo Cristo di Castello* was history. But then while I was having lunch in the cafeteria about to call you I met Dr Teresa Everett, who I'd known since I was a student. She's just been put in charge of part of the Prize Papers Project.'

'What's that? Costas said.

Jack turned to him. 'One of the most exciting developments in maritime historical research in recent years. The National Archives holds papers from more than 30,000 ships captured by the English as prizes between the mid-seventeenth and the early nineteenth century. Every time a ship was captured, all of the papers on board were collected and sent to the High Court of Admiralty to prove the ship's nationality and the validity of the prize. They include everything you can imagine, from mercantile documents to personal correspondence. IMU has recently become involved through a grant from Efram Jacobovich to fund a series of doctoral projects focussing on accounts of shipwrecks among the papers.'

Jeremy tapped a key and the image on the screen changed to a pile of dusty papers heaped on a table, and behind them a large cardboard box overflowing with more. 'I told Teresa about my dead end and she had a brainstorm. It turns out that one of the ships taken as a prize in that year was a Genoese merchantman out of Amsterdam called the *Sacrificio d'Abramo*, Captain Antonio Basso. She was lading cargo at exactly the same time as the *Santo Cristo di Castello*, in the spring and early summer of 1667, but finished earlier and Basso decided to leave straightaway. It was a risk because the Anglo-Dutch War was still on, and even though she was Genoese with the papers to prove her identity any ship coming out of Amsterdam was considered fair prey by the English. She sailed north around Scotland to avoid the contested waters of the English Channel but had the bad luck to be captured by an English squadron in the Irish Sea. Her papers were sent to the High Court of Admiralty and remain intact today in The

National Archives, down to every last scrap. What you see in that photo is only about half of it.'

'I'm guessing where you're going with this,' Jack said. 'Consignments split between the two ships?'

Jeremy nodded. 'That was Teresa's suggestion. You have two ships lading alongside each other in Amsterdam with goods for the same wealthy patrons in Genoa represented by the same merchants and middlemen. It was common for merchants to hedge their bets by splitting consignments between several ships, and we thought that might be the case here.'

'Hedging bets between one ship that ends up wrecked and another that was captured,' Costas said. 'That's what I call bad luck.'

'It was a brilliant case of lateral thinking on Teresa's part, not just focussing on the linear history of one ship but jumping sideways, so to speak, to look at another ship with a parallel trajectory. Studying the papers from the *Sacrificio d'Abramo* might result in new information about the *Santo Cristo di Castello*.'

'This was yesterday?' Jack said.

'In the final hours before the archives closed. Teresa invited me down into the research department where the Prize Papers are under detailed study. She quickly retrieved the boxes for the *Sacrificio d'Abramo* for me to examine and photograph in the time I had available. It was fantastic, as if by going downstairs I was diving on a wreck site, except instead of one ship there were 30,000 of them. The papers are just like the artefacts from a wreck, a time-capsule of the period with fascinating insights with each page that you turn. One bundle had never been opened and was full of black dust from the seventeenth century. I can still smell it on my hands now.'

'And this is where Athanasias Kircher comes in,' Jack said.

Jeremy looked at him intently. 'The papers contained documents related to the ship's construction and ownership, letters between Basso and his Genoese patrons, tables of accounts while the ship was in Amsterdam, and so-called plague passports, issued by ports to certify that departing ships were free of plague. But by far the largest number of papers were related to the ship's cargo, including more than a hundred bills of lading from different merchants as well as a more detailed ledger made by the captain's secretary. The range and quantity of goods on board was astonishing. We've already come across some of it in Paynter's letter, the cinnamon and cloves and Russian hides that were among her most valuable commodities, as well as iron and lead. But there was also pepper, indigo, sugar, ebony wood from the Caribbean, Indian textiles and silk, whale baleen and walrus ivory from Iceland, textiles from the Netherlands and a vast range of manufactured goods. And there were the other great exports of Amsterdam during the Dutch Golden Age, paintings, maps and books.'

'Aha,' Jack said. 'Books means Kircher.'

'I thought you said Kircher was based in Rome?' Costas said.

'Yes, but his publisher Janssonius was in Amsterdam. Most of the bestselling books at this period were published in Amsterdam. Kircher sent his manuscripts to his Jesuit superiors in Italy to be vetted, and if approved they went straight to the printing press in Amsterdam. There was a thriving maritime trade in books out of Amsterdam at this period, with cases of books being shipped not only to Europe but also to all corners of the world that were being colonised and had Jesuit missions, from New France and New Amsterdam to Spanish America and Brazil and the outposts of the Far East.'

'So what have you got?' Jack said.

'Prepare to be amazed.'

CHAPTER 7

Jeremy took a sip of coffee and brought up another image on the screen. It showed a printed slip of paper, grey with dust and age, with spaces deliberately left in the text that had been filled in with beautifully precise handwriting. 'This is one of the bills of lading from the *Sacrificio d'Abramo*, printed in Italian,' he said. 'They were standard forms, essentially receipts or promissory notes, which were completed in duplicate by the captain or the captain's secretary with one copy staying on the ship and the other going to the merchant who had delivered the goods at the wharfside. They always included a copy of the mark of the merchant that was inked or branded on the case or bale, so that it could be identified by the agent or merchant at the port of delivery. Here you can see a **CP** with a cross above it, the mark of the Cadiz merchants Diego Cornelissen and Giovanni Battista Porrata, and also the names of the Amsterdam merchants Benzi and Voet who had despatched the goods and for whom this was a receipt. It translates something like this:

I, Antonio Basso, Master by the Grace of God of my ship, named the Sacrificio d'Abramo, which at present stands at anchor in the port of Tessel of Amsterdam waiting for the first good wind that God will grant me, for my voyage for Cadiz and Genoa where I will discharge, know and declare that I have received in my ship, and have stowed as cargo for you uno Cassettino con alcuni Libri e Carte, *which I hereby promise and am obliged to deliver for you,* menandomi Dio a buon salvamento con detta mia Nave, *trusting to God for the good salvation of my ship, unto Signori*

Cornelissen and Porrata of Cadiz, or to their assignees, who will pay me for the freight two ducats of 12 Spanish reals per ducat. Signed Antonio Basso, Amsterdam, 10 May 1667.'

Fascinating, Jack said. 'Uno Cassettino con alcuni Libri e Carte. A case of books and charts.'

'So this consignment was for the *Sacrificio d'Abramo*, not the *Santo Cristo di Castello*?' Costas said.

Jeremy nodded. 'Cases of books and maps like this were being shipped out of Amsterdam on a daily basis through the summer months. The overseas book trade had become big business by the 1660s. It was only when I looked at the captain's ledger, showing more detail than the bills of lading, that I began seeing the names Viviano and *Santo Cristo di Castello* as well. What appears on the bills of lading for the *Sacrificio d'Abramo* for high-value products such as spices and metal had often only been half of the consignment, the other half being on the *Santo Cristo di Castello*. And then I came to the ledger entry for the case of charts and books on the *Sacrificio d'Abramo*.'

He tapped a key and another image of an old document came up on the screen. 'There it is. The titles of all the books in the consignment and their authors. You can see the name of the Amsterdam bookseller clearly at the top of the list.'

Jack peered closely at the writing. 'Pieter Blaeu,' he said. 'He was the other great Amsterdam bookseller and printer of the age, alongside Jansonnius. Blaeu is famous for his twelve-volume *Atlas Maior*, the most expensive book published in the seventeenth century. The merchants Benzi and Voet evidently acquired the books through Blaeu, who would also have had an arrangement with Jansonnius if any of Blaeu's clients wanted books printed by him as well.'

'There were five charts and 15 books in the consignment,' Jeremy said. 'The charts include a general map of the world with the description in separate sheets, and a more detailed world map in six sheets. Charts were Blaeu's speciality. He was cartographer to the Dutch East India Company, providing charts and globes as navigational aids and benefitting from meeting with captains such as Viviano and Basso who brought back new knowledge that allowed the charts to be constantly updated. But it was the books that really excited me.'

Jack looked closely at the list of titles. 'There it is. *Kirker*. That's Athanasius Kircher.'

'Bingo,' Costas said.

'I can also see the name Kepler,' Jack said. 'Amazing.'

'That's right,' Jeremy said. 'None other than Kepler's *Epitome Astronomie Copernicae* of 1621, the book that spread the idea that the sun was at the centre of the universe. Another volume, advocating the old-fashioned geocentric view, was Andrea Argoli's *Pandosion Sphaericum* of 1644. But the rest of the books were all by Kircher, and represent an astonishing collection of his works: *Musurgia universalis*, arguing that musical harmony reflects harmony in the universe; *Ars magna Lucis et umbrae*, on an early form of image projection using a magic lantern; *Iter extaticum Coeleste*, on astronomy; *Magnes sive de arte magnetica*, on magnetism; *Diatribe de prodigiosis crucibus*, explaining the mysterious appearance of crosses in Naples; *Scrutinium Physico-Medicum Contagiosae Luis*, a study of the blood of plague victims; *Oedipus Aegyptiacus*, his attempt to decipher hieroglyphics; and *Obeliscus Pamphilius*, a study of the Egyptian obelisk in Piazza Navona in Rome.'

'And *Mundus Subterraneus*, famous for his attempt to identify the site of Atlantis,' Jack said. 'Published in 1665 as I recall, so hot off the press.'

'*Obelisci Aegyptiaci* was published even more recently, in 1666. That book was subtitled *nuper inter Isaei Romani rudera effossi interpretatio hieroglyphica*, meaning that it was based on finds made around the Temple of Isis in Rome. Kircher had become obsessed with Egyptian artefacts uncovered at the site of the temple, and that book was pretty well his last word on hieroglyphics.'

'Incredible that these books should have been on the ship only a matter of months or even weeks after they were published,' Jack said.

Jeremy nodded. 'They represent a period of transition between the medieval and the modern, between the Geocentric and Copernican models and between occult mysticism and proper science. What makes them so fascinating is that they provide a snapshot of titles being read at one moment in time, at the beginning of the Enlightenment when a revolution in scientific thinking was about to take place.'

'But no mention here of part of the book consignment being on the *Santo Cristo di Castello*,' Jack said.

'You haven't seen the next entry in the ledger yet.'

'Another page?'

Jeremy shook his head. 'No. You're looking at it. The lower part of this page, where it appears to be blank. The writing has been deliberately erased. It was only written lightly in pencil.'

'Have you been able to read it?'

'First, some background. We know that the *Sacrificio d'Abramo* sailed from Amsterdam in early June, but that the *Santo Cristo di Castello* was delayed until September.'

'Viviano was waiting for two paintings by Rembrandt to be completed, under Sauli's orders.'

'Correct. As we know, that's been another revelation of the archival research, among the Sauli family papers in Genoa last year. They were two *modelli* for large paintings to be hung in the family chapel of Santa Maria Assunta. But that's not the whole story. Rembrandt's procrastination in getting the paintings done may have been something to tell the merchants and agents who would have been getting increasingly anxious about the delays, concerned about the change in the weather. But what you're about to see suggests that the delay was for something even more important, but that Sauli had ordered to be kept secret. Athanasius Kircher was preparing another work that was taking longer than anticipated to complete and deliver to Amsterdam. Soon after Captain Basso's secretary completed the ledger for the books and charts I think word came through from Blaeu that there would be a further delay, and Basso let his frustration be known. Unlike Viviano, he was not a personal client of Sauli so did not have to follow his demands. I think Basso stated his intention to leave without the final work and as a result Sauli ordered that the entire consignment from Blaeu be transferred to Viviano to await transport. I now believe that all of the books and charts that you see in this list were on board the *Santo Cristo di Castello* when she was wrecked off Cornwall.'

'Along with this secret additional document from Kircher,' Costas said.

'Show us what you've got, Jeremy,' Jack said.

'I could see a very faint impression of writing in that space,' Jeremy said. 'Teresa was able to expedite a short-term loan of that page of the ledger for shortwave infrared hyperspectral imaging in the IMU lab. When I arrived back from London last night I took it straight there. This is what they came up with.'

He tapped a key and the image transformed into another view of the same page in a digitally enhanced format with writing visible in the lower part. 'That's Basso's handwriting, isn't it?' Jack said. 'I recognise it from his signature on the bill of lading. As you said, it looks as if he added something in pencil, but then erased it.'

'There are four lines of writing,' Jeremy said. 'It says that the aforementioned *Cassettino con alcuni Libri e Carte* is instead to be laden on Giovanni Lorenzo Viviano's ship the *Santo Cristo di Castello*. You can just see Viviano's mark in the margin, a **V** with a cross through it. But then something else was added, another item in the list of books and charts. It says *Carta con Insula Orichalcum ex Hieroglyphicis et description Solonis*. That's the secret document they were waiting for.'

Jack got up for a closer look and translated the title.

'Chart with the island of Orichalcum from hieroglyphics and the description of Solon. Amazing.'

'It's similar to the caption for the map of Atlantis in the *Mundus Subterraneus*, except instead of the island of Atlantis it's the island of Orichalcum, instead of 'Egyptian sources' it's specifically hieroglyphics, and instead of Plato it's Plato's mentor and source Solon.'

'Kircher was obsessed with hieroglyphics,' Jack said. 'It's always been suspected that some of the hieroglyphic inscriptions in Rome on which he placed great store were Renaissance forgeries, so his mention of Egyptian sources in addition to Plato on that map has never been followed up. But they may be genuine.'

'Orichalcum was the Atlantis metal, wasn't it?' Costas said. 'Thought to have been an alloy similar to brass or bronze.'

'Or mythical,' Jack said. 'A wondrous metal, something of the gods.'

'It's not like us to dismiss something as mythical, is it?' Costas said. 'Fact until proven myth. That should be the IMU motto.'

Jeremy increased the magnification so that the word orichalchum filled the screen. 'It may have been another term for Atlantis, perhaps used here as a way of avoiding stating the more familiar name.'

'Everything about this looks secret,' Jack said. 'Especially the fact that it was only pencilled in and then erased.'

Jeremy nodded. 'If you look at the final line it says *sub mandatis a Sig. Francesco Sauli*, under instructions from Signor Francesco Sauli, and then repeats the names Cornelissen and Porrata as the recipients in Cadiz. Mentioning Sauli, and not his Amsterdam agents Benzi and Voet, is highly unusual. Everything was usually handled by middlemen, by the merchants and agents whose names are in the bills of lading. That's how they made their money, and they were covetous of it. Whatever this *carta* was, it was something that Sauli had arranged personally with Kircher to send to Amsterdam, and for it to be sent on to Cadiz by Sauli's client Viviano. What little we know about Viviano suggests that he would have been beholden to Sauli, that he was a man who could be trusted to do his patron's bidding and to keep a secret, not least because Sauli had helped him out after a previous shipwreck and kept him financially afloat. And this carta seems to have been a one-off, not something despatched by Kircher to Amsterdam to be printed and published. It seems to have gone not to his printer Janssonius but directly to Blaeu, another man who was known to Sauli personally as he had supplied him with books and maps for his palace in Genoa. Something was going on here, something involving these five men - Kircher, Sauli, Blaeu, Basso and Viviano - and the two agents in Cadiz. And somehow it involved a map which appears to have been on board the *Santo Cristo di Castello* when she was wrecked.'

'The *Mundus Subterraneus* was completed only the year before,' Costas said. 'Perhaps this chart was a revised version, something he wanted added as an insert into the book.'

'If so, why be secretive about it?' Jeremy said. 'Why deliberately erase this entry? It looks as if Basso knew enough to be cautious by adding it in himself, not using his secretary. Perhaps Viviano himself then told him to erase it.'

'Perhaps the chart was not a revision, but was the original version intended for the book based on those Egyptian sources,' Jack said. 'Perhaps the map of Atlantis that was then published in the *Mundus* was deliberately vague and misleading. From what we know of Kircher he would have been loath to excise completely a reference to Atlantis from his book, but perhaps he didn't want to lead others to search for it.'

'But we've already found Atlantis,' Costas said. 'Whatever this is about, it can't be the citadel in the Black Sea.'

'Not Atlantis, but perhaps a place where something from Atlantis was taken and concealed.' Jack turned to Jeremy. 'What do we know about those Cadiz merchants Cornelissen and Porrata?' Jack said.

'Teresa pulled up everything she could find about them. They were a prominent Dutch-Genoese company in Cadiz, acting as middlemen for trade between Amsterdam and Italy as well as import agents for goods shipped into Cadiz itself. There are a couple of points of interest. One is that Benzi and Voet, the merchants in Amsterdam who shipped the books, were agents for Francesco Sauli, who we know was scion of one of Genoa's wealthiest families and Captain Viviano's patron. Another is that Cornelissen and Porrata's import trade at Cadiz was not just for wealthy clients in Spain, but also for Spanish and Portuguese islands in the Atlantic. They seem to have specialised in the Canaries and the Azores. The silver decoration in the Cathedral of Las Palmas in the Canaries was supplied by Cornelissen and Porrata, sourced from Andalucian workshops. They were experienced captains as well and seem to have taken their own ships on voyages to the islands.'

Jack sat back, his hands behind his head. 'I want to know more about that. Any contacts they had in the islands, anything more on their trading activities. Maria should be able to help with the archives in Cadiz. And I also want to know more about the hieroglyphs that Kircher claimed were his sources.'

Jeremy nodded. 'I'm on it.'

'Where do we go from here?' Costas said.

Jack checked his phone for messages. 'I've got a meeting lined up this evening on the Lizard peninsula, at Gunwalloe. I've been following my own lead on the fate of Viviano and his crew.'

'And I need to package up a ground-penetrating radar unit and have it flown out to the Sinai. An urgent request from Lanowski.'

'Is he there with Maurice?' Jeremy said.

Jack nodded. 'Those two have turned into a team. For years nobody knew that Jacob had a passion for ancient Egypt. He was just our resident computer genius from Texas. And now he and Maurice are virtually inseparable.'

'Good that they've been able to get a toehold in Egypt again,' Jeremy said.

'It's a precarious one,' Jack said. 'Literally on the edge of Egypt, on the Mediterranean coast where the Sinai Desert hits the sea. The Egyptian authorities have only allowed it because it's an environmental project under the banner of UNESCO. IMU archaeology is still a no-go after our little adventure under the pyramid last year.'

'I still find it strange that you were released so quickly,' Jeremy said. 'One moment you were in solitary confinement under threat of torture and execution, and the next on a flight back to London.'

'They realised that they weren't going to get anything out of us about what we might have seen under the pyramid,' Jack said. 'And the new regime needed to present a clean face. The disappearance of two western archaeologists in the bowels of the Interior Ministry would not have served their cause well.'

'I wonder whether there were other forces at play,' Jeremy said. 'Maybe the regime decided that releasing you and keeping a close eye on what you did next was the best way of finding out if you'd discovered anything. That may even have been behind your return to Egypt, this project in the Sinai. Allowing IMU a small amount of latitude, but not too much for it to raise suspicions that something else was going on.'

'The regime, or someone powerful within the regime.' Costas said. 'Remember where we've been in the past with this kind of thing. Secret societies within the Church. A Chinese cult of tiger warriors. The latter-day Nazi Ahnenerbe. Maybe there's something similar here.'

'It's possible,' Jack said. 'At the moment we're just going with the flow and seeing what will happen next. We're doing our best to provide all the equipment needed for the survey in the Sinai and to please for the authorities. One thing might lead to another.'

'Ground penetrating radar is a bit of a stretch for a study

of turtles and flowers,' Costas said. 'Maurice must be on to something.'

'Let's hope they don't make it too obvious,' Jack said. 'When Jacob and Maurice are following a lead they wouldn't notice the second flood if it was happening all around them.'

Costas got up. 'Well, count me in if there's any diving to be done. Right now I need to return to Little Joey Six.'

'How is he?' Jack said.

'I need to tweak his sonar array. It's amazing how underwater drone technology has advanced. When I began my career submersibles were the size of actual submarines and now I can fit them in my pocket.'

'All the better for exploring submerged passages under pyramids,' Jeremy said.

'We live in hope,' Jack said. 'I need to swing by the conservation lab to see how they are getting on with cleaning the Corpus Christi figure from the wreck. And I want to put a card for Maurice in that package you're sending to Lanowski. It's Maurice and Aysha's fourth wedding anniversary. A reminder that he's a husband and a father now and not just an Egyptologist.'

'Good luck with that,' Jeremy said. 'Anyway, Aysha is his boss out there, being not only an Egyptologist herself but also Egyptian. She told Rebecca once that the only way to manage all of you is to equal you at your own game. And she and Rebecca are part of the next generation at IMU after all.'

Jack eyed Costas. 'That sounds like a challenge.'

'Plenty of mileage in this generation yet,' Costas replied. 'As long as R&R on the beach and gin and tonics are factored in.'

'How's the new property in the Caribbean?'

'I bought it hoping for lots of off-time there but then something came up. It always does. Come and dive under a pyramid, Jack asked. Come and spend a week in solitary confinement in a Cairo detention centre, he should have said. Since then there's been too much going on here. Little Joey, for a start. Anyway, it's more of a nature reserve, bought to preserve a few hectares of coral reef with a tiny beach and just enough room for a portable bar and a sun umbrella. No snakes or spiders.'

'Huh. I knew about your thing with snakes. Spiders is new to me.'

'Mainly the hairy ones.'

'Well, I suppose we all have our sensitive sides. Even Dr Costas Kazantzakis. See you in a bit, Jack.'

They both left and Jack stared at the writing on the screen. *Insula Orichalcum.* He thought of what he had said to Costas, about the survivors of Atlantis. Almost eight thousand years after that event, something secret had been sent from a bookseller in Amsterdam that might offer another opening into that extraordinary story, another loose end to be tied up. Finding Atlantis had been remarkable enough, but tracing the legacy of that civilisation in world history from the Neolithic to the present day had become a long-term quest for him. He was brimming with excitement, the same excitement he had felt when Maurice had phoned him from the desert all those years ago to tell him about the discovery of the Atlantis papyrus in the mummy necropolis. He glanced at his phone again, wondering what new revelation the meeting this afternoon might bring. It was time to go.

CHAPTER 8

Early that evening Jack walked along the edge of the dunes towards the church behind the headland at Gunwalloe about a mile to the north of the wreck site. To his left the rising tide lapped the beach of Church Cove, a line of surf that rippled along the foreshore and over the rocks on the edge of the headland. To the west the horizon was orange with the afterglow of sunset, lighting up Land's End and the open Atlantic beyond. Gunwalloe was familiar territory for him. A few years earlier a storm had swept away the sand and revealed a Phoenician wreck in the outer reaches of Church Cove, leading to an excavation that had transformed understanding of early Mediterranean contact with Cornwall. On the other side of the headland in the cove of Jangye-ryn they had excavated the wreck of the *Schiedam*, a Dutch ship captured by Barbary pirates that had then been used by the English in 1684 to transport people and equipment back from the failed colony at Tangier. Both projects had brought Jack to familiar waters where he had first dived as a boy. After years exploring exotic locations and working in places far from any backup it had been a new experience to make such exciting discoveries so close to home, within an hour of the International Maritime University campus with its state-of-the-art conservation labs and the museum that allowed artefacts to be displayed soon after their discovery on the seabed. The Mullion Pin Wreck offered the same prospect, and he had been excited that afternoon to see the finds from yesterday's dive laid out in the lab for the first time.

He crossed the stream that flowed through the marshy valley leading to the cove and looked up at the sky. Another wave of storm clouds was approaching from the west, and it would only be a matter of time before the wind whipped up the sea and the rain swept in over the headland. He felt a brush of cold against his cheeks and could taste the salty air brought in from the sea. The clear sky on the horizon where the sun had gone down was rapidly being eclipsed by the clouds, and he used the last vestiges of light to navigate the path between the tufts of grass that grew on the dunes on the way to the church.

He reached a knoll on higher ground and turned back to look at the valley. People had lived here for thousands of years, enclosed by the low hills and the sea, eking out a living by fishing and tending cattle along the marshy edges of the stream and almost completely cut off from the world outside. And then in the sixth century AD a monk had arrived across the Channel from Brittany, seeking a remote place where he could devote himself to God. He carved himself out a cave in the headland and a community sprang up to serve him and his successors, living for generations in crude huts among the dunes until they could no longer cope with the storms and moved away to the towns that were springing up nearby. The site of veneration remained, at first no more than a sacred cave and holy well but then a building of driftwood and rubble and slate. By the time of the completion of the Domesday Book in 1086 it was a chapel of the manor of Winnianton, with a stone font and eventually all the trappings of a medieval church.

It was a place that looked more to the sea than to land, something that had drawn Jack to it since he had first come here as a boy. After the community which served the monks had departed it became isolated, a church in the dunes barely protected from the storms by the headland and standing like a lone pillar of faith against the power of nature. The Church of Saint Winwaloe became the Church of the Winds and then the Church of the Shipwrecked Mariners. The congregation were the brethren of the sea, the mariners who were cast ashore in ever-greater numbers as shipping increased through the centuries and the sea claimed more victims. The priests found purpose in the succour they could give to a few and the last rites that they gave to many. For centuries before a change in the law in 1808 allowed bodies washed ashore to be buried in consecrated ground, they had filled the surrounding dunes with the bodies of these people. Sometimes the dunes seemed restless with their souls, as if the rustling of the wind and the blowing of the sand were the sounds of their movement as they rose and gathered on the foreshore, looking out to sea for comrades whose bodies would never be found.

A few minutes later he reached the boundary of the churchyard and let himself through the gate. The church was an unusual three-hall design of the fourteenth century, with the nave and chancel being the same size as the aisles and a detached bell tower that nestled against the slope of the headland. He ducked under the porch and turned the heavy latch to let himself in through the oak door, smelling the familiar musty odour of old churches as he waited for the sensor to activate the lighting. He put his hand on the thousand-year-old font and turned back to look at the most remarkable treasure of the church, a carved oak screen on one side of the door with delicate perpendicular tracery and in the lower register four panels with paintings of the apostles.

Church tradition was that the screen and a similar one against the north door had come from the *Santo António*, a richly laden carrack owned by the King of Portugal that had wrecked nearby on her way from Lisbon to Antwerp in 1527. In order to test the proposition Jack had offered the church authorities the expertise of IMU to try to date the screen and determine its origin. If it was locally made, and not from the wreck, they knew that it was unlikely to date after the Dissolution of the Monasteries under Henry VIII in the 1530s, as the confiscation of church wealth meant little scope after that for elaborate decorations. The style of the tracery was early sixteenth century, and Jack's colleague Maria de Montijo in Spain had discovered similar depictions of the apostles in church art in Spain and Portugal of the period. The clinching evidence had come from hard science; the wood proved to be *Quercus faginea*, Portuguese oak, and DNA analysis had confirmed an Iberian origin. Dendrochronology had at first been unsuccessful because the tree-ring sequence surviving in the thin panelling was not long enough, but then they had matched it to the oak timbers in another Portuguese wreck of the 1520s found off West Africa. Jack had been sufficiently convinced that the panels had come from the *Santo António* to commission an information board that now stood beside the entrance, as well as funding a conservation programme that had seen the paintings restored and stabilised within airtight glass cases that encompassed the lower parts of each door.

He walked up the nave and glanced at his watch. There was still twenty minutes to go until he was due to meet the curate. He slid into a pew just in front of the chancel and sat down. The sensor light went off and he was in near darkness, the only light coming faintly from the sunset through the stained-glass window above the altar and from a candle flickering in a tray that had been lit by a previous visitor. He reached into his pocket and removed a small bubble-wrapped package, and then carefully unrolled the wrapping and took out the figure of the Crucified Christ that he had found on the wreck site the day before. The conservators had brushed away the green verdigris corrosion, and it had a dull golden glow in the candlelight. He cradled it in his palm, feeling the sheared-off arms and legs and the smooth back of the torso, and then raised it until it was visible in silhouette against the window.

He was thrilled by the discovery, one of his best finds from a wreck of this period. He had sent a photo to a friend in the Courtauld Institute in London and they had determined without doubt that it was the work of Guglielmo della Porta, the Italian sculptor of the sixteenth century whose work he and Rebecca had seen in the Metropolitan Museum in New York when they had gone seeking parallels in paintings for some of the wreck finds. The cleaning had revealed the wound on the right side of the chest where the spear had been thrust in after death, following the account in the Gospels. Despite the erosion from more than 350 years underwater it was still possible to see the quality of the finish in the chiselling of the hair and the drapery of the loincloth, and the excellence of the anatomical study in the musculature and emaciation of the torso. What most beguiled Jack was the face, showing Christ without pain or suffering as if asleep and dating the sculpture to the years after the Council of Trent in 1545-63, when the Roman Church had stressed the need to show Christ in this way to present a more benign image of Christianity and draw people back from Protestantism. In the half century or so between the paintings of the Apostles from the wreck of the *Santo António* and the casting of the sculpture the world had changed irrevocably, leading to a century of conflict that had barely been resolved by the time the *Santo Cristo di Castello* set sail from Amsterdam on its fateful final voyage in the late summer of 1667.

Jack thought of Captain Viviano, of those final hours with the wind shrieking through the rigging and the splay lashing at the hull, and whether this figure was a measure of his faith. The Council of Trent had focussed on private devotion and the need for people to develop a personal relationship with Christ, a way of moving away from dependence on the priesthood and therefore addressing one of the concerns of the Reformation. Small devotional figures allowed people private communion in a way that they had not been encouraged before. Guglielmo della Porta had studied under Michelangelo in Rome but had his main workshop in Genoa, his hometown and that of Viviano. Could this have been a treasured figure passed down from father to son, acquired at the time of its production in the sixteenth century and keeping generations of captains named Viviano safe until that day in 1667 when the protective gaze seemed to turn the other way?

He thought of Viviano in Amsterdam before the ship had set sail. They knew that the ship was carrying the two paintings by Rembrandt, and that her delay in departure was partly caused by waiting for them to be completed. But what Jeremy had revealed about the consignment of books from Blaeu added another dimension to the story. Was Viviano also waiting for something that was due to arrive from the bookseller, something that his patron Francesco Sauli in Genoa had wanted shipped out from Amsterdam that was even more valuable than the paintings?

In his mind's eye he saw Viviano making his way that August through the bustling streets of Amsterdam, retracing a route he had taken many times before between the *Santo Cristo di Castello* in the harbour and the painter's house on the far side of the city. He had already endured more than a year of delay waiting for the ship to be completed, for the Zuider Zee to melt and for the painter to stop procrastinating and get on with the commission. Every further delay now made the voyage ahead more perilous, more likely that they would encounter the south-westerlies that swept in from the Atlantic and drove ships back against the shore of England; it was imperative that he complete his lading and depart. Jack imagined him stopping at the shop of Blaeu to check on the progress of the *Atlas Maior* and seeing the batch of books by Kitcher and the other authors that Sauli had ordered. As he crossed the canal and approached the artist's house he may have been brimming with anticipation, hoping for good news. Peering through the window he may at last have seen them – two swaddled and bound packages propped up by the door ready to be carted to the wharfside. All that would have been needed now was to settle up with the artist and to send word for his sailors to come and take the precious masterpieces to the ship.

Jack imagined Viviano hurriedly retracing his steps to Blaeu. Now that the paintings were ready he would have impressed on Blaeu the need to have the atlases and other books packaged up as well and despatched to the wharf. But was there something else, something even more precious that Blaeu had only just received from Kircher, something that he had kept hidden away until being sure that the ship would set sail? Six weeks later in the teeth of the storm, as the *Santo Cristo di Castello* pitched and rolled towards the cliffs and the sails flew off in the gale like banshees, as Viviano clutched his well-worn Corpus Christi and prayed for a good accounting at the Gates of St Peter, had it been this item that he had chosen to rescue rather than the paintings or the books when the chance came to leave in the ship's boat and pull away to safety?

The door creaked and the sensor light came on again, and a bearded young man wearing a cassock came down the aisle. Jack got up and extended a hand. 'Peter,' he said. 'Good to see you again. Formal attire today?'

They shook hands. 'This counts as a gathering of the brethren of St Winwaloe,' Peter said. 'It's particularly appropriate as this cassock has been unchanged since the seventeenth century.'

'That's where I was just now. 1667, to be precise,' Jack said.

Peter gestured at the pew. 'Don't let me disturb you if you need longer.'

Jack smiled. 'I was having something of a reverie.'

'This church is good for that.'

'It's helpful of you to set this up so quickly. I can't wait to hear what you've got.'

'When Jeremy called and we knew you had been diving on the *Santo Cristo di Castello* we decided it was time. We felt we owed you something after your effort to get those painted screens identified.'

'Do you know Jeremy well?'

'He and I were contemporaries at Oxford. I was reading theology and he had come over from the States to do his doctorate on medieval palaeography, so we had a shared interest in ecclesiastical documents. I gather he's been at The National Archives?'

'We're on a paper trail as well as an archaeological one. Once the ball begins to roll with a project, there's a kind of multiplier effect and every lead must be followed up without delay.'

'Well, what we are going to reveal this evening will amaze you. I unlocked the tower door earlier for another of the brethren who will be waiting for me there. Join us outside in ten minutes.'

Jack picked up the statue of the Corpus Christi from where he had placed it on the pew beside him and nestled it in his hands. 'Before you go, I've got something from the wreck that I'd like you to hold.'

CHAPTER 9

Ten minutes later Jack stood outside the church in front of the tower, a detached structure set into the headland slope that had been the rampart of a promontory fort in the Iron Age. He had his diving torch with him and panned it up the coarse granite dressing to a pair of narrow slatted windows where he could see bats flitting in and out. The tower in its present form dated from the seventeenth century, but much of the granite had been reused from an earlier version built not long after the Norman conquest. It was what the tower had been built to conceal that most fascinated him. He had never been inside, and he knew that the opportunity he had now was rarely granted by the church authorities.

He switched off his torch and made his way up to the entrance, ducking under the bough of a yew tree that had grown over the path. As he did so he saw where rabbits digging in the sand to the right had brought up fragments of human bone, well-preserved in the calcareous shell soil. Like many medieval churches, even ones serving a small community, the burials here over more than a millennium would have numbered several thousand, with the more recent ones marked by headstones cutting through older burials as well as pits where the sextons had reburied the bones that they had brought up each time they dug a new grave. Constant reuse of the ground meant that rather than being orderly burials as suggested by the gravestones the ground beneath was a homogeneous fill in which human remains formed a continuous stratigraphic layer. Among them were numerous shipwrecked mariners whose identities were unknown even at the time of their burial, part of the human imprint on this place where land and sea formed a unitary whole with a reach as far as the distant shores from which many of the sailors had come.

Peter was standing in the shadows beside a man with thinning white hair and a large black cross bordered with gold hanging over his cassock. 'Allow me to introduce Father Paolo Tensini,' Peter said. 'From the Church of Santa Maria Assunta in Genoa.'

'It's a pleasure to meet you at last,' the man said in accented English, bowing his head slightly and shaking hands with Jack. 'I have been following your online reports keenly ever since you started excavating the wreck of the *Santo Cristo di Castello*.'

'Then I'm pleased that Peter has been able to show you one of our best finds so far.' Jack gestured at the Corpus Christ figure in Peter's hand. 'A particularly appropriate artefact in the context of the church.'

'There's a place for it here, should you ever wish to find it a home,' Peter said, handing it back to Jack. 'The Corpus Christi of the Church of the Shipwrecked Mariners. You'll soon see why.'

Jack replaced it in the bubble wrap and peered through the half-open door into the darkness beyond. 'I'm grateful to you for bringing me here. I know this is a rare privilege.' He turned to Paolo. 'Santa Maria Assunta. That was originally the Sauli family chapel in Genoa, wasn't it? Embellished with art by Francesco Sauli, Captain Viviano's patron. And your surname rings a bell too.'

'You would be thinking of Giovanni Tensini, a merchant from Genoa in Amsterdam who acted as Sauli's middleman for the import of works of art for the church as well as books and scientific instruments for his private collection. He was my ancestor.'

'Fascinating,' Jack said. 'That must be more than a

coincidence.'

The padlock was hanging on the latch, and Peter pushed the door open. 'Follow us inside. We will explain everything.'

Jack ducked in behind them, took a few steps and straightened up. In the gloom he could just make out the ropes dangling down from the belfry on the left side. Peter took the padlock, pushed the door shut and dropped the lock through the inside latch, and then struck a match and lit two candles on brass holders attached to the wall. The flames flickered and wavered, casting an unearthly glow around them. Jack could see the interior of the tower rising above him like the shaft of a mine, with the floor of the belfry visible at the top. Peter tried the door to make sure it was shut and then turned to him. 'Everything that is said within these walls is secret, known only to our brethren and now to you as well.'

Jack took a deep breath, smelling the damp masonry and a faint tarry odour in the ropes, probably reused cable from an old shipwreck. 'I'm listening.'

'What I'm about to tell you has never been told to anyone else before. Captain Viviano survived the shipwreck.'

Jack stared at him. 'But Jeremy could find no record of him after that night.'

'Viviano came ashore at Mullion in one of the ship's boats while the *Santo Cristo di Castello* was anchored in the lee of the island. He meant to return to the ship, but fate intervened. A gang of wreckers who had seen the storm coming had gathered in the cove. An armed detachment sent by the Vice-Admiral of South Cornwall, Lord Godolphin, arrived just in time to keep the wreckers at bay. But that didn't mean Viviano and his men were safe. Godolphin's main job was to secure anything of value in the wreck for the king. The Anglo-Dutch war had only just ended, and Godolphin was still jittery about any ships coming from Amsterdam. One of his brothers had died in the Battle of the Medway and he felt that he had a personal score to settle with the Dutch. More than that, he was anti-Catholic and felt that an invasion from

France and Spain was imminent on the coast of Cornwall. Viviano being Italian and therefore Catholic would have put him right in Godolphin's sights.'

'Viviano would have been released soon enough, particularly if the Doge of Genoa had intervened with King Charles of England,' Paolo said. 'But the damage would have been done. He would have been stripped of his valuables and they probably would not have been returned.'

'He was caught between the storm, the wreckers and Godolphin's men,' Jack said. 'Not an enviable position.'

'Salvation came briefly in the form of one of Godolphin's lieutenants, a wealthy squire named William Paynter who led the detachment in person.'

'I know that name too,' Jack said. 'Jeremy found a letter from him regarding the wreck in the Admiralty papers in The National Archives.'

'Unbeknownst to Godolphin, Paynter was a secret Catholic, one of a network in Cornwall who supported James, Duke of York, Charles' brother and the future King James II, who had converted to Catholicism in that very year, 1667,' Peter continued. 'Because of the prejudice against Catholics, Paynter made it his mission to provide assistance to shipwrecked mariners of the Roman faith cast ashore on the coast of Cornwall. And because he lived locally and was deputised by Godolphin to be at the scene of any major shipwreck as soon as he could, he was often able to spirit away Catholic survivors before Godolphin arrived. The local clergy were of course Anglican, but they were sympathetic regardless of the Roman Catholic denomination simply as a matter of offering succour to fellow Christians who might be unjustly treated. Those clergy included the priests of St Winwaloe.'

'You said Viviano's salvation was brief.'

'Paynter and his men rode hard and arrived at Mullion an hour before Godolphin,' Peter replied. 'But there was a melee on the beach with the wreckers and in the process Viviano was wounded by a pistol shot while trying to protect his people. He survived the melee, but eventually the wound proved fatal.'

Jack looked at Paolo. 'And your ancestor Giovanni Tensini? Was he on board the *Santo Cristo di Castello*?'

Paulo nodded. 'He was a passenger with his wife and servants. They all drowned in the wrecking and their bodies were never recovered. When the news reached Genoa, his oldest son took the fastest overland route to the English Channel and then a galley across to Falmouth. He wanted to find the bodies and give them a Christian burial, but he was also acting under orders from Francesco Sauli. There was something that only his father and Captain Viviano and a few others had known about, something that had been on board the ship. Sauli had instructed him to use any means to find it.'

'And did he?' Jack said.

Paolo shook his head. 'He was killed in an encounter with wreckers near Pol Glas while he was trying to claim salvaged cargo. I am descended from his son, who was only an infant at the time in Genoa. Ever since then his descendants have passed down the story of that night and its secret, something that Viviano brought with him to this very place.'

Jack looked around. 'Am I right in guessing that he was brought here after being wounded?'

Peter nodded and looked at Paolo. 'It is time.' They each took an end of a wooden screen that was leaning against the wall on the side of the headland slope, moving it to reveal an entrance about a metre and a half high and a metre wide with a wooden door set inside. Peter took out a key and knelt down to unlock and open the door, pushing it inwards. Jack could see that the granite masonry of the tower had been built directly into the bedrock and that the passage beyond was rock-cut. The two men crossed themselves and bowed their heads for a moment, and Paulo recited a phrase in Italian: '*Menandomi Dio a buon salvamento con detta mia Nave.*'

'Trusting to God for the safe passage of my ship,' Jack murmured. 'Those are the words from the bills of lading that Jeremy found in the National Archives.'

Peter glanced at him. 'That was what Captain Viviano was saying over and over again when they brought him here, like a mantra. The priest gave him a cross to hold, but it wasn't enough. He was inconsolable over the loss of his passengers. Apparently, the boat that had taken him off was meant to return for them, but the ship's anchor cables broke and she was blown into the cliffs. Like any good captain he would never normally have left the ship before the last person was taken off. All that the priest could promise him was that the bodies would be given a Christian burial if they were found.'

'He gave the priests all the gold he had on him for the church and the costs of any burials,' Paulo said. 'It was more than 200 ducats, enough to cover the burials of all shipwreck victims here for the next two centuries.'

'What became of him?' Jack asked.

'He was given every succour but died two days later, still repeating that phrase and clutching the cross. He was buried in an unmarked grave in case anyone who might think he still had riches on him came to dig him up. There were many desperately poor people living hereabouts for whom salvage from wrecks and from bodies washed ashore was a means of survival.'

'And there was another reason for keeping his burial a secret,' Paulo said. 'The reason why we have brought you here. Let us go inside.'

Peter and Paulo each took a candle holder and ducked under the entrance, with Jack following. He could see pick-marks where the rock had been hacked out to form the tunnel and the chamber ahead. It had an earthy, humic smell, different from the musty smell inside the church, and the rock when he brushed up against it was damp and cold. He came out of the passage and stood up beside the others in a chamber about four metres across, with low antechambers leading off at irregular angles. In the wall opposite the entrance was a cross carved into the rock, the surface as dark and mottled as the surrounding rock and evidently very old. Jack took out his torch, put it on the dimmest setting to reduce the glare and peered at it closely. 'The rock of the headland is compacted shale,' he said. 'The cross would have been relatively easy to carve and smooth using a piece of granite.'

'It's reputed to have been made by St Winwaloe himself in the early sixth century,' Peter said. 'This was his hermitage, his monastic cell. So you see the legend that he founded the church here is true.'

'I never doubted it,' Jack said, panning his torch around. 'But one thing I can tell you is that he didn't dig this chamber out. This is what the Cornish call a fogou and the French a souterrain. It's a chambered tomb from the Bronze Age, at least three thousand years old. We knew there were cist burials on the promontory and there are tumuli on the surrounding hills, but this adds a whole new dimension to the history of this place. The people buried here were high-status, lords of the promontory fort. This would have been rich in grave goods, perhaps cleared out when Winwaloe discovered it.'

'He is said to have found treasure in gold that he used to finance the first church,' Peter said. 'Can you confirm the age of the tomb?'

'We can do optical and infrared luminescence dating to show when the surface of the rock was first cut and exposed,' Jack replied. 'It only requires a small sample.'

Paulo knelt down beside a dark mass within one of the alcoves. 'This is what we brought you here to see.'

Jack panned his torch over and saw the matted hairs of an old sheepskin beside a small wooden chest. 'This is where Viviano was brought by Paynter and the priest,' Peter said. 'That black stain on the sheepskin is his blood. It's been left as it was when he lay here, except that his belongings were placed in the chest.'

'Can I see?'

'There's a bible, a pistol, a rosary, a few coins and this.' He opened the chest and passed over a gold ring. 'It's a signet,' he said. 'You can see his initial in the bezel.'

'I recognise it,' Jack said, feeling the weight of the gold. 'The letter **V** with a superimposed cross. It's the same mark that Jeremy showed me on the bills of lading for Viviano's personal goods in the cargo of the *Santo Cristo di Castello*. It was inked on the bales so that they could be identified. All merchants had rings or seals like this to mark their goods and confirm their identity. It's very moving for me to hold this. Only yesterday at the wreck site I found a pair of navigational dividers that I'm certain were his. It's as if he's here with us now, not three and a half centuries ago.'

Paulo reached into the chest and took out a long-barrelled flintlock pistol, the brass of the barrel dulled by age and the steel elements of the lock fused together by rust. He passed it to Jack, who cast an eye over the details. 'Giovanni Battista Gavezzani,' he said, peering at the engraved name of the gunsmith on the plate. 'Early flintlocks are a bit of a speciality of mine. He was active in Genoa in the 1660s, so that's perfect for the date of the wreck. You can see that it's been fired as the cock is down and the frizzen is up, and the rust is worst where the powder residue has been left in the pan. Black powder residue is very hygroscopic, meaning it draws in moisture from the air and causes rust. It's a beautiful piece, something that he must have prized.'

He handed it back to Paolo, who placed it carefully in the chest. 'We think it was fired in the melee at the beach,' he said. 'Probably as a warning shot to keep the wreckers away before Paynter and his men arrived.'

'What else did he have with him?' Jack said. 'The gold coins, the pistol, a rosary, a bible. Anything else?'

'After he had been shot and fallen to the ground the wreckers would have tried to grab anything they could see of value on his person. He was clutching something tight to his chest beneath his doublet, and fortunately Paynter's men arrived before the wreckers could get at it. He wouldn't let go of it until Paynter and the priest had brought him here and laid him down, when he knew he was in safe hands.'

'Do you know what it was?'

'It was a thin book or folio sheet wrapped up in vellum, watertight to keep it dry at sea,' he said. 'Once Viviano was safely here the priest left him with Paynter and returned to the beach to see if he could help any others of the crew who had been wounded in the fray. When he came back, Viviano was unconscious, Paynter had gone and so had the package. Whatever Viviano told Paynter had made it imperative that he leave with it at once. In his last moments Viviano regained consciousness and drew the priest close to him, saying the Latin words *cave Hemnetertepi Isaia*, beware the Hemnetertepi of Isis. The priest later wrote it down in the bible that's now in the chest. After that Viviano died.'

'Can I see it?'

Peter put down his candle and reached into the chest, pulling out an old book with a worn leather cover. He opened it up and passed it to Jack, pointing at a faded ink inscription at the top of the title page. Jack stared at it, his mind racing. 'That's incredible.'

'You recognise it?'

'While I was at school my friend Maurice Hiebermeyer tried to teach me hieroglyphics and some of it stuck. Hemnetertepi is a New Kingdom word for priest. High priest, to be precise. And then that word, *Isaia*, of Isis. In his last breaths, Viviano was telling your antecedent to beware of the high priests of Isis. *In ancient Egyptian.*'

'Well, this will interest you then.' Paolo moved the chest aside, revealing a patch of wall with markings on it. 'In his final hours, between Paynter leaving and the priest reappearing, Viviano carved this symbol on the wall with his knife. In the nineteenth century when ancient Egyptian was first being translated the priest who ran this parish became interested in the symbol and went to the British Museum to try to find parallels, but to no avail. Until Peter and I looked at it again just before calling you yesterday nobody else had tried. It has always been assumed to be some form of hieroglyphic, but undecipherable.'

Paolo moved out of the way and Jack took his place, lying down on the old sheepskin where Viviano had been. He edged closer and shone his torch at the wall. For a few moments he was unable to breathe, scarcely believing what he was seeing. He shut his eyes and opened them again, and it was still there. It was something that Maurice and Aysha had first seen on a papyrus in a mummy necropolis in the Fayum, something that had set off an extraordinary train of discoveries. He raised himself on one elbow and sat up, the adrenaline coursing through him, and looked back at Paolo. 'Do you recognise it?'

Paolo looked at him intently, his voice tight with excitement. 'Of course. That's why we called you. It's on the cover of your first book. It's the symbol that Dr Hiebermeyer found in the desert, that's on the Phaistos Disc from ancient Crete and that you found in the citadel under the Black Sea. The Atlantis symbol.'

'There's something else you should know,' Peter said. 'About the package that Viviano had been clutching and that he must have given to Paynter. After that night, Paynter disappeared, never to be heard of again.'

'Did anyone know where he was going?'

'There was one clue. A day later his horse was found abandoned at Wheal Perran mine near Land's End. The mine was on Paynter's land and had been dug down chasing a lode of tin ore as far as they could go using the technology of the time. The lode followed a natural crack in the granite that went below sea level. It would have been the most secure place he knew, and we think he may have been taking the package there for safekeeping when something happened to him.'

'I know the place,' Jack said. 'It's one of the few mines where the old workings survive mostly intact, because there was a terrible accident in the nineteenth century and the mine was shut down. Nobody has been in the deep workings since.'

'Will you go?'

Jack thought for a moment. 'I know who to contact. A good friend of ours who explores mines in Cornwall. By chance, she's been at Wheal Perran over the last few weeks. The current owners want to erect a proper memorial to the miners who died there in the disaster, and they called on her to do a recce.'

They made their way out of the tower to the path beside the church. Peter locked the door behind them and they walked out of the churchyard. The wind had picked up, and the sea was crashing and sucking along the line of the sand beside the headland. Jack stopped where the path divided, knowing that the other two would be heading back towards Peter's car on the lane, and he shook hands with them. 'I'm very grateful to you for confiding in me. I'll keep you up to speed with anything we find.'

'Good luck,' Peter said. Paolo bowed slightly, and they turned to go. Jack reached into his pocket, thought for a moment and then cleared his throat. 'One other thing. I have an artefact that really should be among Captain Viviano's belongings.'

Peter nodded. 'I was hoping you might suggest that.'

'It will need to undergo more conservation to stabilise it. And we'll do a high-definition laser scan so that we can produce replicas for our museum with a 3D printer. Once you have it under your care I'll always know where it is.'

'The Corpus Christi of the Church of the Shipwrecked Mariners,' Peter said. 'It has a good ring to it.'

Paolo crossed himself. *'Menandomi Dio a buon salvamento con detta mia Nave.'*

Jack raised a hand. 'Until we meet again. And now I need to make a phone call.'

PART 2

CHAPTER 10

Rome, present-day

The man in the robe of a Dominican monk made his way past the fountain in the centre of the piazza and towards the portico of the temple, stopping as he always did to put his hand on the cool granite of the column in the corner and looking up at the famous inscription on the pediment: **M.AGRIPPA.L.F.COS.TERTIVM.FECIT**, *Marcus Agrippa, son of Lucius, made this building when consul for the third time.* Part of the Pantheon, the temple to all the gods, and since the seventh century the Church of Santa Maria Rotonda, the granite had been quarried in the eastern desert of Egypt and shipped to Rome when the emperor Hadrian had rebuilt the temple in the second century AD. He glanced back at the obelisk atop the fountain in the piazza, his eye following the worn hieroglyphs up the side until they reached the crowned falcon of Horus, son of Isis and Osiris and one of the oldest deities of Egypt, god of the sun and the sky. He shut his eyes for a moment and whispered an incantation, and then looked at the Christian cross that had been added on top. The obelisk had been brought to Rome in antiquity from the temple of Ra at Heliopolis and dated from the time of Ramses II in the thirteenth century BC, half a millennium before Rome even existed. It was Athanasius Kircher who had first recorded the hieroglyphs, some three centuries after the obelisk had been discovered in the ruins of the Temple of Isis under the medieval buildings next to the Pantheon. Members of Father Kircher's order, the Jesuits, and his own order, the Dominicans, had erected the obelisk in the piazza in the eighteenth century, capping it with the cross to show the dominance of Christ and placing the Horus symbol directly across from the Latin inscription of Agrippa on the Pantheon, as if in further defiance of the old gods of Rome.

Many in Rome at the time of the emperors thought that the hieroglyphs of ancient Egypt on these monuments were merely decorative; they were only of antiquarian interest to scholars such as Pliny and Strabo. In later centuries it seemed that the appropriation of the monuments of ancient Rome by Christianity was the most striking transition evident in the architecture of the city, with temples such as the Pantheon converted to churches and the Christian cross placed above many of the pagan buildings standing at the time of the conversion of the emperor Constantine in the fourth century AD. But for the man it was not that transition to Christianity but the earlier arrival of symbols and sculptures from ancient Egypt that held the greatest significance. The power of Egypt had not died with the conquests by Alexander the Great and the Romans, but had lived on in this city, brought here by the last survivors of the priesthoods of the Nile who had seen the way the world was turning. They had secretly infiltrated the highest echelons of Rome, had survived under the guise of Christianity and had endured all of the vicissitudes of Roman history through war and plague and decay. And they were still here now and in other places where the Roman Church held sway, spreading the power of Isis and Horus and Osiris to parts of the world that the priests of ancient Egypt could scarcely have imagined existed.

He took his hand off the column and walked briskly along the narrow lane beside the Pantheon to the piazza in front of the Church of Santa Maria Sopra Minerva. In the centre of the piazza was the second obelisk, found in the 1665 excavations at the Temple of Isis, this one placed atop the famous elephant by Bernini that had been erected in 1667. Father Kircher had studied the hieroglyphics on this obelisk too, showing that it had been moved from Saïs in the Nile Delta during the Twenty-Sixth Dynasty in the late sixth century BC, in the same years that the Greek scholar Solon travelled there and heard the story of Atlantis from the priests. To the left of the church was the Dominican Convent, which in 1628 became the seat of the Congregation of the Holy Office, better known as the Inquisition; it was here in 1633 that Galileo under threat of torture renounced his support for Copernicus and the heliocentric universe. For the man there was a certain satisfaction in knowing that this place, next to the greatest temple to the Roman gods and the highest office of the Roman church, was also a focus for worship far more blasphemous than anything Galileo might have supported, a heresy that was being enacted in the underground ruins directly beneath the court of the Inquisition.

He carried on towards the church, its white Renaissance façade one of few in Rome not to have been recreated in the Baroque style in the seventeenth century, and entered by the side door. He sprinkled holy water on his cassock from a hanging brass lavabo and crossed himself before walking down the aisle. He passed the beautiful frescoes that adorned the side chapels, including some of the greatest works of art of the fifteenth century, and stopped briefly before Michelangelo's statue of Christ the Redeemer to admire the musculature and poise that owed so much to the sculptures of the Roman period. He turned abruptly to the left, went down a narrow spiral staircase and came to a low door that he opened with a key from a loop under his cassock, locking it behind him and stooping down a low passageway lit by bare bulbs hanging from a cable on the ceiling. It had been dug out of the bedrock in the Roman period, part of the aqueduct channel to the fountain in the Piazza della Rotonda, and had been cleared of rubble by Father Kircher's workmen when they excavated the temple foundations in 1665; since then it had remained a secret passageway known only to a select few. He passed the marble steps of the Temple of Minerva, all that remained of the ancient structure beneath the church and the adjoining convent, and then came to the former convent garden where the obelisks had been found. Ahead of him was a jumble of column bases and broken statues, some left as Kircher had found them and others reconstructed, with the medieval foundations of the buildings above cutting through the ruins from antiquity and forming another low passageway.

He picked his way through the piles of old masonry and came to the edge of the structure that had been Kircher's objective, the foundation walls of the Temple of Isis. The temple had been constructed at the time of Julius Caesar as an open-air sanctuary with statues and fountains and gardens, but had been rebuilt underground in secret after pagan worship had been banned following the conversion of Constantine to Christianity. There it had remained, surviving the sack of the city by the Goths in AD 410 and the fall of the western Roman Empire, the centuries of decay and then the sack of the city again by renegade soldiers of the Holy Roman Empire in 1527, blocked off from the world and known only to those who kept alive the worship of Isis and guarded the extraordinary secret that the sanctuary contained.

He followed the lightbulbs to an ancient wooden door in a low arch that was part of the foundations of the temple. He took out another key, reached with it into the darkness to the right and found the aperture that only he and a few others knew about, pushing the key into a hole at the back and twisting it until he heard the latch drop. He pulled out his hand and pushed the door open, going through and locking it from the inside. The chamber he was in had once been the basement of the temple; when the priests of Isis had been forced underground, they had taken with them all of the surviving sculpture from the sanctuary and set it up here. They had made this their new place of meeting, below the gardens where they had first gathered when they had arrived from Egypt at the time of Julius Caesar and spread Isis worship among the elite of Rome, hiding their true intent behind the fountains and flowers and statues of nymphs that they had put in the open ground above.

Ahead of him was a space about five metres long flanked on either side by small columns carved from the same Egyptian red and grey granite as the columns of the Pantheon, only capped with lotus-shaped capitals as if they had sprung from the banks of the Nile. To further the illusion of being beside the river they had cut a shallow channel in the bedrock and diverted water into it from the nearby aqueduct, a continuous flow that ran under a stone table in the centre of the chamber and past the man now. Between the columns was a succession of small Egyptian sculptures: a cat, a baboon representing the god Thoth, part of a frieze showing the priests of Isis at Saïs, a plaster wall painting of papyrus blossoms and an Egyptian porphyry fragment with the inscription **ARCVS AD ISIS** from an arch that the emperor Hadrian had built outside the temple. Mid-way along the columns on the left was a black marble sphinx the size of a large dog, the hieroglyphic inscription on its chest showing that it belonged to the Eighteenth Dynasty at the end of the second millennium BC, and opposite it the bust of an unknown pharaoh of the Twelfth Dynasty, his head shaven and the eyes enhanced with black kohl like those of the goddess Isis protecting the canopic shrine in the Tomb of Tutankhamun.

Looming out of the shadows at the far end was the cult statue of Isis itself, flanked by two wooden falcon-headed statues that had been brought here in the nineteenth century from a tomb in the Valley of the Kings. The cult statue had been damaged when the temple had been desecrated by Christians in the fourth century AD, but it still had the carved stalks of wheat on the head, the basket of serpents and the ankh symbol and sistrum, the sacred rattle. Everything in this place was authentic; it made him feel that the world of ancient Rome with its copied Greek statues and stolen works of art was more embellishment than substance, whereas here beside the trickling water he could easily be on the bank of the Nile with papyrus rustling in the breeze and a falcon crying in the sky above, a great pyramid casting its shadow just beyond.

He reached the table and sat down in his usual chair, one of four arranged on either side. He took off the black cap of the Dominicans and put on a white velvet cap that had been laid on the table in front of him. Sewn in the front was the *wedjat*, the Eye of Horus, the protective symbol that Horus had given his father Osiris to sustain him in the afterlife. As he composed himself two others came out of the shadows behind the columns, a man in the cassock of a cardinal and a woman, both of them already wearing the *wedjat*. He bowed towards the cardinal, who sat down opposite him. 'Eminence,' he said in English, his accent Austrian. 'I trust you had a pleasant flight from Bogatá?'

The cardinal bowed in return. 'Father Rauscher. The Holy See provides for my comforts. The ecumenical council that required my presence in Rome this week for the annual meeting of cardinals in the Vatican is richly endowed. And Dr Aslanov here was only a short flight away in London.'

Rauscher looked towards the woman as she sat down. 'I trust that your new job in The National Archives in England is not too taxing?'

She smiled briefly. 'Nothing is too challenging after completing a doctorate in Rome under your supervision.'

'Minister Khalil in Cairo sends his apologies,' the cardinal said. 'But it is important that he remains in Egypt as we may call on him to take action in the desert shortly.'

'It is good that he managed to secure the early release of Howard and Kazantzakis last year,' Aslanov said.

The cardinal nodded. 'The interrogators concluded that getting anything out of those two was going to be a long haul, and it was better to release them and follow their movements. The regime had bad enough press already without having the murder of westerners on their hands. And now Dr Khalil has also facilitated the return of Howard's colleague Hiebermeyer to Egypt under the guise of an environmental project in the

Sinai. It is only a matter of time before Howard flies out to join him.'

'Shall we begin?' Aslanov said.

The cardinal pulled away the linen sheet that had covered the surface of the table, revealing a polished slab of red granite covered in hieroglyphics. Part of the inscription was familiar from the Bembine Tablet, a bronze facsimile of the slab made during the Roman period and then acquired by the antiquarian Cardinal Bembo after the sack of Rome in 1527. In his thirst for all things hieroglyphic Athanasius Kircher had studied the tablet and concluded that there must be more of it to be found in the Temple of Isis, but instead of discovering further sections of the bronze copy he found the original slab in front of them now on which the tablet was based. The Roman copyist had not understood hieroglyphics and had moved the symbols around to make an aesthetically pleasing composition rather than one that made sense, and he had omitted the central part with the symbol that was in front of them now. It stood out because it was not hieroglyphic and was clearly from a much more ancient script, one that that had arrived in Egypt millennia before the pyramids and pharaohs and before Egyptian writing had even been invented.

They all reached out and placed their left hands over the symbol, and the cardinal recited a mantra in an ancient tongue. They withdrew their hands and he looked at them. 'Now, to business.'

'Jack Howard?' Aslanov said.

'Tell us what you know.'

'The discovery of Atlantis, and of that same symbol in the submerged citadel, means that we have been monitoring Howard's activities ever since they revealed it to the world,' she said. 'Last year he and his associate Dr Kazantzakis were arrested on the Giza Plateau after they were discovered diving beneath the Pyramid of Menkaure. There is a flooded underground passageway that leads from the Nile.'

'To the tomb of Akhenaten,' Father Rauscher said. 'To his

repository of knowledge, the fabled Pr-Ankh, the City of Light.'

The cardinal glanced at the cult statue. 'Last seen when Akhenaten's followers took his living mummy to its final resting place there after the priests of the Temple of Isis in Memphis had performed the ritual of akhet-re, and then killed all who had worked on building the tomb before it was sealed up.'

'If Howard and Kazantzakis saw something under the pyramid, there has been no word of it since they were expelled and returned to England,' Aslanov said. 'But then something happened two days ago. One of the younger staff in The National Archives approached me for advice on Father Kircher, knowing that Father Rauscher and I had co-authored the standard text on his works. She said that somebody from the International Maritime University had come seeking information on the *Santo Cristo di Castello*.'

'Captain Viviano's ship,' Rauscher exclaimed.

'Correct. Wrecked off Cornwall in October 1667.'

'Names,' the cardinal said, tapping the table with his fingers. 'We need names.'

'Dr Teresa Everett. She is the National Archives researcher. And Dr Jeremy Haverstock, an American working for Howard.'

The cardinal peered at Rauscher. 'Those people are for you to find.'

'Understood.'

'So how did this woman know about the connection with Father Kircher?'

'She did not say,' Aslanov replied. 'But I think she had found a cargo manifest listing his books. If so, it may be the clue that we have been seeking for more than three and a half centuries. The location of the island where the orichalcum was sent by the priests at the time of Akhenaten was thought to have been lost when the soldiers of Alexander the Great sacked the temple at Saïs in the fourth century BC, killing the high priest. Only he knew the secret, passed down from high priest to high priest for almost a thousand years before that. But Father Kircher in his explorations had also discovered a papyrus in Rome that seemed to have been a sketch of the island drawn by the high priest when he knew his fate. Kircher copied it and had it bound in Amsterdam and despatched in secret with Viviano to a merchant-captain in Lisbon who was going to seek out the island. But Viviano's ship never made it beyond the English Channel.'

'We need to find out what they know,' the cardinal said. 'We need to find the island and the orichalcum before anyone else does. We will let Howard and his team do the work for us, and then deal with them just as our forebears did the workers in the tomb of Akhenaten. Only then will the goddess rule supreme and our power as her priests be complete.'

He drew two obsidian knives out of his cassock and placed them on the table in front of him. The blades had been chipped with exquisite fineness and were black and lustrous, with serrated edges. One with a forked end was the pesesh-kef, the ritual wand that touched the lips of a mummy to ensure that it was ready for the afterlife. The other was the sacrificial knife that was plunged into the body to perform the dread ritual of akhet-re, mummification alive. Both blades had been passed down through countless generations from the people of the sands bordering the Great Middle Sea, those who had first worn falcon heads like the statues flanking the goddess behind them now. They were the ones who had met the seafarers who had escaped from the drowned citadel, those who had brought with them the secret that the priests had come to know and sworn to conceal for all time, bringing it under the protection of Isis and preventing it from being known to the world outside.

The cardinal picked up the sacrificial knife and turned it so that it reflected the light. 'With this blade our forebears performed the akhet-re on the pharaoh Akhenaten,' he said. 'The world knows him as the heretic pharaoh, the one who forsook the old gods to worship the sun, but we know him as the one who in his thirst for knowledge entered the Temple of Isis at Memphis and desecrated the Holy of Holies, bringing away the jewel that was the key to the box in which we had stored the orichalcum. For his desecration we sought him out as he lay dying and made him pay the price demanded by the goddess.'

He placed the knife back on the table beside the other. If the pesesh-kef remained where it was, then there was no need for action. If he pushed it forward, then the goddess was calling them; it showed that Osiris had receded from her embrace, and she needed sustenance to revive him. Rauscher knew what to expect; he would not have been summoned here otherwise. They were the Hemnetertepi, the high priests of Isis, and it was their role to activate the Menfet-hor, the warriors of Horus, the descendants of the Horus-headed warriors of antiquity, those who had passed down their fealty through the generations from the depths of time, who would ruthlessly carry out anything that was asked of them if it meant securing the sanctity of the goddess and the secret that she guarded.

The lights flickered and went out, and then came on again. 'With the sacrifice of Akhenaten, Osiris was reborn,' the cardinal said. 'If the orichalcum is found by others then rebirth becomes not just the preserve of the gods, but of people as well. The power of the goddess will fall away, and chaos will rule. Those not among the priesthood who would seek the secret of immortality must suffer the same fate as Akhenaten, and their lifeblood will flow through the fingers of Isis to the lips of Osiris, reviving him for all time.'

He pushed the sacrificial knife forward, leaving it pointing at the symbol in the centre of the table. The decision had been made. Father Rauscher stood up, kissed the outstretched hand of the cardinal and then looked towards the statue of the goddess. He took off the cap with the Eye of Horus and replaced it with his Dominican one. 'Eminence,' he said, bowing slightly. 'I will await your instructions.'

The cardinal stared at him, a cold, hard look that Rauscher knew from meetings that had been called here in the past, and then stood up and spoke. 'We are the descendants of the high priests who came when the Caesars held sway, bringing knowledge of the Atlantis jewel and the orichalcum, the elixir of life that had been taken away by our forebears at the time of Akhenaten. For two thousand years the priesthood has met here to plot its recovery, to find clues to its location and find the treasure that will make Isis arise once again and those who serve her become immortal. At the time of Father Kircher the secret was nearly discovered, and now we are on the trail again. We may no longer have the falcon-headed warriors to serve us but we have their modern equivalent. It is time to summon those who will find Howard and finish what the interrogators in Cairo started. Go now.'

CHAPTER 11

Jack stared at the image of a chart that he had photographed from Kircher's *Mundus Subterraneus* and projected on the wall of his study. The book itself was where Jeremy had put it on the table, the protective wrapping now open to reveal the old leather binding and the letters and decorative borders in gold leaf on the cover. The binding was just as it was when it had left Kircher's publisher Johannsen in Amsterdam in 1665, preserved in the library of this house since Jack's ancestor John Howard had acquired it soon afterwards. The chart was the one showing Atlantis that Kircher had decided to include in the book, captioned *Insula Atlantidis* rather than *Insula Orichalcum* as on the version that was to be shipped on the *Santo Cristo di Castello*.

He sat on one of the chairs that had been set up for the students for their question-and-answer session, leaned forward and thought hard. The chart was upside-down - a convention for some Dutch cartographers of the period - with south at the top and the Atlantic in mirror-image with the Americas to the right and Europe and Africa to the left. That took some mental adjustment to understand, as did the size of the island that occupied nearly the entire expanse of the Atlantic Ocean. That was the feature that had led most scholars to dismiss Kircher's *Insula Atlantidis* as fantasy; an island the size of a continent could not somehow be missing in the Atlantic Ocean. In the view of most scholars, Kircher had located Atlantis in the Atlantic simply because he equated the name Atlantis in Plato's account with the similar one that the Greeks used for the western ocean, the Ocean of Atlas. But now after Jeremy's discovery Jack was not so sure. If the name in Kircher's original chart was *Insula Orichalcum*, then its location could not be explained by the Ocean of Atlas. What was it that had led Kircher to place the island in the western ocean?

There was a knock on the door and Jeremy came in carrying his laptop and a coffee from the canteen. He sat down on the chair to the left of Jack, flipped open the laptop and took a sip from his drink. 'Have you had a chance to see the finds from the wreck?' Jack asked.

'Costas showed them to me in the conservation lab just now. Fantastic, especially the Corpus Christi. He's coming over to join us after he's taken Little Joey for a swim.' He pointed at the screen. 'Are you re-thinking Atlantis?'

'I'm trying to work out what Kircher was pointing us to.'

'You think he was leaving something for posterity?'

'I'm wondering why he produced two versions of the same chart, one that he published in the *Mundus Subterraneus* for all the world to see and the other a secret version that was entrusted to Captain Viviano. I think that one, the chart mentioned in the lading manifest, was meant as an actual navigational aid.'

'What you said on the phone about your meeting at the church is incredible. A secret kept for three and a half centuries about the mortally wounded captain of a Genoese ship and what he was carrying.'

'I'm waiting for a phone call that might move us forward.'

Jeremy gestured at a small book with a green paper cover lying on the chair in front of Jack. 'That's the Loeb edition of Plato's dialogues *Critias* and *Timaeus*. I know it well from my undergraduate major at Princeton in ancient philosophy. I can guess which parts of those books you've been looking at.'

Jack picked up the book and looked at it pensively. 'Kircher used the word orichalcum for the island, changing it from Atlantis. The metal orichalcum is somehow the key to this whole thing. I think he meant that orichalcum was brought to that island, not mined there. Plato says that it was mined in Atlantis itself, which we know was at the site of an active volcano in the Black Sea. The word orichalcum comes from *oros*, meaning mountain, and *chalkos*, copper. I think *chalkos* must be the Greek rendering of the word told to Solon by the priests in Saïs from the original Indo-European vocabulary of Atlantis. 'Mountain copper' makes sense as the term for a metal that was mined in a volcano. The original Indo-European word might have been retained by Solon because there was no other word in Greek for what was being described. It could have been a unique metal otherwise unknown, something brought up from the earth's mantle by that particular volcano and no other.'

'Plato described it being used in Atlantis as a facing for buildings,' Jeremy said.

'It may have been used decoratively in that way, like polished copper,' Jack said. 'But it may have had other qualities that were more important - medicinal, for example. There are instances of ground-up metals being taken for their therapeutic or curative qualities in antiquity.'

'Perhaps the medicinal use of metals was something that Kircher had come across in his study of ancient Egyptian sources.'

Jack put the book down and stared again at the screen. 'People decry Kircher's work for being an *omnium gatherum* of intellectual debris that he had swept up around him in Rome and put into a grand unifying theory of everything. But I don't buy that, not for all of it anyway. In 1667, in the year of the wreck, he was 66 years old, at the height of his powers and with twelve years of incredible productivity still ahead of him. That chart of the island is not just one of those bits of debris but is the work of a man of extreme curiosity who knew he was on to something big, really big.'

Jeremy tapped on his laptop and angled it towards Jack.

'I've been looking at the sources that we know Kircher studied in his attempt to decipher hieroglyphics, anything that might have given him further clues about Atlantis and possibly be the origin of that chart. Kircher himself never went to Egypt, but he had rich pickings among the antiquities that had been brought to Rome after Egypt was annexed in 31 BC. Some of that stuff was buried after Rome fell, and Kircher worked out where to dig for it. Amazing, isn't it - digging for artefacts of ancient Egypt in the ruins of Imperial Rome. His greatest success was at the site of the Temple of Isis in the Campus Martius, under the garden of the Dominican monastery that stands over the remains.'

'The same place that produced the two small obelisks, the one in the Piazza della Rotonda outside the Pantheon and the other just round the corner in front of the Church of Santa Maria sopra Minerva,' Jack said.

'That's right,' Jeremy said, pointing at two images on the laptop screen. 'The first had been found in the fourteenth century, but the second was unearthed in 1665 and set up on top of Bernini's elephant in the piazza in 1667.'

'The same timeframe as the *Santo Cristo di Castello*,' Jack said.

'Exactly. And there were other artefacts said to have been found in the same location that led Kircher to dig there.'

He tapped a key and brought up an image of a bronze plaque densely covered with figures of gods and goddesses and hieroglyphics, the details picked out in enamel and silver inlay. 'Of course,' Jack said. 'The Bembine Tablet of Isis. I've seen it in the Egyptian Museum in Turin.'

'Said to have been found beneath the monastery after the sack of Rome by soldiers of the Holy Roman Empire in 1527. Cardinal Bembo, who acquired it, was a keen antiquarian and believed in its authenticity, as did Kircher. Since then scholars have wavered between ascribing it to the Roman or the Renaissance periods, either as a piece of Egyptianising decorative art or as a deliberate forgery. Kircher's attempt at translating it got nowhere, at least as far as he presented it publicly.'

'What do you mean?'

'Do you remember my friend Marco Carandini from the Pontificia Università Gregoriana in Rome?'

'You introduced me to him at the conference in Oxford last year that you and Maria organised on the new papyrus finds from Pompeii. I told him to apply for a postdoctoral fellowship at IMU.'

'Then you'll remember that Marco's doctoral supervisor is Father Rauscher, the Kircher expert. He also supervised Teresa Everett's immediate superior in The National Archives, Dr Petra Aslanov.'

'Katya's cousin,' Jack said.

'It's a small world.'

'What's Marco's involvement?'

'He's made a new study of the tablet. He thinks that rather than being a random collection of Egyptian symbols, copied into a decorative scheme by someone who didn't know their meaning, there was an original Egyptian text that provided the basis for the tablet, something that was copied only in part and with certain key elements of the original inscription deliberately left out.'

'You think Kircher knew of this?'

'It's possible that he had seen the original but carried on with his study of the Bembine Tablet as a kind of smokescreen, because he'd seen something in the original that he wanted kept secret. It's only a theory but Marco thinks it fits with his new analysis of the tablet. There's nothing else in the hieroglyphic inscriptions known to Kircher that provides a clue to where he got the reference to the island. The inscriptions on the obelisks are all well-known and formulaic. This is the best lead we've got.'

'It would be worth passing it by Maurice. He could read hieroglyphs while we were still at school, and he has a keen eye for anything unusual. That is, if we can extract him from the

Sinai Desert.'

'I'll get on to it as soon as I've met up with Marco and seen what he's got.'

'Are you going to Rome?

'In two days' time. I've booked the IMU Embraer.'

'I might join you. Paulo Tensini, who I met in the church at Gunwalloe, has invited me to visit the Sauli family archive in Genoa to see whether we can find any more connection between Francesco Sauli and Captain Viviano. If there is correspondence between Sauli and Kircher it might help us to understand the relationship between something Kircher could have found in Rome and the departure of the *Santo Cristo di Castello* from Amsterdam in 1667.'

'And meanwhile Maria is seeing what she can dig up in Lisbon about Cornelissen and Porrata, the merchants who were to have been the recipients of the consignment of books and charts.'

Jack's phone flashed and he read the message. 'That was Françoise Mayet,' he said. 'She's from the French Speleological Society, but moved to Cornwall when she was asked to apply her caving knowledge to the exploration of nineteenth century tin and copper mines. That was the call I've been waiting for.'

'I've heard about her,' Jeremy said. 'Didn't Costas fix her trimix valve when it blew up on a U-boat wreck off Lizard point?'

'Fixed it underwater, to be precise. While they were both hanging on a shotline forty metres deep in a five-knot current. Françoise does things on a wing and a prayer. She's a bit like Costas and I were twenty years ago.'

'You mean you're not still like that? Diving under a pyramid last year with your air running out and the entire Egyptian police force training their weapons on you?'

The door swung open, and Costas came in munching a sandwich. He sat down on the chair beside Jeremy looking unshaven and dishevelled as usual. 'What's that I just heard you saying about pyramids?'

'That was Françoise on the phone. Not pyramids for us this time, but a mine.'

Costas stopped eating. 'Uh-oh. That's her speciality, not ours. Of all the possible ways of going, being buried under tons of mud and fallen beams in a Cornish mine is not even near the top of my list.'

'She's been down one of the side shafts at Wheal Perran near Land's End. The old tin mine on the Tregawarren estate.'

'You mean the site of the disaster in 1873?' Costas said.

Jack nodded and turned to Jeremy. 'One of the worst in a Cornish mine. A level collapsed while a team of more than thirty men and boys were trying to hack their way into a rich seam of tin. The rescuers could hear their cries for days afterwards, and they knew that some of the men had tried to escape by digging down into the deeper galleries but never made it out. That's why Françoise is there. The landowner wants the mine properly sealed off and a memorial put in place. Even a century and a half later there are still local families who want closure.'

'That map is interesting.' Jeremy got up and peered at an old tithe map of the Land's End peninsula above the fireplace. 'It dates from 1682 and shows the land at Wheal Perran as being owned by Geo. Paynter. He's the brother of William Paynter, the Vice-Admiral's man at Mullion five years before, the one who took charge of material salvaged from the *Santo Cristo di Castello*.'

'That's why I was stopped in my tracks by what Françoise told me on the phone last night,' Jack said. 'Before going out to the mine she researched its early history. There's a natural fissure in the granite at Wheal Perran that drops down below sea level. The early miners chased a seam of cassiterite, tin ore, far down the fissure, and when they couldn't get any deeper because of flooding they hacked out galleries on either side. The fissure was used by smugglers to hide contraband, and there were rumours that the Paynter family had used it to conceal a fabulous treasure in gold that was buried in a rockfall and inaccessible below sea-level.'

'So that's why Françoise is really there,' Costas said. 'She has a nose for old treasure underground. She discovered some of the best prehistoric rock art ever found in a cave in southern France before moving up here, submerged off the Mediterranean coast.'

'She's found something that has a direct bearing on the *Santo Cristo di Castello*. And she thinks there's more to be discovered.'

'So we're really going diving in a mine?' Costas said.

'The lower workings are submerged. The deepest part of that fissure goes out under the sea. And it can't wait. The rain over the past few days has saturated the ground, and there's more on the way. Françoise thinks there's still a window but only for the next few hours.'

'The rebreather units would be the best bet,' Costas said. 'With the new 5000 psi cylinders the backpack is very compact. I'm guessing we're looking at some tight spaces.'

'And e-suits,' Jack said. 'Even before we reach the water level it's going to be wet and cold.'

'I'm on to it,' Costas said. 'Meet me at the Land Rover in half an hour?'

'I'll come along too,' Jeremy said. 'Not to go down the mine, but to act as surface cover in case I need to call in an IMU rescue team.'

'Has Rebecca been telling you to look after us?' Jack said.

'She said she can't control what you and Costas get up to when you're diving under a pyramid or inside an iceberg, but she can try to when you're this close to home. I'm supposed to keep an eye on you.'

'I'm not sure if we'll be within easy reach of rescuers. Not if Françoise has anything to do with it.'

Costas swallowed the rest of his sandwich, wiped his hands and pointed at the screen. 'By the way,' he said. 'That's a blow-up. It's zoomed in.'

'What do you mean?' Jack said.

'The island of Atlantis. Orichalcum Isle, or whatever it's called. There's no way that was meant to show a continent of that size. That image in Kircher's book is deliberately misleading. It was probably meant to put people off hunting for it because it was so obviously wrong. By his day mariners had crossed the Atlantic many times and knew that there was no lost continent out there. If you examine the detail of the coastline I'd say we're looking at a small island, possibly with three central peaks. Imagine that being a modern composite map with a small-scale outline of the Atlantic and then a large-scale depiction of the island superimposed. What's missing is a box around the island and converging lines from it pointing to a speck on the background map showing its true scale. My money's on one of the island groups in the eastern Atlantic - the Cape Verde Islands, the Canaries, the Azores. Those would also be a first landfall for a boat leaving the Strait of Gibraltar in antiquity, remote and uninhabited and with no certainty of anything beyond other than the fiery edge of the world, so a good place to take something and conceal it. Just a suggestion from a nuts-and-bolts engineer, but I think that's where we should be looking.'

'You mean it's a treasure map,' Jeremy said.

'It has everything except X marks the spot.'

Jack shook his head at Costas. 'You never cease to amaze me. Now that you've said it, it's obvious.'

'What's the betting that Lanowski knows a programme that can search that island outline among all recorded islands and islets in the Atlantic.'

'It would be using satellite imagery via NASA, so right up his street. I've got to get in touch with him anyway about a software issue with Little Joey. If I can get him to get his head out of the sand in Egypt as well, that is.'

'Aysha's the best contact, I find,' Jeremy said. 'Jacob and Maurice are as bad as each other when they've got Egyptology in their sights. She's out there with them and will make sure he replies.'

'OK,' Jack said, glancing at his watch. 'Françoise is waiting for us and is concerned that we get there before the weather closes in again.'

'Roger that,' Costas said, standing up. 'Let's get this show on the road.'

CHAPTER 12

Jack pulled the steering wheel hard to the right and the Land Rover lurched over a pothole on the dirt track that led between the coastal road and the old mining ground near the edge of the cliff by the sea. Jeremy was sitting beside him, and Costas was wedged among the gear in the back. Twenty minutes earlier they had passed the turning to Land's End and seen the flash of the Longships Lighthouse at the most westerly point of Cornwall on the islet offshore, a warning of bad weather to come. As they crested the ridge he stopped for a moment to take in the view. What had once been a hive of industrial activity was now a scrubby wasteland, with piles of mine tailings concealed by rough vegetation and only the exposed base of the mounds showing that they were made up of broken and pulverised rock.

In the centre of the valley a meandering stream marked the place where the tin had first been found, chunks of cassiterite that had been collected in prehistoric times and traded with Phoenician and Greek merchants who had sailed into the sheltered waters of Mount's Bay to the east. From the sixteenth century miners had followed the seams underground, using hand tools to widen the fissures into passages and galleries and then sinking shafts hundreds of metres down to the level of the sea, following the ore as far as they could. To keep the galleries and shafts free of water they had built pumping houses, beautiful stone structures with towering chimneys that still stood like stark sentinels all over Cornwall where mining had flourished. Three of them were visible ahead, the beam engines long gone but the empty shells of the buildings remaining, the largest one standing at the end of the track about half a mile ahead of them now.

The engine houses had become an elemental feature of Cornwall alongside the rock and sea and play of light that had attracted so many artists to this place, the mine ruins seemingly as timeless as the stone circles and barrows on the moorland and ridges behind them. But unlike those ancient monuments there was nothing enigmatic about the ruins; they were a reminder of the reality of mining, of the hardship and loss. The hummocks and vegetation may have smoothed over the scars on the surface but underground it was all still there, as stark and dangerous as it had been on that day in 1873 when so many had died in this place.

Jack looked beyond the mine to the horizon, seeing the line of dark clouds slowly advancing over the sea towards them, and then put the Land Rover into gear and drove down the final section of track towards the engine house, pulling up beside two other vehicles that were parked there. He and Jeremy got out and opened the back doors on each side, removing the gear and letting Costas ease his way out. They had brought their e-suits – all-environment drysuits with an integrated helmet and intercom that they had first used in the exploration of Atlantis in the Black Sea - and rebreathers that would allow them to go underwater. Jack and Costas each slung a suit over their shoulders and they walked with Jeremy towards three figures standing among a pile of gear just beyond the engine house, beside the circular opening of the shaft. One of them came up to meet them, a woman about thirty years old with short dark hair wearing an orange caving suit and climbing harness. 'Jack! All right?'

He dumped his gear beside the shaft and smiled at her. 'Good to see you, Françoise. This is Jeremy. He's a diver too but is staying topside. He's done a lot of research on the Paynter family, the ones who owned this place.'

'Hello, Jeremy. And Costas, always good to see you.

These are my colleagues Tom and Lucy from the Cornish Mine Exploration Group.' She spoke with a French accent but with a hint of Cornish, a result of almost a decade spent in Cornwall as a caving expert with a passion for exploring old mine workings. 'They're our top-watch in case of emergency and will be looking after the ropes.'

'We've warned the IMU rescue helicopter to be on standby just in case,' Jeremy said. 'We do that for all IMU projects, so it's not as if we're expecting any particular problems here.' He peered cautiously over the raised stone collar of the shaft, which was like the opening of a well but much wider, about five metres in diameter. 'Though I have to say this would not be everyone's cup of tea. How deep is it?'

'The old-time miners measured in fathoms, like sailors. It's 400 fathoms to the deepest workings. That's 2400 feet, or over 730 metres.'

Costas whistled. 'More than 2,000 feet below sea level. That would only have been possible once they'd built this engine house and got the steam pump going to get the water out. What date was that?'

'It's a good question,' Françoise said. 'People often assume that prehistoric tin mining, in fact most mining before the sixteenth century, was mainly surface collection, following shallow cuttings on fractured ground to find alluvial cassiterite that had broken away from the seams and was in the gravel of the stream beds. I don't want to give away too much, but one thing you're going to see is evidence of miners going underground much earlier than had previously been thought.'

'I did a search in the county archive before we came out here,' Jeremy said. 'Wheal Pennan is one of the few mines in western Cornwall named in John Norton's *Speculum Britanniae*, which was completed in 1610. That makes it one of the earliest known.'

Françoise turned to Costas. 'You asked about the engine house. Most of the engine houses in Cornwall date from the time of the Industrial Revolution, after James Watt had introduced his steam engine in the late eighteenth century. But we've unearthed correspondence showing that William and George Paynter's father was experimenting with an atmospheric steam engine as early as the 1650s, a precursor of the Watt engine. The early engines were not particularly efficient and relied on coal that could only be got in sufficient volume from south Wales, but they were an attractive option for mine-owners who could afford them and were confident that the deep seams were rich enough for a profit to be made. If Paynter was considering installing one in the 1650s, the implication is that they had already reached sea-level by that date.'

'So how deep does this first shaft go?' Jeremy asked.

'50 metres straight down,' she said. 'At the bottom there's a platform that provides access to the upper levels. Below the platform there used to be a narrower continuation of the shaft dropping down a further 120 metres, to below sea level. The beam engine in the pump house used to draw water all the way up from the base of that shaft to keep the lower workings from flooding. But the lower shaft collapsed in on itself in 1873 and is inaccessible.'

'Is that where the accident took place?' Jeremy asked.

'That was further along the first level about 200 metres north of the platform, where there are more workings that follow a fissure down below sea level. Those workings are not a shaft like this one but a stope, the term for a space left after the miners had chased a seam and shored up the workings with timbers as they went progressively deeper. A stope is inherently more unstable than a regularly cut shaft or level, as it follows the ore wherever it goes. That can mean under rock weakened by seams of minerals that make it more likely to fracture if it's undermined, resulting in slippage and rockfalls that can't be held up by even the strongest timbers. That's how the miners in 1873 came unstuck.'

'How deep does the stope go?' Jack asked.

'We may find out today. We think it goes far out under the sea. It was originally pumped clear of water from the engine house, by way of a drainage adit that connected the main shaft with the stope at the deepest level. And there isn't just one passageway leading out to sea. It's a honeycomb of shafts and levels down there, some with galleries like huge caverns where the cassiterite seam was really big.'

'Does the cassiterite seam eventually come up on the sea floor?'

'We don't know. If so it would be at least half a kilometre offshore, as we've explored the seabed directly off the mine up to that distance and found nothing.'

'Not such a fun place to dive,' Costas said, gesturing at the sea visible beyond the cliff.

'It brought back memories of that drift dive I did with you in the tidal current off the Lizard,' she said. 'This close to Land's End it can be very bad if the tide is ebbing or flooding. Add some wind and swell, and it's not a place you want to be.'

'Who else has been in the mine apart from you?' Jack said.

'Nobody in recent times. I'm the only one to have gone beyond the platform at the base of this shaft. Everything is still as it was in 1873. The little railway track with the trucks for bringing up ore, the tools, everything.'

'Are you recovering human remains?'

Françoise shook her head. 'When we were contacted by the family trust which owns this land, we agreed that anything we see should remain undisturbed. That's the wish of the descendants. They were concerned about the possibility of mine explorers coming here illegally and breaking into the workings, so they want it permanently closed and a memorial placed here beside the entrance.'

Jack gestured at the build-up of clouds on the horizon. 'Do we have enough time?'

'The wind has veered from north to west while we've been here today, but it's still only about 10 miles an hour. It's due to pick up by mid-afternoon and will bring the weather in. That gives us a couple of hours anyway.'

'I thought the mine was already flooded,' Jeremy said.

'It's not more flooding from the sea that I'm as worried about,' Françoise said. 'It's rainwater seepage opening up cracks and saturating the gallery ceilings, putting pressure on timber revetments that are already half-rotten. It's a recipe for another collapse like the one in 1873.'

'We could call it off and wait for a better window.'

'The forecast is for sustained heavy rain for days ahead. And there's another reason why we should do it now. Where we're heading, I've had to open up a blocked shaft that could become like a waterfall with the rain, taking all kinds of debris down into the lower workings that I want to explore. This is our only chance before that happens.'

'You said on the phone that you'd found something,' Jack said. 'What have you got?'

'I dived with Rebecca on the *Santo Cristo di Castello* last year, remember? So I knew the history. When I saw the name you're about to see I was stunned. After you told me about the Paynter connection and the possibility that William Paynter had come to this mine with something from the ship, everything fell into place.'

She took out a bubble-wrapped package from a bag beside her and handed it to him. He carefully unwrapped it and gasped as the artefact was revealed. He had not seen gold like that since Costas had discovered the ankh beneath the pyramid. It was a cross about the size of his palm, on a length of fine chain. 'It's solid gold rather than gilded,' he said, peering at it closely. 'And there are holes for pins at the bottom of the cross and the ends of the arms. This once held a Corpus Christi, a figure of the Crucified Christ.'

'The Corpus Christi you found in the wreck?' Jeremy said.

Jack took out his phone and looked at a photo he had taken of the figure that morning with a five-centimetre scale beside it. 'It's the right size. It could be.'

'Now take a look at the other side,' Françoise said.

Jack turned the cross over and stared. Engraved across the arms of the cross was a name in cursive script: *Gio Lo Viviano*. It was Giovanni Lorenzo Viviano, captain of the *Santo Cristo di Castello*. He held it up to the light and angled it so the others could see. 'Well I'll be damned,' he said. 'It's incredible.' For a moment in his mind's eye he was on the deck of the *Santo Cristo di Castello* as it heaved and swayed towards the coast, the wind shrieking through the rigging and ripping off the sails. *What treasure had been aboard? What had Viviano been hiding?* He took a deep breath, handed the cross and the bubble wrap to Jeremy and glanced at the black clouds on the horizon. There was only one way to find out, and it meant going down the forbidding hole in the ground in front of them. He looked at Françoise. 'Where exactly did you find this?'

'In the deepest part of the mine at the base of that stope, just before a sump that went below sea-level. There's an old rockfall partly covering the sump that cuts off the way forward. The chain was entangled in the rocks, so I think Paynter must have dropped it while the rockfall was actually happening.'

'And as far as we know he never got out,' Costas said.

'There's no record of him after that night,' Jack said.

'Could he have been trying to reach a chamber just beyond?'

'Or returning from it,' Françoise said. 'A stope or a natural cavern, perhaps something he used as a hideaway.'

'For smuggling?' Costas said.

Françoise shook her head. 'It's too deep for that. Most of the contraband at that period was wine, and you weren't going to lower bottles and barrels almost 200 metres down a treacherous shaft only to have to bring it all the way back up again when you were ready to sell it. And the Paynters were wealthy enough already.'

'William Paynter was an agent for the Vice-Admiral of

Cornwall,' Jeremy said. 'The full force of the law was brought down on anyone of his status involved in smuggling. Not just hanging, but hanging, drawing and quartering.'

'There's another aspect to this,' Jack said. 'Another reason why he would have wanted to stay above the law, and another possibility for what might lie at the end of that tunnel. It's just speculation, but it came up yesterday evening after my meeting at Gunwalloe Church when I first heard of the Paynter connection with Viviano.'

'Go on,' Françoise said.

'Paynter was a secret Roman Catholic, and a supporter of James, Duke of York, the future King James II. The wreck took place only seven years after the restoration of the monarchy following the rule of Oliver Cromwell. James was riding a wave of popularity at the time. As Lord High Admiral he had just won the Battle of Medway, ending the unpopular war with Holland. It was what allowed the *Santo Cristo di Castello* to sail that summer without risk of capture by the English. And it was well known among his followers that James was considering conversion to Catholicism. For Catholics in England, many of whom had kept their faith secret for fear of persecution, James would have seemed the answer to their prayers. With the help of troops landed from France, they could have marched on London. Louis XIV had ambitions to rule Europe and would have been all too happy to fund such an enterprise.'

'Fund being the operative word,' Jeremy said. 'I can guess where you're heading with this. Gold from France and perhaps Spain secretly landed on the coast of Cornwall, and local Catholic sympathisers needing somewhere to hide it until James gave the word and they could use it to raise and pay an army.'

'Down at the bottom of the deepest mine worked at the time would seem an obvious place,' Jack said. 'And if Paynter made a pact with the dying Viviano to hide away something that he had saved from the ship, where better to take it? A pact could have been sealed by their shared Catholic faith, with Paynter believing that he was doing something to support a fellow Catholic. Viviano may have given Paynter the cross to increase the chances that God would protect him, knowing that he was beyond help in this world.'

'It seems that the Almighty had other plans, if Paynter never made it out of here alive,' Costas said.

'Maybe God's plan was for us to find it,' Françoise said.

'Only one way to find out,' Costs said, reaching for a climbing harness. 'Before those clouds roll in. Time to rig up.'

*

Twenty minutes later Jack held on to the rope with all of his strength, only relaxing his grip when he was certain that the belay was taking his weight and his harness was correctly positioned. He began to rappel down the shaft, glancing up at Costas' face peering over the edge and then looking down at the light from Françoise's head torch far below. The shaft was so deep that the sides seemed to constrict almost to nothing, and he had to look at the mossy timbers on either side to reassure himself that it was an optical illusion. He has a flashback to the mineshaft that he had dived in as a boy where he had nearly died after his air had cut off, something that had left him with a lingering claustrophobia that he confronted every time he and Costas went into confined spaces. He spun round, paying out more rope until Françoise came into clearer view, and then landed in a slurry of mud at the base of the shaft. He unclipped the carabiner from his harness that held the rope and helped Françoise to haul their backpacks on to a dilapidated wooden shelf on the edge of the platform. 'There's more water than the last time I was here,' she said, her voice magnified in the space. 'It's going to be slippery.'

Jack sloshed over to a dark hole just beyond the shelf where Françoise had anchored another line. With his head torch switched on he could see through into the level, the rusty tracks of the railway for the ore carriages just visible. An old fall of timbers and rock had blocked off most of the entrance but left a narrow gap. Françoise came over and knelt beside him, her face and helmet already splattered with mud. 'That's where I went two days ago,' she said. 'The torrential rain of the last few weeks opened up that channel through the rockfall just enough for me to squeeze through.'

Something crashed into the mud behind them, and Jack turned to see Costas rolling around as he tried to disentangle himself from the rope. He got up, slipped and fell again, splattering himself even further. 'Why does it always have to be like this?' he said, raising himself on his elbows and wiping his face. 'I mean, every time I go down a hole I end up sprawled on my back. It was like that under the pyramid.'

'I blame your new Caribbean property,' Jack said. 'I did say that if you spend all of your off-time in that place one day you'll never be able to leave it.'

'But it's mostly seafood,' Costas muttered, raising himself on his knees. 'Really healthy. And the gin and tonics are mostly tonic. I feel as fit as I've ever been.'

The ground shuddered and rumbled, and a small geyser of water erupted beside Costas and poured into the hole in the rockfall. 'That happens when there's been heavy rain,' Françoise said. 'The water seeps underground and puts pressure on the timbers. It's like an old wooden ship creaking and flexing in heavy seas.'

'And then sinking,' Costas said. 'That's reassuring.'

'Don't worry,' Françoise said, helping him up. 'They used oak in the upper workings and it's still pretty strong. It's only down below that everything's badly saturated and coming apart.'

'*Don't worry*,' Costas repeated, clipping the carabiner to his harness and looking at Jack. 'When have I heard that before. It's a Howard catch-phrase.'

Jack looked back up the shaft, flinching as a drop of water splashed off his cheek. The light at the top seemed a long way off and made the space they were in now seem even more constricted. He took a deep breath to calm himself. Whatever lay ahead, he would keep that glimmer of light, that escape route, in the forefront of his mind. He tugged on the rope for reassurance, feeling it shimmer and vibrate as it strained against the anchoring point far above. *There was always a way out.*

Costas edged cautiously towards the hole in the rockfall, sniffed and crinkled his nose. 'Rotten eggs. Hydrogen sulphide.'

'You get used to it,' Françoise said, tying the rope to the hook. 'There's iron pyrites down one of the shafts and it gives off that smell when it reacts with water.'

'Anything else toxic down there?'

'Carbon monoxide, excess carbon dioxide, some methane. Oh, and radon. That's released from granite and is radioactive. Methane can be explosive in the right amounts. Don't light a match just in case in confined spaces. Come to think of it, there might not be enough oxygen to do that anyway.'

'Now she tells us,' Costas said. 'Bad just became worse.'

She pulled on the rope to test it and hung over the hole. 'I thought you guys were used to this kind of thing. I mean, it's hardly the first time you've gone into the unknown with the odds stacked against you returning.'

'I'm not sure I like the not returning bit,' Costas said. 'Life is different for me now. I have an idyllic tropical island to look after. And Little Joey.'

'Well,' Françoise said, grinning at him. 'We do this for fun then.'

'Glad you think so.'

'You've got rebreathers in case you feel dizzy or start to black out. Think of it like diving. You've only got a finite amount of time underwater before the nitrogen gets you. More than a couple of hours down a mine and the cocktail of gases that accumulate underground starts to be bad news. You just need to stay one step ahead of it. I didn't like the look of that weather offshore and I don't want to be down here if there's another deluge. Let's get cracking.'

'Costas looked at Jack. 'Good to go?'

Jack, peered one last time at daylight far above, steadying his nerves. He gripped the rope behind Françoise and nodded. 'Good to go.'

CHAPTER 13

Jack clipped the carabiner from his harness to the safety line that Françoise had laid on her previous exploration from the platform to the tunnel ahead. He glanced back at Costas, watching him clip on as well, and waited while Françoise ducked into the tunnel and disappeared from view, the glow from her headlamp showing where she had gone. With her caving suit and climbing gear she was less encumbered than they were in their e-suits, though the oxygen rebreathers were streamlined and as lightweight as the materials would allow. Jack followed her, ducking down and crawling through, the mud from the walls smearing his suit in dripping brown streaks within a few metres. He stood up as the tunnel widened, and Costas followed. The level had originally been open from the platform below the shaft, allowing ore to be pushed up the narrow-gauge railway that was now visible ahead of Françoise. Massive timbers shored up the sides and the ceiling, green and orange with algae and fungal growth. She turned back towards them, taking care not so shine her head torch in their eyes. 'The timbers are under a lot of strain. Try not to lean on them just in case.'

'I'm remembering load-bearing physics from a course I did on mine engineering while I was at MIT,' Costas said. 'I'm not sure this would have passed the test.'

'It would have been fine back when the mine was operational,' Françoise said. 'They knew what they were doing. But after a century and a half of saturation some of the timbers are like sponges.'

They reached an opening where the tunnel widened into a chamber and the ground dropped away into darkness on either side. The only remaining part of the tunnel floor was a ridge across the middle with the rails of the track hanging in mid-air near the far side. 'This is the first of two collapses that seem to have taken place when the miners were down here that day in 1873, the one probably setting off the other,' she said. 'The bigger collapse is about eighty metres ahead of us. I call this first one the bridge of doom.'

'More encouraging words from our tour guide,' Costas said.

'Don't fall to the left whatever you do. The fall to the right is probably better, but it's still bad. You need to be steady with your footwork. Double-check that you're clipped on before you follow me.'

She went carefully over the raised section, holding the rope with one hand ahead and one behind, leaning forward with each step to press her feet into the soft mud to prevent herself from slipping. Jack and Costas slowly followed until they reached a small platform at the end of the ridge. Ahead of them the rails hung over an abyss before resuming their course in the tunnel on the far side. Wedged over the abyss was a tangle of timbers that had once been the shoring for the ceiling but had collapsed during the rockfall, with one of the timbers providing an uneven walkway that ended in a gap about two metres wide before the tunnel resumed. 'This bit I call walking the plank,' Françoise said cheerfully.

'Oh good,' Costas said, peering into the darkness below. 'I think I just realised why I prefer being underwater.'

'You first, Jack. Nice and steady now. I'll bring up the rear, so I can be an anchor for the rope in case either of you slips.'

'That's reassuring,' Costas said.

'If one falls, we all fall. Like roped-up climbers on a mountain. All for one, and one for all.'

Costas contemplated the gap. 'You people must have

nerves of steel.'

'I could say the same about you.'

'If it's like this here, what's it going to be like when we get down below?'

'One step at a time. That's the number one rule in mine exploring. Only think about what you can see ahead of you.'

'Or better still, close your eyes so you can't see it.'

'True. If you don't see it, it doesn't exist.'

'If you don't mind, it doesn't matter.'

'That's the attitude.'

Jack walked along the beam, took a deep breath and leapt forward, pulling the rope taut and landing on the other side. Costas followed, the timber flexing ominously beneath him, and then threw himself over the gap, landing heavily and crawling back to his feet. Françoise followed, splattering them with mud and water. Already they were dripping wet and streaked with colour from the minerals that were leaching out the walls of the tunnel. Jack peered down at the ground in front of them. 'Look at that,' he said. 'Hobnail boot imprints, preserved in the mud where it's solidified. That must be from the last time the miners came through here.'

'The footprints are only heading in one direction, and not coming back,' Françoise said. 'The fact that they're in dried mud shows how wet it was from leached rainwater when they came down here that day, undoubtedly a factor in the collapse. They would have known the danger but still pressed on. The writing was on the wall for tin mining in Cornwall by 1873 with the price of tin having dropped through competition with overseas mines, and they must have been worried about their livelihoods, taking every opportunity to work and be paid while it still lasted. It turned out to be one risk too many.'

She led them along the safety line that she had laid beside the railway track, wading and sloshing through puddles filled with copper-red water. Ahead of them Jack could see where their lights played off the walls of another open space, and she held up her hand as they came to the end of the tunnel.

It was a vast cavern, the far side just visible in their beams but the bottom lost in the darkness below. She took out a flare, struck the igniter and tossed it as far as she could. It spun like a Catherine wheel and landed on a ledge, lighting up the space in a dazzle of colour. The cavern was at least thirty metres high and a similar distance across, as large as the interior of a cathedral, and dropped away into a yawning chasm of blackness.

Just as in the previous cavern the railway tracks continued out a short way as twisted girders of iron and resumed again where the tunnel continued on the far side, but here there was no way of getting across. It was not only the scale of the place that took Jack's breath away. Everywhere the rock was covered in vivid colours - blues, greens, yellows - where the minerals had leached out. Just below the flare was a billowing mass of blue, like a giant frozen waterfall cascading into the darkness below. As the flare spluttered and waned, he saw other shapes in the shadows, stalagmites and stalactites where the minerals had combined with calcium, some of them dripping over the rails to form rusticles like those he had seen on iron shipwrecks. It was like some mythical entrance to Hades, a place of awesome grandeur but also a tomb for those who had been trapped on the other side a century and a half ago and whose remains must still be there today.

'The colours are from the lode, which contains copper and iron pyrites as well as cassiterite,' Françoise said. 'The copper produces the blue and green, and the pyrites the iron oxides and hydroxides. The cassiterite is the black stuff sparkly with quartz inclusions that you can see on the other side where the lode is exposed.'

'It must be high in tin content to look so black,' Costas said.

'The lode is rich but narrow and nearly vertical, meaning that the miners quickly got deeper as they followed it down. This was the location of the fissure where the earliest miners chased the lode down from the surface, reaching this level already in prehistoric times. From the sixteenth century the fissure was widened as they went for outlying seams, and then steam technology and the opening of shafts and levels meant that more ore could be raised to the surface. Up above us the stope left by the digging was widened into a ventilation shaft, but that was capped after the mine disaster to seal everything in.'

'So what we're seeing is part natural, part mineworks and part collapse,' Costas said.

'Correct,' she said. 'Most of the void areas below us are stoping, but this cavern was mainly a result of the collapse in 1873. You can see where it took away the rails that originally spanned the space, linking the level we're on now with the continuation of the track you can just make out on the other side of the cavern. There was a wooden and iron bridge across it from here.'

'So what happened to the miners?' Jack asked.

'By early 1873 they'd dug down below sea-level, following the fissure as far as they could out under the foreshore with the pumping engine keeping it clear. They thought that they'd exhausted the lode, but then a small rockfall up here revealed a previously unknown horizontal extension, the lode you can see opposite. Unfortunately, that discovery was what did for them. You could follow a seam vertically with reasonable safety, shoring up the stoping as you went down, but going horizontally was always risky.'

'What caused the collapse?' Costas said.

'Groundwater. That's the biggest danger here. It had rained heavily for days, and a massive storm rolled in while they were underground. They took a calculated risk going down that day. The owner had presented them with an ultimatum, that they had to produce a certain yield of ore by the end of that week or he would have to shut the mine down. That made it even more tragic because many joined in who would not normally have gone, including boys and older men.'

'So they were trapped by the rockfall in the

continuation of this level on the other side?'

'Not all of them. A small group had been working on shoring up the level where you can see it on the far side of the cavern, making it safer and ensuring that the trackway was strong enough to support the cars full of ore that were meant to have been pushed along back to the shaft where we entered. But the rockfall that cut them off from the others also destroyed their exit route, taking away the railway line and the bridge that had supported it and leaving them trapped on that ledge where the flare fell. With a zoom lens you can see a tally chiselled into the rock, showing that they were there for more than a week. Their candles and gas lamps would have run out and they would have been in pitch darkness at the end, unable to light a fire as the timbers that they had used for shoring up the level would all have been damp. Even with light all they would have seen would have been the chasm below them, with no hope of crossing to the other side.'

'Was there any attempt at rescue?' Jack said.

'The rescuers got to the bridge of doom, but by the time they had cleared enough of the obstruction to get through to where we are now there was nobody left alive, with only one body to be seen dangling from a piece of ironwork below the ledge. As they had died one by one, they must have been rolled off the ledge by those still alive, and the last ones may have thrown themselves off in despair. It doesn't bear thinking about. There was no hope of retrieving the bodies or of reaching the men trapped in the level beyond, and when the rescuers realised what had happened the decision was made to close up the mine forever.'

'So where do we go from here?' Costas said.

'Follow me to the edge. Watch your footing.' Jack could see where the safety rope had been attached to a piton driven into the rock and then hung down at a steep angle to the left out of sight. He peered over and saw that it was a slope about three metres wide that had been cut along the side of the stoping, with the rails for the ore cars still intact and the safety rope dangling down the side of a wooden ladder that seemed to be missing most of its rungs. The bottom was out or range of their headlamps, somewhere in the darkness at the base of the slope. Françoise tugged at the rope to test it, attached her belay and turned to them. 'The miners cut this beside the old stope for the first hundred metres or so down, to allow a sloping trackway to be laid for cars of ore to be pulled up. They used a weighted pully system, with lines attached to the carts that looped around iron posts set into the rock behind us, dropping down where they were weighted below. Slipways like this become more dangerous the deeper you go, with more and more rock above you and the possibility of a car breaking free and hurtling down, but they went as far as they could. At the bottom we move over carry on down the stope itself, following the line of the original fissure.'

'I'm hearing that word dangerous quite a lot,' Costas said. 'The bridge of doom was bad enough. This sounds like a one-way ticket to the underworld.'

She reached over and clipped Costas' belay on to the line. 'As you can see, the slope is just off vertical for the first few metres, and then about 45 degrees. There's a platform at the bottom beside the stope. That's what we're aiming for, where the trackway ends. I'll go first so I can check that everything's OK, then you follow, then Jack. Happy with the rigging? Right, I'm off.'

She disappeared over the edge, the line tensing as it took her weight and the beam from her headlamp bobbing out of sight. The flare had died away completely now, and their vision was restricted to the pool of light from their headlamps. After a few minutes there was a shouted OK from below, the sound echoing in the chamber around them. Costas turned around, checked that his belay was secure and lowered himself over the edge. 'See you at the bottom,' he said.

'Last time you said that we were diving under a pyramid,' Jack said.

'What was it Françoise said at the bridge of doom? If

you don't see it, it doesn't exist.'

'I think she meant don't look down.'

'Right.' Costas said. 'I'm off.'

Jack watched him go over the edge. A few minutes later there was another shout from below and it was his turn. He pulled the rope tight, turned around and began to walk backwards down the slope, conscious that everything depended on the belay holding and the rope remaining securely attached to the rock above. To his left the rotten ladder with its broken rungs showed where the miners had made their way down, and to his right the rails for the ore wagon were still intact. He abseiled down until he reached the wagon on the rails, wedged in by a shoring timber from the ceiling that had fallen during the collapse that had sealed in the miners, and he made his way carefully around it. The remaining twenty metres or so of the slope presented another spectacular sight. The lode had leached into the slipway, streaking it with vivid blues and greens, and the rust from the rails and the cart added to the colours. It was as if the rock itself were bleeding, dripping down into the underworld in the darkness below.

He turned back around to face upslope, concentrating on his footing, and a few minutes later reached the platform beside the other two. He had felt the change in air pressure as he descended and blew on his nose to clear his ears. On the platform were the rusting remains of iron buckets and shovel heads with copper residue still on them. He unclipped his carabiner and pointed at the ore cart on the tracks up the slope. 'It wouldn't take much for that to come down,' he said. 'It's tilting in this direction and is almost off the rails. One end of that timber wedging it in is completely rotten.'

'That's why we're moving into the stoping as soon as you're ready,' Costas said. 'If the cart fell it would block our exit route.'

'If we were cut off we could by-pass this place, find other tunnels and cross-link back,' Françoise said. 'The lower levels are riddled with passageways.'

'With a lot of dead ends,' Costas said.

She gave him a grin. 'Some you win, some you lose.'

'And then your torch batteries die and you join those miners down here for all eternity.'

'Where to now?' Jack said.

Françoise pointed to the void beside the slope. 'It's a bit of a mission, but it's only about thirty metres now to sea level. You won't be able to abseil but I've attached another rope that drops to the bottom, so you can clip your belay to it and let yourself down with that.'

'I can't believe you went down there alone,' Costas said.

'It's like climbing a mountain. Once you're committed, you have to reach the top. In a mine, you have to reach the bottom. And it was worth it. You'll see.'

'So this was where Paynter got down in the seventeenth century?' Jack said. 'Seems incredible.'

'Back then this was a natural fissure with much of the lode still intact. It was only as the lode was dug out that the void was widened and the rock became unstable.'

'That's another word I don't like,' Costas said.

'There are several places where you can see rock-cut steps in the original fissure that could be from the sixteenth or seventeenth century,' she said. 'It would have been a challenge working the rock down here with only candles for light, but the Cornish miners could do it.'

'Whatever Paynter was concealing down here was evidently worth the risk of coming all the way down by himself,' Jack said.

'We'll go in the same order. Me first, then Costas, then you. Watch your footing. Some of the ground is soft and liable to slip, as this is a watercourse when there's heavy rain and the sediment gets trapped behind ledges that protrude into the stope. Try not to dislodge rock fragments, as they could tumble on whoever's below. You'll see rocks stacked on the edges of the stopeway, what the miners called deads, chunks they hacked out that didn't have enough ore to send up to be processed. The wooden props you can see holding up the deads aren't doing very much. They were probably only put there for reassurance, and most of them are rotten now anyway. And there are some narrow bits. Wait until I shout before following, like before. See you down there.'

She turned and let herself down into the stope, reached a large fallen rock just below them and disappeared around it. There was a tremor in the ground, and a trickle of water appeared down the slope beside them. 'The storm must have rolled in,' Costas said. 'At least we've got our rebreathers if it starts to fill up with water below.'

'The biggest problem is probably rainwater dislodging rocks above us,' Jack said. 'I don't like it, but Françoise knows what she's doing.'

A muffled shout came from below and Costas turned and lowered himself over the rock, holding the rope with his belay clamp attached. 'Once more unto the breach,' he said. 'At least this should be the final descent.'

Jack watched him slide down the mud out of sight. He remained stock-still, keeping his breathing slow and measured, listening to the dripping of the water increase to a tinkling sound all around him. As long as he knew that there was a way out his claustrophobia was in control, and the space around him was still cavernous. Within a few minutes the water had formed a small stream down the slope where Costas had gone, and a few minutes later a shout came up for him to follow. The descent was less controlled than the previous one, slipping and sliding down the slope, trying not to jam his rebreather into the side and avoiding the wooden props that held up slabs of rock on the way. He reached a point where he could stand upright and make his way between tightly packed piles of rock on either side, but the space narrowed and he was forced to crouch and crawl. Behind the piles of rocks were side-chambers back-filled by the miners with more tailings, much of it blue-green copper-bearing rock stained with mineral precipitate.

Ahead of him was a collapsed chamber where he had to crawl around huge slabs of fallen rock, and beyond that another constricted passage where the rope dangled into a space lit up by the headlamps of the other two. After squeezing through the final section he dropped down beside Costas and saw another yawning hole like a shaft, with a shimmer of water perhaps fifteen metres below. 'I've just got to re-rig this final drop,' Françoise said. 'The rope you can see dangling in the hole was my reserve when I came here before and isn't really safe enough. It's pretty sketchy down there. There's not a lot of room, and these rocks on either side could let go at any point. Go steady as you descend.'

'Yet more words of reassurance from the tour guide,' Costas said.

'You did sign up for the high-risk option.' She tied a knot in her belay rope. 'And the bigger the risk, the bigger the reward.'

'We trust you,' Costas said. 'And you have been down here before.'

'True. Only once, though.' She turned to face them and lowered herself into the hole, extending her arms and legs towards the rock on either side. 'I'm braced out here,' she said, looking up. 'I can't extend my arms any further, so we can't climb down. We'll have to abseil the whole way.'

They watched as she belayed down into the pool of water, and then they followed her. As Jack landed and unclipped from the line, he could see that they were at a junction between a man-made tunnel on one side, probably a drainage adit, and the continuation of the lode-bearing fissure on the other, now going off horizontally. 'The tunnel was dug during the eighteenth century to allow groundwater to be pumped out from these lower workings,' Françoise said. 'You can see the rusted remains of the pump rod coming out in front of us. They didn't yet have pumps powerful enough to clear out the water needed to mine below sea-level, so the workings finished where we are now. The adit goes back to the base of the shaft we came down from the surface, below that first platform. I dropped a line down there as a safety backup because in theory we could crawl back along the adit and exit up the deep shaft that way. That is, if the adit hasn't filled with rainwater by then.'

'Or been blocked by a rockfall,' Costas said.

'It's pretty sketchy. That's a helpful word I've picked up from my Cornish mine-explorer mates.'

'Who have sensibly stayed at the surface,' he said.

'Essential topside backup.'

'Sketchy, dodgy, insanely dangerous, it's all the same to me.'

'We need to move out from under this hole and the stoping.'

'I know. I'm getting used to the drill. In case of rockfall. Or a flood.'

'You're catching on.'

They left the rope dangling and ducked into the first part of the fissure, their headlamps reflecting off seams of cassiterite dotted with speckles of quartz. 'There's a lot of ore to be seen because they didn't finish with it,' she said. 'Beyond here, they didn't do any extraction at all. There was plenty to be going on with higher up. The fissure is mostly in its natural state, formed by minerals dissolving around the lode and leaving gaps between the outcrops of granite. The miners widened some parts ahead of us for access, but it's still pretty narrow.'

'When did they get this deep?' Jack said.

'Probably in prehistory,' she replied. 'Some of the pick marks look as if they were made with antler tines rather than metal tools. But I don't think they got all the way to sea level until the sixteenth or early seventeenth century, at the time of the first intensive exploitation of the mine under the Paynter family. It would have taken a lot of effort to remove the granite to widen the fissure, for little purpose from a mining viewpoint with so much ore still being found higher up. When William Paynter came down here that final time in 1667 a rockfall blocked off the fissure where it went under the sea, and as far as I can tell nobody has got beyond it since then. In the eighteenth and nineteenth centuries they only came down here to dig out that adit to keep the workings above us from being flooded during times of high groundwater and surge from the sea.'

'Jeremy's research shows that Paynter and his brother had actually shut down the mine several years before he disappeared, despite it being a time when the ore yield was increasing and it was becoming more profitable.'

'They were obviously using this as a hiding place,' Costas said. 'Before he came down here with whatever he had brought from Captain Viviano.'

'That's for you to find out with your gear,' Françoise said. 'The only access beyond the rockfall lies below sea level, through a sump.'

'How far ahead is it?' Costas said.

'Fifty metres. Maybe a little more.'

A jet of water burst out of a crack beside Costas' head, hitting the wall opposite and flowing down to the base of the fissure. 'That's worrying,' he said. 'The pressure of the groundwater is now so great it's firing it into the tunnel.'

Françoise put a finger into the water and tasted it. 'That's not just rainwater,' she said. 'It's salty, mixed with surge coming up from the sea. That's why they dug that adit. When the storm conditions are right the combination of rain and sea surge can drive the water in these workings many metres above sea level, and it can take hours to subside. It happens quickly and could trap miners in the deeper levels where they were often a long distance from the shafts and safety.'

'Do you want to carry on?' Jack said.

'We have no redundancy if things go wrong. But you know that.'

'There hasn't exactly been a safety net so far,' Costas

said.

'It's your call,' she said.

'Costas and I have rebreathers,' Jack said. 'Right now, you're the one taking the bigger risk.'

'I'll guide you down to the rockfall and point the way. I should then have time to return and exit the mine before the water situation gets critical.'

Jack stared into the crack ahead of them. All his instincts told him that this was a bad place to be, that drew on his worst fears of confined spaces, that was as dangerous as anywhere they had ever dived before. But they had come too far to turn back now, and he needed to know what lay beyond. He turned to Costas, who nodded at him. 'OK,' Jack said. 'Let's push on.'

CHAPTER 14

Jack followed Costas and Françoise through the fissure at the base of the mine, dropping down on his hands and knees and squeezing through gaps in the granite. Water came gushing in from an opening above them and they sloshed through a pool almost thigh-deep, bracing themselves against the rock as they pushed forward. After a final narrow passageway they came to a chamber about five metres across and ten metres long with a mass of fallen rock at the far end, partly submerged in a pool. Françoise pointed at the water, which was crystal-clear in the beams from their torches. 'That's the sump,' she said. 'Before the rockfall happened I'm certain that a further chamber was accessible, but the only way to get to it now is underwater. This is as far as I got in my exploration and is why I wanted you here with your gear.'

'So the rockfall was what deterred any of the miners who came down here afterwards?' Costas said.

She nodded. 'As far as they would have seen there was nothing more down here for them. We're beyond the main seam of the lode, which trends off to the left at this point.' She pointed at the edge of the rockfall. 'That's where I found the cross, with the chain partly buried in the rocks. I was nearing the end of my planned time underground so I didn't dig out any more, especially when I saw that there was no way I was going to get through.'

Costas knelt down and began removing rock fragments from where Françoise had indicated. After a few moments he stopped and stared. 'My God. Look at this.'

The other two came up beside him. Protruding from under a rock were bones, recognisable as the radius and ulna of a forearm. He removed more rock and revealed the bones of the hand, dislocated as if it had been pulled apart. 'I caused that when I extracted the chain,' Françoise said. 'He'd been holding it.'

Jack lifted a rock on the other side, exposing the crushed remains of a skull. 'It looks as if he was caught in the rockfall and tried to claw his way out, but then was struck by a heavy stone on the head. It would have killed him instantly.'

'You can see from the orientation of the body why I think he was making his way out,' Françoise said. 'He'd been to a chamber beyond, deposited what he was taking and was returning when he was killed.'

'Are you sure this is Paynter? Costas said.

'The cross with Captain Viviano's initials makes it pretty certain,' Jack said. 'Nobody else could have brought that down here.'

'And look at this,' Françoise said. She lifted a fragment of rock from the forefinger of the right hand, revealing a glint of gold. 'It's a signet ring with a bundle of three arrows as the design. I recognise that from the documents I was researching on the history of the mine. It's the Paynter family crest.'

Jack peered closely. 'That clinches it.'

While they had been talking the water had risen perceptibly, lapping the bones and rising up the pile of rock. There was a rumbling sound and then a terrible screeching noise, followed by a percussion that sent a shock wave through the chamber. 'What was that?' Costas said, holding his head. 'My ears are ringing.'

'The ore wagon on the slope,' Françoise said. 'That timber holding it up must finally have given way.'

'If it's wedged at the bottom that might block the exit route.'

'Then it's plan B,' Françoise said, hitching up her gear. 'Going along the lower adit until it reaches the base of the shaft beneath the engine house. I've got pitons and rope and should be able to make my way up to the platform we reached when we belayed down from the surface. I'll leave the rope attached for you to climb up if you exit that way as well.'

'You mean the adit at this level, that's going to be filling up with water as fast as this chamber is?' Costas said.

'That's the one,' she said. 'So I haven't got much time.'

'What about plan C?'

'Which one is that?'

'The one for Jack and me. If the ceiling above this sump collapses while we're in the chamber on the other side and we can't get back.'

'You'll have to hope that the fissure beyond the chamber comes up under the sea and is wide enough for you to get through. Once I'm back at the surface I'll get Jeremy to call in the IMU helicopter. If you do make it out that way any rescue attempt will be sketchy as hell in this weather.'

'Our crew are ex-Navy Search and Rescue,' Costas said. 'If anyone can do it, they can.'

'OK,' Jack said, looking at Françoise. 'Good luck.'

'And to you too.'

They watched as she sloshed her way back through the chamber and ducked into the entrance tunnel, where there was now only about a metre of clearance above the water. The beam from her head torch became a smudge and then disappeared. Another rumble from somewhere high up caused the surface of the water to shake and shimmer, and a small cascade of fragments fell from the side wall, bouncing off the pile of rock. Jack pressed a control under the sealing ring on the neck of his e-suit and the visor snapped down over his face from the helmet, the head-up display inside flashing red and then green to show that the suit was watertight and the rebreather had activated. Costas did the same and pressed the intercom. 'Are you hearing me?'

'Loud and clear.'

'Let's do this.'

Jack crawled into the sump and floated on the surface, waiting while the suit sensed the pressure and automatically adjusted the trim of the water reservoirs on either side of the rebreather to maintain neutral buoyancy. The water ahead was still crystal-clear, but he knew that the slightest movement would stir up the sediment and quickly reduce the visibility to zero. The jumble of rocks looked precarious in the extreme, and he was glad that the rebreather was closed-circuit; bubbles from exhalation might have worked their way into the cracks between the rocks and cause loose fragments to dislodge. He slowly descended into the sump and swam forward, feeling the movement in the water as Costas dropped in behind. He reached a narrow gap between two slabs of rock, just wide enough to squeeze through, and a few metres on saw a shimmer where the light from his beam reflected off the surface of the water. 'I'm through,' he said. 'You've only got a few metres to go.'

'I wish I'd eased off on those seafood platters,' Costas said, his voice sounding strained. 'It's a bit tight.'

Jack turned and saw a billowing cloud of sediment where Costas had pulled himself along. They surfaced at the same time, their beams playing off the rock-cut walls that had once been the far end of the previous chamber, blocked off by the rockfall. Ahead of them was a crack where the fissure carried on out under the sea, and to the right a raised antechamber with chisel and pick marks clearly visible on the rock. The water was already lapping the base of the antechamber; they had to press on if they were to get inside before it was inundated and anything delicate and organic that might have been hidden there was destroyed by the water.

They opened their visors, clambered out of the sump and made their way into the antechamber, panning their beams inside. At first there was nothing but rock to be seen, but then an astonishing sight met their eyes. On a rock-cut ledge were three wooden chests, each about a metre long with domed lids and iron and brass strappings, the outer surfaces encrusted with concretion where the iron had corroded. Jack stooped into the space and Costas followed, and they knelt down in front of the first chest. 'This is what it's all about,' Costas said. 'Unless I'm mistaken, these are treasure chests.'

'Only one way to find out.'

Costas pulled out a small pry-bar from the tool belt around his waist and pushed the chisel end into the gap between the lid and the chest. There had once been a lock, but it had almost entirely rusted away. He gave a tentative push, to no avail, and then pushed the bar down with both hands. The lid gave way with a crack and tilted open. He returned the bar to his belt and they pushed the lid up together, raising it until it was nearly vertical. They stared inside, speechless for a few moments. 'Bingo,' Costas said.

'Unbelievable,' Jack said. 'If only those nineteenth century miners knew what lay beneath them.'

The chest was full of gold coins, thousands of them, all of the same size and denomination. Costas picked up a handful and then let them fall through his fingers, keeping hold of one and peering at it. 'I've seen that before. The crowned shield with the little castles on the obverse, and the cross on the reverse. Portuguese?'

Jack picked up one and peered at it. 'Four cruzados, Alphonsus VI, 1663. Looking at the others, I'm only seeing dates in the 1660s, with nothing later than 1667. That fits the scenario exactly.'

'Which is?'

'What I suggested earlier about William Paynter and a Catholic conspiracy. Secret shipments of gold were made to Paynter, whose credentials as an agent of the Vice-Admiral would have put him above suspicion in the eyes of the King's agents sent to root out potential Catholic rebels in Cornwall. Gold landed under cover of darkness in one of the coves along this coast could have been brought here in secret. Almost certainly France was behind it, with the Sun King Louis XIV ostensibly an ally of King Charles II but harbouring ambitions to have a Catholic monarch on the throne of England once again. The fact that the coins are Portuguese reflects the Portuguese origin of much of the gold in circulation in Europe at the period; it would have deflected suspicion from the French had the shipments been intercepted. The amount of gold here shows that the Brazilian mines run by Portugal were producing in quantities never before suspected, as early as the 1660s. This must be where a lot of the gold from those mines ended up.'

'There's enough here to fund a small war.'

'A small war that could have grown into a revolution. There were sleeper cells of diehard Catholics across England waiting for the fire to be lit. If Paynter hadn't come down here on his mission for Viviano, if that rockfall hadn't killed him, then the course of history might have been very different. He was probably the only one who knew the location of this treasure, with even his brother George being of uncertain allegiance, and the secret would have died with him. Without the treasure, the uprising could never have happened. The wreck of the *Santo Cristo di Castello* was a turning point in English history, in a way that could never have been guessed.'

'Speaking of Paynter and Viviano. Check out the third chest.'

Jack followed Costas' gaze. On top of the furthest chest in the corner was a shape the size of a document case covered in a blue-green mineral precipitate that had dripped down from the ceiling, nearly encasing it. He sloshed over and carefully prised it from the chest, causing much of the precipitate to fall away. It was old leather wrapping, almost certainly vellum, bound up as books would have been for seaborne transport but only thick enough to contain a narrow volume or a single folio sheet. The leather that had been covered by the precipitate was well-preserved and he could see the faint outline of an inked mark on the surface. He stared in amazement and then showed it to Costas. 'It's the mark that Jeremy found in the bills of lading for the ship, the letter V with the cross under it that Viviano used to identify his own goods. This must be what Paynter left here almost 350 years ago. Whatever is inside is the key to our mystery.'

'Bingo,' Costas said. 'Now let's get out of here. Look at the water level.'

Jack turned towards the chamber entrance. In the time that they had been inside the water had risen rapidly, creeping up until it lapped the base of the treasure chests. A massive influx of groundwater from the storm was pouring down the shafts and was clearly going to fill up the chamber completely. He thought of Françoise, hoping that she had made it through the adit in time. He looked at the package, his mind racing. It had only been wrapped up against the damp of a ship's hold, not to survive full immersion underwater. He turned his back to Costas, holding his arms out. 'Unzip my suit,' he said. 'I'm going to put it inside.'

'You're crazy. The water will be over our heads in seconds.'

'Just do it.'

Costas pressed the retaining clips on Jack's helmet, uncoupled the hose and placed the helmet on the nearest treasure chest. The ceiling was dripping wet, and Jack blinked hard as rivulets of water ran down his face. He could survive being damp inside his e-suit after it was sealed again, but not if the suit was flooded. Costas sloshed back to him, the water now at waist level, and grasped the zip on Jack's right shoulder. 'As soon as it's open I'll grab that package from you, shove it inside and zip you back up again. Ready?'

'Go for it.'

In one movement Costas yanked the zip from one shoulder to the other. Jack braced himself against the sudden intake of cold air and concentrated on not slipping into the water. Costas took the package, pushed it inside and round to an internal pocket in front of Jack's chest, and then pulled the zip shut, yanking hard. He grabbed the helmet, locked it in position and clicked in the air hose, snapping the visor shut and hitting the control on the side to activate the breathing system. Jack's head-up display came online just as the water rose over the level of his face. 'That was close,' he said. 'Thanks.'

'On a wing and a prayer,' Costas said. 'Right. Let's move.'

They pulled down their fins from behind their calves and locked them in place, and then swam back into the main chamber. Another rumble shook the water and the rockfall shifted and collapsed, blocking off the sump at the entrance. Jack stared at it, feeling a rising tension in his chest, a tightening in his breathing. They were cut off at the bottom of a submerged mine with no chance of getting back the way they had come and their only hope being in the other direction under the seafloor. He forced himself to focus his mind ahead, imagining swimming free in the sea. Costas turned to him, checking that he was alright. 'You can see the cassiterite of the lode where the fissure goes forward,' Costas said. 'That's promising, because it's the other minerals with the lode that leached out millennia ago and left the open space of the fissure. We just have to hope that it's wide enough for us to get through it and out under the sea.'

Jack powered forward behind Costas, their headlamp beams reflecting off speckles of quartz in the lode. If the tunnel connected to the sea then the depth readout on his console should be close to that of sea level, with several metres of additional depth from the rainwater flooding that had been rising around them. After a short distance the tunnel dropped almost vertically, and he watched Costas' light become a smudge in the gloom. He activated the override on his automated buoyancy system and expelled air from his suit as he plummeted down, equalising the pressure in his ears and bleeding air back into his suit to prevent it from squeezing him. He followed Costas closely, pulling himself though cracks where the fissure narrowed, trying not to think of the consequences if one of the gaps were too narrow. Twenty minutes after leaving the chamber Costas slowed and turned back to look at him.

'Good news,' he said. 'The fissure is going back up.'

Jack glanced at his depth readout: 42 metres below sea level. A few metres ahead he could see where the tunnel inclined sharply, and he pulled himself towards the bend. Looking up he saw Costas just above him, his torch illuminating the sides of the fissure. 'Lights off,' Costas said. 'I might be able to see daylight.'

Jack switched off his head torch and the fissure was plunged into darkness. He closed his eyes, waiting for them to adjust, and then looked up again, still seeing nothing. Gradually a faint haze appeared, barely perceptible. 'Is that what I think it is?' he said.

'It's sunlight through the sea floor about ten metres above me. But we have a problem, Jack. The fissure narrows and there's no way I can squeeze through. Come up and you'll see what I mean.'

Jack switched his headlamp back on and rose alongside Costas below a ceiling of rock. Costas shone his beam into the fissure and put his right hand through, showing that it was barely wide enough for his arm. Jack stared at it, trying to keep his breathing calm. *So near, yet so far.* There were no other obvious cracks or fissures that they might get through. 'Any suggestions?' he said.

Costas reached into his toolbelt and pulled out a small orange package labelled C-4. 'Plastic explosive. You know I never dive without it.'

'That could bring down everything on top of us,' Jack said. 'And the shock wave would be channelled through the fissure. It would be like being hit by a wall of rock.'

'I can feel a ledge above this overhang where I might be able to place the charge,' Costas said. 'That would project most of the shock wave upwards but might be enough to crack the ledge and bring it down. I'd need to set the detonator timer with enough leeway for us to get back beyond the bend of the tunnel so that the rock doesn't fall on us, and away from the worst of the shock wave.'

'Where the rock fall might seal us in permanently.'

'This ledge is all that's in our way. Above it the passage to the surface looks wide enough for us to get through. And we can always try to dig through a small rockfall.'

'How's your air supply?'

'I've got about twenty-five minutes left at this depth.'

'OK. Let's do it.'

Costas broke away the packaging to reveal the dull brown of the explosive, pressed his forefinger into it to create a hole for the detonator and then reached up into the fissure and pushed it along the ledge as far as he could. 'You're going to have to do it, Jack. You've got longer arms than me. The further back the better.'

Jack traded places with him and felt along the ledge, reaching the explosive and pushing it against the rock face. He backed out and Costas passed him a brass pencil detonator. 'It's set for five minutes. Shove one end into the explosive and then press the other end to activate it. I made it myself in the IMU lab. It should work.'

'It should work?'

'I've never actually tried it with real explosive. My usual kit is still on board *Seaquest* and I just threw this together before we set off this morning.'

'And if it doesn't work?'

'Boom.'

'And you're using me as point man?'

'That's 16 ounces of C-4. If it goes off this close, it's taking both of us out. It doesn't matter who has their hand on the detonator.'

'What are dive buddies for,' Jack said.

'Inseparable, in this world or the next.'

Jack took the detonator, made sure it was correctly positioned and pushed his arm back up through the fissure, reaching around until he felt the explosive and the hole that Costas had made in it. He pushed the detonator into the hole and then pressed the activator at the other end. He moved his arm away, being careful not to dislodge the explosive, and dropped down beside Costas. 'Right. It's ticking. We need to move.'

They pressed the manual overrides on their buoyancy systems, dumped air from the chambers and dropped down to the bend in the tunnel, swimming as fast as they could back the way they had come. Costas stopped behind a slab of rock that protruded from the side and Jack came behind him. 'We've only got about 30 seconds left. It's more important now that we shelter than put any more distance between us and the explosive. There's going to be an almighty shock wave.'

Exactly on cue there was a shudder and Jack felt the air sucked from his lungs. A few seconds later the water rushed by, and they clung to the rock knowing that it would soon surge back in the other direction. As it did so it brought a mass of silt with it, reducing the visibility to zero. They waited for the surge to settle down, and then pushed off and swam back towards the bend in the tunnel, Jack in the lead. He kept his headlamp on even though all he could see was the reflection of silt in the water. Where the bend had been he swam into a cascade of freshly fractured rock that filled the space completely. There was a crack and a shudder somewhere behind them and the water seemed to shimmer. 'That's the way back behind us blocked off as well,' Costas said. 'Our only chance now is to dig through this rockfall.'

Jack glanced at his head-up display. It showed only eighteen minutes of breathing gas left. It was going to be touch and go even if they were able to dig their way out. He began to remove rock fragments, prising them out and pushing them behind him, trying to keep his breathing slow. After a few minutes they had cleared a hole large enough to see open water in the fissure above. Together they heaved away a large fragment and Costas pulled himself through, with Jack following him. They reactivated their automated buoyancy systems and finned upwards. Where the ledge had been was now an opening just wide enough to pass through. A few minutes later they were out on the seabed, floating among swaying fronds of kelp. Jack closed his eyes for a moment, letting the groundswell take him, feeling a huge flood of relief. *They had made it.* He looked down at the black hole below them and then across at Costas. 'You alright?'

'The helicopter is already here.'

The visibility was good enough to see the surface twenty-five metres above, and he could make out the concentric circles where the rotor-wash was beating against the waves. He felt another wave of relief. That meant Françoise had made it out too and had directed the rescue crew to where she thought they might come up offshore. As they ascended through the fissure the beacons on their helmets would have transmitted a GPS fix, leading the helicopter to its current position directly overhead.

They were not out of danger yet. There was at least a Force 6 gale blowing and the swell would make recovery difficult. But the pilot and the winchman knew their job, and it was not the first time they had been extracted from a tricky situation. The important thing now was to conserve their remaining air and rise slowly enough to avoid decompression sickness or an embolism. Jack needed to forget about the stress and claustrophobia and become a diver again, back in his natural environment where all of his instincts and training would kick in.

He gave an OK sign to Costas and then a thumbs up. 'Good to go?'

'Good to go.'

He watched as Costas rose above the kelp towards the wavering pool of light on the surface from the helicopter's searchlight. He could feel the bulge of Captain Viviano's package inside his e-suit, and he felt a rush of excitement. He wanted to get it to the conservation lab as soon as he could, to peel it open and see what lay inside, to discover what it was that had been so important that a dying captain 350 years ago had thought of nothing else on his deathbed and had entrusted it to another to conceal in one of the most dangerous places that he and Costas had ever explored. He could hardly wait.

PART 3

CHAPTER 15

The Great Middle Sea, 5521 BC

The man in the stern of the boat turned, placed his feet squarely on the thwarts and swayed with the rhythm of the waves, a motion that came easily after so many days at sea. It was as if the power of the ocean were in his own body as well, surging through his blood from one side to the other. The same could not be said for the others in the boat, curled up on the keel or splayed on the thwarts, one of them clutching the edge and retching over the side. They were tough men, strong in body and spirit - carpenters, metalsmiths, stonemasons - but some of them had barely left the temple precinct all their lives, and none were sailors. They were Elik, Enkidu, his own brother Shamhat, Shuruppak the son of Ubara-Tutu, and Utnapishtim. He himself was Shamash, named after the sun, the life-giving force that made all of the new gods of the priests seem meaningless, no more than empty-faced statues. The days spent rowing against the current as the floodwaters rose and then sailing beyond the Strait of the Bosporus on to the Great Middle Sea had been the biggest ordeal of their lives, and now they were yearning above all for sight of the promised land to the south, for an end to the misery of seasickness and for fresh food and water once again.

It had not helped that the night before they had decided to drink the last of the wine, a rough red made from the grapes that had grown on the slopes of the volcano. The wine had made them forget the sway of the boat and they had told tales as the shamans once had, stories of the origins of their people as hunters on the steppe before they had come down to settle on the shores of the Black Sea. They had spoken in hushed tones of more recent times, of the rise of the sea until it drowned the citadel and the departure of the priests in their boats for the distant corners of the world. Shem told of Noah, son of Lamesh, the first to leave, and as the wine flowed they had laughed at the story until their bellies ached. Noah had built a boat far larger than the rest, adzing the planks along with his sons and lashing them together, and then filling it with sheep and goats to provide food for the journey as well as the pet monkeys and cats from the temple. He had tried to persuade a pair of aurochs on as well, the last of the breed of wild oxen that had been brought down from the steppe. The aurochs had stomped and bellowed and swept their horns from side to side, and then lumbered off into the water and swum by themselves into the mist, never to be seen again. By the time Noah finally departed his boat was surrounded by hundreds of gulls and birds of prey diving down to get at the food for the animals, and as it slowly made its way out to sea with the goats bleating and Noah disconsolately looking for his aurochs it had been the funniest thing that any of them had seen. For a brief time it had relieved their anxiety as they looked to their own boats and provisions, the last timbers being shaped by feverish hands as the floodwaters rose towards the temple and the great pyramid in the centre of the citadel.

Noah had been one of the elder priests who still sought to commune with the spirits of animals in caves, with mammoths and mastodons and sabre-toothed tigers that were now little more than a distant memory among the oldest hunters, those who had roamed the steppe in the days before Adam and his sons Cain and Abel and Seth had discovered the secret of farming and brought their people to the rich soils beneath the volcano on the edge of the sea. Other departing priests had been of the new order, those who had first set up faceless statues of Anu and Anil and Enki, gods of sky and wind and water, and who had brought the people under their yoke. But for Shamash and his companions their focus was neither animals nor statues, but wood and stone and metal. They were taking with them not the age-old rituals of the shamans or the inventions of the priests but the knowledge and skills that were the greatest achievements of their people, the ability to work in stone and metal and construct monuments far in advance of any of the peoples around them. That would be the legacy of their drowned civilisation, the gift that they could bring to others willing to take them in and conceive of monuments even greater than those that now lay submerged beneath the floodwaters of the sea.

He looked at the man lying asleep between the thwarts in front of him, his repose more peaceful than the others. *Utnapishtim, how is it that you have lived so long? Are you immortal?* He was old, but not old. Young, but not young. His hair and beard were white, but his skin was as fresh and taut as that of a man in his twenties. It was Utnapishtim who had first warned them of the flood, coming back one day in his fishing boat from the Strait of the Bosporus and telling them how the waters of the Great Middle Sea had broken through, cascading down where once there had been a land bridge and filling up the basin of the sea. And it was Utnapishtim who had led them here now, taking them back beyond the strait on a voyage he had made generations before when he was truly young, far south to the desert shore where he had given the people seeds of grain in exchange for water, seeing great swathes of green on either side of the river running through the desert and remembering it years later as a place to which refugees from the flood might return to rebuild their citadel and bring all that they had learned to a new land.

But there was something else besides their knowledge and skill that they had brought with them, something that lay wrapped in a cowhide beside Utnapishtim as he slept. It was Utnapishtim who had named their boat *An-tiki*, the Prolonger of Life, and last night they had found out why. Before they had become too drunk to listen Utnapishtim had told them the story of his youth and the secret of his longevity. As a boy he had been among the first to come down from the steppe to the slopes of the volcano by the sea, to watch how the seeds of grain fell and learn to sow it themselves, to smelt copper from the ore that lay all around to fashion tools that allowed them to fell trees and split rock and begin to build the first houses and walls. While their fathers and uncles had laboured on the citadel the boys had gone deep into the volcano to the cave of the shamans, and seen two streams of fire meld into one, seeing it cool into a metal of strange colour and brightness. They had watched from behind a rock as the shamans prised out chunks of the metal with antler picks, ground it into powder, mixed it with water and consumed it. The youngest of the shamans, those with many years of natural life still left, had died agonising deaths; but the oldest had arisen revitalised, just as Utnapishtim was now, old but not old, young but not young.

Later the boys had stolen back to the cave when the shamans had left and taken away some of the powder themselves. They had known not to consume it until they too were near death, but when they did so they lived for generations beyond the normal span of men. They became the elders of the citadel, the *atrahasis*, the wisest ones. No others knew the source of their longevity, something that allowed them to oversee great building projects that would have faltered had they not lived for centuries, that depended on vision and determination over many years to see them through. Great temples were completed, and the pyramid that mimicked the shape of the volcano itself. Inside the pyramid they had placed the last of the powder in the Holy of Holies, and it was Utnapishtim who had consumed it, lying on his bier near death with the sun playing on his aged skin and wisps of hair, waiting in flickering consciousness to see whether he would convulse and die in terrible pain or come to life again.

And now he was the last of the *atrahasis*, the last of

those who might bring the wisdom of Atlantis to a new shore. With the floodwaters rising he had gone back into the volcano, seeking the confluence of the rivers of fire that he had seen as a boy. The shamans were long gone, but he had found the place and hacked out a chunk of the precious ore, the metal that the shamans called orichalcum. It was what lay beside him now, wrapped in the cowhide. There was no telling whether it was the correct mixture of elements, or whether the shamans in preparing the powder had added a secret ingredient that the boys had not seen. But it was their hope for the future, a symbol of the strength of purpose that had led them to seek out a new beginning, a hope that they too might follow in the footsteps of Utnapishtim when their time came and live long enough to see great monuments rise over their new land as they had once done in Atlantis.

Shamash leaned on the tiller and felt the warmth of the sun on his face. *Shamash, life-giver*, he whispered, repeating the words that his mother had said every night as he fell asleep. A raven flew over, croaking and flapping, a bird of the land and not of the sea, heading into the haze to the south. For several days there had been a yellow tinge to the air, a dust that made their throats even drier than they already were, and a smell like brackish fresh water. It was stronger now, and the dust had settled in a thin sheen on the thwarts of the boat. Utnapishtim raised himself on his elbows and looked to the south, his eyes piercingly blue, almost luminescent. 'We are close,' he said, his voice sounding distant and hoarse. 'I can see the channels where the fresh water of the river runs into the sea. This is the place.'

'You see well, Utnapishtim,' Shamash said. 'I see only haze.'

'I see well, but my vision is fading fast. My time is coming. This boat will be my bier.'

'Will they welcome us? Or will they be people of war?'

'I gave them seeds of grain. I gave them the secret of farming. For some, that means peace and prosperity. For others, war. That was many generations ago, and the course that men take is unpredictable.'

Ahead of them a dense patch of mist covered the sea, swirling at the edge where it was caught in the breeze. The boat scraped over something; Shamash could see that it was a sandy shoal, partly awash. A great sea-turtle looked up and stared at him with huge eyes, its eggs in a hole in the sand behind it. Elik reached out for the eggs in desperation, but the boat was over the shoal with the next surge of the sea and the turtle was behind them. The wind drove them in towards shore and up over the surf, the waves slapping the sides and breaking over the stern. Utnapishtim lay back down, his skin now translucent and his hair coming away with the wind. He reached into the pouch on his belt and took out the jewel that he often held, its colour brilliant even in the murky light and the symbol of Atlantis visible on one side, picked out in gold. 'Take this when I am gone, Shamash,' he said, his voice little more than a whisper. 'It will be your guiding light. And beside it in the pouch is a small amount of the powder of orichalcum.'

'It is you who must consume it, Utnapishtim,' he said. 'We need your wisdom above all else.'

'It will have no effect on me now. I have had all that I can, and I have lived two score the normal lives of men.' His eyes had faded to blackness and were staring sightless up at the sky. 'But for you and the others, it may offer hope.'

'We are young men. It will only hasten our end.'

'You are young, but you are near death. It can only be taken at the end of life by the very old or the very ill, those with nothing to lose. Even if you were to be given water and food now, some of you are too far gone to recover. The powder may hasten the end for some but give a new lease of life for others, a life that may last as long as mine. Perhaps, Shamash, you who are named after the sun, you will be the new god of the people who live in this place, the one who shapes their destiny.'

Shamash looked at the body of Utnapishtim. His skin had become yellow and brittle, and his cheeks hollow. He was crossing the waters between life and death and was accepting it. The others had stirred now, some of them too weak to raise themselves, but Elik and Shamhat were peering over the bows into the mist. Suddenly the boat rammed into the sand and grounded with a shudder. This time they were stuck fast, and Shamash could see the rippling surface of the sand on the foreshore and beyond that a line of piled-up dunes that seemed to loom in and out of the mist. They had beached on a great desert shore just as Utnapishtim had predicted. He could see nothing green or alive, but then he saw a mound of turtle carcasses, gutted and stripped of their meat. People had been here, and they might return. If they were fishermen and turtle-hunters, there was hope. Above all they needed water. With the sun beating down and the dunes blocking the breeze this place would become as hot as the volcano, worse even then being out at sea. The others had slumped back into the boat, moaning and wheezing. They had little time left.

He left the tiller and crawled over the thwarts to Utnapishtim, feeling light-headed and dizzy. With the power of the orichalcum having left him the old man's body had shrunk to little more than skin and bones, like a desiccated corpse in the desert. Shamash prised open his hand to take the jewel, and then removed the pouch from his belt, feeling the weight of the powder inside. He crawled back and sat in the stern, swaying and retching, falling in and out of consciousness. He remembered what Utnapishtim had said: *only to be taken at the end of life*. He squinted at the shore, his eyes burning hot and no longer able to water, and seemed to see a mirage, a haze of heat rising off the sand and shimmering into the sky. He saw two figures walking towards him, one a woman with flowing dark hair and the other a child. To his joy he recognised his wife Leah and their son Enil, here from the headland of Ilion where they had left the women and children in safety before sailing south, with Enil banging on the wooden drum he had made for him. He got to his feet, arms outstretched to greet them, but then he tottered sideways, falling heavily in the boat and blacking out. He came to with someone shaking him, and saw that it was his brother Shamhat, his lips cracked and his eyes half-shut, lying where he had pulled himself alongside. 'Shamash,' he said, his voice a rasping croak. 'Sit up. They are nearly upon us.'

Shamash raised himself on one elbow and squinted at the shore. The figures were still advancing, but now he could see that his earlier vision had been an illusion. They were not his wife and son but were several men coming down from the dunes. Silhouetted on the horizon behind them were a dozen or more men in loincloths, shackled at their feet and chained from neck to neck, the figure of a goddess with a snake on her head being carried at the head of the procession. A man cracked a whip and the line shuffled on, marching to a drumbeat, until one of them fell sideways and was immediately set upon by two dogs. Shamash shifted his gaze to the figures advancing towards him. They were taut, muscular men, their skin darkened by the sun, made taller by fearsome headdresses in the shape of a falcon, the beaks blood-red. Each of them brandished a spear in one hand and a dagger in the other. The skin around their eyes was blackened by paint and they were covered by red weals in the shape of strange symbols. They came inexorably, splashing into the water where it lapped the shore, like hunters intent on finishing off a stricken prey.

Shamash stared, paralysed. Something was not right; these were not fishermen and farmers. What Utnapishtim had brought the people who lived by this shore generations ago had taken them on a different course. These were slave-traders, men of violence and oppression, wearing the symbols of a goddess whom he did not recognise and who might show no mercy to his people. They would find no slaves of any value here, only broken men unable to drag themselves along. The daggers carried by those traders were for one purpose only, to finish off those who were of no value to them and leave them as carrion for the birds of prey who followed, the falcons and eagles that were already circling overhead.

He had to act now. With shaking hands he took the pouch and poured its contents into a wooden bowl that had been by his feet. There was no water, so he took a copper knife from his belt and thrust it into his forearm, letting the blood drip into the powder until it was a thick liquid. He leaned over and held Shamhat's head up, tipping the bowl into his mouth and forcing him to swallow. If it killed him, it was better than the death that awaited him at the hands of the men who were now bearing down on them. He tipped the remainder into his own mouth, swallowing it in great gulps, tasting the iron in the blood and trying not to gag. He held the sides of the boat, forcing himself to breathe deeply, trying to keep down the only thing that had been in his stomach for days. He felt a searing pain and saw Shamhat convulse and roll over, blood trickling from his mouth. And then he felt a great awakening within him, greater than the surge he had felt on the sea, and a fire rose up through his lungs and his neck and his face, making his eyes light up and see the world as Utnapishtim had done. As the men came up to the boat he rose to his full height and roared, his arms outstretched with the jewel held high until it flashed in the sunlight, dazzling the men and making them cower in its rays. 'I am Shamash, the Sun-God,' he bellowed, his voice deeper than it ever had been before, in words that they could not understand but would know to be divine. 'I have come from the sea to rule over you. Kneel down and pray to the god of Atlantis.'

CHAPTER 16

Lake Bardawil, Egypt, present-day

Maurice Hiebermeyer took off his pith helmet, pulled up his googles and wiped the sweat off his brow. The glare from the salt flat was blinding, and he quickly put the goggles back in place again, tightening the cord behind his head to stop them from slipping down his nose. The view through them was opaque, otherworldly, as if he were looking at a photographic negative, and he stood still for a moment to regain his bearings. They were a legacy from his grandfather, a surveyor with the German Afrika Korps during the Second World War who had volunteered his services to the British after being captured and had been put to work tracing a road in the desert. It was his grandfather's stories of the antiquities he had discovered that had fired up his fascination with Egyptology as a schoolboy, and he wore the goggles out of respect for a man who had committed his life to Egypt after the war and had helped to reopen the German Archaeological Institute in Cairo. He knew that modern polaroid technology would give a significantly better image than the heavily tinted lenses of the 1930s, but somehow that view with its murkiness and strange refractions allowed him to see into the past with a special clarity, as if the deficiencies of the lenses filtered out the distractions of the present. He associated them with his greatest discoveries in Egypt over the past thirty years, and he fervently hoped they would not fail him now.

He put the helmet back on, checked the flap to make sure that it covered his neck and looked around. Behind him he could hear the crash of the surf against the spit of sand that separated the sea from the lagoon, a shallow lake that extended almost a hundred kilometres parallel to the shore and had dried out at the eastern end to form the salt flat. Beyond the flat lay the edge of the Sinai Desert, a vast expanse of dunes and ridges that extended hundreds of kilometres south to the Red Sea. He could see nothing else, no crumbling hillocks of mudbrick from ancient settlements, no modern buildings, no roads. Yet he knew that the emptiness was an illusion, and in his mind's eye he could populate it with the great movements of history that had passed this way, seeing the silhouettes of camels and caravans and people shifting in and out of view like a mirage on the horizon. This had been the *Via Maris*, the Way of the Sea, the bridge between Egypt and Asia during Pharaonic times. From here Thutmose III in the Eighteenth Dynasty had taken his army deep into the land of Canaan, creating the largest empire Egypt had ever known. A millennium later Alexander the Great had come in the other direction, leading his army to conquer Egypt and carve out his own place in history. In the seventh century AD it had been the holy warriors of the jihad, and then the Crusader King Baldwin III who had died here and given his name to the place, the Sabkhat al Bardawil. The British had confronted the Ottoman Empire here during the First World War, Israelis had fought Egyptians in the skies above and now it was the new regime whose outposts were springing up along the coast, making his presence here a tenuous foothold back in the land that he loved.

The tides of history had not just swept from east to west and back again, but had also come from the north, bringing refugees from war and pestilence and natural disaster who had found landfall here before making their way west to the fertile floodplain of the Nile Delta. He reached into his pocket and felt the ancient artefact there to remind himself why he was here, not as a rather unusual member of an ecological team studying the flora and fauna of the lagoon but rather as an archaeologist yearning to get back into Egypt under the new regime, one that had expelled him along with all other foreign archaeologists more than a year previously but was now beginning to suffer the economic impact. He had already made a discovery that had found favour with the regime, an Islamist inscription on an ancient stone monolith protruding from the desert, carved when the Arabs moved west over the Sinai in the seventh century AD. For two days now he had been waiting on tenterhooks while the inspector who had been attached to the team applied for an excavation permit to the new Ministry of Culture in Cairo, two days in which he had scoured the edge of the lagoon in the vicinity of the discovery ostensibly recording the flora but really looking for any further clues that they were in the right place for what he was seeking.

The northern Sinai and the Nile Delta were the great unknown in Egyptology, a region barely scratched by archaeologists while the focus of attention was on the pyramids and temples and tombs to the south; yet it was here under the sand and the alluvium of the Nile that the biggest questions might be answered, about the origins of Egyptian civilisation and whether or not it had been influenced by people coming over the sea from the north. It was well-known that waves of refugees had arrived at the end of the Bronze Age, the so-called 'Sea Peoples' fleeing the collapse of civilisation at the time of the Trojan War, but he was seeking evidence of a migration much older than that, of people fleeing a great natural catastrophe who may have brought with them the seeds that made Egypt great in the following millennia. If he could do that, if he could find something that would link Jack's discovery of the lost citadel in the Black Sea with his own revelations among the pyramids and tombs along the Nile, then the blank canvas of the desert here in early prehistory would become populated by people as important as the pharaohs and pyramid-builders who were their successors to the south.

It was Jack who had set this ambition in train by giving

him the artefact that was in his pocket now when they were at boarding school together in England. He took it out, held the polished black basalt up and saw the image engraved on one side. It was part of a palette, used for mixing pigments and cosmetics, and dated to the predynastic period or earlier - no later than the fourth millennium BC. The carving showed a line of slaves chained together with one of their number fallen and being attacked by jackals, and behind them fearsome warriors wearing headdresses in the shape of falcons; above them was a sun-disk and to the right the prow of a boat drawn up on a shoreline, cut off where the palette was broken. The sun-disk was not the familiar Aten of Akhenaten but the sun-symbol of the Mesopotamian god Shamash, dating thousands of years earlier than Akhenaten and suggesting that the scene depicted the arrival of people from distant lands. It had been his most treasured possession and had sealed his friendship with Jack, who had known about his grandfather and his passion for Egypt and had been with him over the years that followed, through their studies together at university and his foundation of the Institute of Archaeology at Alexandria. The profiles of the jackals and the falcon-headed warriors seemed such clear antecedents of the later gods Anubis and Horus, and to represent the missing elements of Egyptian history that the sands of this shoreline might conceal.

Jack had been given the artefact as a boy when he had lived in New Zealand by the wife of an officer who had fought in the Sinai during the First World War. She had known little of its origin, only that he had been part of the New Zealand contingent in the Egypt Expeditionary Force that had pushed across the Sinai in the campaign against the Ottoman Turks in 1916; it had been sent to her with his possessions after he had been killed near Damascus in 1918. But several months ago Jack had been sent a diary by their granddaughter who had found it among her mother's belongings after she had died. In it the soldier had described how he had discovered the artefact as well as an inscribed stone pillar when his unit had dug a channel to the sea in order to flood the western end of the Sabkhat al Bardawil, to prevent the Turks from using the sand bar to advance west again. The scheme had been abandoned and the unit had moved on as the Turks were pushed back into Palestine, and the wind and the sea had quickly concealed all trace of their work in the sand.

Jack had immediately contacted him as well as Jacob Lanowski, IMU's computer genius who also had a passion for ancient Egypt. Lanowski was here now, hunched over in a tent on the other side of the dune, putting together a satellite-aided survey of the sedimentary characteristics of the lake for the ecological project but also doing a palaeoenvironmental reconstruction of the shoreline six thousand years ago to give a best-fit for its location within the present-day salt flat. It was Jacob who had pinpointed the location of the 1916 find, combining map references in the war diary of the New Zealand unit with satellite imagery to lead them almost exactly to the inscribed pillar in the sand, something that Maurice knew was far older than the Arabic inscription they had found on its upper surface. The IMU bid to carry out the ecological assessment of the lagoon had partly been Jack's effort to bring him back to Egypt, and he was very grateful for that. This had become a personal journey for him, a return not only to Egypt after his enforced absence but also to the passion of his childhood and the earliest foundations of the civilisation that had fascinated him all his life, not to pyramids and sculptures and mummies this time but to the small clues in the sand that were so often the key to resolving the great mysteries of the past.

He put the artefact back in his pocket and took a deep breath, feeling the hot air in his lungs and tasting the familiar tang of the desert. Until an archaeological permit arrived, if it ever did, he was going to have to content himself with his official role as a counter and recorder of the tiny scraps of flora that dotted the desert, something that he had found unexpectedly satisfying. He stared out over the salt flat, wondering if he were seeing something black sticking out in the distance, unsure whether it was a mirage or an effect of the goggles as he turned from left to right and made the image shift and distort. He raised the goggles and squinted at a tiny flower in the crack in front of him where the sand dune reached the crust of the salt flat. He bent over and peered closely, shading his eyes. It was *Iris mariae*, one of the threatened species, named after Mary, mother of Jesus, with delicate lilac-coloured leaves, pinkish and violet. It was really rather pretty, he thought. He took out his GPS receiver, held it close to the flower and photographed it with his phone, making sure that the readout for the fix was visible.

He straightened up, pocketed the receiver and phone and pulled down his googles again. That was good, he thought. The representative from the Egyptian ministry who was with them to oversee the ecological project would see that his focus had been in the right place, and not on archaeology. He peered out over the salt flat again. There was definitely something there, like a blackened stump. It was probably just a piece of flotsam washed through the channel from the sea, but it needed checking out. He thought for a moment, and then looked down again at the edge of the crust. They had been warned by the local fishermen not to go on it, but the fishermen themselves did so and none of the team had tried. They were probably erring on the side of caution. You won't know until you try, Jack always said. It was probably hard enough.

He put his right foot out, gingerly placing it on the surface. Nothing happened, and he put more weight on it. At that moment he heard the roar of a diesel on the crest of the dune and a Land Rover pulled up. A door slammed and a woman's voice came down loud and clear. 'Maurice. *Maurice.*'

'What is it?' he said, pirouetting back to see Aysha, then slipping sideways on the salt and regaining his balance. 'What do you want?'

'Don't do it,' she said, enunciating each word forcibly.

'Don't do it.'

'But the Egyptian fishermen do it. We watched them yesterday.'

'Yes. Along marked trackways. We agreed that we would not do it. *You* agreed. And the fishermen weigh about one third as much as you do.'

'There's something out there. About three hundred metres south-west. I'm sure of it.'

'Well, if it fits with Jacob's prediction of the location of the ancient shoreline then we'll get a trackway laid on the flat to look at it. Right now you need to come with me. I'll tell you my news from the ministry when we're with Jacob.'

Hiebermeyer peered out again into the haze and then took his foot off the crust. As he did so a large crack appeared with a lattice of hairline fractures going off in all directions, and the briny water oozing out where he had been. He backed off and made his way up the slope towards Aysha. Seeing her there in her wide-brimmed hat and white abaya robe, with her tool belt and desert boots, it was hard to believe that it had been fifteen years since they had first dug together in the mummy necropolis in the Faiyum when she had been a graduate student and they had found the papyrus with the account of Atlantis that had led Jack to his extraordinary discovery in the Black Sea. Now they were married, had a son almost old enough to wield a trowel and were back again in the sands of Egypt. He reached her and they set off together down the far side of the dune towards the breaking surf and the shimmering expanse of the Mediterranean Sea.

In a small depression at the end of a track about halfway down was an old army tent with one side open, the canvas flapping in the breeze and a figure seated inside at a table behind a laptop. Hiebermeyer bounded and slid down the dune until he arrived at the tent, Aysha behind him. Lanowski looked up, his eyes barely visible through the film of dust covering his glasses, and then quickly turned back to the screen. He was a picture of devotion to the task at hand, his long lank hair plastered on his forehead and neck and with a growth of stubble to rival Costas. Aysha shook her head in despair as she looked at the two of them together. 'The marine biology team have finished their report,' she said. 'That's one of the things I came here to tell you about. And we haven't got much time.'

'What's the story?' Hiebermeyer said.

'The lagoon has become the main wintering and foraging ground for turtles in the eastern Mediterranean, and the place where they haul out to lay eggs. But they are being caught up in the nets of bottom-trawlers in the lagoon. The fishermen think the turtles are competing with them for sea bass, but it's not true. It's overfishing that has reduced the numbers of sea bass, and anyway the turtles mainly eat shrimp and crabs. But the reduced sea-bass numbers in turn have increased the numbers of shrimp and crabs, bringing in more turtles. And there's another factor. Global warming has increased evaporation in the lagoon, resulting in higher salinity. And shrimp love salt.'

'Resulting in yet more turtles,' Lanowski said.

'Correct. And the turtles are not just being killed as by-catch in nets. The fishermen are getting increasingly desperate, seeing the sea bass numbers fall but the numbers of turtles rise. Some of them are being deliberately killed.'

'But the turtles are protected under international law.'

'We're talking livelihoods here. People on the poverty line.'

'Are all of the species affected?'

'All of them. Loggerheads, Green Turtles, Leatherbacks.'

'Solution?'

'Education. Demonstrating to the fishermen that the turtles are not the problem and turning the Sabkhat al Bardawil into a marine protected park. The IMU team will develop a sustainable fishing strategy and liaise with the Egyptians to make sure it is properly implemented. The fishermen will need an additional income source so we are suggesting that they be trained as park rangers, to protect the turtles rather than seeing them as a threat. Efram Jacobovich from IMU's Board of Directors has agreed to provide a relief fund to pay them. If the government here agrees, that will give us a toehold back in Egypt again, even if it's just in the Sinai. One thing might lead to another, with ecology perhaps opening the doors again to archaeology in the long term.'

Lanowski looked at Aysha. 'You said we haven't got much time.'

'Before you arrived in Egypt yesterday we dammed up the channel between the lagoon and the sea that normally keeps the lagoon under water. My uncle's machinery was used to create a simple sand barrier that can easily be dug away again. We did this in order to expose enough of the lagoon bed to collect the data we needed for the environmental study. The UNESCO advisory team has recommended as a matter of urgency that the dam be opened up to allow the salt flat at this end of the lake to be flooded again, in order to keep the ecosystem stable. I've just received the finalised schedule for the machinery to move in. If it's not done soon the ecology of the lagoon may be permanently altered and it will look as if IMU has done more harm than good.'

'That's one of the things you came to tell us,' Lanowski said. 'What's the other?'

'It's about the excavation permit. My uncle is an irrigation engineer and decided to stay on in Egypt despite the regime change, as it's crucial to maintain the canals and channels from the Nile in order to sustain agriculture. The new regime has enough sense to see that and have given him some leeway. It was his team that we used to dam up the channel and provide boardwalks to get over the flats. I presented a case that the Arabic inscription we found on the stone could be of great historical significance and really put the archaeology of early Islam in this region on the map. We have another friend in Minister Khalil, the one government minister from the old regime who was retained because he was a world-renowned Islamic scholar before he became a politician.'

'I remember his name,' Lanowski said 'Wasn't he the one who secured Jack and Costas' early release last year?'

'Correct,' Aysha said. 'Without him they would probably still be in solitary confinement, or worse.'

'So what's the decision?' Hiebermeyer said.

'We've got the green light.' She smiled at him and held his arm. 'An excavation permit for the site of the pillar and a survey permit for the western sector of the Sabkhat al Bardawil. But we've only got three days to explore the salt flat of the lagoon until it's flooded again. They've made that the time limit for the pillar excavation as well.'

'*Wunderbar*.' He clapped his hands and heaved a sigh of relief. 'How many people can we have?'

'Only a small team. We must keep a low profile in case anyone with influence from the government who doesn't like the idea shows up and has the clout to shut us down. The main thrust of IMU's activity here still must be the ecological project. But Rebecca is on her way, and you are here for us too Jacob if you can unglue yourself from your computer. Three of my uncle's assistants have worked on archaeological sites with us in the past so we can call on them, and there are also the machine operators. My uncle is going to helicopter in a couple of mini diggers this afternoon to clear the sand from around the pillar.'

Hiebermeyer looked back in the direction of the salt flat, just visible through a gap in the dune. The sun was low now, a great golden orb that would soon disappear behind the delta of the Nile. The ancient Egyptians had another name for the route along this shore, the Ha-Horus, the Way of Horus, the road leading to the place where the Sun-God sank beyond Egypt in the west, drawing with it the lifeblood of the people of the Nile and then returning it from the east the next morning. The three days ahead were not just about what lay out there under the dunes and the salt flat, but about where it would lead, about how it might help to explain the rise of the most remarkable civilisation the world had ever seen.

Three days. That was a tall order. Three days to bring together the equipment needed to mount an excavation in one of the most difficult places he had ever worked. Three days not only to dig out that stone pillar but also to see whether his instinct was right, whether that blackened timber sticking out of the salt flat was what he thought it might be. He remembered one of Jack's favourite catch phrases: *on a wing and a prayer.* It felt like that now, as if everything hung in the balance. He owed it to everyone, to himself, to Aysha, to Jack, to do the best he could, to seize this chance to put his foot back firmly on the map and not to let anything push him away.

He took a deep breath, swallowed hard and turned back to them. Aysha knew what he was going to do and was already holding out her phone. 'It's ringing,' she said. He held it to his ear, barely able to contain his excitement. 'Hello, IMU? This is Maurice Hiebermeyer. Please put me through to Jack Howard straight away.'

CHAPTER 17

Over the Tyrrhenian Sea, Italy

The IMU Embraer had begun its descent early, banking sharply over the Tyrrhenian Sea as it headed towards the Italian coast. Jack had slept for almost the entire flight from England and was cradling a cup of coffee as Jeremy worked on his laptop beside him. He had woken with the final image from the mineshaft dive two days ago seared in his mind, the view of the open sea and the sunlight above as they had swum up the shaft, but he had not dwelt on the dangers that he and Costas had faced. All he could think about was the leather-bound package from the seventeenth century that they had discovered and what it might contain. After being winched up to the helicopter and flown to the IMU campus he had taken the package straight to the conservation lab, where a team of experts had been on hand to begin the process of stabilising and opening it. He had hoped that they would have had success before his flight, but the leather had stiffened to form a compact mass and they had been worried that exposure to light might damage any inked paper inside. They had done the work in an infrared chamber, and the chemicals used to soften the leather had taken effect too slowly to see anything before he had left.

He tried to put that from his mind and focus on the day ahead. Just before flying he had received a call from Maurice Hiebermeyer in Egypt that had tightened the schedule even further. With a window of less than three days for the excavation in the desert it was imperative that he get out there as soon as possible to help, and Costas would be joining them. That meant that they only had a few hours to meet up with Jeremy's friend Marco Carandini from the Pontificia Università Gregoriana to find out all they could about Father Athanasius Kircher and what he had been up to in Rome in the summer of 1667. With any luck there would also be word from Paolo Tensini in Genoa about whether there was anything further in the archives on Captain Viviano and his patron Sauli and their connection with Kircher. Jeremy was planning to stay on in Rome to pursue any leads, but Jack very much hoped that he would come away today with enough to take the quest forward once he had heard back from the conservation lab.

'I've just had a message from Maria in Spain,' Jeremy said. 'In the state archive at Simancas she found a cargo list for the *Santo Cristo di Castello* sent by the Spanish consul in Amsterdam, and in Lisbon she found notarial documents referring to the merchants Porrata and Cornelissen. It seems that having specialised in the transshipment of goods to Madeira and the Azores, including paintings and chandeliers from Amsterdam, from the late 1660s they focussed their attention on acquiring guano from the outlying islands, mostly uninhabited. It's a strange change of tack, from being specialised art dealers to collectors of bird droppings, but potassium nitrate was always in high demand for making gunpowder. Anyway, they disappear entirely from the records after one outward voyage to the islands in 1673. It's as if they vanished into thin air.'

'Shipwreck?' Jack said.

'That's the obvious conclusion. One curious record exists for the provisioning of their ship for that final voyage from Lisbon. Merchant ships were quite heavily armed at that period, but she was taking on additional arms, all of them anti-personnel: twelve bronze breechloading swivel guns of one-inch calibre, twelve muzzle-loading rail guns, twenty muskets, pistols, shot, three half-quintal barrels of gunpowder and two boxes of *granadoes*, grenades. Those last are particularly unusual for a merchantman.'

'Were they worried about pirates?'

'Pirates from the Caribbean in the early eighteenth century used the islands as a base for attacking East Indiamen coming up from the south Atlantic as well as treasure ships from Brazil and Spanish America. But the 1660s and 70s is a bit early for that, at the beginning of the age of Caribbean piracy.'

'Perhaps they were being pursued by someone else. Maybe guano was not all they were after in those islands, and someone else was after it too.'

'Pirate treasure?'

'I was thinking of something else. Something that may have been taken there millennia ago.'

'Perhaps what we hear today will give us some clues. Marco has sent a car to pick us up at the airport and take us into Rome. We're meeting in the piazza outside the old Dominican convent beside the Pantheon and the church of Santa Maria sopra Minerva. We couldn't do any better than that, next to the site of the Temple of Isis and the place where Kircher made his Egyptian discoveries.'

Jack turned and stared out of the window as the plane crossed the coast and descended through the clouds towards the airport at Fiumicino. Below him he could see the great hexagonal harbour built by the emperor Trajan, and beyond that the ruins of Ostia, the original port of Rome on the river Tiber that had silted up after the river changed course in the early medieval period. He had flown into Rome many times before, first as a student of archaeology and then on the trail of one of the greatest mysteries that he had ever confronted, exploring the catacombs beneath the Basilica of St Peter in the search for the earliest evidence of Christianity. But now he was having to adjust to thinking about Rome in the seventeenth century, to the city as a hub not of an empire but of something with an even greater geographical reach - a religion that by the time of Captain Viviano and the *Santo Cristo di Castello* had spread to every corner of the world, going hand-in-hand with the explorers and traders who left the ports of Catholic Europe in search of new worlds. The Church had become a promoter as well as a suppressor of ideas, creating in Jesuits such as Athanasius Kircher some of the greatest scholars of the age and yet also stoking the fires of the Inquisition, putting Galileo on trial and yet in so doing creating the very constraints in which new ways of thinking so often flourish. And through it all ran an extraordinary seam dating back to ancient Egypt, an import less obvious than Christianity but no less powerful, a belief from the age of the pharaohs that had survived the fall of Rome and the darkness of the medieval period and was confronting them now.

A little over an hour later they were in the heart of the city, driving past the Colosseum and the Palazzo Venezia and plunging into the narrow streets of the Campus Martius, the region between the Capitoline Hill and the river Tiber where many of Imperial Rome's greatest monuments had been built. It was Jack's favourite part of Rome, where buildings of the medieval and Renaissance periods lay over ancient structures in the streets surrounding the Pantheon. They pulled up next to the rear wall of the Pantheon in the Piazza della Minerva and got out, thanking the driver and walking over the cobbles towards the centre of the piazza. 'Marco will be here in about ten minutes,' Jeremy said, glancing at his phone. 'I'll see if I can grab us a coffee somewhere.'

Jack went over to Bernini's statue of the elephant with the obelisk on top of it, dodging between boys playing football in the square. Behind the sculpture was the Renaissance façade of the church of Santa Maria sopra Minerva, and to the left the former Dominican convent. He mounted the steps of the plinth and put his hand on the feet of the elephant, something that drew him back to the time of the *Santo Cristo di Castello* and Athanasius Kircher. The sculpture had been installed in the very year of the wreck, 1667, and the obelisk had been found only two years before that, buried beneath the convent where the Temple of Isis once stood. In 1667 Kircher had only just completed his *Obelisci Aegyptiaci*, published in time to be included in the batch of books that were on board the *Santo Cristo di Castello*. As he looked at the obelisk he thought of Amsterdam and the ships and streets of Rome, imagining them as they had been in that fateful year; it took little effort to envisage the piazza as almost nothing had changed since the seventeenth century.

He read the dedicatory inscription in Latin on the plinth in front of him: *Sapientis aegypti insculptas figuras ab elephant belluarum fortissimo gestari quisquis hic vides documentum intellige robustae mentis esse solidam sapientiam sustinere. Whoever sees here the images carved by the wise Egyptian and carried by the elephant, the strongest of beasts, realise that it takes a robust mind to carry solid wisdom.* He looked up at those images now, at the hieroglyphs that would have seemed so mysterious to the people of Rome when the obelisk was brought here from Egypt for the Temple of Isis in the first century AD, and that Kircher more than fifteen hundred years later had still struggled to understand. It was an inscription of the pharaoh Apries and showed that the obelisk had originally been set up in Saïs on the Nile Delta some time between 588 and 568 BC. That was another reason why Jack had wanted to touch the sculpture today. Maurice Hiebermeyer was convinced that the obelisk was from the same temple in Saïs that had been visited by the Greek scholar Solon in the sixth century BC, the place where he had heard the story of Atlantis from the priests. For Jack that was a link to another part of the story, far back at the dawn of civilisation when refugees from a drowned citadel on the Black Sea may have brought with them something more precious than Jack could ever have imagined when he and Costas had first dived on the site more than 15 years previously.

A man in a black cassock came up beside him and followed his gaze. 'Giver of life on earth as the sun is in eternity,' he said, his English slightly accented. 'I believe that is the correct translation of the hieroglyphs that so taxed Father

Kircher.'

Jack turned and recognised him, and then looked back at the obelisk. 'A link between heaven and earth, between terrestrial and divine, the pyramidal shape of the obelisk representing rays from the sun just as the pyramids do in Egypt.'

'It was the genius of Bernini to combine the baroque elephant and the obelisk, something that might have been jarring in other hands but represents the assertiveness and confidence of Rome at the time of the counter-reformation, with antiquities being used once again to strengthen the message of the Church.'

'Capped by the insignia of the Pope with the cross of Christ on top, where once there would have been the sun-disk with gold plating to reflect the sun when the obelisk was outside the temple at Saïs,' Jack said.

'Indeed,' the man replied. 'Divine wisdom, ever-present since God created the world, reached Christianity by way of ancient Egypt even though those people at the time of the pharaohs lived before salvation in the form of Christ had come.'

Jack gestured towards the Pantheon. 'And yet there we have perhaps the greatest sun symbol of them all, the circular temple radiating its wisdom over the city. Most people who stand outside don't see it as a church but as a temple. One of the achievements of Christianity in Rome was to preserve evidence of pagan belief, not to subsume it.'

'Spoken as a true archaeologist.' The man smiled and held out a hand. 'Dr Howard. Your reputation precedes you.'

'As does yours, Father Rauscher. Jeremy has shown me your monograph on the works of Father Kircher. I also know that you supervised Marco Carandini's doctoral thesis at the Pontificia Università, on the reception and understanding of ancient Egypt in Renaissance and early modern Rome.'

Rauscher bowed slightly and gestured towards the Dominican convent. 'I've just been with him in the library discussing the publication of his thesis. He told me he was meeting you down here and I wanted to say hello.'

Jack looked at the building. 'Formerly the Casa della Inquisition. A nerve-wracking place for a doctoral candidate.'

'Fortunately, times have moved on since the trial of Galileo, and we no longer put students through quite that degree of rigour. I should tell you that I have followed with great interest your excavation of the wreck of the *Santo Cristo di Costello*. It is fascinating to know that one of the ships leaving Amsterdam in 1667 was carrying a consignment of books by none other than Athanasius Kircher. I await with much excitement any further revelations of your research.'

A compact, well-dressed young man came round the side of the building accompanied by Jeremy, who was precariously holding two paper cups and trying not to let them slosh over. Rauscher shook hands with Jack again and strode back to the entrance to the convent, nodding at the other two as he passed them. Jeremy passed Jack over one of the cups. 'Marco has stashed my bag in the convent,' said. 'He knows you're only here for a couple of hours.'

Marco held out a hand to Jack. 'Jeremy took me along to a lecture you gave on the search for the gospel of Christ while I was a visiting student at Oxford and he was finishing his doctorate. You put me in touch with Maurice Hiebermeyer to help with the transcription of the hieroglyphs that Kircher had been studying in Rome.'

'I remember. I've just been trying to work through the one on this obelisk. Father Rauscher tells me that he is still involved with your research.'

'His full surname is actually Ritter von Rauscher. His great-grandfather was the prince-archbishop of Vienna. Generations of his family have served the Vatican and been Jesuit scholars in Rome. Pretty daunting really, but he was the best person to supervise my research and gave me many insights into the Egyptians in Rome, something that has been a passion of his since he himself was a student here.'

Jack took a sip of the coffee and glanced at his watch. 'So what have you got for us?'

Marco looked at him intently. 'Something that nobody else has seen except me. You are going to be amazed.'

'That's what we're here for.'

'I take it you don't mind getting wet?'

Jack squinted at the sun reflecting off the fountain in the square. 'At the moment, that sounds positively inviting.'

'Good. Follow me.'

*

Marco led them to the rear wall of the Pantheon and along the narrow lane that led to the Piazza della Rotonda in front of the temple. In the centre of the piazza was the other small obelisk from the Temple of Isis, discovered in the fourteenth century beneath the church of Santa Maria sopra Minerva and erected on the fountain in 1575. Jack stopped and looked at it for a moment, knowing that Father Kircher had spent many hours standing here pondering the hieroglyphs in his attempt to translate them. The obelisk was much older than the one in the Piazza della Minerva, dating to the reign of Ramesses II in the thirteenth century BC, at a time when the traditional religion in Egypt had been re-established following the heresy of Akhenaten in the previous century.

He turned and followed the other two beneath the huge granite columns of the portico, made from stone freshly quarried in the eastern desert after the Roman annexation of Egypt in the first century BC. As he entered the building his eyes were drawn from the coloured marble of the floor to the stark concrete of the dome, its concentric coffers rising to the central opening through which sunlight streamed. The name Pantheon meant all the gods, but the Roman historian Cassius Dio speculated that it came not from the statues of gods that had been set up inside but instead from its resemblance to the dome of the heavens, a place that channelled the energy from the sun itself – a place more properly dedicated to the Roman Sun-God Helios, the god known as Shamash in ancient Mesopotamia and the Aten in Egypt. Walking under the opening and feeling the warmth of the rays Jack could empathise with those who had fallen under its spell, the life-giving heat of the sun more real than the imaginary existence of so many of the other gods.

Marco reached an apse at the rear where a small door was set behind the tomb of one of Italy's kings, unlocked it and then locked it again behind them. Ahead was a gloomy brick-lined passageway lit by a string of bare bulbs, and then a brick stairway going down. 'This follows the outer wall of the rotunda,' Marco said. 'About six weeks ago water began welling up on the floor of the Pantheon, meaning a blockage in the aqueduct channel beneath. The authorities of Santa Maria Rotonda knew that I'd studied the ancient plans of the area during my doctoral research and thought that I might know a way of getting beneath the floor. They appointed me as archaeologist to carry out the watching brief while the work went on. Apart from the contractors and myself nobody else has been down here in living memory, as that door we came through was sealed behind a veneer of marble slabs. I only found it by consulting a plan from the sixteenth century when the church was being renovated and we discovered this passage, part of the original Roman construction.'

The steps were narrow but long, dropping gradually around the perimeter of the rotunda. At the bottom Marco ducked under a low arch and they followed him into a space too low to stand upright. Marco gave them each a small LED torch and switched on one of his own. They could see that the concrete base of the rotunda was bedded on solid rock, the grey-white tufa that underlay most of Rome. Running across the centre of the floor was a rock-cut channel with water flowing through it, clear and sparkly in the torchlight.

Marco panned his torch down the channel to another low arch where the water flowed out beneath the western foundations of the rotunda. 'That's where the problem lay,' he said, his voice dull and muffled in the confined space. 'There had been a small seismic event, barely noticeable but enough to topple a foundation stone from the original Republican temple into the channel. It blocked up the exit and trapped other debris brought down the channel as a result of the earthquake, causing this chamber to fill up and the water to rise through the drains to the floor of the Pantheon above. The contractor cleared the blockage easily enough using divers.'

'And you found something here?' Jack said.

'After the contractor left I waited two days for the water to subside so that I could see if there was any need for further work. Once it had drained away I got down here and explored as far as I could under the arches at either end of the channel. During the Roman period the Campus Martius was supplied by the Aqua Virgo, famed for the clarity of its water. What we're looking at mostly seems to be a result of renovation work carried out on the old Roman aqueduct in the fifteenth and sixteenth centuries. Under Pope Nicolas V the entire aqueduct was restored and extended, culminating in its consecration as the Acqua Vergine in 1453, but further work was carried by the architect and sculptor Giacomo della Porta in the 1570s. The purpose of that work was to extend channels to a further 18 public fountains, including the one under the obelisk in the Piazza della Rotonda about fifty metres from where we are now. That's where this channel leads.'

'I'm guessing you were interested in going in the other direction,' Jack said.

Marco nodded. 'I knew that the water in the channel came through the site of the Temple of Isis immediately to the east, just beyond the Dominican convent. Most temples needed running water, particularly the Temple of Isis with the water garden that was said to have been its main attraction. I thought of getting in touch with one of the teams that explores underground Rome, but I decided to keep it to myself. You can never know which groups have been infiltrated, and who might be an informer. There are secret organisations with religious affiliations in Rome and many people beholden to them, sometimes within families running back centuries. You'll understand why I was worried when you see what I've found.'

'So you went into that tunnel alone?' Jeremy said.

'I've read all of Jack's books. Going through submerged underground passageways seems to be necessary if you want to find treasure.'

'It's not without risks,' Jack said. 'When this is over I'll tell you where Costas and I have just been. But carry on.'

'It's about 120 metres long. It goes under the road and the Dominican convent to the foundations of the Temple of Isis.'

He led them to the entrance of the aqueduct on the east side of the chamber. Jack could see that the arch was made up of blocks of travertine probably reused from the Republican temple that had preceded the Pantheon, but that they had then been reworked and stabilised in the sixteenth century; the keystone bore the date 1570 and the inscription **GIA DELLA PORTA ARCHITECTUS FECIT**, 'Gia della Porta architect made this'. It seemed a deliberate evocation of the famous inscription of Agrippa from the Republican temple that had been retained on the front of the Pantheon, as if Giacomo della Porta had been trying to show that his work represented continuity from the great works of the past rather than an attempt to replace them. Giacomo was from the same family of sculptors in Genoa as Guglielmo della Porta, creator of the Corpus Christi figure from the *Santo Cristo di Castello*, and as Jack passed under the arch he reached up to touch the inscription, feeling the same connection with the past that he had felt when he first picked up the sculpture on the wreck site.

Marco and Jeremy led the way, their backs bowed in the narrow space and the water up to their knees as they sloshed against the flow. The channel curved slightly to the right, and within twenty metres the entrance was no longer visible. After another twenty metres it opened out into another space that was high enough for them to stand upright. As Jack panned his light around he remembered doing the same in the catacombs beneath the Basilica of St Peter's several years before, but here it was different. Instead of niches and shrines dug out of the bedrock there were massive concrete and rubble foundations of the Roman temples that had stood above where they were now. The air was different too, not the musty odour of decay in the catacombs but the smell of limestone and the fresh water that flowed around their feet. It made the place seem less sepulchral than Jack had expected, and more connected with the modern-day city that could be heard in the dull reverberations of traffic from the streets above them.

Marco aimed his torch at a series of low arches in the wall opposite, and Jack did the same. He could see the smashed-up amphora sherds that had been used as a tempera in the concrete, showing that it was Roman. The water channel came out from under the central arch but the tunnel was completely submerged, with only the top of the arch visible. 'That's the original Roman waterway that ran under the Temple of Isis from the Aqua Virgo,' Marco said. 'Giacomo della Porta tapped into it to create the offshoot that we've just been along, supplying the fountain in the Piazza della Rotonda, but he didn't need to make any modifications to the main channel so he left it unaltered. I think it's been submerged since the Roman period, the result of a settling pool on the other side of the temple that always fills up above this level. If I'm right it should take us straight to the basement chambers beneath the Temple of Isis.'

'There's no other way in?' Jeremy said.

'A passageway leads from the northern apse of the church of Santa Maria sopra Minerva to a locked metal door in that wall in front of us now. But any attempt to break our way through that would leaving signs of our presence. It's imperative that whoever comes down here and uses that door doesn't know that others have been here as well.'

'So you're saying that we're going underwater,' Jeremy said.

'Every exploration with Jack Howard has to be underwater.' He grinned at them. 'We'll strip down to the essentials and leave our clothes here. I'll take my phone, which is waterproof like the torches. The submerged section is about fifteen metres long. How's your breath-holding?'

'Jeremy looked at the channel sceptically. 'Rusty. I've been in archives recently.'

'I'll hold my light at the end of the tunnel when I get there to guide you. And Jack can always push you along.'

'Great. And it's against the flow.'

'Good to go?' Marco said, taking off his shirt.

'You *have* been reading my books,' Jack said. He shone his torch into the tunnel and took a deep breath. 'Yes. Good to go.'

CHAPTER 18

They stripped off their clothes and sat on the edge of the channel. 'Once I'm safely through I'll flash my torch five times and then leave it on to guide you,' Marco said. He knelt in the water, inhaled sharply three times and then held his breath, pulling himself forward under the arch. They watched the glow from his torch recede as he kicked against the current, and then Jeremy got in the water to wait for the signal. After about two minutes there was a dull banging and they could hear Marco's voice, muffled but distinct. 'There's an air pocket about ten metres in,' he said. 'Stop there first.'

Jeremy took deep breaths as Marco had done and then ducked under the arch, pulling himself away. Jack got in behind him, wanting to be close behind in case Jeremy got into trouble. The water was cold, but refreshingly so, and he tried to calm his heart rate and his breathing, blanking out any thoughts of confined spaces as he exhaled forcefully to expel as much carbon dioxide as he could. The tunnel was narrower than he had anticipated, only a metre and a half or so from floor to ceiling. He took a final breath and plunged in, aiming his torch forward as he pulled himself along the sides. Through the blur he could see Marco's light far ahead and the silhouette of Jeremy's legs kicking through the water. After about thirty seconds Jeremy stopped, and Jack could see a puddle of reflection along the top of the channel where air had been trapped. He came up beside him in a gap about half a metre high, blinking and gasping. 'This is mostly going to be carbon dioxide after Marco was here too,' he said. 'We can't linger here or we'll black out.'

'His light's flashing,' Jeremy said. 'He must have got through.'

They both took deep breaths and ducked down again, Jeremy in the lead. As they approached the light Jack saw Marco's legs in the water and they surfaced just in front of him, pulling themselves up on the sides of the channel and catching their breath. Jack wiped the water from his eyes and panned his torch around. They were in a space as large as the one under the Pantheon but crossed by brick arches that divided it into a series of vaulted chambers. The water channel came through from another large chamber beyond an arch ahead of them, and Marco led the way towards it. 'This is all Roman,' he said, pointing with his torch. 'The brickwork, the hydraulic concrete with sherds in it. It's the basement foundations of the Temple of Isis.'

'Look at this. Incredible.' Jeremy had stopped in front of a life-size statue of a jackal on a plinth with its ears upright. 'Anubis,' Jack said, kneeling in front of it and putting his hand on the stone. 'It's just like one from the tomb of Tutankhamun, except this is black diorite. The god of death, mummification, embalming, the afterlife and burial.'

'I'm not sure if I like the sound of that,' Jeremy said. 'Down here it seems a bit close to home.'

Marco came over and peered closely. 'The hieroglyphs down the front are of Ramesses II, very similar to those on the obelisk in the Piazza della Rotonda. I bet this came from Heliopolis as well, brought here by the priests of Isis in their attempt to recreate their temple in Rome.'

'Egyptians who brought Egypt to Rome,' Jeremy said.

'That was the conclusion of my dissertation,' Marco said. 'Father Rauscher tried to edge me away from it, saying it would be too controversial. But I'm certain he believes it himself. We know the Romans plundered the places they conquered and brought back art and other treasures. But the idea of Egyptian priests seeing which way the wind was blowing deciding to bring their most sacred rituals to Rome and recreate them in secret under the very noses of the emperors is a new one. I'm not talking about the flowery rituals in the Temple of Isis for the idle Roman rich, but the serious stuff.'

'Is that what you think was going on here?' Jeremy said.

'I think that's what Father Kircher was on to when he conducted the excavations that produced the obelisk. He may well have broken through down here. This statue is not something that fell from the ruins of the temple above and got buried. It has been deliberately placed beside the water channel. It fits with my theory that there was a secret inner sanctum down here.'

'It's not the only statue,' Jack said. 'Take a look.'

They stood up and panned their torches around. Evenly spaced along the sides of the channel were more statues, all of them intact and many of them lustrous from polishing. They were animal rather than anthropomorphic, and Jack recognised several from his time as a student with Maurice Hiebermeyer studying Egyptian sculpture in the British Museum: the lioness Sekhmet, goddess of war; the mother goddess Hathor, with cow's horns; Babi, the baboon god; and most impressive of all, Sobek, crocodile god of the Nile, half-submerged in the channel. 'Amazing,' he said. 'These are sculptures equalling in quality anything I've ever seen from ancient Egypt. I wish Maurice could see this.'

'It's a kind of processional way towards a final chamber, a holy of holies,' Marco said. 'There's one thing I want to find here above all else, and that's where it might be.'

They followed him along the side of the channel towards the crocodile. It was life-sized, made from green marble with eyes of red crystal, and the flow of water made it seem alive, ready to lunge out of the channel towards them. Jack remembered seeing the extraordinary statue of the crocodile-god Sobek beneath the pyramid with Costas the year before, and suddenly that discovery seemed immediate, as if he were viewing the same thing from a different angle, refracted through a different lens. He followed the other two under the arch beyond and an astonishing scene met his eyes. The chamber was wider and longer than the one they had just come through, with a higher vaulted ceiling. In the centre was a long stone table with a polished surface flanked by four stone seats. Just behind the head of the table dominating the room was a red granite statue of the goddess Isis, holding a papyrus staff in one hand and an ankh symbol in the other, with a royal cobra rearing up from her crown and behind that a headdress of cow horns enclosing a sun disk. Mounted on the walls on either side were four beaten gold masks of the falcon-god Horus, son of Isis and Osiris, with wings folded back in the shape of a cape. Jack touched the nearest one, feeling the smooth surface of the metal. 'These are old, incredibly old,' he said. 'Predynastic certainly. Maurice always thought that Isis and Osiris and Horus had their origins in early prehistory. The ability to work cold metal like this was already there in the early Neolithic.'

'I wonder what went on here?' Jeremy said.

'It's not just what went on here. It's what *goes* on here,' Jack said. 'Look at the candle holders beneath the masks. There are fresh candles in them.'

'My guess is the *inventio Osidiris*,' Marco said, his torch aimed at the statue. 'The ceremony for re-enacting Osiris' death.'

'And Isis' success in restoring him back to life,' Jack said.

'Osiris rises from the dead just as Christ does,' Marco said. That's why the Cult of Isis was attractive to early Christians, who also saw similarities between Isis and the Virgin Mary. What we know from the ancient sources about the Cult of Isis in Rome would suggest that the ritual of the *inventio* was little more than a mystery play, one of many from imported cults enjoyed by the elite of Rome. But what went on for the public in the temple above concealed something for more serious underground, a continuation of the actual ritual carried out by the priests of the Temple of Isis in Memphis in Pharaonic times.'

'Check this out.' Jeremy had gone into a smaller space beyond the statue of Isis, where the water channel came through. 'It looks like a mortuary slab. There are runnels carved around the outer edge that lead to a central hole over the water channel, a neat arrangement for flushing away whatever liquids came off the slab. And there's a knife.'

Jack followed him and picked up the knife. It had a beautiful flint blade, ground down and then pressure-flaked on one side with the ripple pattern extending to a finely serrated edge, and a grip of ivory carved in the shape of a falcon. 'This is very old as well, from the Naqada culture of the Nile Delta,' he said. 'Maurice studied these knives for his Masters' project and I helped him to record the British Museum's collection. The falcon decoration on the grip is fascinating because it may represent Horus, and therefore support his theory about the very early origins of those gods.'

'Didn't he cause a bit of a stir in the media by suggesting that these were used for human sacrifice?' Jeremy said.

'People used to think these knives were just for display. Maurice suggested that the origins of mummification lay in an ancient tradition of human sacrifice, something well-documented among the Semitic peoples of the Near East but never before suggested for Egypt. He thought that these knives could have been used for that purpose.'

Marco stepped up behind Jack and panned his torch over the slab. 'My God,' he said, his voice wavering. 'The akhet-re. That's what this slab was used for. So it's true.'

'What do you mean?' Jeremy said.

Marco paused. 'It's what I've been working on in the past couple of days. I haven't even told Father Rauscher yet. It's one of the papyrus transcriptions from the Kircher papers in the Sauli archive in Genoa, sent to me by Paulo Tensini. Kircher couldn't translate the hieroglyphics, but I can. For years scholars have suspected it, and now I can confirm it. The Egyptian priests carried out the ritual of akhet-re, mummification alive. The account includes a depiction of a slab just like this and flint knives.'

'How do you do that?' Jeremy said, incredulously. 'I mean, mummify and keep someone alive?'

'The Egyptian embalmers were incredibly skilled. They knew exactly what they could take out and how to do it. They paralysed the victim with snake poison, keeping them conscious and feeling pain but unable to move. They would then remove one lung, one kidney, the intestines, the eyes, part of the brain. They knew how to staunch the bleeding and sew the body up again. By the time the poison wore off the victim would be wrapped up in linen and inside the tomb. They might live for hours, even days.'

'Why do such a thing? Punishment?'

'Possibly. But it was also part of the *inventio Osidiris*. The hieroglyphic text tells how Osiris could only be restored to life through the soul of a sacrificial victim, but in order for the life-force to enter Osiris the victim had to be suspended half-way between life and death. The priests achieved that through the akhet-re. The life-force was most powerful if it came from someone who had disrespected the goddess, who refused to offer her proper worship. One of those in the papyrus described as having suffered this fate was the heretic pharaoh Akhenaten. History tells us that he died a natural death as a result of his final illness, but that was not the whole story.'

'That explains something horrific,' Jack said. 'Costas and I saw his mummy when we entered his tomb beside the Pyramid of Menkaure. It was off the slab and on the floor, as if he'd come alive and struggled in his death throes.'

'And today?' Jeremy said. 'Are you saying that this still goes on?'

'If it does, anyone who violates this place is going to be at the top of the list of potential victims. That means us.'

'Mummification alive,' Jeremy said. 'That's just great.'

'There is one other thing.' Marco went back under the

arch into the main chamber with the table. 'The Sauli archive contains a letter from Kircher to Sauli in Genoa regarding Egyptian antiquities that he'd found in Rome. We know that Kircher found the obelisk and sculptures when he dug under the garden of the Dominican convent. But I think he came down here and saw what we're seeing now. He may even have been responsible for setting up some of the sculptures.'

'You think he was part of some latter-day cult of Isis?' Jeremy said.

'I think in his single-minded search for hieroglyphs Kircher broke through into this place, and those who followed the cult found out. I think they tried to induct him, perhaps believing that with his occult interests he might easily be swayed to their beliefs. They may have seen him as an asset, with his knowledge of hieroglyphics and his discovery of sculptures and inscriptions from the original Roman Temple of Isis that would have had a cult significance for them. They may have persuaded him to bring most of his finds into this underground complex. They may have included senior members of the Church, including those from his own order, the Jesuits, who may have made it impossible for him to refuse and tried to bind him to their secrets.'

'But he could never have been a true believer.'

'The letter that Kircher wrote to Sauli shows that he found something down here, something very close to his interests that had been part of this place since Roman times. It was the original Egyptian inscription that was the basis for the Bembine Tablet. If we can find that inscription then it may be the breakthrough you need. Kircher told Sauli that it was the source for the location of the island on his chart.'

Jack stared at him. 'Are you sure of this?'

'I read the letter two days ago.'

'The Bembine Tablet is metal, right?' Jeremy said. 'Then look at the table. It's a slab on top, and you can see a thin metal sheet below. I think the slab is moveable.'

Marco and Jeremy went to either end of the slab while

Jack pushed the edge with both hands, easily sliding it off. As he did so they angled it down until it rested on the floor, wedged against one of the stone chairs. He shone his torch on the metal surface that had been revealed and the other two came round to see. It was lustrous, highly polished, and dazzling in the glare. He angled his torch away and an astonishing image came into view. The metal was covered with hieroglyphs in cartouches divided by figures of gods and people, including falcon-headed warriors and bearded men in a boat. The hieroglyphs radiated out from a central symbol the size of his palm that sent a jolt of excitement through him, a memory of the first time he had ever seen it on the papyrus that Maurice and Aysha had unwrapped from the mummy in the Egyptian desert fifteen years previously. He stared at it, his mind racing. *It was the Atlantis symbol.*

'That symbol is missing on the Roman copy, on the Bembine Tablet,' Marco said. 'There can be no doubt that this is the original Egyptian inscription that Kircher saw.'

'Can you read it?' Jeremy said.

Marco peered closely at the inscription. 'The Bembine Tablet is a random collection of hieroglyphs copied by someone who didn't know what they meant, made in Rome at a time when their meaning had been lost. For some reason they didn't include the Atlantis symbol. Maybe it looked odd, out of place, not consistent with Egyptian decorative motifs. But I can see that the hieroglyphics as they are arranged here in their original setting tell a coherent story. I can translate it, but I'll need time.'

There was a distant clanging and a sound of muffled voices. 'Someone's coming down from the church,' Marco whispered. 'We need to get the marble slab back on so that nobody knows we've been here. And then we need to get out of here, pronto.'

He removed his phone from where it had been velcroed on his forearm and quickly photographed the tablet, and they then pulled the slab back into place. He led them back through the arch and into the chamber with the sculpted animals. 'Torches off,' he whispered. 'Same order as before, me going first. The flow of the water should take us back beneath the Pantheon in one breath-hold.'

For a few moments they were in pitch darkness, and then a faint smudge of light came from the direction of the voices, enough for Jack to see the outline of the aqueduct channel in front of them. Marco knelt in it, took a deep breath and launched himself towards the arch in the wall, followed a few seconds later by Jeremy. Jack lingered for a moment on the edge of the channel, seeing the wavering beam of a torch and then someone lighting the candles around the table. He saw the swish of a cassock and heard a woman and a man in low conversation in Italian. The candlelight cast a luminous glow over the crocodile, its jaws agape and the rush of the water making its tail seem to move to and fro as if it were swimming towards him. It sent a cold shiver down his spine, and he suddenly needed to be away from this place. He lay down in the water, feeling its cool embrace as it rippled over his body, took a deep breath and plunged in.

*

A little over an hour later they sat on the steps of the fountain in the Piazza della Rotonda looking up at the inscription above the portico of the Pantheon. Jeremy had just returned with food and drink from the takeaway taverna where he had found coffee on their arrival three hours before, having made his way through the tourists who were now thronging in the square. Jack had not eaten since leaving England and he was relishing the food while the sun dried off the dampness from their swim underground. He had been running over the extraordinary things they had seen and thinking ahead to the next stage of his plans, with the car due to arrive in half an hour and the Embraer waiting at Fiumicino to take him on the next leg of his journey to Cyprus and the excavation in Egypt.

'Beer and pizza in the Piazza della Rotonda,' Jeremy said, finishing eating and taking a swig from his bottle. 'You just can't beat it.'

'You're beginning to sound like Costas,' Jack said.

'Nobody enjoys food like he does,' Jeremy said.

'I've forwarded my photos of the inscription to both of you and Maurice,' Marco said. 'If we can brainstorm it we could have a translation within a few days.'

'Maurice is up to his neck in sand at the moment,' Jack said. 'This will be your job. We need it as soon as possible.'

'I'm on it.'

'Hopefully your translation will come at the same time that the conservation lab at IMU opens the package from the mine. Something precious was taken from Egypt in antiquity to a hideaway in an island to the west, something that those here in Rome wanted to remain concealed but that Father Kircher knew about. We need to pick up the trail that went cold when the *Santo Cristo di Castello* went down in 1667.'

Fifteen minutes later they stood in front of Michelangelo's statue of Christ the Redeemer inside the Church of Santa Maria sopra Minerva, just off the square on the other side of the Pantheon where they had been dropped off when they had arrived. The statue was something else that Jack had wanted to touch, another connection with the quest that they were on; it had been the inspiration for Guglielmo della Porta when he had created the Corpus Christi figure that Jack had found on the wreck. He looked up at the face now and then at the body. It was a supreme example of contrapposto, with one leg flexed and the head turned to the other side, a balance that Guglielmo had retained in the lifeless body hanging from the cross with the head turned down. He could also see how Guglielmo had been influenced by Michelangelo's anatomical study, by the musculature and the expression of the face. It took him back to the moment when he had lifted the figure from the shingle, green with verdigris and with the cannon lying behind it, and then to the evening in the

Church at Gunwalloe when he had shown it to Peter and Father Tensini. It was hard to believe that only a week ago it had been on the seabed where it had lain for almost 350 years, part of the wreck whose secrets were still being unravelled and had brought them here to Rome now.

They walked back out into the square beside Bernini's elephant so that the driver would see them when he arrived. Jack thought about what Father Rauscher had said when they had met in the square earlier. 'How do you think Rauscher knew about the bill of lading for the *Santo Cristo di Castello* and the consignment of Kircher books?'

'It wasn't me,' Marco said. 'When Jeremy contacted me I agreed to keep it secret.'

'I've been wondering about that,' Jeremy said. 'Outside our circle the only other person who knew was Teresa Everett, my contact at The National Archives who showed me the Prize Papers from the *Sacrificio d'Abramo*. She may have told her head of department, Dr Petra Aslanov. Before taking up the position at The National Archives Aslanov worked for many years at the Pontificia Università Gregoriana alongside Rauscher and collaborated with him on the Kircher project. Anything new relating to Kircher would have been of great interest and she may have told him.'

'She has an interesting surname,' Marco said, turning to Jack. 'You once knew a warlord named Aslan. During your search for Atlantis.'

'She's his niece,' he replied. 'And our colleague Katya's cousin. They were both fascinated by ancient languages at students but took slightly different directions. Katya says that Petra is more like her father than she is.'

'That doesn't sound too good,' Jeremy said.

Jack pursed his lips. 'There's something disquieting about this. I can't quite put my finger on it. Telling me that he knew about the Kircher books was deliberate, almost a warning.'

'Do you think Rauscher is part of the Isis priesthood?'

Jeremy said, turning to Marco. 'Have you ever suspected it?'

Marco was quiet for a moment. 'Suspected, but never certain. In Rome we are used to scholars coming from within the Church, for their scholarship to be dispassionate and objective, independent of their beliefs. There are many societies, some of them openly known such as Opus Dei and others secret. For me, Father Rauscher was the foremost scholar of Athanasius Kircher and a senior professor at the Pontificia Università, an ideal choice as supervisor. It seemed natural that he should have a special interest in Kircher's quest for ancient hieroglyphs and where that had led him. It was when he hinted that he believed a cult of Isis may have outlived the Roman period that I began to wonder whether his interest was purely scholarly.'

'Do you think he may have been preparing you for induction?' Jeremy said. 'He's been letting you get pretty close to what may have been going on.'

Marco thought for a moment. 'He was very enthusiastic about you coming here. He knew that you and I were old friends, and that Jack was stopping off here on the way to Egypt. He will have known that Jack Howard doesn't come to Rome as a tourist, and that you'd just been excavating the *Santo Cristo di Castello*, the ship that the Isis priesthood have known was carrying the chart of the island. And someone, maybe Dr Aslanov, had told him that we'd made the connection with Kircher through the papers in the National Archives. It is all beginning to add up.'

'I think that we're being led on,' Jack said. 'If the chart is still to be found, then we are the best people for the job. Rauscher himself told me that he is a keen follower of our work. And when we've got what they want, they'll be there to take it off us.'

'With whose army?' Jeremy said. 'We're talking about a secret society of priests and scholars.'

Jack gestured at the Dominican convent, the former home of the Inquisition. 'Rauscher told me times have moved on since Galileo was tried here. I'm not so sure. The Inquisition in some ways was similar to the akhet-re of the priests of Isis, both of them forms of human sacrifice to placate a deity. Both show how ritual and belief, how adherence to apparently higher ideals, can quickly translate into repression and brutality. And those who worked the racks and stoked the fires, those who administered the poison and carved up the bodies, required henchmen to bring them their victims. Those falcon masks we saw in the chamber may be decorative now, but the ancient iconography shows Horus-headed men as guards and slave drivers and warriors, as mercenaries whom the priests would pay to do their bidding. Today those mercenaries would not carry spears and knives but AKs and MP5s. A secret society thousands of years old is going to have the resources to call up their own private army. We need to be careful.'

'I have many friends here in the church,' Marco said.

'That's not necessarily a safety net. We have no idea who might be among them. Petra Aslanov in the National Archives. Father Rauscher, in all probability. People hiding in plain sight, holding positions of power in the church, in academia, in other organisations. Like many secret societies, that's the best way to remain concealed and to persuade others to follow you if they can see that membership can advance their own careers.'

The car pulled up outside the Pantheon and they walked towards it. 'Say hello to Rebecca for me,' Jeremy said. 'She's flying to Cairo from Accra today. She's just messaged to say she's finally got through customs there.'

'What exactly are you looking for in Egypt?' Marco said.

'I want to know where all this originated. I want to know about the link to Atlantis. Maurice may have found something that will bring it all into sharper focus. Something incredible.'

'You've only got three days?' Jeremy said.

'That's what the Egyptian authorities have allowed. Three days before they flood the lagoon where the finds have been made.'

'Hopefully the conservation lab will have unpicked that leather package you found in the mine by then. And then all going well we might be taking a sea voyage out to the west following something that went there thousands of years ago.'

They reached the car and Marco turned to Jack. 'Four hundred years ago Galileo was condemned in this place for showing that humans were not the centre of the universe, and yet the Inquisition made people feel exactly that, mere specks in the Cosmos. Father Rauscher often spoke to me about Nietzsche and the idea of the *Übermensch*, of a world without religion in which people are supermen. He was opposed to the concept and pointed to the Nazis and others who have been empowered by it. But if this elixir from Atlantis, the orichalcum, gives people greater strength, a greater sense of self-worth, through longer and more productive lives, then surely the risk that it will make some of them *Übermenschen* can be borne. It's got to be better than the alternative, one where opportunities to free the human spirit are suppressed in order to keep power in the hands of a few.'

Jack glanced back at the building where Galileo had been tried. He remembered that one of the books on the Index Librorum Prohibitorum, the list of books banned by the Inquisition, was Kepler's *Epitome Astronomie Copernicae* of 1621, the very book had been carried in the consignment on the *Santo Cristo di Castello* in 1667 – a ship from Genoa with a Roman Catholic captain who would have crossed the Inquisition at his peril. It made the ship seem a beacon of light in an age when repression and enlightenment went hand-in-hand, and made Jack more determined than ever to know the truth of the document being carried by Captain Viviano and the secret it contained.

'I can only speak as an archaeologist,' he said. 'Keeping artefacts hidden, concealing history, never works. If there is something to be found that illuminates the past and may improve the future, then I'm all for it.'

'That sounds like the makings of a motto for IMU,'

Jeremy said. 'I'll see if I can do a Latin translation.'

Jack shook hands with Marco and got in the car. 'Keep me in the loop with everything. Jeremy, I'll see you in two days. And watch your backs.'

CHAPTER 19

Egypt, Lake Bardawil

A black Mercedes with government plates drew up in a swirl of dust beside the crumbling limestone wall, joining half a dozen other vehicles that were parked at the end of the desert track. In the distance the twinkling lights of the Nile Delta could be seen along the line of the river, the first light of dawn revealing the undulations of the dunes in a pale wash of colour. The rear door opened and a man got out, checked his watch and straightened his tie. He was impeccably dressed in a black overcoat and designer shoes, his long hair tied back and his beard trimmed close. From the front passenger seat another man got out, an AK-12 assault rifle with a folded stock held to his chest, and more men with weapons got out of the three vehicles that pulled up behind, fanning out and taking up positions along the edge of the desert. From somewhere to the south a jackal howled, an eerie sound that split the night, and a raven rose from where it had been feasting on carrion beside the wall, its raucous cry sending a tremor through the air. Dawn was nearly upon them, and the man knew that he had to be in position before the first shafts of sunlight lit up the sky from the east.

He made his way over the nearest dune until he was out of sight of the vehicles, putting his hand up for his bodyguard to remain behind. Once he was sure that he was out of earshot he took out his phone and tapped a number. 'We are ready, your Eminence,' he said in heavily accented English. 'I can have them in custody in half an hour.'

'There is a change of plan,' the man at the other end said. 'We believe that Howard may have discovered the original map to the island that was being carried in the *Santo Cristo di Castello*. We need to know for certain before we make a move.'

'Has the woman from the London archives talked? The younger one?'

'We threatened her family and she told us everything she knows. But she is not enough. We need someone closer to Howard. There is one in Rome now, Jeremy Haverstock, and we will take him.'

'The governing council in Cairo are impressed by the discovery of Arabic inscriptions at this desert site. They have given permission for further archaeological work. They would also like to offer the German Egyptologist Hiebermeyer permission to resume investigations inside the Pyramid of Menkaure at Giza because there are more Islamic inscriptions there. That was where Howard was arrested last year.'

'At the place we knew was next to the tomb of the heretic pharaoh.'

'It may be that there is something further in the tomb that they wish to find. Something that will help them on their quest. We must let them look for it.'

'You are the minister, Dr Khalil. Let them do it. They will lead us to what we want to find, and then we will strike. Rauscher has already contracted a team of mercenaries and a vessel and they are on standby. We will soon be able to convene in the temple and make the offering that the goddess has been awaiting for three thousand years, the offering that will keep the priesthood in power until the end of time. I will keep you informed of developments.'

*

Jack lifted his binoculars, peered through them at the tent and the two figures on the dune to make sure that he was heading in the right direction and carried on trudging through the sand, slinging the binoculars over his shoulder and dropping his sunglasses back over his eyes. Behind him the swirl of dust below the helicopter's rotor had settled, and ahead he could see the whitecaps on the sea. In the two days since Maurice had phoned him a meltemi wind had blown from the north-west, pushing conditions in the east Mediterranean to an unseasonable Force 5. The flight from Fiumicino to Cyprus had been straightforward enough, but things had got bumpy on the helicopter ride from the Royal Air Force base at Akrotiri to *Sea Venture* and then on the voyage south to the edge of Egyptian territorial waters. *Sea Venture* had already been on station in the East Mediterranean in case the IMU team at Lake Bardawil required rapid extraction; they did not want a repeat of the emergency last year when the new regime had taken over and expelled foreign nationals.

The IMU presence in Egypt now was above board, with the ecological project under UNESCO supervision and Maurice having a permit for limited excavations, but even so they were taking no chances. He and Costas were still persona non grata to many in the regime and they had not announced their arrival in the country; they were simply IMU personnel accompanying equipment brought by the helicopter. By way of reassurance the RAF had agreed to extend its exercise zone to the edge of Egyptian airspace, with two Typhoon jets doing a fly-by over *Sea Venture* an hour earlier and a joint aircraft carrier task group including US and French warships within range. The new regime in Cairo had made its point last year but would know that there would be nothing to be gained from threatening foreign nationals again when there was a powerful international task force in position ready to carry out air strikes if necessary.

It was only nine in the morning but already he could feel the heat of the sun and the sweat on his forehead. He seemed to be making little progress, sinking up to his ankles with each step, and for a moment the two figures ahead seemed like characters in an existentialist play, moving without apparent purpose in a landscape that reduced them to ciphers. He pushed up his hat, wiped his forehead and carried on, seeing the expanse of Lake Bardawil between the dunes and the sea and the area to the west where it had been reduced to a salt flat. It was now the final day that had been allowed by the ministry before the channel would be opened again and the lake flooded. To ask for more time would be to raise suspicions that they had embarked on something more ambitious. He looked beyond the tent to the dune overlooking the lagoon where he knew that the excavation was taking place, just out of sight. They had less than 24 hours to reveal everything they could, for Maurice to prove that he was right and with any luck to put this place on the map as one of the most important archaeological sites to have been discovered in recent times, not just in Egypt but in the entire cradle of civilisation.

'Jack! Wait up. I can't move any faster.' Costas trundled up behind him, wearing an Arab headdress and ski goggles and unshaven as usual. 'I'm carrying the backpack, remember? I just hope Jacob really needs this stuff. As if he hasn't got enough gadgetry out here already.'

Costas had met up with him in Akrotiri and spent most of the time on *Sea Venture* surrounded by the dismembered parts of the device in the backpack, a state-of-the-art scanning drone designed to save time recording any structures uncovered during the excavation. He had been behind Jack as he had wanted to activate it in the helicopter cabin to test it before stepping out into the dusty air. 'Did you get it working?' Jack asked.

'Roger that. I just need to keep the sand out of it.'

'Good luck with that. We're in one of the biggest deserts in the world.'

'Got any water left? I'm parched. Couldn't fit any into the bag with all this weight.'

Jack pointed towards the tent. 'I don't, but they will.'

'Right. Let's keep moving.'

'Nice headgear, by the way. Costas of Arabia.'

'I'm just blending in. We're supposed to be anonymous, remember? We are just two additional scientists flown in to help with the turtles. Most definitely not Jack Howard and Costas Kazantzakis. After last year's escapade under the pyramid they'd put us in a dungeon and throw away the key, and more importantly Maurice's excavation would be terminated.'

'So to blend in you're the only foreigner wearing Arab gear between the Nile and the border with Israel.'

'Well, it's not as unusual as those two,' Costas said, pointing towards the tent. 'They look like Vladimir and Estragon in *Waiting for Godot*.'

'Just what I was thinking. Except they're a little more exuberant than Beckett's characters.'

They clambered up the dune and stooped under the awning of the tent, taking off their headgear. Hiebermeyer and Lanowski had reached the tent just before them from the other direction and were sitting in front of a laptop. Costas took a small water bottle from the table and downed it in one go, splashing the final drops on his face, and bent over beside Lanowski to peer at the screen. Hiebermeyer looked up and smiled. 'Good to see you, Jack. And Costas.'

'Good to be in Egypt again,' Jack said. 'Not like last time, I hope.'

'The gods willing.'

'Where are the others?' Jack said.

'Aysha and Rebecca are working on the excavation just over the brow of the dune. They've been at it since dawn. We've got two sites, one on the dune and the other on the salt flat. We've only got a couple of hours until it gets too hot, and then the evening and the night. The machinery from the Egyptian contractor is already in place to open up the channel and flood the salt flat first thing tomorrow morning.'

'For my benefit,' Costas said. 'Give me a rundown on how we end up being here.'

Hiebermeyer turned in his chair and opened his arms expansively towards the desert. 'The Sinai, the bridge between Egypt and the Near East, where Africa meets Asia. And just over the dune is the hundred-kilometre-long lagoon that Herodotus in the fifth century BC called the Serbonian Bog. You would have had a good view of it flying in.'

'A Gulf profound as that Serbonian bog/Betwixt Damiata and Mount Casius old/Where Armies whole have sunk,' Costas said. 'Milton, *Paradise Lost*.'

Hiebermeyer peered at him over his glasses. 'Was that Costas Kazantzakis I just heard declaiming poetry?'

'I've been brushing up on my seventeenth century literature. Seemed appropriate given the date of the wreck we've been working on off Cornwall.'

'The ancient Greek historian Diodorus Siculus in the first century BC wrote that that it was narrow but marvellously deep, and surrounded by great dunes,' Jack said. 'While Costas has been in the seventeenth century, I've been reading the classical sources.'

'The same Diodorus who wrote about Cornish tin traders?' Costas said. 'He got around.'

Jack leaned over the computer in front of Lanowski. 'OK, Jacob. Show us what you've got.'

Lanowski tapped a key, bringing up a satellite image of the coast. 'That's the Sabkhat al Bardawil six months ago, visible over its entire length,' he said. 'You can see the channels cut in 1953 to keep the lagoon flooded, including the one at this end that we had blocked up to reduce the level of the lagoon by a metre or so in order to expose the salt flat so that we could do the environmental assessment.' He tapped the key again, bringing up the same view but with more yellow exposed at the eastern end of the lagoon. 'That's a Landsat image I accessed this morning as the satellite flew over us. The exposed flat is a salt-crusted depression saturated with hypersaline water, with the salinity of the lagoon twice that of the sea outside. We've done spot-depths and the average for the lagoon is only 1.5 metres.'

'I can understand the urgency of opening the channel to flood the lagoon again,' Jack said. 'That's got to be way too saline for the turtles.'

'Blocking it was only a temporary measure, done during the part of the year when the turtles are unlikely to show up to lay their eggs.'

'One and a half metres is hardly the 'marvellous depth' described by Diodorus Siculus,' Costas said.

'I'm coming to that,' Lanowski said. 'Basically, when you look at the landforms of the lake today you're seeing a low ridge barrier on the seaward side, the salt flats of the lagoon and then the dunes of the desert itself, some mobile, some stable, with the usual interdune depressions and hummocks. Everything is fairly stable now but in the past there have been rapid accumulations of high-energy beach sand driven in by the sea, topping the barrier and silting up the lagoon.'

'Maybe Diodorus was exaggerating the depth,' Costas said.

Lanowski tapped the key again, bringing up a multi-coloured 3-D geomorphological image. 'This is a geological cross-section of the eastern part of the lagoon, showing the bedrock rather than the sand. You can see that the bedrock lies fifty metres or more below the present level of the flat. It's part of an elongated synclinal trough, an oblique-slip fault trend that forms a compressed tectonic feature between the Mediterranean crust to the east and the Oceanic crust to the west. Since the time of the Flandrian Transgression about eight to six thousand years BP there's been a gradual regional tectonic uplift, as well as an accumulation of some fifty metres of sediment depth pushed in by the sea.'

'So at the time of Diodorus the lagoon could have seemed pretty deep.'

'Relative to the sea outside, yes. To someone coming from offshore you would have had the gradually sloping sandy shallows that are still there today, then the high sand dune barrier just as described by Diodorus, then the deep blue depths of the lagoon.'

'Good to confirm the veracity of the ancient sources,' Jack said.

Costas pointed to a rise in the bedrock close to the eastern end of the lake. 'I'm guessing that's where your pillar is. Just north of where we are now, a few hundred metres away.'

Lanowski nodded. 'It's a structural ridge elevated above the trough, brought closer to the surface by tectonic uplift. The pillar was sculpted out of metamorphized limestone in the bedrock, a hard stone like marble. That's why it's survived so well. The ridge must have been exposed in antiquity but most of the time since has probably been covered in sand.'

'Where's this leading us?' Jack said.

I've been trying to model the seashore at the time of the Black Sea flood, to work out where any refugees from Atlantis might have beached a boat. I've modelled the sea-level rise from meltwater since the last glacial maximum, 18 to 20 thousand years ago, when it was about 120 metres lower in the Mediterranean than it is today, and I've factored in the slight drop in sea level caused by the breaching of the Bosporus and the flooding of the Black Sea. Then there's tectonic uplift and sand ingression to factor in. Lots of variables. Spatio-temporal data, geocomputational algorithms to extract and delineate it. I developed a layers paradigm to organise input data and produce layers of thematically mapped output. I've never done hydrological modelling like this before. It's been fun.'

He tapped a key, leaned back with his hands behind his head and broke into a smile. A line appeared across the satellite image through the middle of the lake, veering closer to the landward dunes at the western end. 'And there it is,' he said. 'That's the shoreline in 5500 BC, give or take fifty years. A boat coming in from the north would have gone first over a sandbar, about where the present barrier dune is located along the seaward edge of the lagoon. It was probably only a few metres deep and awash in places. It would then have gone over the lagoon proper, where they would have seen the bottom drop away, and then up over a shallow sloping seabed to run aground on the beach. If I were going to look for the remains of a boat of that date abandoned on the shore, it would be along that line.'

'OK,' Costas said. 'That's one line across the map. It's still more than a hundred kilometres of coast to explore. Now you need another line to intersect it to give us a tight search area.'

'That's where the New Zealand connection comes in,' Lanowski said. 'Jack, you can give us the lowdown on the First World War archival stuff? That's more your area of expertise. The notes you sent me are up on the screen.'

'The lady who gave me the artefact was a friend of my parents in Nelson where we lived for five years when I was a boy,' Jack said. 'Her husband Frank Hunter had been a history teacher at Nelson College and an officer in the local militia, the tenth Nelson Squadron of the Canterbury Mounted Rifles. When war broke out in 1914 he went with them to Egypt and then to Gallipoli, where he was wounded, and then was with them through the Sinai and Palestine campaigns until he was killed near Damascus in early 1918. The artefact came back with his belongings, but it was only two months ago that their granddaughter found a box in the attic of their house with his diary inside. Before then I'd only known that it came from somewhere in the Middle East during his war service, but in his entry for 8 May 1916 he describes how he found it while they were digging a water channel near Mahamdiya, the name of the nearest village to the east from here.'

'So he was part of the ANZAC force?' Costas said.

Jack nodded. 'The Australia and New Zealand Army Corps. The Canterbury Mounted Rifles were part of the Anzac Mounted Division. They'd come from Gallipoli a few months earlier where they'd fought as infantry and lost more than half their men. They then regrouped in Egypt and formed part of the Egypt Expeditionary Force when the British decided to go on the offensive against the Turks from the south, pushing them back across the northern Sinai where we are now and over the Suez Canal into Palestine. That was in the late spring and early summer of 1916. The regimental history of the Canterbury Mounted Rifles records how on the seventh and eighth of May they were occupied in cutting a channel from the sea to the western end of the Sabkhat al Bardawil, the object being to flood the lagoon in order to create a defensive obstacle to any Turkish counter-offensive.'

'The officer who wrote the account in the regimental history was something of an archaeologist,' Hiebermeyer said. 'He describes the very hot days and then the heavy dews that cause mist at dawn, just as we've experienced, and the salt flat as white as if it were covered with snow, with hard, sharp crystals and black mud underneath. He wrote about how the wind laid bare a stone trough with a perfectly preserved plaster interior that he thought was a Roman watering station. In 1916 finding water for themselves and their horses was the biggest issue crossing the desert, just as it had been in antiquity.'

'Were there any maps or sketches in the box?' Costas asked.

'No, but there was more detail in the war diary of the regiment,' Jack said. 'The commanding officer of every unit in the British and Imperial forces had to keep a daily diary, written in pencil on standardised forms. On the seventh of May Colonel Findlay, the commanding officer, went to Mahamdiya to inspect the place where the canal was to be cut. He called it a canal, but really it can only have been a narrow channel given the time and manpower available. On the eighth of May the Tenth Squadron proceeded to cut the canal to connect with the sea. That's the Nelson squadron, Hunter's unit. On the following day the first Squadron joined them, but then they received orders to proceed to Romani to the east beyond Lake Bardawil. The Turks had withdrawn more quickly than expected, and the lake was no longer strategically significant. But the regimental history makes it clear that the exercise was futile anyway. Colonel Powles wrote that 'as fast as the cutting through the sand was made the waves filled it up again and the project was abandoned.'

'And then there's this crucial bit of information,' Lanowski said, scrolling down Jack's notes. 'The war diary of the Fifth New Zealand Engineers.'

'That's right,' Jack said. 'Whenever you're trying to pinpoint the location of work carried out at the front, on trenches or fortifications or other features, it's the diaries of the engineers that you turn to. They were trained surveyors and were more likely to give detailed map references. The Fifth were the Divisional Engineers of the Anzac Mounted Division, and were sent in advance to trace a location for the channel in the spit of sand that cuts off the lagoon from the sea. They describe it as point 56, near Mahamdiya.'

'It was Jeremy who provided the next step,' Lanowski said, tapping the keyboard and bringing the satellite image back on the screen. 'He found a set of 1916 maps in the National Archives that showed the location of point 56, which I've transposed on to the modern-day satellite image.' He tapped a key and a small red arrow appeared on the line of the coast. 'By drawing a line from that point perpendicular to the coast on my sixth millennium BC map, we come up with a fix about 500 metres from us now over the dune in the middle of the salt flat. It coincides closely with the place where Maurice saw the timber sticking out of the mud.' He looked up at Jack, his eyes gleaming. 'X marks the spot.'

'Bingo,' Costas said.

'And we found something in the excavation of the pillar that clinches it.' Hiebermeyer picked up a plastic finds bag with an object inside it and passed it to Jack. 'Recognise that?'

Jack took it out and held it to the light. 'Well I'll be damned,' he said. 'A brass cap badge of the Nelson Squadron of the Canterbury Mounted Rifles. A stag's head with the motto *Rem gero stenue*, fight with zeal.'

'Do you remember what you told me when we went

on our first archaeological outing together from school?' Hiebermeyer said. 'You said that archaeology was everywhere that humans went, in the shape of the land, in the soil, in the trees, even if there were no monuments or artefacts to be found. Well, it's like that here. All you see is desert, nothing but sand, and yet this place saw some of the greatest movements of people in history: the migration of hominids from Africa to Asia, the arrival of refugees from the sea in the Neolithic and Bronze Age, the Israelite exodus from Egypt, the campaigns of the pharaohs, the Arab jihad, the Crusades, the two World Wars. And they are not just faceless and nameless people but include known individuals who shaped history: Thutmose, Moses, Alexander the Great and others. It's just that they didn't linger here, so left no monuments. Or so we used to think.'

'What do you mean?'

'Get ready for one of the most amazing things you've ever seen.'

CHAPTER 20

Jack approached the crest of the dune and saw the outer ridge of sand that separated the sea from the lagoon, with the channel through the ridge clearly visible where the machinery would in position to open it up again tomorrow morning to let the sea back in. A few steps further and he saw the full width of the lagoon itself, a vast expanse of salt flat that shimmered in the sunlight and was covered in cracks where it had dried out. To the right where the remaining waters lapped the edge of the flat hundreds of seabirds were wheeling and swooping, picking up crustacea and fish left dry as the water evaporated and the shoreline of the lagoon receded still further. The birds were taking advantage of a lull between the end of the meltemi wind from the north and the arrival of the khamsin dust storms from the south. He had already felt the first brush of hot air from the khamsin on the nape of his neck, scalding and dry like the heat from a fire, another reason why the excavation had to finish today before the dust enveloped them and further work became impossible.

He reached to the crest and stopped in his tracks, stunned by what he saw. Just over the other side where the dune sloped down towards the lagoon was an outcrop of rock about twenty metres across and five metres high, the feature that Lanowski had spotted on the landform map. It was what lay in front of the rock that made him gasp with astonishment. A large pit about ten metres across had been dug in the sand, with two mini diggers standing idle on either side and the Egyptian drivers sitting together in the shade of the rock drinking tea. In the centre of the pit Aysha and Rebecca were kneeling side-by-side brushing the base of a stone pillar about two metres high on a plinth. Encircling them at about a three-metre radius were six T-shaped pillars almost as high, evenly set on a base of unworked stone. He could make out carvings on them, some in low relief, others in such high relief that they were almost detached: animals, birds, strange symbols, and on the sides of the pillars representations of human arms, the hands just visible at the bottom where the sand lapped the pillars.

Hiebermeyer came up beside him. 'See what I mean?'

'It's incredible,' Jack said. 'It's almost exactly the same as Enclosure A in the early Neolithic sanctuary at Göbekli Tepe in Anatolia, except with one central pillar instead of two.'

'And very similar to the shrine you found in Atlantis.'

'The surrounding pillars have the same anthropomorphic features, with those arms and the incised belts and loincloths.'

'And the faceless heads represented by the T-shape at the top.'

'It's a sun temple,' Costas said, coming alongside and wiping the sweat off his face. 'It's like the Pantheon in Rome as it was originally conceived. Statues of gods surrounding the interior, with the sunlight streaming through the centre. Is this the refugees from the Black Sea staking their claim, arriving here with their gods and saying this will be the new Atlantis?'

'Arriving with gods, or as gods themselves?' Jack said.

'The same question is asked at Göbekli Tepe,' Hiebermeyer said. 'The anthropomorphic figures that we call gods may in fact have been representations of priest-kings, rulers of the first settled communities who then became part of the foundation myths of those societies, like the Patriarchs of the Old Testament.'

'*Übermenschen*,' Jack said. 'Supermen, with supernatural characteristics such as extreme longevity.'

'Arriving here and being venerated as gods,' Hiebermeyer said. 'Building this enclosure would have been beyond the abilities of a single boatload of exhausted refugees. They must have guided local people in the design and shown them how to work in stone. It's the earliest example of monumental architecture in Egypt by over two millennia, dating from the sixth millennium BC.'

'Can you be sure of that date?' Jack said.

'When the new regime took over last year they left my radiocarbon lab in the institute at Alexandria intact, and the technicians are still there. Those pillars were originally coloured and we found the residue of vegetable die in the relief carvings, as well as charcoal in a crack beneath the central plinth. Aysha took the samples away and got them analysed within twenty-four hours, and we had the results back just before you arrived. 7540 BP plus or minus 50 years.'

'That's 5520 BC, give or take,' Costas said. 'Bang-on for the Black Sea exodus.'

'Wait till you see what else we've found.'

They slid down the sand to the enclosure and waved at Rebecca and Aysha, who looked up from their work and waved back. Jack went up to the nearest pillar, dropped down on his knees and peering at it closely. It was covered in low-relief carvings of predators – a lion, a wild boar, a vulture, and a huge feline with incisors that could only be a sabre-toothed tiger, a species that had been extinct for several thousand years by the time of the Black Sea flood. 'It's amazing that predators of the Ice Age should still be among the sacred symbols of these people several millennia after the Neolithic had begun,' he said. 'It shows the strength of the hunter-gatherer belief system, the survival of the spirit world alongside the inception of the first gods in human form.'

'Theirs was a world of shamans and priests,' Hiebermeyer said. 'Perhaps a world of uneasy cohabitation between the two, with the gods beginning to subsume the old beliefs. Maybe those who escaped here from the flood were of the old order, keeping belief in the spirit-world alive.'

Costas went round to the other side of the pillar and suddenly jumped back. Jack followed and saw a large arachnid carved in high relief, a fat-bodied form that must also represent an extinct species. He traced his hand over the human arm carved on one side of the pillar, long and thin and angled at the elbow, and then over the belt and the strange symbols on it. Costas recovered his composure and crouched down in front of the pillar. 'We've seen that before,' he said. 'The symbol at the base.'

Jack followed his gaze. 'Well I'll be damned,' he said. It was the unmistakeable shape of a bull's horns, a bucranion, the shape that the world had come to know through the discovery of the Bronze Age palaces of Knossos in Crete more than a century before, but which they now knew originated thousands of years earlier when it had represented the shape of the Bosporus, the Strait of the Bull, before the floodwaters of the Mediterranean cascaded into the Black Sea basin and drowned the citadel of Atlantis.

'At Göbekli Tepe one of the abstract symbols was an H shape,' Hiebermeyer said. 'It's more developed here and a bit more familiar. Look at the next pillar.'

Jack went over and gasped with astonishment. Just above the base where the bucranion had been on the previous pillar was the Atlantis symbol, an H but with the distinctive small lines extending out on either side. He turned back to look again at the belt on the previous pillar. 'Now I know where I've seen those symbols before. Not just at Göbekli Tepe, but on the original of the Bembine Tablet that Jeremy and Marco and I found under Rome two days ago.'

'Now look at what Aysha and Rebecca are revealing.'

They went over to the central pillar behind the two women. That pillar too was covered in relief carvings, but very different from the others. 'That's an Arabic inscription at the top,' Jack said. 'It must be the one you found first, poking out of the sand.'

'Its archaic Kufic, the early angular form of Arabic calligraphy,' Hiebermeyer said. 'Aysha can translate it.'

She put down her brush, got up and backed off so that they could see the inscription more clearly. '*In the name of God the whole, merciful, the compassionate, this inscription is set up by 'Amr ibn al-'As in Djumâda II of the year nineteen,*' she said. 'That's the Hijri year, counted from the year Muhammad went from Mecca to Medina, the first year in the Islamic lunar calendar. Year 19 corresponds to AD 640 and Djumâda II to January. That was the year of the Arab conquest of Egypt, and 'Amr ibn al-'As was their leader.'

'It's one of the oldest Kufic Arabic inscriptions ever recorded,' Hiebermeyer said. 'Before this the earliest Islamic monument in Egypt was a tombstone dated to the year 31, AD 652. In fact it's the earliest known Arabic inscription of Islamic date not just in Egypt but anywhere. Finding this was our breakthrough with the regime in Cairo and allowed us to propose an excavation. Without it I doubt whether we'd have been given a permit.'

'The Arab conquest was one of the great movements of history that passed along this shore, but unusual in leaving a marker like this,' Jack said.

'It was because the Arab army lingered here,' Aysha said. 'It took them two months to take Pelusium, the fortress on the eastern edge of the Nile Delta that was the first large place west from here and one of the last outposts of the Byzantine Empire in Egypt. The top of the pillar must have been sticking out of the sand and been an obvious place for an inscription. By doing so they were stamping their authority on something they knew was much older from the very worn carving that was already there. Move sideways to get a better angle and you'll see what I mean.'

Jack did so and then saw it. 'Unless I'm mistaken, that's the solar disk of Shamash.'

'Akkadian Shamash, Sumerian Utu,' Hiebermeyer said. 'The sun-god of ancient Mesopotamia. A circle with four points emanating from it and four wavy diagonal lines between.'

'You said Shamash was a god of ancient Mesopotamia,' Costas said. 'How does that relate to Atlantis on the Black Sea?'

'Göbekli Tepe lies in southern Anatolia on the edge of the Syrian desert,' Hiebermeyer said. 'That's not far from the headwaters of the Euphrates river, so within the fertile crescent of the Levant and Mesopotamia and Anatolia with Atlantis at its northern edge. What we hadn't realised before our discovery of Atlantis was that the southern Black Sea region was at the heart of the agricultural revolution, not on its fringe.'

'What's is the date of the solar disk carving?' Costas said.

'The same as the surrounding pillars, mid-sixth millennium BC,' he said. 'But whereas those pillars are limestone from the bedrock here, this central pillar is granodiorite. The lab in Alexandria has done a thin-section petrological analysis that pins it to Aswan on the upper Nile, the main source of granite in Pharaonic times. That's over 500 kilometres by river and sea from here. Not only is this the oldest monumental inscription in Egypt by almost two millennia, but it's also the earliest evidence for the transport of stone by boat.'

'A lot of firsts here,' Costas said.

'Egyptology is like that,' Hiebermeyer said. 'One small site can answer more questions than all the pyramids and temples put together.'

'It also shows the involvement of local people from Egypt in this monument, not just the new arrivals,' Aysha said. 'Only they would have known where to source the higher-quality stone. And they knew that granite was harder than limestone and that the inscription would be longer-lasting.'

Jack stood back and surveyed the enclosure. 'A difference with Göbekli Tepe is that there's only one central pillar here, not two. If this pillar represents Shamash, then his consort Inanna is missing.'

'It's like Osiris without Isis,' Hiebermeyer said.

'Perhaps there were no women on the boat,' Aysha said. 'If these pillars were set up by the Egyptians to represent those who arrived rather than a fully developed pantheon, then they may represent those who came ashore, among them one called Shamash. It could be as simple as that.'

'What does the absence of the female consort mean?' Costas said.

Jack paused for a moment. 'Let's assume there was a priesthood already in Egypt, a cult of Isis. The people in the Sinai who first encountered these new arrivals may have been overawed by what they were seeing, by men who may have had something supernatural about them. But when the priests from the early temples on the Nile came here and saw the monument that had been built, this temple or sanctuary, they may have been alarmed. Isis could have been their main god, the early Egyptian manifestation of the mother goddess common across this region and Europe in the early Neolithic, and the origin of Shamash's consort Inanna as well. If the priests saw that these Übermenschen threatened to eclipse their own gods, not only Isis but also the others in the Egyptian pantheon that were developing at the time - Osiris, Horus, Seth, Ptah, Anubis - all of the anthropomorphic and animal gods, then there was a problem.'

'The Egyptians could absorb and syncretise gods from surrounding regions, but this may have been different,' Hiebermeyer said. 'The arrivals may have come at a time when the priesthood was solidifying its power base, becoming locked into the deities and rituals that were to characterise Egypt over the coming millennia and give generations of priests control over the country and people.'

Jack nodded. 'The arrivals may at first have been welcomed for the skills that they brought in metalwork and masonry and architecture, paving the way for the great achievements of ancient Egypt. But the priests might have been looking ahead to the time when these men had passed on, when their presence could be eclipsed. And that may have meant taking and concealing whatever it was these arrivals brought with them that prolonged their survival. It may have meant reasserting the dominance of Isis, the mother goddess, and of locking the threat away in her temple under the charge of her priesthood.'

'Check out the bottom of the pillar,' Hiebermeyer said. 'Just above where Aysha and Rebecca have been cleaning.'

Jack knelt down and peered at it. Below the Shamash symbol was a fragment of a polished stone palette, fractured on one side. He looked up at Hiebermeyer. 'Amazing. The artefact found by Captain Hunter in 1916. It's the other part of it.'

'This is also where we discovered the cap badge of the Canterbury Mounted Rifles,' Aysha said. 'In the sand where you are now.'

Hiebermeyer knelt down beside Jack, his part of the artefact in his hand. 'The soldiers must have seen the top of the pillar sticking out when they came here to excavate the channel and decided to dig down to have a closer look. If I place my fragment alongside you can see how they fit together. It shows a boat beached on a foreshore, and a procession of men leading away from the boat up a slope. There's some incredible additional detail. As well as beardless men in loincloths, several of them with the Horus headdress, you can see six larger figures with long braided hair and beards. In front of them is an emaciated bearded man being carried on a bier with something on his chest. Above him is an ankh symbol, the cross with the teardrop-shaped loop, the earliest representation of the ankh by over a millennium. And beside that is a smaller version of the Shamash sun symbol.'

'It looks like a funerary procession,' Costas said.

'That's what I thought at first glance,' Hiebermeyer said. 'But the ankh is the symbol for life, eternal life. The man on the bier may have been ill or injured, perhaps weakened by the voyage, but I believe that he is alive.'

'The braided beards show that these are men of Mesopotamia and Anatolia,' Aysha said. 'It's how they're portrayed later in Egyptian art. They may have been naturally taller, but there is something extra to their dimensions. They are being portrayed as larger than life.'

'Seven pillars, seven men,' Jack said. 'That can't be a coincidence.'

'The ankh symbol is directly above the object on that man's chest,' Costas said. 'It looks like a box, about twice the width of the man's hands.'

'When I first saw that I also thought of funerary rites, of mummification,' Hiebermeyer said. 'It looks like the canopic chests used to contain organs. But with the ankh symbol above and the man alive, I'm convinced it contained something else. And take a close look at the side of the box.'

Jack peered at it. He could just make out a circular impression containing the Atlantis symbol, surrounded by the four cardinal points of the Shamash solar symbol. He beckoned Costas over. 'Do you recognise that?'

Costas knelt down beside him. 'It's what we saw under the pyramid in the tomb of Akhenaten. The Atlantis jewel.'

I think that box contains the elixir of life,' Hiebermeyer said. 'The substance that gave these men their god-like qualities in the eyes of the Egyptians.'

'Orichalcum,' Jack said quietly. 'The most precious substance of Atlantis.'

'In the Sumerian flood myth, in the Epic of Gilgamesh, the Sun-God appears as the flood waters begin to subside, as the sun breaks through,' Aysha said. 'That would seem a pretty obvious time to be thankful for the life-giving qualities of the sun. In early Mesopotamian depictions Shamash is shown as an old man with a beard and long arms, tall and outsized as he is here.'

'Except that here he's a man, not a god,' Costas said.

'Maybe he's part-way there, being carried ashore from

his mortal existence to a place where he's reborn as something else.'

Jack pointed to a tray of stone fragments beside the base of the pillar. 'Are there any more inscriptions?'

Rebecca reached into the tray and handed Jack a fragment of shiny black stone not much bigger than the palm of his hand. 'Another imported stone, this time black basalt from the Faiyum region to the west of the Nile, near the mummy necropolis where we found the Atlantis papyrus,' she said. 'It's even harder than granodiorite, so was brought here by someone who really wanted the inscription on it to survive the millennia.'

Jack traced his finger over the incisions on the surface. They were familiar Egyptian symbols, fully fledged hieroglyphs of the pharaonic period. 'It's a cartouche, indicating royalty or divinity,' he said. 'New Kingdom, Amarna period, mid to late fourteenth century BC.'

Hiebermeyer pointed at the hieroglyphs. 'There's the ripple of water for the letter n, and above that the ibis, meaning spirit or divine, and above that a group made up of another ripple of water, then a reed, alphabetic for the vowel i, then a half-moon shape and finally a circle with a dot in it for the Sun-God. That group reads 'itn', which transcribes as Aten, and the whole cartouche reads 'the Spirit of the Aten'.'

'The royal cartouche of the pharaoh Akhenaten,' Jack said. 'Incredible.'

Rebecca handed him another fragment. 'On this one you can see the hieroglyph of the sun disk with extended arms below, the symbol of the Aten,' she said. 'And below it there's another inscription, but not hieroglyphic.'

Jack could see four symbols made up of horizontal, vertical and diagonal lines. 'Remarkable,' he said. 'That's proto-Canaanite.'

'Not just proto-Canaanite, but proto-Hebrew,' Hiebermeyer said. 'From the early Hebrew version of the Canaanite alphabet. You can see the symbol like a backwards E for the letter H, and the Y for W.'

'**YHWH**,' Jack said, spelling it out. 'The Hebrew word for the one god, Yahweh, the creator of the cosmos and the one true god of all the world.'

'With the sun-symbol of the Aten directly above it, and higher up on the pillar the solar disk of Shamash. They're all connected.'

'What's the date of the Yahweh inscription?' Costas said.

'The same as the Akhenaten cartouche,' Hiebermeyer said. 'It's the late Bronze Age version of the Canaanite alphabet, the earliest example known. The hieroglyphs and the letters were clearly carved by the same hand.'

'That letter like the backwards E is like one half of the Atlantis symbol,' Costas said. 'There seem to be a lot of similar symbols here, but I don't get how a Hebrew symbol can appear alongside the cartouche of Akhenaten.'

'Remember the story of Moses and Pharaoh in the Old Testament,' Jack said. 'Moses was the leader of the Israelite slaves, and Pharaoh was Akhenaten. The relationship between the two has fascinated scholars through the ages, because they both believed in the one God. Sigmund Freud thought they were the same man, but you can take a literal view of the Bible story and see Moses for what he was and Akhenaten as the pharaoh who found more sympathy with the views of his Israelite slave than he did with his own priests, who may even have allowed the Exodus of the Israelites across the Sinai to the Holy Land.'

'So how did Akhenaten come to be here in the Sinai?' Costas said.

'He had a thirst for knowledge, for the wisdom of the ancients,' Hiebermeyer said. 'Liberated from belief in the old gods, he sent his scholars to all corners of the land to garner what they could, forcing the priests to give up their secrets and taking the scrolls and inscriptions that had been hidden away in the temple repositories. Rather than destroying evidence of older gods and beliefs, the priests had subsumed them, locking them away where their own gods could forever keep them under their heel. In the Temple of Isis at Memphis he found something that led him to this place, and word of a long-hidden treasure that the priests of Isis had despatched somewhere far away for safekeeping, something too valuable and dangerous for them to keep in Egypt. And here half-buried in the sand Akhenaten found a sanctuary that seemed to confirm for him the ascendancy of the Aten, the Sun-God that had come to enthral him.'

'This coast is the Way of the Aten,' Aysha said. 'Akhenaten renamed this route between east and west after his new god, and now we know what brought him here.'

'He came with his Israelite slave and stamped his authority on this place,' Hiebermeyer said. 'And Moses went from here with his image of the one god, the one whose power shone down like the sun and cast light on the darkness.'

'The story of the lost treasure set Akhenaten on another quest, a quest for orichalcum, something that the priests of Isis could not allow,' Aysha said. 'He paid the ultimate price for that, and after his death this inscription was desecrated like everything else to do with Akhenaten and his new religion.'

'And then this monument was lost to history, buried in the sand and forgotten,' Rebecca said. 'Through the final dynasties of the pharaohs, the conquest of Egypt by Alexander the Great and the arrival of the Romans, until an Arab commander almost two thousand years after Akhenaten saw the top of the pillar poking out of the sand and decided to inscribe his message on it as well. And then for more than a thousand years it was lost again, until a soldier in the First World War dug down and found that fragment of stone carving. By an amazing chance it passed on to us and here we are now.'

'I can't stop thinking about the jewel under the pyramid,' Jack said. 'The Atlantis symbol within the Shamash symbol, shining red like the descriptions of orichalcum. I think that jewel is what's depicted on the box with the man on the bier, with Shamash.'

'Perhaps it's a key,' Aysha said. 'Perhaps the priests kept it when they sent the box off to be hidden, knowing it could not be opened without it.'

Jack looked over at Hiebermeyer. 'If the regime in Cairo really does look on you in a better light, what do you think the chances are of you and Aysha making a little visit to the Pyramid of Menkaure? You could take up where Costas and I left off.'

'We're already on to that,' Aysha said. 'I've told our contact in the ministry that the Kufic is very similar to the lettering in the Arabic graffiti inside the tomb chamber in the pyramid, the inscriptions that you and Costas saw last year. If we can prove that Amr ibn al-'As went to Cairo directly after taking Pelusium, stamping the authority of Islam first on this pillar and then inside one of the pyramids at Giza, we would be looked upon even more favourably. We've requested that my uncle be allowed to bring in a pump to drain that submerged chamber under the pyramid where you dived, on the grounds that there might be more inscriptions down there. Then we'd be able to get equipment in to open that crack again and see what you saw, only this time with a chance of getting the jewel out.'

'Be careful with it,' Costas said. 'Look what happened to Akhenaten.'

'Before you ask, I don't think the jewel is cursed,' Jack said. 'But it does bring with it the legacy of a priesthood more than seven thousand years old who are hardwired to do everything in their power to prevent the orichalcum being discovered, just as they were in the seventeenth century when Kircher came close to finding it. The only curse likely to come down on us is out of the muzzle of a silenced Beretta or in a burst of AK rounds.'

*

Jack stared at the procession on the carving and realised for the first time that he was looking at the people of Atlantis. He had seen incredible things years before under the Black Sea - a pyramid, a temple complex, the houses where the people of the early Neolithic had lived and worked - but one thing missing had been the people themselves; there had been no bodies, no images. Touching these carvings allowed him to stand alongside those men with their beards and braided hair and see the future as they had done, to understand how their vision and determination to survive the calamity of the flood had led to the spread of agriculture and language and technology, ideas that more than anything else were responsible for shaping the world to come.

'I've just realised something,' he said. 'The arms on the sides of the pillars are the same as the rays of the sun on the Aten symbol, flexed at the elbow with hands outstretched. And the hieroglyphs of the rippled line and the disk and dot in the Akhenaten cartouche are the same as those on the Shamash solar disk. There's a continuity here, symbols in use in the Bronze Age that were derived from something much older, something that's beginning to lock into place.'

'The focus on Shamash and the Aten sheds a whole new light on these circular enclosures,' Hiebermeyer said. 'Sun worship, worship of the one god, monotheism, is deeper rooted than we might have thought, going back at least to the foundation of the gods at the time when the spirit world of the shamans was being eclipsed by the new priest-kings of the Neolithic. Costas was right to compare this site to the Pantheon.'

'Those animal and birds on the pillars and the tablet in Rome are a link between this place and the Temple of Isis and the seventeenth century, between Athanasius Kircher and the shipwreck and the secret it was carrying,' Jack said. 'I'm hoping that we'll have a translation of the tablet and an image of the document from the mine so that we can brainstorm all that before we leave Egypt.' He stood up, blinking the dust from his eyes and feeling the sweat pricking on his forehead. 'But before that, I'm yearning to see what you've got on the salt flat. Some exciting nautical archaeology I hope.'

'Amen to that,' Costas said. 'I'm burning up. Anywhere closer to the sea would be good.'

Hiebermeyer dropped his goggles over his eyes again. 'I was wondering when you were going to say that. We've got maybe an hour before the heat and dust make it impossible. Rebecca will lead the way.'

CHAPTER 21

Jack shaded his eyes and peered over the salt flat. The haze was like heat rising from hot asphalt, and all he could see ahead was shimmering air and a dark smudge in the distance suspended over the flat like a mirage. He set off again behind the others, keeping his pace slow and measured in order not to overheat. With each step the salt crackled beneath him like a thin crust of ice on a frozen lake, an unnerving sensation as if he were about to fall through every time. The analogy with ice ended there, though. The heat was as intense as he had ever experienced, dry and fierce, with the sunlight reflecting off the surface and the wind from the south only making it worse, bringing a waft of hot dust from the desert rather than any relief. The dust storm that they knew was building up had reduced the glare from the sun but in all other respects was bad news, limiting the time they would have at the site before having to turn back to the tents and the helicopter was grounded. The clock was ticking with *Sea Venture* holding offshore and *Seaquest* nearly ready to make way from Falmouth towards the Atlantic, to a destination still unknown but that Jack fervently hoped would become clear before the day was out.

Hiebermeyer was just ahead of him and stopped to take a swig from his water bottle. 'See anything yet?' he said.

'The view was better from the top of the dune above the heat haze,' Jack said. 'Down here all I can see is that dark smudge ahead.'

'The dust storm will soon obscure even that,'

Hiebermeyer said. 'We'll only have time for a quick look, but I promise you it will be worth it.'

Costas stopped and bent over with his hands on his knees. 'I take back what I said about wanting to be closer to the sea. I don't think I've ever been this hot before.'

'Drink plenty of water,' Hiebermeyer said. 'Only about two hundred metres to go now.'

Jack watched Rebecca as she walked ahead of them. She had an easy stride, confident and self-assured, as if she knew where she was going in life. He remembered the girl he had comforted twelve years earlier after her mother had been killed by the mafia in Naples. He had not seen her for several months now, but he was used to long gaps between meeting up with friends and colleagues on excavations that might carry on season after season for years. It was always as if the intervening time had not happened at all, as if the deep time of history that they were trying to reveal eclipsed the passage of time in their own lives. Rebecca looked more like a woman now than a teenager, with her hair cut short from her time working in the refugee camp in west Africa. He was glad that she was back with them, with Aysha and Maurice and the others who had been her family as she had grown up, guiding her in ways that he knew her mother would have been pleased to see.

She stopped and waited for them to catch up. 'Jeremy says hello, by the way,' he said. 'He's planning to fly back from Rome to Cornwall to join us on *Seaquest* if we get what we need to navigate a way ahead.'

'Don't let him do anything dangerous. He may be part of the family, but he's not used to putting his life on the line for archaeology. Not yet anyway.'

'Part of the family?'

'The IMU family.'

'I was just wondering for a moment.'

She gave him a look and walked forward again, shouldering the magnetometer that she had carried from the excavation on the dune.

'Daughters,' Costas said, shaking his head.

'Dads,' Hiebermeyer said. 'Sometime they say the right thing, sometimes not.'

Jack looked at him. 'Has Uncle Hiemy got any better suggestions?'

'Rebecca will steer her own course. She is a Howard after all.'

A narrow boardwalk lay ahead of them, stabilised by wider cross-planks every five metres or so that extended over the sides and were pinned into the salt flat with iron stakes. All around them rivulets of water and shallow pools reflected the haze and reduced the visibility to a few hundred metres. As Jack mounted the boardwalk it was as if he were walking into a mirage, out of the present into a world almost unfathomably far back in time, through the waves of armies and invaders who had passed this way back to the first seafarers to reach these shores almost eight millennia before. The sense of time elapsed increased as they walked further and the shape that materialised out of the haze ahead became the only feature in view, a blackened beam sticking out of the flat that looked more and more like the prow of a boat with other timbers visible behind.

'Aysha's uncle and his workers put this boardwalk in two days ago after I first saw that timber,' Hiebermeyer said. 'This part of the salt flat is a shallow basin that lies below the level of the lagoon to the east, so it's waterlogged with dangerous patches of liquified clay like quicksand on either side. John Milton wasn't making it up in his poem when he wrote that the Serbonian bog swallowed up armies. Diodorus Siculus said that the entire army of the King of Persia was lost here.'

A few moments later they stood on a raised wooden platform almost within touching distance of the timbers. For Jack it was an incredible sight, the oldest wooden boat he had ever seen, pre-dating the boats of the Bronze Age by at least three millennia. 'Amazing,' he said. 'Right back at the beginning of seafaring in the Mediterranean.'

'You can see where the planks were sewn together with rope, like early Bronze Age boats,' Hiebermeyer said. 'There are holes bored into the edges of the planks with the remains of twisted willow withies that served as rope. The pole lying across the thwarts was a mast, but it was probably mainly paddled. We didn't find any loose artefacts inside, as if it had been stripped but the boat itself deliberately left with all of its timbers intact, almost as a monument.'

'It was probably quickly buried in the sand, bearing in mind that this was exposed seashore at that point,' Jack said.

Rebecca's phone rang and she answered it. 'I need to get back to help Aysha,' she said, putting the phone away. 'She's closing down the dig at the enclosure before the khamsin sets in. The mini diggers are going to backfill the site to keep it protected and then Aysha's uncle is going to airlift them to the sandbar to open up the channel from the sea tomorrow morning. He needs to do the airlift before the khamsin because the dust could choke the filters in the helicopter's engine.'

'OK,' Hiebermeyer said. 'We won't be far behind you.'

As she left a buzzing sound came from above and a drone dropped level with them, panning along their faces and tilting from side to side. 'Hello Jacob,' Costas said to it. 'What gives?'

The drone tilted towards the boat and bobbed up and down enthusiastically. 'He can hear me, but he hasn't yet got the speaker working,' Costas said, taking out his phone and reading a message. 'He says the drone has just finished its job. Three thousand three hundred photos, a multi-beam scan and half an hour of video footage, all successfully uploaded. That should allow us to build a life-size 3-D model of the boat back at IMU.'

'You're not going to give the drone a name, are you?' Hiebermeyer said.

'Her. Not it.'

'Oh no.'

'I'm glad to see all the work you did while we were on *Sea Venture* has paid off,' Jack said.

'That reminds me. Some tweaking is still needed on Little Joey.'

'He'll be waiting for you on *Seaquest*.'

The drone bobbed up and down as if waving, backed off and sped away. 'The timbers will be preserved *in situ*,' Hiebermeyer said. 'Once the sea floods back in when the channel is re-opened the sediment will bury it again, and the salinity level in the lagoon is too high for shipworms, *teredo navalis*. The boat has survived like this since Neolithic times and should continue to do so into the foreseeable future.'

'Did you take wood samples?' Costas said.

'From the prow,' Hiebermeyer said. 'We put a climbing harness and rope on Rebecca and she managed to crawl over and get them. It's Turkish oak, *Quercus cerris*, consistent with the location Atlantis in Anatolia. The lab in Alexandria gave a provisional radiocarbon date of 7500 plus or minus 100 BP, closely matching the dates for the pigment and charcoal from the enclosure. And it gets even better. Wood from Atlantis and the other Neolithic sites that have been found along the submerged shoreline of the Black Sea has produced a complete tree-ring sequence for the period, one that has been linked to a sequence up to the present day. It gives us a date for when the tree was felled of 5,522 BC.'

'Fantastic,' Jack said. 'That's the first absolute date we have for the Black Sea flood and the end of Atlantis.'

'Rebecca's inspection showed that the boat was built in haste, that it was functional but crude,' Hiebermeyer said. 'With more time they could have made a better job of the joinery. It's indicative of rapid construction in the few weeks between realising that the Bosporus had been breached and the floodwaters beginning to inundate the citadel.'

'Is this the reality behind Noah's Ark?' Costas said.

'There's no evidence that this particular boat was carrying animals, but others very probably did. A boat such as this would have been large enough to take several breeding pairs of the main domesticated species, though perhaps not as big as aurochs, which went extinct about this time.'

Jack put a hand on Hiebermeyer's shoulder. 'So early Neolithic Egypt is no longer a blank canvas.'

'It's everything I've ever dreamed of,' Hiebermeyer replied, his voice hoarse with emotion. When you gave me that stone artefact with the carving when we were boys I knew even then that it was old, older than the pharaohs. Do you remember when you helped me record the Egyptian flint knives in the British Museum? That was about getting back as far as I could, about trying to understand where it all began. What it was that led to the pyramids and temples and mummies.'

'That reminds me,' Jack said. 'Something we found at the Temple of Isis in Rome that I need to tell you about. It might confirm your theory about what those knives were used for.'

Hiebermeyer pulled his phone out of his pocket and glanced at it. 'That was Aysha. The Egyptian inspector has just arrived and wants to talk to me. Tell me about it while we make our way back.'

He lowered his goggles and pulled down the flaps of his hat to protect his face from the sun. The Afrika Korps gear made him look like an apparition from the past, as if one of the soldiers who had passed by this place in the wars of the last century had come back to life. Jack had tried on those goggles and knew what they were like, opaque and murky with the imperfections of the lenses causing ripples and distortions in the view. He seemed to see the prehistoric boat in that way now, with the dust giving a brownish tinge to everything as if the world were fading to sepia. He remembered a line from the Epic of Gilgamesh about Shamash riding his chariot over the heavenly sea, and he imagined that now, not a desiccated salt-flat but a sparkling shoreline with the sun shining through. In his mind's eye he saw ghostly figures stir in the boat, men with braided beards and long hair tied back, men parched and starving who had almost forgotten how to walk, who staggered and fell as they slipped over the side and went up through the surf. Coming down towards them were others wearing the headdress of the falcon, fearsome warriors who were cowed in awe and wonder when they saw the men somehow revive and tower above them, men whom they had thought they might plunder and enslave but now would be treated as gods. The image seemed to meld with the procession on the carving until all movement ceased and he saw only that, and then the ghostly outline of the boat fell away to the bare skeleton of the wreck and the sea became sand.

He blinked hard and turned to see Hiebermeyer and Costas leaving on the boardwalk. He could smell the dust of the desert more strongly now, a cloying dryness in the back of his throat that seems like the distilled essence of all that had passed this way, from the dawn of civilisation to the present-day. He was coursing with excitement at what he had seen, extraordinary discoveries that already rivalled anything they had ever found, but he knew there was a greater prize somewhere ahead and he prayed that they would soon have what was needed to take the quest forward. He lingered for a few moments to take pictures of the boat with his phone and then followed the other two into the haze.

*

'Jack!' Lanowski looked up from his laptop, his face beaming with excitement. 'Perfect timing. I've just had the results from the IMU conservation lab on your package from the mine.'

Jack dropped the flap of the tent behind him and took off his sunglasses. He and Costas had left Rebecca and Hiebermeyer at the ancient enclosure on top of the dune and had carried on to the tent where Lanowski had remained while they looked at the boat on the salt flat. Lanowski had lowered the sides of the tent to keep the dust out, a mixed blessing as there was still enough sunlight for it to act as a greenhouse. Jack quickly downed a small bottle of water and then looked at his phone. 'Hang on. It's Jeremy. He wants a video call, right now. Let's put him on your screen.'

A few moments later Jeremy and Marco appeared side-by-side, their faces heavily pixelated because of the poor reception. 'We've translated the inscription from the table in the Temple of Isis,' Jeremy said. 'The first revelation is that it doesn't date to the time of the Romans in Egypt but to the reign of the pharaoh Akhenaten, in the second millennium BC. Does that make sense with what you've got there?'

'Yes, it does,' Jack said. 'I'll explain later. Carry on.'

'The hieroglyphs tell how a sacred object that arrived on the shores of Egypt with Shamash was taken by the priests of Isis and hidden in their temple, but then put in a ship and taken from there beyond the Pillars of Hercules to an island in the ocean of Atlas. Two ships went, but only one returned.'

Any indication of the date?'

'Akhenaten sent a ship to pursue them, but it never returned. So this must have taken place during his reign, when he was searching the temples in Egypt for the secrets of the ancients for his library. The priests of Isis must have got spooked and decided to conceal their greatest treasure as far away as they could, somewhere at the limits of the sea that Egyptian mariners had explored.'

'That's fantastic,' Jack said. 'Anything more?'

Jeremy started talking but the image disintegrated and a notice came up saying that the connection had failed. 'Damn,' Costas said. 'It must be the dust storm.'

Jack turned to Lanowski. 'I can't wait to hear what you've got.'

'What Jeremy said fits beautifully,' he said. 'The IMU conservation people couldn't prise it open the package without destroying it so they put it through an infrared scanner. Shortwave hyperspectral infrared to be exact. Something Costas and I have been working on. It's a real ground breaker.'

'Show us the image.'

Lanowski tapped a key and an irregular outline appeared on a white background with lettering above it. 'I put it through a lot of filters and came up with this. It's the outline of a land mass with the Latin words **INSULA ORICHALCUM** above it. As well as Captain Viviano's mark on the leather you can see that of the Cadiz merchants Cornelissen and Porrata, for whom the package was evidently intended.'

'Exactly as we'd hoped,' Jack said, staring at the image with mounting excitement. 'It's similar to the land mass for Atlantis island published in the *Mundus Subterraneus*, but crucially different in the details of the coastline. This must be a copy of the actual image that Kircher found on an Egyptian papyrus, something that was brought out of Egypt in the Roman period but must have originated much earlier.'

Lanowski looked at him, beaming. 'Well? Do you want to hear what I've found?'

'Spill it, Jacob,' Costas said.

'It was your doing, actually,' he said. 'The idea that Kircher's image might represent a small island rather than a continent. As soon as I refined this image I fed it into a shoreline detection programme developed by a friend of mine at NASA who was in the same PhD group as me at MIT. The algorithm combines the latest Landsat-9 and Sentinel-2 imagery with more than thirty years of satellite-derived shoreline imagery. It's the most robust sub-metre resolution I've ever seen, almost sub-pixel, but it takes a while to work because the shoreline you see in any given image fluctuates with the tide and waves so needs to be estimated by the algorithm before it can be used to find a match.'

'OK,' Jack said. 'So what have you got?'

Lanowski pointed at the screen. 'You might think all those indentations and wiggles around the shoreline were just artistic or approximations, but you'd be wrong. Take a look at this.'

He tapped a key and a satellite image of an island came

up, brown on the surface and surrounded by the blue of the ocean, a white line of surf along the shore on one side. 'Well I'll be damned,' Jack said, bending down and peering closely at the island and then at the seventeenth century image. 'It's the same.'

'The algorithm doesn't allow 100% certainty, as that's impossible. But by drawing the resolution back to 30 metres, to about the degree of accuracy that a good cartographer might have attained from shoreline sketches and survey data in the past, we're looking at a 90% match. There's no reason why Egyptian seafarers couldn't have depicted a coastline with that degree of accuracy. So yes. That's Kircher's island. The island drawn on the papyrus from the time of Akhenaten. The island that the priests of Isis didn't want anyone else knowing about.'

'Where is it?'

Lanowski tapped a key and the image reduced in scale to show the island as part of an archipelago. 'It's between Madeira and the Canaries. A small cluster of islands under Portuguese control about 200 nautical miles off the coast of Morocco.'

The Ilhas Selvagem,' Jack said. 'The Savage Islands. I've never visited them, but I know of them by reputation. Captain Kidd was rumoured to have buried treasure there, taken from Portuguese ships bringing gold from Brazil. Several expeditions went to find it in the nineteenth century. There are strong tidal currents, and it was a lethal place for sailing ships that strayed too near.'

'Kircher's island is Selvagem Grande, the largest of them,' Lanowski said. 'Volcanic, about two kilometres across. It's a nature reserve with a research station manned part-time by two rangers, and the Portuguese Navy mounts an occasional fisheries patrol nearby. Otherwise it's uninhabited and it's rarely visited.'

'And cut off by Atlantic storms for much of the year, I imagine,' Costas said.

'That whole archipelago from Madeira to the Canaries is the most likely place for an ancient boat sailing beyond the

Strait of Gibraltar to have made first landfall,' Jack said. 'If they were taking something to conceal, it's far enough for them to think they'd pretty well reached the ends of the earth.'

'Isn't Madeira another place where IMU did an ecological project?' Lanowski said.

Jack nodded. 'About ten years ago. Sea turtles again, in fact. They're really turning out to be our friends. We have an open invitation from the Portuguese Government to carry on with the environmental monitoring that we began then. That should work in our favour now.'

'I take it that's where we're going next?' Lanowski said.

Jack gave him a steely look. 'I want the most advanced 3-D visualisation of that island you can get. Digital elevation models, the lot. Get me everything you can.'

'I'm on it.'

'I'll get Jeremy to find out everything he can find on the history of the island. The Portuguese discovery, any shipwrecks, the treasure hunts. And to see what Maria's been able to find in the Lisbon archives about those merchants Porrata and Cornelissen. Maybe when they were taking goods out to Madeira and the Canaries they were going to the Savage Islands as well.' He turned to Costas. 'Where is *Seaquest* now?'

'Working up in Falmouth Bay after her refit.'

'She needs to be underway as soon as possible. Full expedition kit and security team. You know the drill.'

'I'm already writing the checklist in my head. Little Joey too?'

'Everything.'

'I take it you're expecting trouble.'

'That's why I want us underway as soon as possible. When our friends in Rome get wind of what's happening, they'll do all they can to stop us. They may have the resources to put something as powerful as *Seaquest* in the water after us.'

'Isn't that archipelago in Portuguese territorial waters?'

'Yes, but volcanic islands are problematic. Territorial claims out to sea are generally only made over the continental shelf and those islands rise directly from abyssal depth. The Portuguese navy and maritime police may only have jurisdiction close inshore. Outside that, it would be a free-for-all. We need Captain Macalister on *Seaquest* to get confirmation from the Portuguese on where they can operate.'

'I'll call him as soon as we're on *Sea Venture*,' Costas said.

Jack raised a flap of the tent and walked outside, seeing the orange glow in the west where the sunset was refracted through the dust of the khamsin. He thought of what had brought them here in the first place, the artefact discovered by a soldier from New Zealand more than a hundred years previously. He remembered the words of the commanding officer of the Canterbury Mounted Rifles as he tried to express his feelings about this place even as he and his men were driving hard against the enemy: *night after night on outpost one watched and marvelled at the wondrous tints. As the sun sinks below the rim of the horizon, the whole sky glows with coloured bands of light, then these gradually fade out, leaving a clear blue sky studded with innumerable stars*. That same vista had been seen by those who had come this way through history, from Thutmose and Alexander the Great to Crusader kings, from warriors of the jihad to merchants with caravans of riches and soldiers from far-off lands brought here to do battle in a world at war, thinking of little but the heat and the sand and the need to find water. Above them the chariot with the sun had emerged from the gates of heaven as it did every day at dawn and then disappeared at dusk to travel through the night around the underworld in preparation for another sunrise to come.

As Jack watched the sunset now, trying to imagine how the ancients had explained it, he thought of an island in the far-off Atlantic whose shape was now seared on his mind, a treasure map as exciting as any that had led him on expeditions of discovery in the past. In his mind's eye he saw a vessel again, not the one he had visualised on the salt flat but a deep-bellied ship of the Bronze Age able to sail across the Mediterranean and out into the Atlantic, leaving a wake through history that they were now trying to follow. He could not yet visualise the people on that ship, something that he knew might come if they found the wreck, but he had already seen on the bier in the stone carving an image of what she contained that would remain imprinted in his consciousness until they had reached as far as they could on this quest.

Costas came out beside him, tipped up his hat and took a swig from a water bottle. 'Rebecca said she's staying here to help finish up the excavation. So it's just the two of us for this jaunt.'

'Along with Macalister and the crew of *Seaquest* and an IMU security team,' Jack said. 'And the Portuguese navy, if we can persuade them to take seriously that we are in search of the secret of immortality but are being chased by priests of the temple of Isis who want to mummify us alive.'

Costas nearly choked on his water, swallowed hard and peered at Jack. 'What?'

'I was going to tell you on *Sea Venture* but you were too absorbed in fixing the drone. We found evidence in Rome the akhet-re is still performed. They use one of those obsidian knives to take just enough out of you while leaving you alive. And a kind of pick to get at your brain through your nose. Something about nourishment for the goddess. We think that's what they did to Akhenaten, but probably the life-force from him is wearing a bit thin. It was over 3,000 years ago after all. They'll be wanting a new victim.'

'Don't look at me.'

'Aysha and Maurice have a pretty good track record in unwrapping mummies, so if it happens you'll be all right. Probably.'

'Reassuring as usual.' Costas took another deep swig and squinted at the horizon. 'Yet another routine outing with Jack Howard. Nearly die in a mineshaft, nearly fry in the Egyptian desert and then get mummified alive.'

'But if you survive, there's beer at the end on me.'

'So, the helicopter to *Sea Venture,* sail back to Cyprus, then the Embraer to Cornwall and another helo to *Seaquest*?'

Jack nodded. 'We can spend the journey to Cyprus checklisting all the gear we'll need.'

'Roger that.' Costas finished the bottle. 'Do you think there might be pirate treasure out there as well? Gold, like in the mine? This time we might get our priorities right and actually raise some.'

'I'm hoping for a bigger prize than that.'

'Immortality or gold,' Costas said. 'It's a tough call.'

'Or both.'

'That's more like it.'

'We're due at the helicopter in twenty minutes. The pilot is worried about dust from the storm getting into the engine. Good to go?'

'Good to go.'

PART 4

CHAPTER 22

The Savage Isles, the Atlantic Ocean

Jack peered out of the observer's side window as the Lynx helicopter began its descent towards the ship visible on the ocean some three thousand feet below. They had followed its wake for the last fifteen minutes but that had become less clear as the captain slowed down in anticipation of the helicopter's arrival. It had been a three-and-a-half-hour roller-coaster ride since they had left the IMU Embraer at Casablanca in Morocco, heading due west over the Atlantic through the eastern side of a cyclonic system that had become more concerning as the morning progressed. They had been unable to see the ocean as they approached the centre of the system, and *Seaquest* was the first ship they had spotted since leaving the coast of Morocco. They knew that there were others converging on the same course, one that was pursuing *Seaquest* as well as vessels of the Portuguese Navy, but for now Jack was thinking solely about *Seaquest* and their destination ahead, a goal that would only become real once he saw the shape of the island that he had memorised from Athanasius Kircher's map and from poring over the satellite image that Lanowski had shown them of the archipelago somewhere in front of them now.

He glanced at the pilot. 'How are we doing?'

The pilot was focussed on the instruments and the view below, his hands on the control sticks as he guided their descent. 'We're nearly at the limit of our range with the external fuel tanks. Fortunately the wind has eased off so we should have a reasonably smooth landing.'

Jack looked at the navigation screen with the small-scale chart that marked their progress. To the north-west lay Madeira, and some three hundred nautical miles south of that the Canary Islands. Between them were two archipelagos of volcanic islands, the Ilhas Desertas near Madeira and the Ilhas Selvagens further south, both Portuguese territory. The largest of the Selvagens lay dead ahead of them now some 20 miles away, meaning that they were only half an hour by sea from the 12-mile limit that marked Portuguese territorial waters. Being within those waters would not protect them from confrontation but it would mean that they could call on the police and military for assistance, something that Captain Macalister on *Seaquest* had been discussing with the Portuguese authorities since the ship had left Falmouth three days previously. The fact that IMU had carried out a collaborative ecological project off Madeira two years before and that Jack was a patron of the Portuguese Centro de Arqueologia Subaquática worked in their favour, but any assistance would still depend on Portuguese vessels being within range and having the authority under international law to intervene.

He craned his neck around to look at the sole occupant of the passenger compartment, a familiar figure in a flight suit with his arms braced against the sides and his face concealed beneath his helmet and visor. 'All well?' Jack said. 'We're nearly there.'

'I'm just glad I didn't have breakfast in the airport at Casablanca,' Costas said, his voice sounding strained. 'It would have been all over the interior of this compartment by now.'

'The chef on *Seaquest* does an excellent omelette.'

'Don't say that. I can't think about food until we land.'

A few minutes later the Lynx bounced on the helipad near the stern of *Seaquest,* the pilot throttled the engine down and the crewmen who had been waiting alongside sprang forward to secure the landing gear to the deck. Jack disconnected his harness, unlatched the door and got out, glad to feel the deck beneath his feet, and then reached over and put a hand on the nose cowling of the Lynx. She had served them well for more than 15 years since their expedition to the Black Sea but was nearing the end of her working life, and he knew that Captain Macalister was keen on an upgrade. Costas clambered out beside him and they both ducked under the rotor and made their way amidships to where Macalister was standing beside the hatch that led up to the bridge. He had a close-trimmed white beard and was immaculately turned out as usual, his sweater bearing the shoulder insignia of a captain in the Royal Naval Reserve. They took off their helmets and shook hands with him. 'Good to see you, James,' Jack said. 'And good to be back on board *Seaquest*. It's been a while.'

'A few improvements since you last saw her,' Macalister said. 'Upgraded defensive armaments, retuned dynamic positioning system and enlarged internal docking bay for the Aquapods, allowing safer egress and recovery in heavy seas.'

'Do you still think that's our best option?'

'Much of the island is ringed by cliffs, so your best access to the shoreline will be from the sea. The surface currents are too strong to dive from a RIB and get safely ashore. Your best bet will be to go in deep with the Aquapods below the worst of the current and make your way up against the undersea cliff.'

'Do we have any further clues on where we should go in?' Costas said. 'Jeremy and Maria were following some leads.'

'I've heard nothing from Jeremy for almost twenty-four hours,' Jack said. 'I expect he and Marco are absorbed in the archives in Rome. Maria left a message saying that she's going to contact us as soon as she knows we're on *Seaquest.* It sounds as if she might have had a breakthrough.'

'Good,' Macalister said. 'I'll get a link set up as soon as I'm back on the bridge.'

'Is the security team prepped?' Jack said.

Macalister pointed to several men in camouflage and webbing who were loading gear into the passenger compartment of the helicopter. 'Ben and a four-man team will be flying out to the island to establish a position on the upper plateau. They may not be able to help if you are on the shoreline and can't get up the cliffs, but they should be a reassuring presence. I've told them to go soon because the western side of this cyclonic system is likely to come sweeping over the islands within the next few hours, potentially grounding the helicopter. It also means that it's out of harm's way on the island in the event that anyone fires a shell or a missile at the ship.'

Jack waved at Ben, who did a thumbs-up in return. 'Strip off your flight suits and then we'll head to the bridge,' Macalister said. 'I'll get some coffee and sandwiches sent up.'

'I'm just going to nip below,' Costas said. 'I need to check on Little Joey.'

'Ah, yes,' Macalister said. 'Little Joey. Multiple complaints from the engineering department. He was supposed to be in sleep mode when we put him aboard, but then he woke up and he snaps at anyone who comes near.'

Costas looked apologetic. 'Of course. The new facial recognition software. Jacob set it so that Little Joey would only respond to him or to me. Everyone else is a threat. It will need an iris scan from both of us to override the command.'

'Jacob is in a tent in the Sinai desert two thousand miles away.'

'He can do it remotely. I can set up a satellite link.'

'You've got fifteen minutes,' Macalister said. 'If there's no progress by then, Little Joey goes to the brig.'

'Roger that.'

*

Half an hour later they stood on the bridge of *Seaquest*, Costas having come up from below with his breakfast in a carton that he put on top of the binnacle. Macalister had given them a briefing and Jack was waiting for Costas to finish eating before going down with him to the internal docking bay to check that the Aquapods were fully charged and their e-suits were ready to go. He had felt increasingly on edge, watching the clouds on the horizon swirl and thicken and hoping for a message from Jeremy or Maria on the satellite phone. Everything was in place except the critical information on where exactly on the island they should make landfall. Without that, they would be going in blind, with more than a kilometre of difficult coastline to explore and no idea of where the most likely location might be.

'Incoming from Maria Gonzales,' the communications officer said. 'She's on video link.'

'Put her on the main screen,' Macalister said.

A woman with dark hair tied back and glasses appeared on the screen, sitting in front of a backdrop of white-washed walls and the sea. 'Hello everyone,' she said. 'I'm outside on my laptop and the reception's not great.'

'Where are you?' Jack said.

'In the Canary Islands. Fuerteventura to be exact, on the remote southern coast. I've got some exciting news.'

'You were researching the seventeenth century merchants Cornelissen and Porrata,' Jack said.

'Right. In Cadiz I found more records of their role as middlemen between Amsterdam and Genoa. They were the main brokers in Cadiz for the arrival and distribution of silver from the Americas, supplying it to the Dutch and English East Indiamen which stopped there on the outward journey and taking a healthy commission. That meant that Cornelissen and Porrata had a secure source of wealth, and little need to develop new interests of doubtful profitability. But as we've seen, in the early 1670s they suddenly become involved in a venture to collect saltpetre for gunpowder from the guano to be found in the Ilhas Selvagens and the Ilhas Desertas, remote archipelagos with a reputation as ship killers.'

'We know they already had business interests in the Canaries,' Jack said.

Maria nodded. 'Before the silver trade took off much of their focus had been on Las Palmas, where they supplied paintings and brass embellishments for the Cathedral of Santa Ana. It turns out that the cathedral was the destination for the candelabras and chandeliers being carried on the *Santo Cristo di Castello*. When she was wrecked they had been waiting for her to arrive in Cadiz, and they were then going to tranship the consignment out to Las Palmas in their own vessel.'

'But we now know that the transport of those items was a smokescreen for something else,' Jack said. 'The discovery of their merchant's mark on the chart from the mine clinches it. The chart was destined for them, entrusted by Kircher and Sauli to Captain Viviano, and was meant to provide what they would need to identify the island where the hieroglyphic text on the plaque in Rome said that the object taken from the Temple of Isis had been hidden. They laid the groundwork through the saltpetre venture, allowing them to explore the islands without provoking suspicion by the followers of Isis who might have been on to Kircher and sent to follow them.'

'It's also what sealed their fate,' Maria said, holding up a scan of a document in old handwriting. 'I hit a dead-end in Lisbon so decided to come out here and look at the church archives in Las Palmas. I found the name of the merchant they dealt with in Las Palmas on behalf of the church, Pietro Del Forno, and a dossier of his correspondence. I finally struck it lucky yesterday when I found a letter he'd written to another merchant in Lisbon in 1673. By then it seems likely that Porrata and Cornelissen would have had a duplicate of the map you found, one that Sauli and Kircher must have got to them when they realised that the first one had been lost after the wreck of the *Santo Cristo di Castello*. Del Forno remarked on how unusual it was that Porrata and Cornelissen had arrived in their own ship with the purpose of visiting the islands to oversee the collection of guano, which Del Forno regarded as beneath them as upper-end merchants. He remarked on how their ship had extra armament, something that we already knew from the Cadiz archive. Then he said that the day after Cornelissen and Porrata had sailed from Las Palmas for the islands another ship put in, asking after them and then hastily setting off in pursuit. It was a large Italian vessel and heavily armed. It was not a naval vessel or a pirate ship but seemed to have been privately hired.'

'And what then?' Jack said.

'I couldn't find anything more in the seventeenth century records, but that's not the end of the trail. Knowing of my interest, the curator of the archive put me in touch with an old fisherman and diver who knew the Islas Selvagens and Islas Desertas well. The fisherman told me they're full of all kinds of traps for the unwary, with currents and whirlpools and areas of shallows that look safe as anchorages but are death traps when the wind changes. He said there are numerous shipwrecks but only one he knew of that contained cannon. It's in the Ilhas Desertas, in a shallow lagoon-like area where the fishermen never go. He said there's a jumble of cannon only a few metres deep surrounded by jagged volcanic rock just below the surface. He only ever dived there once, but he took some photos.' She put two faded prints up to the camera. 'I'm not a cannon expert, but those look the right period.'

Jack peered closely at the screen. 'The two on the left are breech-loading swivel guns of bronze. The document you found in Lisbon about the additional armament for Cornelissen and Porrata's ship lists bronze swivel guns.'

Maria held up another photo. 'This is a close-up of one of them.'

'Ah, that's beautiful,' Jack said. 'The armillary sphere and coat of arms of Portugal.'

'The refitting was carried out in Lisbon,' Maria said. 'Cornelissen and Porrata had another warehouse there, and that's where they had their ships built.'

'The larger gun in the other photo is Italian, possibly Venetian,' Jack said. 'I'd be comfortable putting all of these in the 1660s or 1670s.'

'Then here's my hypothesis,' Maria said. 'Cornelissen

and Porrata were clearly expecting trouble even before they set out from Lisbon or else they wouldn't have bolstered the armament in their ship. But the Italian ship was too big for them to confront even so, and instead of engaging their pursuers at sea they lured them away from the Selvagens towards a place they knew in the Ilhas Desertas, that lagoon that was a known ship trap. It would have been a one-way trip for both vessels, but it would have kept their pursuers away from the location of the treasure.'

'Sounds like a suicide mission for Porrata and Cornelissen,' Costas said.

'For the greater good,' Jack said. 'I think these men, Kircher, Sauli, Viviano, the merchants, knew the importance of what they were after, something that promised the possibility of prolonging life. They were willing to put their lives on the line to keep it from the priesthood who were sworn to conceal it for all time.'

'How does get us closer to pinpointing where we should be looking on the island?' Costas said.

'Wait for it,' Maria said. 'And jump forward almost three hundred years. As I was about to leave, the old fisherman asked me whether I was interested in U-boats and the Ilhas Selvagens. It seemed a pretty big disconnect from the seventeenth century, but I was intrigued. He said that his brother lived in a house on the island of Fuerteventura south of Gran Canaria that had been the base for a Nazi agent during the war, and that he'd recently found a stash of papers hidden in the wall of a room that detailed his activities. He and his brother had not told anyone else or studied them in detail yet. He knew about IMU, and after I'd contacted him, he thought we might be the right people to approach.'

'Go on,' Jack said.

Maria picked up a typed page and showed them. 'This is a copy of a 1947 document on suspected former Nazi agents in Spain from the Madrid bureau chief of the US Office of Strategic Services, the precursor of the CIA. The man was called Gustav Winter. It describes him as a 'German agent in the Canary Islands in charge of observation posts equipped with wireless transmitters and responsible for the supplying of German U-boats.' By 1947 the activities of wartime agents in Spain were of limited interest and the story was shelved. But the presence of Winter on the islands may have been a factor in prolonging the Battle of the Atlantic and shows how Franco in Spain was actively assisting the Nazis, something that Franco tried to conceal after the war. That's why Winter's activities were never widely known and why he hid the papers rather than destroying them, as he wanted to reveal the truth of his wartime role after Franco had gone.'

'But Winter died before then?' Jack said.

'Correct. The papers confirm what the OSS had suspected. U-boats frequently came into the shallows on the south side of Fuerteventura for revictualling and refuelling, with the fuel being pumped from a concealed reservoir filled by a tanker masquerading as the ship that carried fresh water from Gran Canaria to Fuerteventura. That significantly increased the range and duration of the U-boat patrols, allowing them more time to shadow convoys going along the coast of Africa and across the Atlantic. Winter's base also provided a haven for U-boats damaged by Allied attack but still seaworthy, including several thought by the Allies to have been sunk but that managed to make it this far. One of those was U-182, Kapitänleutnant Nicolai Clausen, which was thought to have been destroyed by depth charges from the destroyer USS *Mackenzie* near Madeira on 16 May 1943. In fact it was too badly damaged to make it to Fuerteventura and was gradually sinking, and Clausen drove it into a semi-submerged cavern on Selvagen Grande.'

'That's our island,' Jack said. 'So Clausen evidently managed to contact Winter from the U-boat to tell him this?'

'The U-boat's radio had been destroyed in the attack, but Clausen managed to rig up a transmitter by taking a wire high enough in the cavern to act as an antenna. The radio ran off a small battery they managed to salvage from the U-boat, but that only lasted a week. Fifteen men made it out of the U-boat, but they died one by one, some from thirst and starvation and others by trying to swim out and getting caught in the tidal current which is very severe at that place. After six days it was only Clausen and a British Merchant Navy radio officer, James Gillespie, who had been taken on board as a prisoner several weeks earlier after U-182 had sunk the SS *Aloe* off South Africa. Clausen had surfaced among the lifeboats and provided the crew of the *Aloe* with food and other means to survive so that they could make it ashore, but he had taken the master and the radio officer prisoner. In those final days together in the cave he and Gillespie seem to have struck up a friendship, probably after realising that the war for them was over and they would not be getting out of that place.'

'Couldn't Winter mount a rescue operation?' Costas said.

Maria shook her head. 'That was out of the question. The Spanish couldn't risk being seen overtly to aid the Nazis, with Allied long-range reconnaissance aircraft overflying the islands and long-wave radio transmissions being monitored. So it wasn't feasible for Winter to alert the Spanish authorities on Las Palmas, and he didn't have the means to mount a rescue himself. The local fishermen told him that the place where the U-boat had grounded was impossible to reach by boat because the currents were too strong. It was another ship-trap like the lagoon that wrecked those two ships in the Ilhas Desertas in the seventeenth century. Clausen and Gillespie couldn't get out of the cavern to climb to the top of the island, there was no fresh water and they were too weak to forage for eggs or fish.'

'How does this help us?' Costas said.

'Winter copied down everything that the two men said on the radio. I think he was tormented by the fact that he couldn't save them and he wanted there to be a record. The final transmission was from Gillespie to say that Clausen had died, and that he had slipped him back into the sea to be with his men. Gillespie was half-crazed with thirst, his voice rasping and barely audible, but he had dragged himself as far as he could into the back recess of the cavern and in the dim light had seen something carved on the walls. He said he had visited the museum in Cairo before the war when his ship had gone through the Suez Canal and he was certain of what he was looking at. He said it was hieroglyphics. Ancient Egyptian hieroglyphics.'

'My God,' Jack said. 'Did he say anything more?'

'The transmitter went dead. That was the last thing Winter heard.'

'Did he work out the location?'

Maria showed a black and white aerial photo of a jagged cliff with white water below and a narrow inlet going into a cavern. 'This is the place identified by the fishermen. It's a good fishing spot just offshore because of the currents but is also dangerous for the same reason. Nobody has ever taken a boat in there and come out alive. I've just emailed you the position on a satellite image.'

Costas looked at Jack. 'Bingo.'

'That's brilliant, Maria,' Jack said. 'It's just what we were looking for. We'll send the Lynx from the ship to pick you up as soon as we can. And thank the fisherman from us. Hopefully I'll have the chance to do so in person soon.'

'Look after yourselves. Be careful.'

The screen went blank and Jack turned to Macalister. 'How soon can you get us there?'

'We're fifteen nautical miles offshore now,' the chief officer said, checking the navigation screens. 'We should be in position to launch the Aquapods in about an hour.'

'I'll be more comfortable when we're within the twelve-mile territorial limit,' Macalister said. 'There are no Portuguese assets within close range, but at least then we'll be able to send out a mayday if we're attacked.'

'Are you expecting that?' Costas said.

'I know the vessel that's pursuing us. There are three in

its class, and this is the latest. They were built by a shipyard in the Far East and are open to hire with crew to anyone with the right money. They've been designed to look like superyachts but strip away the veneer and they're actually warships. Ideal for anyone wanting to transport large consignments of drugs or other illegal cargo through international or territorial waters where nations have limited capability for maritime interdiction.'

'Mercenaries at sea,' Costas said.

'Exactly. The company provides everything for the client including a weapons team, mostly ex-Russian special forces with experience in Chechnya and Syria and Ukraine.'

'Experience meaning murdering civilians,' Costas said.

'If that's what the client pays for, that's what they get.'

'What are its armaments?'

'Medium-range lightweight anti-ship missiles with active radar homing, probably Marte Mark 2 Sea Killers with the usual 70 kilo semi-armour piercing warhead. Also fixed armaments at least equivalent to our own, probably a 30 or 40 mm cannon on a forward mount and a couple of 20 mm Oerlikons.'

'But not a Phalanx close-in weapon system.'

'That's where we have the edge. The Phalanx is not available to private buyers, and we only have it because *Seaquest* is a reserve auxiliary vessel of the Royal Navy. The Phalanx is a good defence against missiles but is of less value as an offensive weapon, with an effective range of only about a mile. All they need to do is keep beyond that range and they are the ones with the edge.'

'And you know they've flown off a helicopter,' Costas said.

'About an hour ago. An H160M. We tracked its heat signature as far as we could. It was heading towards the island.'

'They're waiting for us to show them the way,' Jack said. 'That's another advantage of going in with Aquapods. We'll be underwater so under their radar screen. With any luck we'll be able to enter that cavern without being detected, if we can get through the swell and the current.'

'That's the next thing I was going to ask,' Costas said. 'The latest weather forecast.'

Macalister glanced at the navigation console. '4 to 5 foot swell, visibility only about two miles. It's due to rise to Force 6 by this afternoon with driving rain from the west. It won't last long, just until the front blows over, but it's enough to ground the helicopters for a critical window or four or five hours.'

'And what about the inshore currents?' Costas asked.

Macalister pointed to another screen showing a detailed view of the bathymetry around the island. 'There are strong currents off the western side where you'll be going in, exacerbated by the tide. IMU collaborated with the Oceanic Observatory of Madeira two years ago when we helped with the ecological assessment, providing a microstructure profiler to measure turbulence and temperature variations. What we found was great for biodiversity, but not so good for us today. The submarine canyons around the island cause what's known as a warm wake, with the steep slope of the ridges causing oscillations in water movement. Solar radiation at the surface creates convective cells of greater salinity that sink into the currents, causing yet more turbulence. Combined with the swell slamming into the coast, this translates into a perfect storm underwater with tidal currents of up to ten knots parallel to the shore and violent lateral and vertical movements. And it's worse when there are high spring tides.'

'As there are now,' Jack said.

'It sounds like the mythical Siren Island,' Costas said. 'A place that lures you in and from which there is no escape.'

'But you can turn that on its head,' Jack said. 'It means nobody else would try what we're planning now. Nobody else has the equipment or the experience.'

'You mean nobody else is crazy enough,' Costas said.

The chief officer motioned Macalister over to the port

bridge wing, and they both trained their binoculars astern. Macalister came back in and spoke to the helmsman. 'What's our distance to the island now?'

'Just under thirteen nautical miles.'

'That's the vessel following us,' Macalister said, turning to Jack and Costas. 'They're bearing down fast, trying to get within range before we reach the territorial limit.' He pressed the alarm beside the helm and spoke into the microphone. 'This is the captain. Actions stations. I repeat, action stations.' He took the radio transceiver that was handed to him by the Chief Officer, listened intently and then turned again to Jack. 'I'm going to drop you close in and then get back out to sea again to draw our pursuer away. I've just had word that a Portuguese Navy frigate and patrol vessel are on their way, but they are at least four hours out and will not engage unless there is a clear and present danger. Until they arrive, we're on our own. It is time for you and Costas to go below and kit up.'

CHAPTER 23

An hour later Jack stood in *Seaquest*'s internal docking bay with his e-suit pulled up around his waist, the suspender straps holding it over his shoulders. Beneath the suit he was wearing lightweight boots, hiking trousers and a fleece, with a radio receiver and a compact tool kit strapped to his thighs. He released the magazine from his 9 mm Beretta, pulled back the slide to check that the chamber was empty and snapped it forward again, replaced the magazine and slotted the pistol into the shoulder holster beside a spare magazine. He watched as Costas did the same and then they both put their arms into their suits and their heads through the neck rings, the two crewmen who were helping them zipping them shut over the shoulders and locking the helmets in place.

'We're not the only ones who are armed,' Costas said. 'Little Joey has a .22 automatic with a thirty round belt integrated into his forward sensor array.'

'Another one of your tweaks with Lanowski?'

'You never known when a little extra firepower might come in handy.'

Jack flexed his fingers in the gloves that were attached to the wrist seals and pressed the controls on the side of his helmet to activate the system. The e-suits were all-environment suits with internal heating designed to be used with various breathing systems depending on the depth and conditions, housed in a streamlined backpack and with a battery-powered control module that locked into the helmet. They were expecting most of the dive to be inside the

Aquapods with the suits allowing shallow-water egress close to shore, so they had opted for compressed air over the oxygen rebreathers that they had used in the submerged mine. The two small cylinders within the backpack were filled to three times the pressure of a normal recreational scuba tank, meaning that the weight and volume of the backpack were minimised while allowing enough air for an hour at twenty metres depth. He eased himself into the backpack as the crewman held it up, connected the hose and snapped shut the visor, activating the internal readout that showed pressure in the air tanks, depth, external and suit temperature and his heart and breathing rate, with the option of a head up virtual display of the immediate surroundings created by a scanner on the helmet for low visibility conditions. He pressed the intercom control on the side of the helmet and turned to Costas. 'Buddy check?'

Costas' voice crackled over the intercom. 'Cylinders full, all systems functional. Breakfast eaten and coffee drunk.'

'Jack to bridge, are you reading me?'

'Loud and clear. You're good to egress in five minutes. We've just activated the dynamic positioning system to give the ship maximum stability.'

Jack opened his visor and Costas did the same. They reached down to check their fins, which were retracted around their calves ready to be deployed, and then walked over to the open cockpits of the Aquapods, which were suspended side-by-side in the docking bay. The Aquapods were sleek submersibles, the newest configuration of a tried and trusted design first deployed in the search for Atlantis, with a water-jet system that allowed close manoeuvrability but could also propel them at nearly ten knots, as well as a pressurised internal atmosphere and an ejector seat like that of a fighter jet in the event that they needed a quick exit underwater.

They did a quick walk-around to inspect the exterior surfaces, knowing that the crew chief would already have done so but following standard procedure for double-checking, and then climbed on to the overhead gantry above the Aquapods and lowered themselves into the cockpits. The seats were moulded to fit the e-suit backpacks and they strapped themselves in. The display monitor in front of Jack flashed up and he checked that everything was functioning correctly, testing the waterjet unit and hearing the hum of the electric motor. The Aquapods were operated like aircraft, with a control stick, pedals and a throttle lever, but with a computerised autopilot that could take them to a pre-set destination while making real-time adjustments and using a 360-degree scanner to avoid obstacles. He tested the control stick and then looked up at the crew chief. 'What's the latest on the sea conditions?'

'It's slack water but the flood is beginning,' she said. 'It's a new moon with high spring tides, meaning a tidal range of about four metres. I've programmed in the GPS position for your destination which means you can fly on autopilot. You'll be dropping deep to avoid the worst of the currents near the surface.' A green light lit up on the gantry and an alarm sounded. 'Okay. That's your cue from the bridge. Good luck.'

Jack heard the throb on the deck above them of the helicopter taking off, feeling the vibrations through the ship and knowing it was Ben and his team heading towards the island. He gave a thumbs-up to the crew chief, snapped his e-suit visor shut and lowered the canopy on the Aquapod, seeing Costas do the same. The screen readout showed that the seal was successful and the atmosphere pressurised to ambient. The crew chief flipped open a cover beside the gantry and pulled down a handle. There was a rumble as the doors opened in the hull below them and the water rose up, a bubbling foment that settled below the level of the gantry where it was held back by the air pressure in the docking bay. He activated the autopilot and looked across to Costas. 'Good to go?'

'Good to go.'

Jack gave another thumbs-up and the crew chief pressed the red control above the handle in the panel. The gantry released the two Aquapods simultaneously, and for a few seconds they pitched and rolled on the surface of the water. Then the autopilots took over, expelling air from the ballast tanks in a hiss of bubbles and white water that seemed to envelop them. When it cleared Jack was in the open water below *Seaquest* plummeting into the depths, feeling the current take him as the Aquapods came side-by-side to face it head-on. Within a few seconds the silhouette of *Seaquest* was no more than a black smudge on the surface and then he lost sight of it completely, seeing only the dim light above and the gloom in the water around him. They continued dropping until the autopilot levelled them off at 200 metres depth. They were in the ocean twilight zone, the sunlight almost gone, and all that Jack could see was the glow from their instrument panels and the occasional flash of bioluminescence in the darkness below. He overrode the autopilot and put the Aquapod in stationary mode, seeing that Costas had done the same. 'Everything OK?' he said.

'Roger that.'

A robotic face appeared beside Costas, its electronic eyes close to the canopy and looking around, blinking. 'Little Joey looks a little freaked out,' Jack said.

'He likes to swim free. Not to be confined.'

'Hopefully he'll get his chance soon.'

'Have you seen the depth below us? For a moment back then I thought we were on a one-way ride into the abyss.'

Jack looked at the bathymetric display: below them it was 2,294 metres to the seabed. It was unnerving being over such depths, knowing that they could plummet for over two kilometres in pitch darkness and still not see the bottom. A movement in the water made him push the control stick sideways, and he saw a flash of silver. 'Switch on your headlamps, low beam,' Costas said. 'We don't want to spook them with too much light, but I think we're not alone.'

They switched on their lights and an extraordinary scene came into view. All around them was a school of marlins, cobalt-blue on top and silvery white below, with prominent dorsal fins and long spear-shaped upper jaws. They were stationary in the water facing in the same direction as the Aquapods but swimming hard to hold their positions against the current. The marlin above Jack seemed almost as large as his Aquapod, but it was not as large as the tiger shark that had taken up position immediately below. Other sharks were visible among the marlins, coming in and out of the darkness. They seemed to have joined a great curtain of predators suspended at mid-depth, waiting for what they knew must come their way in the smaller fish that would be swept down by the current and seek their own food in the nutrient-rich waters below.

'No wonder Little Joey was terrified,' Jack said. 'He could see what we couldn't.'

The shark below Jack lunged at a small fish that seemed to come tumbling out of the darkness ahead, snapping is jaws and swallowing it whole, and then resumed its place between the Aquapods. 'We seem to have become part of the food chain,' Costas said. 'Fortunately, at the top end of it, though I'm not sure those tigers would think so if we were outside the Aquapods.'

'I'm activating my autopilot again,' Jack said. 'We need to press on.'

'Roger that.'

The hum of the waterjets increased and they moved forward. Jack switched on the virtual reality display and could see why the marlins and sharks had been in that position. They were only about two hundred metres to the left of the canyon wall that led up to the shore of the island. The fish were like a net extending from the wall out to sea at exactly the point where the display showed the current dipping down from the surface to about 200 metres depth and then going back up again. Fish from the shallow schools would be swept down by the current down just like the one they saw, easy prey for the predators. He could also see why the autopilot had taken them to that depth and was maintaining it as they progressed forward now. It was keeping them below the worst of the current until they reached the cleft to the shoreline. He could see it now on the display, a fissure in the canyon wall at about a 45 degrees angle, with basalt forming ledges like steps that carried on up to the surface.

'You can see why fishermen would have been tempted by this place, but also its dangers,' Costas said. 'That's the greatest density of marlins I've ever seen, but the current dropping at 8 or 10 knots to 200 metres depth would be enough to drag down a net and the boat along with it.'

The canyon wall came into sight out of the gloom, their lights picking out jagged protrusions of lava that looked as if they had been formed only yesterday. They were ascending now, parallel to the wall at about a thirty-degree angle, the dark shape of the cleft just visible in front of them. At one hundred metres' depth Jack saw the first sponges and gorgonians and fans of black coral, somehow clinging to the lava just outside the current. Looking up towards daylight he saw vast schools of mackerel and amberjack, and far above that a loggerhead turtle dive down into the current, riding it out of sight along the shoreline. The visibility was stunning, almost as if they were suspended in mid-air, yet he knew that any sense of safety was an illusion, that to get from where they were now to the surface meant crossing through an eight-knot current that formed an invisible torrent in the water above and would sweep them back down into the depths in a matter of seconds.

The virtual reality display showing the slope of the canyon was progressively replaced by the actual view as their lights played along the outcrops of lava. After a few minutes the cleft appeared in front of them, a dark crack about ten metres wide that led up from the depths to the tumult of white water now visible against the shoreline some fifty metres above. 'It looks like a collapsed lava tube, split further by seismic activity,' Jack said. 'It should provide protection from the worst of the current at this depth.'

'I think we just found our U-boat,' Costas said. 'Look into the cleft directly ahead.'

Costas' Aquapod pulled round to the right so that it was facing the cleft, and Jack followed suit. He saw great sheets of twisted metal, wedged against each other and darkened with corrosion. The current was too strong for much marine growth, meaning that the entire wreck was visible from the propellor and rudder array far below to the bow casing in the shallows above, with the collapsed remains of the conning tower and the forward deck gun directly beneath them. 'Switching to manual,' Costas said. 'I'm dropping down to be sure of its identity.'

Jack did the same, feeling the jolt as he took over the control stick and the current pushed the Aquapod sideways. He pushed the throttle lever with his left hand, expelled air from the ballast tanks and pressed the right pedal to tilt the Aquapod to starboard, bringing it round just above Costas and pushing the control stick forward to pitch it towards the wreckage. Costas switched to full beam and panned his lights along the casing, revealing vivid yellows and reds where the metal had rusted and was covered in tubeworms and barnacles. 'It's definitely a Type IXB, consistent with U-182,' he said. 'I can see the 10.5 cm gun, two 2 cm guns aft of the tower, the three Daimler-Benz diesels where the stern has opened up and the four torpedo tubes where the bow has sheared off. There's a lot of damage consistent with depth charge explosions, not only from the USS *Mackenzie* in the action that was thought to have sunk her but also from a B-24 Liberator that apparently attacked few hours before. It's amazing that it managed to limp this far. One of the propellors is missing, presumably having been destroyed in the attack. It looks as if the captain tried to ram it into the inlet above but it twisted round with the current, breaking off just behind the torpedo room and then being caught in the cleft as it slipped into the canyon. It might still be pretty unstable.'

'I can see something unusual through the floor of the torpedo room,' Jack said. 'It's angular in shape, not like the basalt.'

Costas slowly descended into the gap where the bow had sheared off. 'Some tight manoeuvring needed,' he said. 'I'm worried about the waterjets dislodging any of the wreckage. It could set off a chain reaction and the whole thing could slide down the slope into the abyss, taking me with it.'

'We've identified the U-boat, so you don't need to go in there.'

'You're going to want to see this, Jack.'

'What is it?'

'What you just spotted. The U-boat isn't the only wreck in this cleft.'

Jack eased his Aquapod into the space beside Costas. A tangle of wiring and panels lay ahead, shrouding the torpedo tubes. The propellor of one of the torpedoes was only inches from his forward light array, and he pulled back slightly on the stick to avoid bumping into it. He tilted forward and then the object he had seen was in his beam only a few metres away. He stared at it, stunned. 'Incredible,' he said. 'It's Egyptian. Ancient Egyptian.'

'It looks like the same black stone as the plaque in the desert, the one attached to that pillar,' Costas said. 'You can see the hieroglyphics clearly. I'm scanning and photographing it now.'

Jack's mind was racing. The object was carved from a single block of stone shaped like a seat, with hieroglyphs on the back surface. In front of the hieroglyphs was a small sculpture in the round of a woman, her arms outstretched and her head surmounted by bull's horns encompassing a solar disk. She was stepping on a high relief carving of a crocodile, its mouth agape and staring outwards. 'It's a shrine, a shipboard shrine,' he said. 'And that's Isis, subduing the crocodile. I can see the royal cartouche of Nefertiti in the hieroglyphs.'

'Akhenaten's wife, who was also the High Priestess of Isis.'

'That's what Maurice believes.'

'The we've hit paydirt.' Costas panned his beam under the U-boat plating where the seabed at the base of the cleft was visible. 'I can see a stone anchor, just like one of those on the Bronze Age wreck we excavated in the Aegean. And there's a white marble container like one of those canopic jars from the Tomb of Tutankhamun. And you can see the edge of an oxhide copper ingot and what looks like a bronze dagger blade.'

'There's a shipwreck here, and it's ancient Egyptian,' Jack said. 'Incredible.'

'Does that mean that what we're looking for, the orichalcum, is under this somewhere? Removing any of the plating to search for it could bring the U-boat wreck down around us.'

'James Gillespie said he saw hieroglyphs on the wall of the cavern in 1943. They can only have been inscribed by survivors of this Bronze Age wreck, trapped there just as Gillespie and the U-boat captain Clausen were three thousand years later. Those Bronze Age survivors would have done everything they could to bring ashore their precious cargo. That's where we need to be looking.'

'Roger that. And the tide's really beginning to flood now. We need to get in there before the surge is too great.'

'Autopilot or manual?'

'Manual. This is one place where human reactions might be the safer option. We need to be able to respond to the current in ways that the computer might see as illogical. We may not get a second chance as we'll have to do this at full throttle and that will be a big drain on the batteries. I'll go first.'

They rose above the wreckage until Jack felt the tug of the current ripping along parallel to the cliff face. Above him an explosion of white water churned up the surface as if he were looking up at a breaking surf. The current lay between them and their objective and would take them on a rollercoaster ride into the abyss if they did not get the next move right. Costas dropped down a few metres, gunned his waterjets so that the wake was visible corkscrewing behind him and drove as far as he could towards the left side of the cleft. He suddenly shot upwards, turned around until he was nearly facing Jack and then for a few seconds rode the current at terrifying speed, before veering left and disappearing behind the protrusion of basalt that marked the right side of the cleft and the entrance to the inlet. A few moments later his voice came over the intercom. 'As Françoise would say, that was sketchy as hell. The illogical bit is keeping your waterjet at full power while riding the current. You'll need it to get into the cavern, using the current like a slingshot.'

Jack took a deep breath, pushed the control stick forward to drop below the level of the current and increased the throttle to maximum, watching the battery percentage drop at an alarming rate as he gunned the Aquapod forward. He passed over the bow of the U-boat, glanced to his right and saw the hazy yellow of Costas' Aquapod in the dark recess of the inlet, the image blurred by the current that was rushing between them. A few metres further and he would be able to turn into the current, a seemingly suicidal move but one that he had just seen work. As he braced himself for the turn he felt a jolt and the Aquapod dropped five metres, scraping over the top of the U-boat. In that split-second he realised that he had been caught in a wobble in the current, something that would make it difficult for him to repeat Costas' manoeuvre. With the current dipping down and swerving from side to side the cleft no longer provided protection. He felt the Aquapod being driven backwards, the current tilting it up and creating a much larger surface area for the water to push against.

He jammed the control stick forward as far as it would go to depress the elevators at the back of the Aquapod and activated the waterjet that fired directly below in the hope of raising the stern and righting it. The additional waterjet put more stress on the battery, and he watched the percentage readout go into the red. From being seconds away from joining Costas in the relative safety of the inlet he was now in the worst possible situation. The current had driven him back to their start point beside the canyon wall and he would not have enough power to repeat the attempt. He had to make a snap decision. 'I can't make it,' he said. 'I'm ejecting.'

'Can you hold position against the cliff face?' Costas said.

'The battery's down to five percent. It's giving me four minutes.'

'I'm going to deploy my anchor line so that the current takes it round to your position, and use that to try to reel you in. I've wedged my Aquapod into a fissure and set the automated throttle control to compensate for the drag from the anchor. But there isn't enough power to pull in your Aquapod in a ten-knot current once your battery dies, so you are going to have to pop your canopy and get hold of the line yourself as you eject. Whatever you do, don't attach the line to your Aquapod. It will just pull mine out and we'll both be on that one-way ride into the abyss.'

Jack felt another surge and shifted the waterjet power to the port side just in time, bringing the Aquapod back against the canyon wall facing the current. A second's hesitation and the Aquapod would have spun out of control and he would have had no way of recovering. The display was showing only two minutes of power left, dropping faster than real time. When the power went he knew it would be sudden and that would be it. 'Any time now would be good,' he said. 'I've got less than a minute left.'

A line with a small grapnel anchor appeared in front of him, swaying violently to and fro in the current and nearly smashing into the nose cowling. He knew that he was going to have to grab the anchor the instant after he opened the canopy and let go of the steering. 'Another metre,' he said. 'No more.'

'OK,' Costas said. 'My own battery is almost out of juice too.'

'Ejecting now.' Jack snapped down the visor on his e-suit helmet and hit the switch on the side to activate it. The internal display lit up and he felt the rush of air into the system from the rear-mounted cylinders. He braced himself and pulled the red eject handle beside his seat. The cockpit filled with a rush of water and then the canopy tore off, spinning away behind. The power of the current pinned him back in the seat, and he crouched forward as far as he could behind the instrument panel. With his left hand holding the control stick he reached up blindly with his right hand for the anchor. Several times he nearly had it but then it swung violently away. He could see the Aquapod power indicator flashing red and the battery time at zero. He had only seconds left.

Everything happened at once. The anchor caught on the rim of the cockpit and held fast just as the power display went blank and the waterjet ceased. He heaved the control stick sideways to bring the Aquapod at an angle to the current in an attempt to dislodge the anchor. He let go of the stick and grasped the two arms of the anchor that were sticking up over the rim, squatted on the seat and then pushed off until he was caught in the current, holding on at full stretch with the Aquapod beneath him. The current was terrifying, ripping past him like a storm-force wind, and he knew he could only hang on for a few seconds. The anchor slipped sideways, still caught under the rim, and then slid further along and wedged in the corner of the cockpit.

For a horrifying moment his world stood still, the anchor just outside his visor, his fingers slipping on the grapnel and his breathing ragged as he put all of his strength into his hands. And then with a sudden tearing sound he was free, flying in the current at the end of the line, the Aquapod tumbling away behind him into the depths. He could feel the line being ratcheted forward and he continued to hold on with all of his strength. After a few moments he rounded the corner into the inlet and saw Costas' Aquapod, the waterjets on maximum as the winch drew him out of the current and the line went slack. He cautiously moved one hand from the anchor and tapped the back of his calves to release his fins, allowing him to swim forward until he was in front of Costas' canopy, and then he let go of the grapnel completely and pressed the intercom on the side of his helmet. 'Thanks. That was close.'

'What are friends for.' Costas snapped down the visor of his e-suit and a few seconds later his canopy opened and he swam out, coming up level with Jack. 'I've lost comms with *Seaquest*. Hopefully we'll be able to establish them again once we get ashore.'

'But you've got Little Joey.'

'Right behind me.' Costas turned back and activated a control on the panel on his wrist. Little Joey came swimming up from the Aquapod cockpit, blinked at Jack and then went forward, hovering in mid-water above the cleft. Costas quickly pulled out a thin tether line from the console on his wrist and attached it to a hook on Little Joey's back. 'We don't want him taking a look back round the corner into that current, do we?'

'No, we do not,' Jack said. The adrenaline was still coursing through him, and he felt the exaltation of survival and the excitement of what might lie ahead. He glanced back into the abyss, seeing the bow of the U-boat and the flashes of silver in the gloom far below, and then he looked into the recess ahead of them. 'OK. Let's move.'

CHAPTER 24

Jack swam up beside Costas into the inlet and the entrance to a large cavern beyond. After the tumult of the sea outside the inlet was a limpid backwater, full of fragments of seaweed and small jellyfish that had somehow escaped the current. He floated just underwater, watching the sunlight shine through the jellyfish and sparkle on the surface, feeling his breathing and his heart rate lower after his exertion only a few minutes earlier in the very different world outside, a place of terrifying currents and abyssal depths. It was as if having broken through the current they had entered an enchanted isle, and yet he knew that it was an illusion, that this vivid community of life and colour would be swept inshore with the rising tide and pummelled against the rocks, a process that had gone on twice a day with the tide since time immemorial and in which he and Costas were briefly a part.

They surfaced at the same time, pulling themselves out over the smooth volcanic boulders that lay at the entrance and coming to rest on a flat shelf beside the cavern wall about two metres above the level of the sea. They unlocked and snapped open their visors, and Jack enjoyed his first breath of sea air in this place, cold and salty after the air from his cylinders. He could hear the birds now, crying as they swept low over the sea in search of small fish and flying in and out of their burrows in the cliffs, a raucous cacophony with the crash of the sea as a backdrop. 'Cory's shearwaters,' he said, raising his voice against the noise. '*Calonectris borealis*. They're the main reason the islands were made into a nature reserve. They're very rare and overfishing was depleting their main food source.'

Little Joey came out of the water, extended his six articulated legs and began walking carefully over the rocks towards Costas, who still held him on the leash. He stood on the platform beside Jack and raised himself on his forelegs beside the cliff face, the protective hoods over his eyes completely retracted. A few inches away were the equally wide-open eyes of a gecko, upside-down on the rock with its head extended. Its tongue flickered in and out, and Little Joey recoiled, cocked his head and stared again. 'I think he's met his match,' Jack said.

'Or he's in love,' Costas said.

'Don't look to the left of the gecko behind the rock.'

'What is it?'

'Fascinating,' Jack said, peering closely. 'These are only supposed to be found on the Ilhas Desertas. They're critically endangered, so this is an exciting discovery.'

'Oh no. I'm not looking.'

'I hadn't realised that they grew this big. It's an excellent example of island gigantism. Darwin would have loved it. *Hogna ingens*, the Desertas wolf spider.'

A spider the size of Jack's hand with black and white legs and a large thorax crawled into view and stopped beside the gecko. Little Joey made a whimpering noise and jumped back, followed by Costas. 'This place just got a whole lot worse,' he said. 'I'm putting my visor back up.'

'It's only mildly venomous,' Jack said. 'Nothing to worry about.'

'A famous Jack Howard catch phrase.'

'The tide's coming in and we need to get to the back of this cavern before it's on top of us,' Jack said. 'We'd never get out again in the surge. And Macalister is certain that our pursuers have already put a helicopter down on the island. We need to move now.'

They made their way into the cavern, with Little Joey clambering over the rocks beside them. The entrance was at least twenty metres high, and above that the cliff towered for a further fifty metres or more. The rocks at the entrance to the inlet blocked off the view of the sea beyond, and without comms there was no way of knowing whether *Seaquest* had made it back offshore before coming into contact with their pursuer. The Portuguese navy were still at least two hours away and until their arrival they were on their own. Two hours was a long time with the helicopter from the other ship having already landed somewhere on the plateau above, and Jack prayed that whatever confrontation might be happening with Ben's security team was going in their favour.

The barnacles on the rocks gave a good grip until they reached high water mark, where the guano from the shearwaters made the rocks slippery and treacherous. After about twenty metres they passed beyond the burrows and perches of the birds on the rock face above and the boulders became easier to traverse. The cavern narrowed, and in the gloom ahead they could see that it split into two smaller caves, both extending further than they could see. 'We need to choose the correct one to look for the hieroglyphs,' Jack said. 'With the tide coming in we may not have the chance to backtrack and look at the other one if we reach a dead-end.'

'This is where Little Joey comes in,' Costas said. He opened the cowling on Little Joey's back and four miniature arms with rotor blades folded out. He unhooked the leash, retracted the line and opened up a remote-control console on his wrist. The rotors began whirring and Little Joey took off, hovering in front of them. 'Sea, land and air,' he said. 'He's our first all-environment drone. This is what I've been working on over the past few weeks.'

Little Joey rose, tilted and flew ahead, the beams from his forward array lighting up the boulders on the floor of the cavern and the walls on either side. As well as a video image the screen on Costas' remote control showed a 3-D model of the cavern as Little Joey progressively mapped it using a multibeam scanner, with enough detail to reveal any features that might be man-made. It reached the point where the cavern split into two caves and Costas chose the right one, and then took his thumbs off the controls. 'Now that he knows which way to go, it's hands-off,' he said. 'He'll stop when he can go no further and then turn back to go into the other cave.'

A few minutes later the scan was complete, showing the right-hand cave ending about a hundred metres beyond. Little Joey came whirring back in front of them and turned into the passageway to the left, stopping in mid-air where a rocky platform came into view on the screen with a section of sheer wall abutting it. Costas zoomed in using the remote and they could see crude carvings in the wall, the details indiscernible but clearly man-made. Just beyond the platform the floor of the cave dropped below sea level and they could see a pool of water extending into a tunnel. 'Bingo,' Costas said. 'That platform must be where Gillespie hauled himself out and made his final radio call. All of that's going to be under several metres of water as the tide rises. We need to get in there pronto.'

They scrambled over the boulders and made their way to where Little Joey was hovering over the symbols in the rock. Jack tried to imagine Gillespie making his final radio transmission, having dragged Clausen's body into the sea and then lying down to die himself. There was no evidence left of their plight, Gillespie's body having presumably been swept away by the tide and nothing remaining to show how they had eked out their final few days. But the symbols carved in the rock by other shipwreck survivors more than three thousand years earlier were still there to be seen, the sharp edges softened by mineral formation but the hieroglyphs clearly visible. 'They're covered in a thin layer of calcium carbonate,' Costas said. 'It shows that the platform was above the high-water mark for a long time after those who carved this were here.'

'I checked the historical sea levels while we were on *Seaquest*,' Jack said. 'The mean sea level in the late second millennium BC in these islands was about six metres lower than it is now.'

He could make out hieroglyphs showing the ripple of water, the reed, the half-moon shape and the ibis, symbols familiar from the pillar in the desert and the shrine they had just seen below the U-boat. He panned his head torch beam over the markings and angled it to the left to enhance the shadows. 'The first cluster is a personal name, possibly Iufenisis, 'He who is belonging to Isis,' he said. 'The next symbol is that of the Sem priests, those responsible for embalming and mummifying. Then there are the first four hieroglyphs of the name Nefertiti, just like that shrine in the wreck, but followed by an image of Isis rather than the usual Aten symbols. And then there's the Atlantis symbol at the end.'

'What does it mean?'

'Iufenisis, Sem priest to Nefertiti, High Priestess of Isis, offers the Atlantis object in this place,' Jack said. 'Iufenisis must have been a survivor of the shipwreck, and this is a waymarker, telling any who might be sent by the priests of Isis to recover the treasure that it's here in this cavern.'

'I think it's more than just a waymarker,' Costas said, shining his headlamp at a point where the platform abutted the cavern wall. 'I think something went on here, a ritual. There's a flint knife embedded in the rock, sealed over by calcium carbonate that must have dripped from the ceiling.'

Jack dropped to his knees and stared at the object. 'Incredible. I can see the ripples in the flint where it's been pressure-flaked. It's Egyptian, of the predynastic period.'

'Exactly like the photo you showed of the knife you found with Jeremy and Marco in the Temple of Isis in Rome.'

'On the table that Marco thinks was designed for human sacrifice.'

'You mean mummification alive,' Costas said. 'The akhet-re. Something about breathing new life into Isis after the death of Osiris. What they did to Akhenaten.'

'What his wife arranged to have done to him,' Jack said. 'Nefertiti, High Priestess of Isis, whose allegiance to the goddess was greater than to the Aten or her husband.'

'Do you think that's what went on here?'

'If they were about to conceal something that they saw as a threat to the power of their goddess, then some kind of propitiatory offering would be expected. And Maurice is convinced that those knives were used for mummification and sacrifice.'

'I'm going to move off this platform,' Costas said. 'It's giving me a bad feeling.'

'That cave entrance where Little Joey is hovering is where we need to go.'

'I'm sending him down it now for a recce,' Costas said, activating the remote control. 'The tide still hasn't inundated it so he should be able to skim along the surface of the water.'

They watched as Little Joey dipped into the tunnel and disappeared, and they clambered after it to the pool of water at the entrance. 'Do you think Gillespie could have made it this far?' Jack said.

'I doubt whether he made it beyond the platform and the hieroglyphics,' Costas said. 'He and Clausen hadn't eaten or drunk anything in days and from the sound of his last communication he was very close to the end. And beyond here the tunnel is below mean low water.'

'But the Egyptian survivors could have got through in the second millennium BC.'

'With the sea level lower back then, the tunnel would normally have been accessible except in heavy seas.'

'If we go in now, we may have to wait inside until the tide drops before we're able to get out again,' Jack said. 'The surge at high water will probably be too great to swim against. We're going to have to take our chances.'

Costas looked at the screen on the remote control. 'OK. Little Joey has got through. There's some kind of chamber at the other end. I'm following him in.'

'I'll be right behind you.'

Costas closed the screen, flipped down his helmet visor

and activated his breathing system. He slipped into the pool and went head-first into the tunnel, kicking hard and pulling himself out of sight. With the rising tide what had been a separate pool was becoming continuous with the ocean, and Jack could already feel the swell coming in and out. He closed his visor, put his head torch on maximum and dropped underwater. Like Costas he kept his fins retracted, knowing that he would need to have his feet free to wedge them against the side walls when the surge came through. He pulled himself forward, waited for the swell and let it push him a further five metres or so. He knew that it would get stronger each time and that he would have to brace himself against the return of the surge down the tunnel if he were to have any hope of getting forward. About ten metres in the width constricted, the jagged protrusions of basalt catching his suit on either side. The constriction would increase the strength of the surge and turn the tunnel into a potential death trap, a place impossible to get out of where each rush of water would send him crashing against the rock on either side.

He switched off his beam in order to see the smudge of light ahead from Costas, guessing that he had made it through. He had no choice but continue following him. If he turned back and made it out they might be cut off from each other for hours until the tide dropped again. He jammed his legs against the sides of the tunnel, waiting for the next surge, and launched himself forward, pulling himself along the rock to get as far ahead as he could get before the surge returned. When he felt the water slacken he wedged himself behind an outcrop and waited. The return was like a wall of water bearing down on him, and he felt his hold slip just as it started to slow down. He waited for the next surge and rode it as far as he could, knowing that he probably had only one more chance before the return became too strong. He could see a widening ahead, pulled himself along the rocks towards it and found another place to brace himself, but this time the return was considerably reduced. He swam forward again with the next surge, saw the reflection of Costas' light in the water and surfaced in a cavern beside him, holding himself against the rock as the surge went up the boulders ahead of them and came back down again. Costas reached out to give him a hand. 'Okay?'

'Piece of cake,' Jack said, pulling himself up on to a rock and kneeling down to catch his breath. 'We're not getting out that way on this tide.'

'There may be another exit. Look to the left.'

Jack switched his head torch back on, hit the control on the side of his helmet and slid the locking mechanism across the front, and Costas did the same. As his visor sprang up he was assailed by the noise of the sea, rushing up and down the rocks and booming in the back of the cavern, and by the smell and taste of the air. He could see where a fissure in the side of the chamber went up at about a 45-degree angle, and at the top there was a hint of daylight. 'I reckon we could get up that,' Costas said, his voice raised against the noise. 'It might get us out of here and allow us to make contact with Ben and his team as well as with *Seaquest*.'

Jack turned towards the rear of the cavern. He had a sudden flashback to their exploration of Atlantis fifteen years earlier, to diving inside the submerged volcano to the Holy of Holies, the inner sanctum where the priests had performed their final rites before going down to the shoreline and fleeing the flood in boats such as the one they had seen in Egypt only a few days before. Something had been missing in the inner sanctum, something that had been on a pedestal and that he and Costas may have seen under the pyramid in Egypt, a key to a legacy of Atlantis that they might be about to find all these years later at the very edge of the ancient world. He felt a strange light-headedness, as if he were elevated above the scene watching Costas in slow motion, unable for a moment to believe that this was reality. And then he was following him to the back of the cavern, to a place where the basalt was less jagged and more bulbous, where they dropped to their knees beside each other in front of a polished wall of basalt about a metre across. In the centre was a rectangular crack, barely discernible, where a cavity had been cut into the rock and then lidded over with a slab of black rock of different origin, similar to the Egyptian stone from which the plaque in the desert and the shrine on the wreck had been made.

In the centre was a concave recess about a hand's width across filled with a mossy growth. He reached in and carefully picked it away, scraping out some deeper cuttings he could feel at the base of the recess. Costas activated the remote control on his wrist and Little Joey lifted off and hovered in close, a miniature nozzle extending from his forward array that he inserted into the recess and used to blow away the remaining debris with a high-pressure air jet. He backed off and settled on the rock between them, and Jack stared at the shape in the recess, stunned. It was the Atlantis symbol, but in reverse. 'I've seen that exact shape and size before,' he said. 'It's the reverse of the jewel that we saw beneath the pyramid, that Maurice and Aysha are hunting for now. And that's not a lid over a recess. It's the front of a stone box slotted into the wall, a box that they must have brought here all the way from Egypt.'

'It's amazing that they managed to cut that recess into the basalt.'

'They were Egyptians, remember. They knew how to work in stone. And if they managed to use that fissure to get out of the cavern to the surface, they could have hunted and foraged for food on the island. A few of them could have survived here for weeks, even months, enough time to make sure that they had concealed their precious cargo properly.'

'You think this is it?'

'I think the jewel is the key to getting the box open. Now I know why Nefertiti and her priests never retrieved the jewel from the tomb of Akhenaten. It was in a place where they could never have expected anyone to find it, and yet the priests would have known where it was should they have needed it. And perhaps it was to taunt Akhenaten, knowing that he would still have been alive for a few hours after the akhet-re, conscious enough to know that he was clasping an image not of his beloved Aten but of something much older whose concealment in his tomb represented the ultimate victory of the old order over his new religion.'

'It's time we got to the surface and made contact with *Seaquest*. We need to see whether Maurice and Aysha have found what we need.'

Jack stared at the carving for a few moments longer, the noise of the water rising and falling over the rocks filling his ears. Little Joey suddenly flashed red and became agitated, bouncing up and down on his legs. Jack heard the unmistakeable click of a pistol being cocked behind his right ear. 'Doctor Howard,' a man's voice said, heavily accented. 'And his sidekick. It seems you have found what we want. Don't move.'

CHAPTER 25

Jack remained stock-still, staring at the polished rock face. They had been alert to possible danger with their Berettas accessible but had not heard anyone approaching because of the noise of the sea in the cavern, and they had been focussed on the carving in the wall. They had guessed that others would be on the island from Macalister having tracked the helicopter, and Jack now realised that the fissure to the surface was a mixed blessing, allowing them an escape route from the cavern but also a place where anyone exploring from above could get down. The man spoke again, his voice guttural and heavily accented. 'Put your hands behind your heads, get up and turn around, slowly.' They both did as instructed, turning towards each other and then facing the man. He was heavyset with a shaved head and tattoos, wearing combat fatigues smeared with mud from his climb down and carrying an AK-12 on a sling as well as the pistol. Behind him were two other men spaced out in front of the pool, their legs apart and also carrying rifles.

As he turned Jack saw that Costas still had the remote for Little Joey open and activated on his wrist. Jack caught his eye and glanced at it, knowing that Costas would be reading his thoughts. Lanowski had programmed Little Joey with a reactive defensive posture, meaning that he would respond to anyone shooting at him, tracking incoming rounds and using his thermal and UV sensors to lock in on the aggressor. He could react faster than a human, the response triggered by rounds already incoming. The mode included a command for

Little Joey to jump sideways to avoid immediate danger and also to provoke the aggressor in order to deflect attention towards him. The programme had been designed to defend whoever might be operating him, and that was what they needed right now.

With a whirr Little Joey took off and flew to the rear of the cavern, flashing red and facing the men. The distraction was enough for the man with the pistol to let down his guard, allowing Costas to kick him and send the pistol clattering to the ground. One of the other men fired a burst at Little Joey, hitting his rotors and sending him spinning away but not before he had fired in return, hitting both men and sending them sprawling onto the rocks. Costas pulled out his Beretta and pointed it at the man in front of them as he staggered backwards. 'Your men shot my drone,' he said, aiming at the man's chest and then his legs. 'And I am not a sidekick.' There was a deafening crack and the man fell, blood welling up from one thigh. He gasped in pain and clutched the wound, blood oozing out between his fingers as he tried to staunch the flow. Costas reached into his tool belt and tossed him a roll of combat gauze and a sachet of clotting powder. 'Deal with it now or you'll bleed out. I take it you know what to do.'

The man ripped open the sachet, poured the powder into the wound and then wrapped the gauze tightly around, his face contorted with pain. Costas kicked him over, glanced up to make sure that Jack had his Beretta trained on the man and ziplocked his wrists behind his back as well as his ankles. 'We'll send someone to get you once we've dealt with any friends you might have on the island.'

'You won't get far,' the man said, his voice rasping. 'Our vessel is about to take out *Seaquest*. And your security team on the island can't do anything. We have a hostage. Give yourselves up now and he will be released.'

Costas squatted down beside him. 'And who would that be?'

'I will say nothing more.'

'No, you won't.' Costas tore off a strip of duct tape from a small roll and slapped it over the man's mouth. He struggled and writhed on the ground, and Costas stood up beside Jack. They stripped off their e-suits, adjusted their webbing pouches and checked the magazines in their Berettas. 'Have you got your backup radio receiver?' Jack said.

Costas tapped the pouch in front of his left shoulder. 'It should allow us to contact Macalister once we get to the surface.'

'A hostage,' Jack said. 'One of Ben's team?'

'There's another possibility.'

'You mean Jeremy.'

Jack gave him a grim look. 'Nobody had heard from him for almost forty-eight hours. I shouldn't have left him in Rome right under Rauscher's nose.'

'If they have him, it may have stopped them from making an aggressive move until now. They will want to use him as a bargaining chip. They won't know that a Portuguese naval force is nearly within range, about *Seaquest*'s latest defensive upgrade or that the first thing Ben would have done on arriving on the island would have been to deploy several of his team as snipers who will still be in position even if there is a standoff with a hostage.'

'Let's hope so,' Jack said. 'Are we taking Little Joey?'

'I think he's doing a good enough job where he is.' Jack glanced back into the recess of the cavern where Little Joey had been shot down. The drone had clambered up on to a rock, his damaged rotor trailing behind him, and was sitting motionless with his eyes staring at the man on the ground, the barrel of the .22 aimed at him. The only sign of life was a flashing red light on the forward array, but it was enough. 'Nobody messes with my drone,' Costas said to the figure on the ground. 'Try to make a move after we've gone and you're a dead man.'

Jack glanced at the crumpled forms of the bodies beside the pool. 'Mercenaries,' Costas said, following his gaze. 'The

H160M helicopter that *Seaquest* tracked going towards the island can accommodate up to ten fully equipped troops, so there could be at least five more on the island.'

They went over to the fissure and began to make their way towards the surface, scrambling over ledges and pulling themselves up cracks in the rock. The fissure had formed as the lava cooled when the island was an active volcano, and the basalt had been smoothed by thousands of years of rainwater pouring down from above. After about ten minutes they could see the sky clearly through the opening. The final section was a nearly vertical pitch with a rope dangling down from above, evidently left by the men they had encountered below. Costas tested it and then used it for support as he climbed up a series of ledges on one side, with Jack following him. At the top they came out on one side of a grassy knoll, the rock forming the fissure entrance concealing them from the main part of the island and the cliff edge overlooking the sea just a few metres away.

Jack lay back for a moment on the grass, catching his breath and taking stock of the situation. Above them the edge of the cyclonic system that had dogged *Seaquest* was rolling away to the east, the dark clouds forked by distant lightning but with clear skies and bright sunlight in the west. With the front receding the wind had dropped off almost completely, but the air was filled with the noise of the crashing sea and the cries of the shearwaters that were wheeling and diving over the cliffs beside them. The top of the island was a plateau less than a kilometre across, barren of trees and affording little cover except for a few rocky outcrops. They had come out near one of the three summits some 150 metres above sea level, with a view over most of the island but not over a low-lying area to the south where the ranger station was located, the only structure on the island. As there were no helicopters to be seen he guessed that the H160M and the Lynx from *Seaquest* must have landed there and that would be where the others would be.

The island was similar in flora to the western Sahara but fed by the Gulf Stream and a waypoint for species migrating along the African and European coasts. It was a place of seeming desolation, exposed to the worst forces of nature and at the very edge of the open Atlantic, yet with an abundance of life where existence seemed distilled to its essence, where the light and the wind and the sea seemed to exclude everything else. It was also a place with barely any imprint of human activity, and yet which they knew might hold one of the greatest legacies from early civilisation that had ever been sought.

Costas took out the radio receiver and a compact monocular from his toolbelt. 'I can see how our pursuers found this fissure within only a few hours of arriving on the island and why they decided to check it out. It would be easy enough to traverse the plateau looking for possible entry points down to the sea, and they were lucky with this one. Or unlucky for them, as it turns out.' He pressed the push-to-talk button on the side of the receiver. 'Costas to *Seaquest*. Do you read me. Over.'

There was a crackling sound and Macalister's voice came back. 'We read you loud and clear. What's your status? Over.'

Costas quickly filled him in as he and Jack made their way a few metres up the slope to the highest point of the knoll, affording the clearest view over the sea to the east. *Seaquest* was only about a mile offshore, and another vessel was a similar distance away closing in on her fast. 'I've got you on visual,' Costas said, peering through the monocular. 'You've got trouble astern. Over.'

'We're on it,' Macalister replied. 'A patrol boat of the Madeira Maritime Patrol and a Vasco da Gama class frigate of the Portuguese navy are less than thirty miles away, with two Super Lynx helicopters of the Esquadrilha de Helicópteros de Marinha already in the air. Because we're within the 12-mile territorial limit they have the right to interdict, but they are standing off to await developments in case they provoke a confrontation. Our enemy must know they are there but seem pretty brazen. Something is giving them the confidence to think that they can get away with attacking us. Over.'

'The hostage must be the reason why. If it's who we think it is, we can't request assistance from the Portuguese navy until the threat to him is removed. Over.'

'Keep me up to date on that. Ben can't communicate because there's a standoff and he must have had to give up his radio. I'm not trying radio contact with his two snipers in case our enemy can track the signal and find them. Over.'

There was a sudden red flash from the attacking ship. 'You've got incoming!' Costas said.

'We've clocked it. Shutting down comms now. Out.'

Jack pulled out the monocular from his belt and watched the missile streak towards *Seaquest*, which was turning hard to port leaving a tight semi-circular wake behind her. 'Macalister is manoeuvring bows-on to reduce his profile, meaning that the radar signature from the chaff they fire will be larger and more likely to distract the missile,' Costas said. 'The chaff is the new SRBOC, the Super Rapid Bloom Offboard Countermeasures. He'll also be deploying infrared flares in case the missile is heat-seeking.'

'And using the Phalanx,' Jack said.

'That's if none of the other countermeasures work. If the Phalanx locks on target, nothing will get through that storm of tungsten. Good old-fashioned gunfire.'

They saw a puff of smoke from the foredeck of *Seaquest* and a shimmer as the chaff burst and then a few seconds later heard the bang, followed by the flash of flares igniting in front of the ship. The missile continued to streak directly towards the bridge but several hundred metres out it disintegrated in a shower of fragments, some of them bouncing off the sea and hitting the side of the hull. A few seconds later they heard the whirr of the 20mm Vulcan cannon firing 70 rounds a second. 'That's done it,' Jack said. 'A Phalanx is an unusual and expensive bit of kit for an archaeological research vessel but it just proved its worth.'

'And now for retaliation,' Costas said. '*Seaquest* still has the old 40 mm Bofors L70, with state-of-the-art gyro stabilization after the refit. The Vulcan doesn't have the range to hit them but the Bofors does.'

The heard a quick succession of bangs as the Bofors emptied its hopper of 26 rounds at the other vessel. Jack turned his monocular on it and watched the splashes as the rounds bracketed the foredeck where the missile launcher was located and then found their target, striking the deck with a mixture of armour-piercing and high-explosive rounds. A fireball rose above the ship and a cloud of black smoke and flames enveloped the bridge. Costas lowered his monocular as the report from an explosion reached them. 'That would be the other missile that was still in the launcher cooking off. According to Macalister they also have a 20mm Oerlikon but that won't have the range and anyway is on the foredeck, so is toast now. Threat eliminated.'

The radio crackled and Costas picked it up. 'It's not on the IMU secure channel, but on channel 16.' It crackled again, and a man with a familiar accent spoke. 'This is a message for Dr Howard. We have a colleague of yours on the south side of the island. If you value his life, you will come to us now.'

Jack pressed to reply, but there was no response. He looked grimly at Costas. 'That was Rauscher. I recognised his voice. We're going to have to do what he says. They must have Jeremy.'

'Rauscher won't know that we've taken out those three in the cavern.'

'He must have been waiting for radio contact from them, and then decided to try us on the open channel.'

'Let's move,' Costas said. 'The sooner we're in clear sight, the less likely they are to harm Jeremy.'

They got up and made their way across the scrub and rock from the highest point of the island towards the low plateau to the south-west. As they crested the final ridge the full extent of the plateau became visible and they could see figures clearly. They stopped and scanned ahead, trying to assess numbers. Jack could make out Rauscher, looking incongruous in city clothes, and in front of him Jeremy, with a man in camouflage behind him holding a pistol to his head. About ten metres away on the east side of the plateau Ben and the men of his security team were kneeling with their hands behind their heads and their weapons on the ground in front, and behind them were two more figures in camouflage with AK-12s trained on them. 'That's three men I can see with weapons,' he said quietly. 'Add to those the three we left down in the cavern and Rauscher and Jeremy, and that's pretty well a full complement for the HI60 helicopter.'

'I count four of our guys from the team of six, meaning the two snipers are still out of sight and in play,' Costas replied. 'There are several areas of rough ground where they could be concealed within 500 metres of the plateau, in range for their AWM rifles. At the moment they can't take out the bad guys pre-emptively without a big risk of casualties on our side. They might drop the man behind Jeremy and one other but that still leaves Rauscher and the fourth man, who could loose off a magazine into our guys kneeling in front of him before he's taken out by the next shot from a sniper. We need something to distract them, to give the snipers the extra edge of a few seconds.'

'Ben would have had no choice other than to give up when Rauscher appeared with Jeremy,' Jack said. 'But with any luck they won't know about the snipers.'

They came to within fifty metres of the group. One of the men in camouflage behind the security team aimed his rifle at them and shouted in fragmented English. 'Weapons on the ground. Slowly.'

They did as instructed and waited as Rauscher came towards them. 'Dr Howard. We meet again. You have led us to the place where the priesthood concealed the orichalcum more than three thousand years ago. Three hundred and fifty years ago others tried to find it, followers of the heretical Father Kircher, but they failed in their quest. If you do not hand over what you have found your colleague Dr Haverstock will die here and now.'

'They have nothing to lose now by killing Jeremy,' Costas said to Jack quietly. 'They could do it and turn to Ben's team and hold them to ransom in the same way. We have to be very careful what we say.'

Jack stared at the scene, his mind racing. He could tell Rauscher that their ship was disabled and the Portuguese Navy was on its way. He could tell him that 350 years ago those sent by the priests had not come to this island because Cornelissen and Porrata had selflessly led their ship to destruction on the Islas Desertas. He could tell him that he and Costas had not found the box and try to buy time that way, or that they would need the jewel to open it. But any one of those responses could destabilise an already precarious standoff, and anything confrontational could tip the balance against them. 'Tell us your terms,' he said, raising his voice against the noise of the sea. 'The safety of my people is more important to me than any artefact.'

'We will take the orichalcum and dispose of it at sea, finally ridding the world of the threat to our order. The priesthood will be secure, and you will not break us. After that we will release Dr Haverstock and he can be on his way.'

'I need to see that he is well.'

'You can approach.'

Jack advanced cautiously, Costas by his side. Jeremy looked pale and defiant but showed no obvious injuries. 'Are you alright?' Jack said.

'I'm fine,' Jeremy replied. 'I've been treated well. That is, until I was taken from Rome to the ship and we met up with this Russian with the pistol and his friends. A big mistake for Rauscher and his priesthood to hire these thugs. They have some romantic notion that they're latter-day warriors of

Horus. Rauscher is out of his depth.'

The man behind Jeremy grasped his right wrist and twisted it up, making him bend over and grimace with pain, and then pulled him back and put the gun to his head, snarling at him in Russian. Rauscher looked alarmed and held up his hand. 'Don't harm him. That was our agreement. It is my call.'

The man waved his gun towards Rauscher and then put it back behind Jeremy's head. 'You stay out of this, Father Rauscher,' he said mockingly, his voice heavily accented. 'This is our show now. Whatever these people have found here will be worth more than you've promised to pay us.'

The situation was on a knife-edge, and Jack tried to keep his cool. 'And Marco?' He said. 'Is he alright?'

'He's my student,' Rauscher said. 'He has nothing to do with this.'

'Nor does Jeremy,' Jack said. 'Let him go and take me.'

The man with the pistol snarled in Russian again and stood his ground. Jeremy was right. Rauscher was not in control of the situation. Whoever he had used to kidnap Jeremy in Rome was not here, having presumably been left on the ship. These men he had hired to come to the island with him were ruthless and brutal and would not respect a man like him. The situation was on the verge of becoming very ugly for all of them with Jeremy no longer serving any useful purpose and the rest of them suddenly expendable, not just Jeremy but also Rauscher and Jack and Costas and Ben and his men. The snipers could only be reactive to what was happening and by the time they saw shooting it would be too late. Jack looked at Jeremy, remembering what Rebecca had said to him when he had last seen her before coming out here. *Do not put him in any danger.* If anything happened to Jeremy he would not be able to live with it. This was not a situation that could be defused. Something needed to change very quickly if any of them were going to get out alive.

Costas spoke quietly to Jack without turning his head. 'Helos in the air,' he said. 'I can hear them. It must be the Portuguese Navy. Macalister will have liaised with them. They're keeping low over the water to reduce the noise. They'll be in radio contact with the snipers to co-ordinate an attack.'

The noise of the helicopters became a thunderous clatter and two machines rose from below the cliffs on either side of the plateau, their rotors kicking up a storm of dust as they held position about a hundred feet above the ground. They bore the red cross of Portugal and the markings of the Esquadrilhade Helicópteros de Marinha, and from their side doors crewmen trained mounted machine guns on the scene below. As their assailants looked from side to side a rifle shot rang out from somewhere up the slope and the man behind Jeremy fell in a spray of blood, and then there was a second crack and one of the other men dropped too. Ben leapt up and overwhelmed the third man, pinning him to the ground and kicking his weapon away, and the other members of the security team picked up their weapons and converged on Rauscher. One of them shouted and he dropped to his knees and then on the ground, his hands behind his head. Another who doubled as the team medic rushed Jeremy away and crouched with him behind a rock. The helicopters landed, powering down but keeping their rotors ticking over, each disgorging half a dozen men with weapons who quickly fanned out over the plateau.

It was all over in a matter of minutes, with Jeremy safe and the perimeter secure. One of the snipers came down from his position in the rocks and Ben took his radio from him, talking intently into it and then to the Portuguese officer in charge of the assault team. He returned the radio and ran up to Jack and Costas. 'I've just spoken to Macalister. We're taking Rauscher and the other man off straight away. The captain of the Portuguese frigate wants them in the brig and then to carry out complete sweep of the island to make sure it's secure. Once we've done that you can carry on with your search.'

'There's a man down below tied up in the cavern, and two bodies,' Jack said. 'The drone is keeping an eye on them.'

'We'll deal with it. Costas, can you show us the way?'

'Roger that. We could do with some climbing gear to get back down there safely.'

'The Lynx will fly it out from *Seaquest*.'

'Did Macalister mention any casualties from the missile attack?' Jack said.

'Midships port side will need a new lick of paint where it was splattered with rocket fragments, but thankfully nobody hurt. The other vessel was not so lucky. It was a burnt-out wreck by the time the Portuguese arrived and there were only a few survivors in a dinghy.'

'We saw the action from the cliff-top,' Jack said.

'Marco was instrumental in what just happened,' Ben said. 'Rauscher was lying about him just now. He had Marco imprisoned in Rome, but as you know Marco is pretty intrepid and managed to escape into the sewers last night. He called IMU and was patched through to *Seaquest* just after you and Costas left in the Aquapods. It was Marco's information about Rauscher's plans and the use of these mercenaries that convinced the Portuguese to attack. He managed to escape with Jeremy's friend Teresa from the National Archives, who had also been held hostage. They're both safe.'

'Does Jeremy know?'

'I'll fill him in now.'

'The crew losses on the other vessel are not something to relish but that's Rauscher's call for bringing them out here,' Jack said. 'The mercenaries I think the world can do without.'

'I recognise some of their faces from Interpol,' Ben said. 'The same ones crop up over and over again. The man holding the gun to Jeremy's head was wanted for war crimes in Syria. Justice is served.'

Costas went with Ben to the IMU Lynx, which was just out of sight at the end of the island alongside the H160. He looked over to where the IMU medic and another from the Portuguese team were giving Jeremy a check-up. Jeremy gave a thumbs-up and Jack turned towards the two prisoners. The

Portuguese officer had cuffed them and was beginning to lead them away, but Rauscher stopped as they passed Jack and turned to him. 'Be careful,' he said. 'What you may have found here could change the face of humanity. We had our duty to the goddess, yes, but we are not fools. If the orichalcum gives immortality, then you risk making men into gods. If it helps to cure illness and gives longer lives, then we were wrong. It is your call. It had better be the right one.'

Jack stared at him as he was led towards one of the Portuguese helicopters. All that mattered now was that Jeremy was free. The threat from a latter-day cult of an ancient Egyptian goddess seemed to diminish by the second as Rauscher was bundled into the helicopter and it took off. He felt a rush of adrenaline as he remembered the archaeology, the extraordinary discovery of the Egyptian wreck and the artefact that was sealed in the basalt wall at the end of the cavern. He knew what he had to do now.

CHAPTER 26

Twenty-four hours later the island was a hub of activity, with helicopters ferrying people to and from *Seaquest* and the Portuguese frigate that was holding position just offshore to the east. The burned-out wreck of the attacking vessel had been sunk by gunfire and the surviving crewmen as well as the prisoners from the island had been transferred to the frigate. An hour earlier the Lynx from *Seaquest* had arrived with Rebecca and Hiebermeyer and Aysha, who had flown to Madeira from Egypt, and earlier in the day it had brought Maria from Tenerife as well as Françoise who had flown in from Cornwall. Captain Macalister's team in the RIBs from *Seaquest* had been working all morning at recovering the two Aquapods, having discovered Jack's in emergency flotation mode some two miles off the north side of the island where it had been taken by the current. The wounded man and the two bodies had been removed from the cavern the evening before, and Costas had returned with Françoise as soon as she had arrived to extract the stone box from its niche in the wall and bring it to the surface. They had done so just before the others arrived in the Lynx, taking it to the high point over the cliffs where Jack and Costas had watched the action at sea the previous afternoon.

They were sitting there now with Maria after filling her in on events since they had spoken to her on the radio about the U-boat the morning before. Françoise had gone down into the cavern again to collect their climbing gear and tools. A familiar form came striding up the slope, his shorts nearly at half-mast and his Africa Korps sunglasses as impenetrable as ever, with slightly more stubble than usual. Seeing his friend coming towards him like that always gave Jack a feeling of well-being, like a memory from childhood of unfettered adventure, and took him back to their first explorations together as boys when he had given Maurice the artefact that had helped to spark off this quest. He stood up as Hiebermeyer arrived and put a hand on his shoulder. 'Brilliant news from Egypt, Maurice. I only heard it from Rebecca on the radio this morning before you flew out of Cairo, and the reception was poor. I can't wait to hear more.'

'It happened yesterday afternoon,' Hiebermeyer said, raising his sunglasses and beaming with excitement. 'The ministry allowed us to pump out that shaft beneath the pyramid where you and Costas found the entrance to Akhenaten's tomb. We had found some more Kufic inscriptions on the pyramid from the early Islamic period, so they were very pleased. Once we were at the bottom of the shaft Aysha managed to reach in and get the jewel out. She's bringing it up here with Rebecca now.'

'Fantastic,' Costas said. 'That was unfinished business.'

Hiebermeyer pointed to a wooden crate beside them. 'Is that the box?'

Jack nodded. 'We've kept it in the crate that Costas and Françoise used to encase it for protection while they hauled it to the surface. We're waiting for everyone to be here before opening it.'

'Even if there's nothing inside, it's still a remarkable discovery. The wreck is the first definitive evidence of ancient Egyptian seafaring in the Atlantic. Are you planning to excavate?'

'You bet,' Jack said. 'I've been in radio contact this morning with CINAV, the Portuguese Navy's Centro de Investigação Naval, and CNANS, the Centro Nacional de Arqueologia Nautica e Subaquática of the Património Cultural. They're very interested in collaborating and making it a joint project alongside our environmental programme.'

'You might even get me learning to dive,' Hiebermeyer said. 'This is the first ancient Egyptian shipwreck found beyond the Nile Delta. I can't miss up on something like that.'

'There's a bit of a current down there, and a slight problem with a U-boat,' Costas said. 'And you can only dive on neap tides. And when there's no swell.'

'Sounds like diving off Cornwall,' Hiebermeyer said.

'You take your chances when you can,' Costas said. 'And sometimes you're lucky.'

'Like doing Egyptology under the new regime.'

'I'm glad you're back in Egypt,' Jack said. 'And finding brilliant things again.'

Captain Macalister came up the slope with another officer wearing the uniform of the Portuguese Navy. 'Allow me to introduce an old friend of mine,' Macalister said. 'Capitão-da-fragata João Rodrigues Brandão.'

The man advanced towards Jack with a broad smile and an outstretched hand. 'Dr Howard. I am delighted to meet you.'

'The pleasure is mine,' Jack said, shaking his hand. 'And call me Jack. We owe you a lot. Without the arrival of your helicopters, things could have been very different.'

'It is fortunate that we were within striking distance of the island. The Madeira Maritime Patrol was carrying out a routine mission around the Ilhas Desertas and interdicted a factory trawler that had crossed into territorial waters. They called on us for backup, so we were already in the area. There is nothing more important for us than asserting sovereignty in these waters, mainly because we are committed to protecting the marine park that encompasses these islands.'

'João and I have just been discussing the next stage in our environmental project,' Macalister said. 'I've been in touch with Efram Jacobovich and he has offered to fund a permanent scientific presence here, providing a state-of-the-art research station to bolster the ranger outpost.'

'Do you guys still have the Inquisition?' Costas said to

Brandão. 'Rauscher had his man hold a gun to the head of my friend Jeremy. Nobody gets away with that.'

The Portuguese officer gave him a steely look. 'I don't yet know what it is that brought you here, though if it involves Jack Howard and IMU then the importance of what you are doing is not in question. All I know is that these people carried out an armed intervention on Portuguese soil that included kidnapping and threatened murder. We've moved on from the Inquisition, but we do have a special maximum-security penitentiary that will make Rauscher think we haven't.'

Jeremy came up beside them supported by Aysha and Rebecca, who helped him to sit down. His arm was in a sling and Jack looked at him with concern. 'Are you alright?'

'Just a few aches and bruises. Mostly a bit miffed that I allowed myself to be kidnapped in Rome when you'd advised me to watch my back. I'm not sure that I'm cut out to be part of your team.'

'Oh yes you are. That kind of thing happens to all of us.'

'You're the best,' Costas said, putting a hand on his shoulder. 'I mean it. You can be my dive buddy any time.'

'You'd have to put up with Little Joey,' Jack said. 'He can be a bit temperamental around spiders and geckos, like his master.'

'I do not have a problem with geckos,' Costas said. 'Spiders, yes, but geckos, no. Little Joey and the gecko became fast friends while Françoise and I were down in the cavern.'

Jeremy smiled at him. 'OK. It's a deal. Maybe somewhere tropical?'

'I have a small island in the Caribbean that might fit the bill,' Costas said. 'Since seeing the turtle conservation project in Bardawil lagoon I've wanted to do something similar, to set up a protected reserve for loggerheads to lay eggs. I need a team of divers to explore the reef and observe their behaviour. That is, if I can draw you away from your parchments and scrolls. Françoise has already said yes.'

'I can do that,' Jeremy said, looking at Rebecca. 'Or

maybe we can?'

'I hope so,' Rebecca said. 'I still have work to do helping with the excavation in Egypt and then it's another stint in the refugee camp in west Africa. I might allow myself a break when I get back.'

'Roger that,' Costas said. 'The drinks are already in the cooler.'

'It's a shame that Jacob's not here,' Maria said. 'And Marco.'

'Jacob's holding the fort in Egypt,' Aysha said. 'The lagoon's flooded now and the ancient boat is underwater, but we still need to finish digging out and recording the stone pillar after it was buried again in the sandstorm. He's been having trouble with the drone for the scan and was asking about Little Joey.'

'Happy to oblige,' Costas said. 'Françoise and I retrieved him from the cavern yesterday evening and I'm itching to get him back on *Seaquest* to my tools to repair the damage. I can be in the desert again as soon as the helicopter and the Embraer can get me there.'

'Little Joey deserves a medal,' Maria said. 'It sounds as if he saved the day down there.'

'A lot of people saved the day,' Jack said. 'Ben's men, the Portuguese helicopter crews, Captain Macalister. A team effort as always.'

'And about Marco,' Jeremy said. 'I spoke to him this morning in Rome. He'd like to be here but he's working 24/7 on getting the underground temple of Isis recorded.'

'He'll have to be careful,' Jack said. 'It wasn't just Rauscher. There are other members of the priesthood out there still. The law in Italy can do little to clamp down on them as it would be hard to connect them to any crime.'

Jeremy held up his phone, showing a newspaper headline. 'I don't think there will be much to worry about. Marco went to the press this morning with the discovery of the underground temple and the modern-day priesthood, and it's gone viral. They've worked out the names of the main players in the priesthood. It turns out that a very senior Cardinal had been siphoning off money from the Vatican to pay for their activities, including hiring the vessel and the mercenaries. Nobody steals from the Vatican and gets away with it.'

'The press are going to love the mummification alive thing,' Maria said.

'Could be a technique to try out on Rauscher in your prison?' Costas said to Brandão.

'I don't think even the Inquisition extended to that.'

Jeremy turned to Jack. 'I did do one useful thing in captivity. Do you remember in Rome saying that concealing the past never works, and my idea that it might make a good motto for IMU? I've been mulling it over ever since, trying to get the translation right. I've gone for medieval Latin, my speciality. Anyway, here it is: Illumina praeteritum melius futurum. Illuminate the past for a better future.'

Jack stared out to sea, watching the swell roll in and break over the rocks on the shoreline below. *Illumina praeteritum melius futurum*. 'That works,' he said. 'I can see it above the entrance to the IMU campus, beneath the Howard anchor and the Atlantis symbol.'

'I didn't know that the Atlantis symbol was part of our coat of arms,' Rebecca said.

'I think we can lay claim to it now, don't you?'

Jeremy looked at Jack intently. 'That motto isn't just about learning from the past. It's about how our discoveries light up the lives of the people who follow us, about the wonder and inspiration that gives life extra meaning.'

Rebecca pointed at the wooden crate. 'And sometimes it's about finding artefacts that might make a difference.'

Costas knelt down beside them. 'So, Jack. Is this the end of the line?'

'What do you mean?'

'I mean, what could be in that box. Immortality. The elixir of life. You can't get much better than that.'

Jack looked at the box and closed his eyes. He felt the brush of the wind against his face, and the warmth of the sun. He opened them again and saw a shearwater hovering over the cliff, searching the sea, the feathers on its wings fluttering in the breeze. He remembered the incredible richness of life they had seen underwater, the schools of fish and crustacea feeding in the current, the larger fish deeper down awaiting their turn in the food chain. Immortality, to live as a god, was a fool's dream, but if there were something in what they had found that might ease illness and misery, some ancient lost wisdom that might allow those who were suffering to enjoy another day, then what they were doing would have been worthwhile.

'We've already found the elixir of life,' Rebecca said. 'What we were doing in the lagoon, what we're seeing here. Protecting places like this. We're part of it, for as long as we can help to keep life going. The oceans are our future, our immortality.'

Jack looked at Costas. 'Anyway, this can't be the end of the road. There's still treasure to be found. Silver pieces of eight from the Spanish Main. Portuguese gold coins. Pirate treasure.'

'Maybe next time we come across gold coins you'll let us get some.'

'And there's that beer I still owe you for saving me in the mine.'

'Roger that.'

Françoise climbed up from the fissure beside them, put down a coil of rope and took off her harness and helmet. Now that they were all there Costas picked up a small pry bar and began to remove lengths of wood from the crate where they had been nailed together, revealing the polished black stone of the ancient box underneath. After a few minutes it was completely exposed, and they could see the intaglio carving at the front with the Atlantis symbol. It was a beguiling artefact, dark and mysterious and giving nothing away, sitting on the rocky platform overlooking the sea like a holy Ark. Aysha took off the bag that she had been carrying and carefully removed a swaddled object, unwrapped it and passed it to Hiebermeyer. The memory of the jewel beneath the pyramid was seared on Jack's mind and yet it had only been a fleeting view the year before; seeing it now close-up took his breath away. It was the size of his outstretched hand, lentoid in shape, with the Atlantis symbol standing out from one face in relief. Even in the sunlight it remained opaque, as if it were revealing the shape of the past but not the detail within, as if the truth would always lie in the realm of imagination and conjecture even when they held the greatest treasures of antiquity in their grasp.

He put his hand on the box, feeling the frisson of immediacy with the past that he always felt when he touched an artefact, seeing the jewel with the symbol of the lost ancient civilisation that had launched his career and brought them to where they were now. Hiebermeyer lowered the jewel and held it in front of the box, showing that the carvings exactly matched and that the jewel was the key to opening it. Jack felt a surge of excitement, not only about what the box might contain but also about the future, about an ancient dream of immortality and also about the team of people around him now and the revelations that still lay ahead of them, about inspiring others to see their own lives as part of the same great adventure. He took a deep breath, stared intently at the box and then looked at Hiebermeyer. 'OK. Let's do it.'

AUTHOR'S NOTE

This novel is a sequel to my first novel *Atlantis* and its follow-up *The Gods of Atlantis*, as well as to my novels *Pharaoh* and *Pyramid*. In *Atlantis* Jack and Costas discover the long-lost citadel of Atlantis beneath the waters of the Black Sea, and in *The Gods of Atlantis* they find evidence for an exodus of priests across the Atlantic. Both novels are rooted in plausible archaeological scenarios that have become even more compelling since I wrote them. The basis for *Atlantis* was evidence that the Black Sea had been cut off from the Mediterranean during the last Ice Age and did not fill up to the same level until the Bosporus was breached by the waters of the Mediterranean in the sixth millennium BC – causing a sea-level rise of more than 100 metres that inundated Neolithic communities along the south-eastern shore of the Black Sea, in modern Turkey. That region may be where agriculture first became established as well as the homeland of Indo-European language, and in my novels I suggest that the spread of these ideas could have begun with the exodus of refugees from the Black Sea.

The possibility that they took with them skills in stonework is revealed by the remarkable early Neolithic site of Göbekli Tepe, designated in 2018 as a World Heritage Site for containing 'one of the first manifestations of human-made monumental architecture.' The stone circles of that site – located not far from my fictional citadel of Atlantis – include T-shaped monolithic pillars that may be the first representations of the gods of that civilisation, my 'Gods of

Atlantis.' My 'Atlantis symbol', comprising two vertical bars, a cross bar between them, and further small bars extending out from the horizonal bars, is one of the symbols on the second millennium BC Phaestos Disc from Crete, and is similar to H-shaped symbols found alongside other carvings on the pillars at Göbekli Tepe, including animals, birds, insects and representations of the human form. That site dates to the tenth to ninth millennium BC, at the dawn of agriculture, and I suggest that the H symbol may be an early representation of a word for 'god'.

The only known source of the Atlantis story is the dialogues *Critias* and *Timaeus* by the ancient Greek philosopher Plato. If we accept Plato's account of the origin of the story – that it was passed to him by Solon, who had heard it from Egyptian priests – and that Atlantis was based in historical reality, then the Black Sea flood and the precocious early civilisation suggested by sites such as Göbekli Tepe may provide a context. In my fiction the story was filtered through the Bronze Age civilisation of the Aegean, which itself suffered a devastating natural catastrophe with the eruption of Thera in the sixteenth century BC. In addition to the Atlantis story, the Black Sea inundation provides a possible basis for the flood stories of the Old Testament and the ancient Babylonian *Epic of Gilgamesh*, including the names of gods that may have been worshipped at sites such as Göbekli Tepe - an extraordinary and previously unknown period of human achievement several thousand years before the first pyramids of Egypt or the megaliths of north-west Europe were built.

*

In the *Epic of Gilgamesh*, the hero Gilgamesh goes to his ancestor Utnapishtim in order to discover the secret of immortality. Utnapishtim - who himself is immortal - instructs Gilgamesh to find it in a plant under the sea, something that he fails to do. Immortality, or extreme longevity, is a theme of many foundation myths, and is seen for example in the lifespans of the early patriarchs in the Old Testament. The idea that there might be an 'elixir of life' is similarly deep-rooted and continues to exert fascination. It is possible that a plant or mineral, known in prehistory but since lost, might have ameliorated some aspects of ageing, but the idea may also have been rooted in the experience of hallucinogenic or stimulant drugs that might seem to have reviving or reinvigorating qualities. A common theme is the tension between the yearning for immortality and the will of the gods to deny it; if immortality is only to be found in the afterlife then the priests could exert control by requiring worship and submission to attain it, whereas their influence would wane if immortality were something that people could discover themselves. For this reason priests such as those of Isis in Egypt might have resisted the idea of an 'elixir of life' had it been propounded, as a threat to their god and their own positions of power.

In my novel that 'elixir' is orichalcum, a metal from Atlantis mentioned by Plato. In the *Critias* he describes orichalcum as 'that which is now only a name but was then something more than a name … dug out of the earth in many parts of the island, being more precious in those days than anything except gold', and how the outer wall of the citadel 'flashed with the red light of orichalcum.' The word derives from the Greek *oros*, mountain, and *chalkos*, copper, so literally means 'mountain copper.' If this were a Greek translation of a much older word used by the people of the early Neolithic, then that original word might have been an amalgamation of the Proto Indo-European *berg*, meaning mountain, and *ayos*, copper. In my novel, the citadel of Atlantis was built next to an active volcano, which could have been the mountain in which the metal was discovered.

The word orichalcum first appears in the Homeric Hymns and in Hesiod (*The Shield of Heracles*, 122, translated by H.S. Evelyn-White in the Loeb Edition of 1914 as 'shining bronze'), dating to the seventh century BC or before, but not in reference to Atlantis and probably referring to a copper alloy with a golden appearance; that seems to be the meaning of the word as it was used in the later Greek and Roman periods, for instance in reference to the alloy used to mint the Roman sestertius and dupondius. Pliny the Elder refers to orichalcum (or aurichalcum) as a copper alloy made with the admixture of a substance called cadmea, probably a zinc mineral (*Natural History* 36, 4), and it may be that this is the 'Mossynecian copper' described by Pseudo-Aristotle as 'very shiny and white, not because there is tin mixed with it, but because some earth is combined and molten with it. They say that the man who discovered the mixture never taught anyone' (*De Mirabilibus Auscultationibus*, 'On Marvellous Things Heard', trans. W.S. Hett, Loeb 1936). Whatever the true identity of orichalcum, the idea of metals and minerals having medicinal properties was well-known in antiquity and is extensively explored by Pliny in Books 36 and 37 of his *Natural History*.

*

In my novel the orichalcum is taken from Atlantis in a boat whose occupants have names drawn from the Old Testament before the flood and from the *Epic of Gilgamesh*. Of those names, Shamash was the name of the Mesopotamian sun-god; his symbol with radiating arms was a precursor to the Aten symbol adopted by the pharaoh Akhenaten when he rejected the old gods and turned to monotheism. Utnapishtim in ancient Mesopotamian mythology was told by the god Enki to make a ship to be called 'Preserver of Life' in order to save humans and animals from a great flood, for which he was deified by the god Enlil. In the earliest extant version of the flood story – on a cuneiform tablet in the British Museum of the early second millennium BC - the protagonist is called Atrahasis, 'exceedingly wise,' a word also found in the Sumerian King List for a king who ruled before the flood.

One theme in the Atrahasis story is the thirst and hunger of the gods during the flood, something that can be imagined for the occupants of a boat during a long open-sea voyage. After much time at sea Atrahasis sent out a raven, and when it did not return he knew that they were close to land. In the flood stories, first written down several thousand years after the Black Sea deluge, a merging of the human occupants of the boats with the gods whom they brought with them – including Anu, Enlil, and Enki, the early Mesopotamian gods of sky, wind and water – might have been a natural part of the storytelling and mythologising process, with the occupants taking on seemingly supernatural qualities such as extreme longevity.

*

The Mullion Pin Wreck, the *Santo Cristo di Castello*, is an actual shipwreck located off the western Lizard Peninsula in Cornwall. Much about the wreck and its artefacts as described in this novel is true to life, including the artefacts that Jack finds – all of which I have been discovered since first diving on the site in 2018. The documentary evidence for the wreck includes Captain Giovanni Lorenzo Viviano's petition to King Charles II (*Calendar of State Papers Domestic*, Charles II, Vol CLXIX, 83, August 1666) and the letter of William Paynter regarding arrangements for salvage of the wreck.

When I went to The National Archives to see that letter I was fortunate to be invited into the research department to examine the 'Prize Papers', where I discovered a treasure trove of documents that had been on board another Genoese merchantman from Amsterdam that can almost be regarded as the *Santo Cristo di Castello*'s sister ship – the *Sacrificio d'Abramo*, which had left Amsterdam a few weeks earlier in the summer of 1667 and was captured as a 'Prize' by the Royal Navy. The evidence of the two ships was complementary, with the *Santo Cristo di Castello* providing artefacts and the

Sacrificio d'Abramo bills of lading and other documents, and they overlapped even more when I discovered that several merchants had split their consignments between the two ships.

All of the merchants, as well as the two captains – Viviano and Antonio Basso – had their own monograms that they used to mark their consignments, including Viviano's mark as described in this novel. Through the Prize Papers and other documents, in Genoa, Spain and Amsterdam, I learned much about the merchants involved as well as Viviano's patron in Genoa, Francesco Sauli. Among the most fascinating records was one for a batch of books exactly as described in the novel, including many titles by the Jesuit scholar Athanasius Kircher. When I saw that those included the *Mundus Subterraneus* - and remembered that this was where Kircher had published his famous chart showing the island of Atlantis - the seed was planted for the storyline in this novel.

*

An outstanding find from the wreck has been a small copper alloy Corpus Christi figure by Guglielmo della Porta, one of the foremost Italian sculptors of the sixteenth century. After discovering the figure I took it into the nearby Church of St Winwaloe, just as Jack does in the novel. The church, known as the 'Church of the Storms', includes painted panels thought to have been salvaged from another nearby wreck, the *St Anthony* of 1527. A striking feature of the church is the detached tower set into the side of the seaward promontory, at a place below the rampart of an Iron Age fort where the original monk's cell of St Winwaloe may have been located. Inside the tower I have seen very old pick and chisel marks on the rock-cut interior; the chamber beyond is fictional, but it is a plausible location for a monastic cell in a prehistoric tomb – an idea inspired by the discovery of a Bronze Age barrow less than a hundred metres away during recent excavations.

The Paynter family, whose crest was a bundle of three spears, owned property in the Penwith peninsula near Land's End from at least the sixteenth century and were much involved in mining. There is no evidence that William Paynter was a secret Catholic, but there were Catholics among the gentry of Cornwall and the possibility that they might support a Catholic claim to the throne was a concern to the king and his agents. The mine in the novel is fictional but based on actual mine workings at Botallack near St Just. In his *Speculi Britanniae*, completed by 1610, John Norton wrote that Botallack was a 'litle hamlet on the coaste of the Irish sea, moste visited with Tinners, where they lodge and feede, being near their mynes' (John Norden, *Speculi Britanniae Pars. A Topographical and Historical of Cornwall*. London, 1728, p 35). This is the earliest reference to a mine in Penwith; although the digging of shafts is not documented at Botallack until the 1720s, it seems likely that underground working had taken place earlier. The nineteenth century disaster in my novel is based on one in 1893 at Wheal Owles at Botallack in which 19 men were drowned when the mine flooded. Their bodies were never recovered.

Many Cornish mines in the nineteenth century went out under the seabed and were pumped clear of water using steam engines in the stone buildings that are such a distinctive feature of the landscape today. The description of the mine entered by Jack and Costas, including collapsed shafts and levels, abandoned tools and vividly coloured mineral extrusions, is drawn from my own experience and that of others exploring abandoned mines along the coast of Cornwall.

*

Athanasius Kircher was fascinated by Egyptian antiquities in Rome, many of which were associated with the Temples of Isis and Serapis (Osiris) next to the Pantheon. The obelisk now in the Piazza della Minerva was discovered in 1665 beneath the cloister of the Dominican convent above the site of the temples; the obelisk in the Piazza della Rotonda, uncovered in the fourteenth century, may have come from the same place. Other Egyptian sculptures thought to have been found in the area include statues of Isis, a lion, a baboon and a cat, and a stone table leg. Whether or not Kircher instigated the 1665 excavation in the cloister is unknown, but his personal museum was in the Collegio Romano directly above the Temple of Isis and he would undoubtedly have been present to record the obelisk and attempt to interpret the hieroglyphs. The aqueduct channels beneath this part of the Campus Martius include extensions and renovations to the Aqua Virgo carried out in the sixteenth century, and it is possible that further exploration was carried out underground when foundations of other Roman buildings were encountered.

The original findspot of the Bembine Tablet is unknown, but it may have come from the same place as the Egyptian sculptures associated with the Temple of Isis. This remarkable artefact, acquired by Cardinal Bembo soon after 1527 and now in the Egyptian Museum in Turin, is thought to have been a Roman creation based on one or several Egyptian originals. Kircher's attempt to use it in his *Oedipus Aegyptiacus* to decipher hieroglyphics failed, but it did focus his attention on the figure of Isis in the centre – for Kircher, who knew no boundary between science and the arts, between occult and reason, seeing a syncretism between the supposed wisdom of antiquity and his own Christian beliefs came naturally, and he might have viewed Isis as he would have viewed Akhenaten's Sun-God, as expressions of the one universal deity.

*

The Sabkhat al Bardawil on the northern coast of the Sinai desert has been a focus of concern in recent years for the deaths of sea turtles that use its beaches for hauling out and laying their eggs. During the First World War, the lagoon – a salt marsh extending for nearly 50 miles along the coast – was passed by British and Allied troops of the Egyptian Expeditionary Force as they advanced towards Palestine in 1916 in the campaign against the Ottoman Turks. On 7-9 May 1916, New Zealanders of the Canterbury Mounted Rifles, part of the Anzac Mounted Division, were ordered to dig a channel from the sea at the western end of the Sabkhat al Bardawil, the object being 'to flood the Bardawil so as to furnish an additional protection to the Suez Canal, but as fast as the cutting through the sand was made the waves filled it up again and the project was abandoned' (Lieutenant Colonel C.G. Powles, *The History of the Canterbury Mounted Rifles 1914-1919*. Auckland, Whitcomb and Tombs, 1928, p. 97). The unit war diary notes the location as 'Mahamdiya', and that digging on 8 May was carried out by the Tenth (Nelson) Squadron – from the town where I lived on the South Island of New Zealand for four years as a boy, when there were still veterans of the campaign among the people that we knew. The ancient boat on the shore of the lake in my novel is fictional, but the north Sinai coast has long been thought of as a place where evidence for early prehistoric seafaring might one day be found. The soldiers themselves were fascinated by the archaeological remains that they encountered, including ancient watering troughs – a matter of particular interest to the mounted troops as watering their horses in the desert was a constant problem (Powles., *op. cit.*, p. 121).

    Among the best-known pictorial carvings of the Predynastic period in Egypt are those on the so-called 'Battlefield Palette' in the British Museum (EA 20791), dated to the fourth millennium BC. The low-relief scenes show prisoners and battle casualties being scavenged by animals; one of the prisoners is flanked by a standard with a falcon, the bird that was to become associated with Horus and is familiar from depictions of the god in Pharaonic times. Other remarkable artefacts from this early period are flint knives, including the 'Pitt-Rivers Knife' in the British Museum (EA 68512) with its beautiful pressure-flaked blade and carvings of birds and wild animals on the grip. The possibility that these knives may have been used in early attempts at mummification may be supported by research published in 2018 on the fourth millennium BC Turin mummy, one of the earliest bodies from Egypt showing evidence for artificial embalming.

The idea that my fictional prehistoric pillar in the desert – with carvings of early Neolithic date such as those found at Göbekli Tepe, as well as a second millennium BC inscription of Akhenaten - might also have included an early Arabic inscription is based on the existence of numerous Arabic inscriptions on the monuments of ancient Egypt, including the pyramids; one of the earliest known is a grave slab of AD 652 in the Cairo Museum that provides the basis for the wording of the fictional inscription in my novel (El-Hawary, Hassan Mohammad, 'The most ancient Islamic monument known dated A.H. 31 (A.D. 652), from the time of the Third Calif 'Uthman', *The Journal of the Royal Asiatic Society of Great Britain and Ireland* 2 (1930): 321-33, Cambridge University Press).

*

The Cadiz merchants Diego Cornelissen and Giovanni Battista Porrata really existed – their mark **CP** with a cross above it is found among the bills of lading for the *Sacrificio d'Abramo*, and they are known to have shipped goods to the Canary Islands and Azores. The Savage Islands are a small archipelago mid-way between the two, with one of the islands, Selvagem Grande, matching the fictional plan of the island sketched by Kircher that Jack and Costas find in the mine. The actual plan of Kircher's Insula Atlantis from his *Mundus Subterraneus* of 1665 – the same year as the construction of the *Santo Cristo di Castello* - is reproduced on my webpage for this book, with the perspective looking south as was common in Dutch cartography at the time.

The account in this novel of a possible Nazi agent on the island of Fuerteventura is also historical, including the quote from a 1947 document from the Madrid Bureau chief of the U.S. Officer of Strategic Services, as is my account of the final patrol of U-182, Kapitänleutnant Nicolai Clausen, except that there is no evidence that it survived being depth-charged by the destroyer USS *Mackenzie* near Madeira on 16 May 1943. Among those presumed to have died in the sinking were the masters of two merchant ships who had been taken by Clausen as prisoners after their vessels had been torpedoed – one of them, Captain Angus Maclennan of the SS *Aloe*, had been on board the U-boat for almost six weeks at the time of the attack. The radio officer in this novel is fictional and is not a representation of any of the officers from the *Aloe* who survived her sinking.

Treasure-hunters are known to have visited Selvagem Grande on at least five occasions since the early nineteenth century, searching for pirate gold – so Jack and Costas were not the first, though the treasure they seek in this novel is of far greater value than anything those earlier explorers could ever have imagined.

*

The references to the 'Serbonian bog' - Lake Bardawil - are from Herodotus, *Histories* II: 6 (Loeb 1920, trans A.D. Godley), Diodorus Siculus, *Bibliotheca Historica* I: 30 (Loeb 1933, trans C.H. Oldfather) ('a lake, quite narrow, but marvellously deep and some two hundred stades in length, which is called Serbonis and offers unexpected perils ...') and Milton, *Paradise Lost* II: 592-4 (1674 edition), first published in 1667, the same year that the *Santo Cristo di Castello* went down. Further details of that wreck can be found in my book *A History of the World in Twelve Shipwrecks*, published in 2024 by Weidenfeld &

Nicolson in the UK and St Martin's Press in the US, and more background material and images related to the novel can be found on my website www.davidgibbins.com.

THE END

Printed in Great Britain
by Amazon